THE ARITHMETIC OF COLOR

Previous works by Bernadette Rule

POETRY

The Window Washer of Chartres

Deep Breath

Earth Day in Leith Churchyard:
Poems in Search of Tom Thomson

The Literate Thief: Selected Poems

Gardening at the Mouth of Hell

The Weight of Flames

Private Places

Full Light Falling

Frames of Mind

CREATIVE NONFICTION

Dark Fire

"Art Waves: A History & Some Highlights", *Hamilton Arts & Letters*,
issue 14:1, Summer 2021

"Cousins", Hamilton Arts & Letters, issue 8.2, Winter 2015/16

"How Babies Are Made: Martha Nelson Thomas
and her Doll Babies" *Brought to Light: More Stories
of Forgotten Women* (Seraphim Editions, 2015)

"A Layer of Ghosts" *Hamilton Arts & Letters*, Issue #6,
November, 2013

THE
ARITHMETIC
OF COLOR

by Bernadette Rule

2023 IRONING BOARD PRESS

IRONING BOARD PRESS

ISBN 978-17776440-2-4

www.bernadetterule.ca

DEDICATION:

For Tom and Mary Johnson, & their family, living & dead
And in particular, in memory of Georgia Ruth Jackson,
Rosa Mae Robinson & Gladys Morse
who kept the stories

Pluck the stars out of the heavens.
The stars mark our destiny.
The stars marked my destiny.
I am tired of civilization.

Fenton Johnson, "Tired"

PROLOGUE

The Arithmetic of Color is a nonfiction novel. My father first told me Tom Johnson's story when I was an adolescent. I began researching it in the early 1990s, interviewing dozens of people, and was richly rewarded with their memories and knowledge of Tom's story, and of that time and place. But I never dreamed I would receive the kind of eye-witness account that Tom's niece Gladys Morse gave me. She was in her 90s then, still living on her own, clear of mind and very grateful someone was going to tell this story to the wider world at last. I owe her a great debt. The italicized passages throughout the book are in Gladys' voice.

GLADYS: I

Course I remember it. The day Uncle Tom got word he was a millionaire? Why, that was a big day fo sho out in Slayden's Crossin. Maybe the biggest day that little old burg's evah seen. Even though it didn't make the paper til the next day, what with them white men askin ev'body where Tom Johnson lived, the news got out fast, and family and friends come in from all over the county. Some even made the three mile trip in from the county seat a Greenberry. They come by train or buggy or on foot. It was near as excitin as a 8th of August Picnic, but it was late January. I reckon, now I come to think on it, that it was a good thing it was winter, and too cold to stand around outside fo much more'n a hour or so. But ev'body wanted in on the excitement, so they just kep on comin and goin. Friends and neighbors filled up that little dirt road in front of Tom and Mary's place, the whole day and into the evening. Yesiree, it was somethin. Ev'body that was there remembers that day.

Uncle Tom look like he didn't know what hit him. He's still in his work clothes. He'd been about to go back to the Capitol Buildin where he'd been doin some plaster work, when this white lawyer from Oklahoma come up on the porch, and behind him a reporter from The Greenberry Daily Leaf. *He said later he felt like he'd had a spell put on him from the minute they knocked on the door. That spell didn't wear off the whole time he had all them bigwigs and newspaper reporters on him. But he come through that first day real good, far as I could tell. He wasn't never a man to shy away from the spotlight, and that was a good thing the way it all turned out, cause he sho nuff had a spotlight on him then.*

He was a handsome, bright complected man, was Uncle Tom. He wasn't tall—stood about five foot eight or nine—but he give the impression that he was. He had a tall personality, you might say, and he was broad—broad as that doorway yonder. Not fat, mind you, but wide through the shoulders, and strong. One time I said I reckoned his life had made him big somehow— made him a person you'd take notice of. But my grandmother, his mama Clara, she said, Naw Gladys, you got that wrong. Tom was borned like that. He never coulda slipped through this world unnoticed.

His wife Mary was so different from him. Small and neat. She jes wanted to please people, and she'd get all confused if she was ever made the center of the conversation. Her and Uncle Tom was as clean a example as you ever gonna find a opposites attractin. That day, when the whole world come up on her doorstep, Mary jes smiled that little worried smile of hers and kep on makin coffee fo people. I teased her once or twice about bein Miz Millionaire, but she'd jes shake her head and ask me did I need mo coffee or anything.

Somebody said to her—oh I know who it was; it was Rita Marie Galbraith—who'da loved bein a millionaire even more'n the rest of us—Rita Marie says to her, What you gonna buy first, Mary, with all a that money?

Mary looked down a minute at the bare ground, then back over her shoulder at the fine clapboard house Tom'd built her, with its porch and its pretty green trim and all, and she said, I done got all I need right here. Ev'body laughed real big and started talkin all at the same time bout what they'd do if the money was theirs. And Mary, she jes stood there with both hands folded on her right hipbone, smilin and listenin to all of us. When the talk wasn't about her and Tom, her smile didn't carry no part of a frown.

I'm a old lady now and I can see things I couldn't see then. When she wasn't no more excited than she was bout becomin a millionaire, we jes figured that was Mary, down to the ground. Now I'd put it this away: The biggest dream Mary Pryor ever had in her life was when she fell for Tom Johnson. That dream come true fo her when she wasn't much more'n a girl and she'd had plenty of time to see what comes of gettin what you wish fo. Maybe she was smarter'n the rest of us on that account.

CHAPTER ONE

The second white person to hurry to Tom Johnson's side the morning he became a millionaire was Judge Arch Wingate. The judge's brother Ted, the banker, had telephoned him that morning to make sure he was hurrying out to Slayden's Crossing. Despite the fact that their grocer father died when they were young and they had received only an eighth grade education, the Wingates were possessed of iron ambition and shrewdness. The decade of the 1920s had seen their steady rise into two of the richest and most powerful men in western Kentucky... until that January morning, when a black man seemed poised to pass them up.

Arch turned his Model T onto the dirt road beside the railroad track where Johnson lived, and saw that crowds of people stood talking in the neighboring yards. At the sound of the motor, three white hens squawked and flapped under the porch next door to the one-and-a-half-story frame house. A dog ran forward, barking. Mixed breed, the judge noted. He could tell it didn't dare come near him, so he ignored the dog's ineffectual threats. As he walked through the gate and up the porch steps, all conversation ceased. A pretty woman of about fifty opened the front door quietly as he raised his hand to knock. Her partially straightened hair framed a round, solemn face.

Mornin, Judge Wingate, she said, looking slightly to the side of his direct gaze.

Well now, you know who I am, little lady, but if you're Tom Johnson's wife you don't appear to be as excited as you ought to be.

I am Tom's wife. I'm Mary Johnson, she said, stepping aside to hold the door. Please come i..., she started, but he was already moving past her into the living room.

Johnson and a short blondish man of about thirty-five stood up from where they'd been sitting. The room was clean and nicely decorated. Its focal point, and biggest surprise, was the mantelpiece that surrounded a tiny coal grate. It was white and featured ornamentation that would have been the envy of the judge's own house: scrolled brackets with gilded leafwork and a swag of brightly painted fruit and flowers. Should've left em unpainted, he thought, but still... Even the ceiling was worked in an elaborate pattern of overlapping leaves. Arch looked around at the upholstered chairs, which though a bit worn, were all tricked out with doilies. There was even a little settee. A parlor, he thought. Hm. Pretty damn nice for darkies.

Though they had never met, Tom and Arch recognized each other. Everybody in the county knew Judge Wingate, and now it seemed everybody knew Tom Johnson as well. This sudden, unprecedented visit from the judge didn't seem to surprise either of the Johnsons. A subtle resignation lay beneath their careful politeness.

Mr. Axley, this is Judge Wingate, said Tom, gesturing slightly with an open hand, the way some dignitary might.

Mary slipped out unnoticed to make more coffee. She carried her blue clay water pitcher to the pump in the backyard, careful to avoid the mounds of damp leaves Tom had never gotten around to burning last fall. A chartreuse cabbage in the dead garden provided the only color. Privy, coal shed, incinerator, cloud-stuffed sky, bare trees—all but the cabbage could've been sketched with a lead pencil.

Straddling the puddle under the pump, she performed the common task without a thought for it. It had begun to look like the two of them would never get to discuss this oil business in private.

They'd been sitting at the table after breakfast—which now seemed like a scene from the distant past. Tom, billfold in hand, was giving her the money to pay the bills for the month, thumbing each dollar down forcefully into its own pile, when they'd heard the first knock at the door. It had been this Mr. Axley with a newspaper reporter in tow, then after him, the whole neighborhood, eager to know what was up. Mercifully the reporter had hurried away after having been stopped from following them inside, but the house and yard had been filling with people ever since. Tom's mother Clara had left only ten minutes ago with some of Tom's sisters and now, just as things had been dying down a little and she sensed—hoped—Mr. Axley might be about to go back to town, here comes Judge Arch Wingate for mercy's sake. When would it stop?

The full pitcher was heavy and painfully cold in her hands; back inside she leaned against the stove, warming them for a minute or two before starting the coffee. This Oklahoma land title again, back to haunt them, when it had seemed things were going so well.

She sat down at the table and rattled some beans from the bag into her grinder, pinching up the ones that rolled onto the oilcloth. Y'all goin in, too, she said in a thin, teasing voice. They surrendered their rich odor as Mary turned the little crank. Funny how they never smelled as good when they were whole. The water was so cold the glass pot fogged up for a moment on contact. She spooned some grounds into the battered little basket and set it down into the water, replaced the lid and put the pot on the stove top. The voices from the front room had never once let up. And now behind her, slowly but inevitably, the percolator's tattoo gathered speed.

*   *   *

They had crept up on him like thieves. Sitting at the kitchen table with Mary, Tom hadn't heard them come up onto the porch. The sudden sharp knocking at the door had the startling effect of gunshots. Who knocks on your door like that at 8 o'clock in the morning? Besides, everybody knew Tom was catching the 8:25 for Frankfort.

Thinking it had to be trouble, Tom opened the door upon two white strangers, one with a notepad and a pencil poised to write down everything he saw and heard. Though his stomach tightened with fear, Tom narrowed his eyes, adopting a sternly quizzical pose. He didn't have to think what to say; the short man in the front took the lead, after pausing for a beat to stare at Tom's blue eyes.

Are you Tom Johnson?

The man's eager, businesslike tone did nothing to alleviate Tom's fears. Who wants to know?

My name is Benjamin Axley. I'm an attorney from Tulsa, Oklahoma. He waited a moment, watching Tom closely.

Tom's guard rose even higher and he reached for the weapon of silence.

The little man cleared his throat and shifted his bag to the other hand. Mr. Johnson—I'm sure it *is* Mr. Johnson—I have some amazing news for you and I've been looking for you for some years in order to deliver it. It concerns a landowner in Oklahoma named Sam Ford. The last word of this statement carried the slight inflection of a question, yet it was, without doubt, a statement and it was made with a knowing smile. A smile of self-congratulation.

Again the man paused a moment as he stared with poorly concealed surprise at Tom's blue-green eyes. Wildcatters on Sam Ford's land have had an oil strike that makes him one of the richest men in the state—and I can tell you there are some mighty rich people in Oklahoma. Sam Ford, Mr. Johnson, is now worth twenty million dollars.

The lawyer pronounced each word of the sum separately and precisely, but Tom kept rigidly still, like a boy determined not to cry out during a whipping. Still probing for the response he felt his message deserved, Axley patted his leather satchel smartly and continued. I happen to have proof right here in my bag that you are Sam Ford.

Still silent, Tom stared at the bag with an expression Axley couldn't read; but somehow at that point, Tom's response ceased to matter. Axley held tightly to the reins.

May I come in?

I's jes leavin to catch the train to Frankfort. I got work there.

Axley looked pointedly at Tom's white overalls and smiled. Mr. Johnson, after you hear what I have to say I hope you'll understand that you never have to work again.

* * *

Axley had stopped the newspaperman at the door, and the reporter had scurried away to make his report. Later in the day Tom noticed that he had returned and was circulating among the crowd, with his notepad before him. Now, in the late afternoon, Tom watched as Judge Wingate lit a cigar and settled in beside the lawyer. Determined to give nothing away, Tom maintained his silence as best he could, barely speaking during this meeting, never mind that it was in his home, on the subject of his future, his fate. The white men didn't seem to mind. They sat in his and Mary's accustomed chairs at either side of the fireplace, while Tom sat on the couch. He could hear Mary behind him, coming and going, was aware of the excited crowd outside, their voices as comforting to him as distant music.

The railroad track was only about thirty-five feet away from the house, and each time a train thundered past, all conversation had to be postponed. During such intervals the two men looked around, studying Tom and his home as if the noise provided a cover for their inspection. One or the other of them would continue as soon as possible, their voices re-establishing dominance over the train's diminishing noise.

Never since he built this house seven years ago had a white person been inside it, let alone two of them.

Tom had based the house on a pattern he found printed in the back of an old *American Builder Magazine* that Noble McCracken had saved off his garbage wagon. He had adapted it, adding a window here, moving a wall there, according to his and Mary's whim. Talking about it had been one of the things that had helped bring them back together. This house was Tom's sanctuary, his monument. It was the gift he'd laid at Mary's feet when he came back to her. Her acceptance of it had made their new life possible. And now two strangers, having first glanced around judgmentally, hunkered at its hearth, discussing the possibility of making huge changes to that life.

Axley, his papers fanned out in front of him on the floor, directed his comments to the judge. The fact is that Tommy here is sitting on a gold mine—a mine of *black* gold.

The two men chuckled.

Black gold, that's right, said the judge. This is an amazing development, that a local—someone from Wills County—could be in on the Oklahoma oil boom. This'll be good for the entire county!

Axley had to collect himself for a moment after the judge's last statement. He stared at Wingate, then gave a small mirthless explosion, masked as a laugh. Well, let's not forget, it's his Oklahoma roots that have created this thing, Judge.

Oh, of course. Of course. Both states are intimately bound up in it. And I have no wish to deprive Oklahoma of its rightful share of this oil strike. But Kentucky, now Kentucky has not had the luck that your fine state has had, Mr. Axley; surely you can see that. A thing like this could make a difference in a place like Wills County. We have our own oil wells, if you will—tobacco, for instance. That's our 'black gold'—dark-fired tobacco. But...

Judge Wingate, please bear in mind that I have had this case in hand for many years.

Then I'd think you'd welcome a little help with it, Mr. Axley. The judge's expansive laugh fell a bit flat when Axley failed to join in. Come now, we mustn't pretend, even for a minute, that this great piece of luck has anything to do with you and I, Mr. Axley. All I'm trying to say is that for a man like Tom Johnson here, this represents possibilities he'd never've dreamed of. Am I right, Tom... uh, Tommie?

Tom came out of his position as a spectator enough to nod, almost imperceptibly, then looked back down at the papers on the floor.

Axley, registering the nod, gave an eye-smile to the judge. He is indeed a fortunate man. However, for a positive outcome, one of the first things that I will have to determine is the identity of our lucky friend here. That, I have discovered, is at the crux of this case. Tom Johnson or Sam Ford? Elbows on knees, he breathed audibly into his prayerfully folded hands, rolling his eyes back to Tom dramatically. Anything to say on that, Tommie?

Tom didn't answer immediately. What, exactly, are you askin me, Mr. Axley?

Well... He opened a hand in Tom's direction as if it were obvious. You have two names: Tom Johnson and Sam Ford. Tom Johnson is a Negro plasterer from Kentucky. Sam Ford is an oil-rich Creek Indian from Oklahoma. Which...

Now, now, Mr. Axley. I wouldn't be too worried about that matter at this particular point. A lot of the nigras around here have some Indian blood in em. I b'lieve you can leave this to me. Here is where I can help you with your case. I have enormous influence, which I think you'll find extends well beyond Wills County. And furthermore, I'm prepared to set all other matters aside for as long as necessary, in order to represent my client here in his oil claim.

Axley straightened and took a deep breath, which he held for a long moment. He opened his mouth slightly.

The judge continued. I don't think we need to stress our boy right now with such a definitive stand. Let me make a suggestion. Why don't you join my wife and I for supper. Axley waved his hand and began to protest, but the judge cut him off. No no, I assure you, Lexie loves having comp'ny for supper. She'll be delighted. Besides, give us a chance to discuss the case. I insist. I insist.

Tom's face remained impassive, his gaze never resting on the two men, but the judge's mention of supper lifted his hope of an imminent end to the meeting. Though Axley had arrived after breakfast, the question of how to manage a midday meal had simply been avoided, both Tom and Mary privately hoping Axley would leave if he got hungry enough. Coffee was all they'd had, and Tom's stomach was rumbling embarrassingly, as was Axley's.

Well, um, thank you, Judge Wingate. I… uh… I appreciate your offer, but…

Come come now, no buts about it, Mr. Axley. In fact, why don't we go on back to town and we can discuss it for as long as you want. Get everything nailed down right off the bat, if you take my meaning. A case like this one doesn't come along every day.

Biting his lip, Axley nodded. He stared into the middle distance, preoccupied, almost cornered. Then he gave in. Alright then. I was gonna take the 5 o'clock train back into Greenberry....

Well then, you see how timely my invitation is. He took out his pocket watch. It's just a little after four, so that'll put you ahead of the game. I'll be happy to have your company back to town. In fact, for the entire duration of your stay in our fair city, Mr. Axley, me and my automobile are at your service.

Well… thank you kindly, Judge Wingate, he said, gathering up his papers with exquisite care.

Please, please. My friends call me Judge Arch. Wingate gave another of his hearty laughs.

Axley and Wingate rose together and crossed the room. Judge Arch it is, then. He looked back at Tom, who stood behind them. I'll see you tomorrow morning, Tommie. I'll be back out here by ten. We mustn't waste any time. And, don't worry about your job. *This* is your job now, and I will be doing all the work for you. With a little extra help from Judge Arch here it seems.

The judge laughed with true relish and slapped Axley on the back. Ain't that always the way. Some people do all the work, while other people—here he stopped to bow his head sideways at Tom—get all the money.

By the time they finally left the Johnson home, the two men of law gave the impression of complete camaraderie. As soon as the car disappeared from view, Tom stepped out to speak to the eager little throng in front of the house, putting his hands out to stem its surge toward the porch.

Is it true, Tom, what they's sayin? called Rafe Emerson.

Look. I know y'all been waitin to hear what's goin on, and I'll tell ya all about it, but Mary and me jes needs a few minutes by ourselves.

Tom's brother Richard called out, Aw come on now. Cain't y'all celebrate after you tell us what happened? We been waiting around seem like a long time. No telling how much longer *you* two'll be. The crowd's raucous appreciation made Richard beam.

Don't pay no tention to him. You know how baby brothers is. Me and Mary jes needs to talk, no kidding now. We ain't had a minute to ourselves all day long. Why don't y'all go home and eat and then come on back? Whadda ya say? I'll tell you all about it after supper. I'm bout to starve to death here.

Convinced by his light tone, the group dispersed. Tom closed the door and turned slowly around to face Mary, who stood in the kitchen doorway. They stared at each other in silence for a moment. Then Mary walked over and put her arms around Tom's waist, resting her face against the stiff bib of the white duck overalls she had made him for the job in Frankfort. Johnson's reputation as an artisan of plaster fancywork kept him in increasing demand. He was making a respectable living, and had seemed happier these past few years than she had known him to be since they were young.

Oh Tom, what're we gonna do? He had one arm around her; only when she began crying softly did he enfold her with both arms. I didn't never want to see Oklahoma again.

I know. I know it, baby. Listen...I been studyin on it while they was talkin, Mary. I'm gonna call up Rev'ren Parsons. He'll tell me what's the best thing to do. He knows my story—how I turned my life around. Knows lawyers, too. He's a smart man, and I believe I can trust him.

Which is more'n you can say about them two that jes left!

Easy, baby. Tom stroked Mary's hair, kissing the top of her head. We got to stay easy on this.

After a moment, he stepped back and adopted the lighter tone he'd taken with the crowd. It's... it's gonna take some fancy footwork, sho nuff, to handle these lawyers. When they get the smell a money...hooowee. But I'll handle it, don't you worry, Mary. We gonna be fine. I'm goin ovah to the grocery fo a minute while you make us some supper. Won't be gone long. Jes long enough to call up Frankfort, and then Rev'ren Parsons.

He drew his billfold out of a hip pocket and fumbled through it for the card. There it was, worn and dirty:

> Reverend James Parsons
> The Society For The Friendless
> 614 Massachusetts Building
> Kansas City, Missouri
> Telephone: Chapel 6-013

When he held the card up, Mary could see that Tom's hand was trembling. He flipped it over and ran his thumb across the embossed phrase on the other side: First Friend.

CHAPTER TWO

James Parsons replaced the telephone receiver into its cradle and sat in silent amazement. *That was one telephone call I would not have wanted to miss*, he thought, shaking his head in wonderment, then running long fingers through what was left of his hair. He had eaten lunch in the office and begged off an afternoon meeting as luck would have it, in order to sift through the details of a new case. The orderly stacks of paper on his desk were even higher than usual.

Though Tom Johnson reported regularly to him by mail, Parsons hadn't heard his voice in years. *It must be seven or eight years by now*. Parson's job had taught him that, ironically, murderers were often the most redeemable parolees. Tom Johnson was a fine example of redemption, and now, like a divine illustration, his efforts to make up for his sin and follow the right path were being rewarded a hundredfold. Parsons sat back, hands joined across his stomach, and gazed at the picture of the Good Shepherd on the wall across from his desk. *No, a million*fold, *by golly!* A smile spread across his face.

Tom had sounded a bit overwhelmed on the telephone, he reflected. But of course, who wouldn't? And the Reverend couldn't help feeling deeply touched that Tom had called on him. He was used to phone calls from men who were at rock bottom, but when things began to go well for them they usually kept the correspondence to the minimum required by law. Well, and who could blame them? Naturally they associated him with their darkest memories. First came the crime and the arrest, then trial and prison, and finally the raw shock of getting out and trying to start over as an ex-convict.

Tom had been as fine a man as any parolee he had ever worked with. It had to've been, good heavens, maybe ten years since he'd shown any signs of... *Let's see*, he mumbled aloud, walking over to his filing cabinet and drawing out Johnson's dossier.

Suddenly Parsons heard the clock in the tower across the street chime four-thirty. He looked at the thick manila file in his hand. If, as he had promised Tom, he was going to travel to Kentucky tomorrow, he had a lot of work to clear off his desk. He laid the dossier on the chair beside the door, where he customarily put the work he was taking home. He would have to forego the strong temptation to read it now, in the light of this tremendous new development. In fact he would just have to wait and read it on the train tomorrow.

His resolve lasted about fifteen minutes. When he found himself unable to concentrate on the cases in front of him, he decided to leave a little early, and buy his train ticket on the way home. All other business would just have to wait. It wasn't every day someone in your circle of acquaintance became an oil baron! Grabbing his coat from the rack and tucking Tom's file under his arm, he whirled out into the hallway and turned to lock the door of his office. Twenty million dollars! he said aloud, then shook his head. From behind the other doors typewriters clacked and telephones rang. He barely registered them. Barely heard his own footsteps echoing along the empty corridor.

Oh my goodness. My, my....

CHAPTER THREE

They had started their married life expecting to raise a large family. Tom himself was one of ten children, and Mary had six brothers and sisters. But fate had had different plans for them.

They were married on December 11th, 1897 in the African Methodist Episcopal Church of St. James, set at the edge of the fields in Slayden's Crossing. Tom Johnson was twenty-six years old and Mary Pryor twenty-two. The community which had known them both all their lives was well pleased with the match, and many commented that they would make mighty pretty babies.

Indeed, within seven months their son, Benjamen Tyree Johnson, was born, delivered by Tom's mother, Clara. A daughter, Alma Emmalia, followed a year later almost to the day. The pattern seemed set that would eventually produce the large family necessary for working a farm.

But in 1901 little Alma died of scarlet fever, and Mary's grief almost consumed her. In December of 1899 they had moved to a farm outside Smith, a community in Indian Territory, which is where the baby died. Over time Mary became convinced that if only they had stayed in Kentucky Alma would've lived. Even if she had been exposed to scarlet fever back home, Clara would have been there to help.

Alma died in the spring. By the time Mary could lift her head again, the heat and wind of summer had swept all the green from the landscape. Except for the copse of scrub oaks in the coulee below the house, Mary felt she might as well have been looking across the dry seas of the moon. She ached for home, the trees, the green fields of corn and tobacco, the warm circle of family.

Burying her baby out here alone had nearly finished her. Back in Slayden's Crossing Alma would've been buried with Mary's little baby brother and sisters, and her parents and grandparents in Heaven's Gate on the hill above the church, where the trees slowed the wind and stirred it into a lullaby. Out here it howled across the land the whole year round, and baby Alma's grave was all alone beside Smoke Creek.

Mary took Ben there every day and sat in silence, sometimes for hours, while the boy waded in the creek or played along its banks. Tom spent most of his time helping his uncle Sax on the farm. When Mary begged to move back home, back to Kentucky, Tom frowned and held her close.

Mary, we cain't go back. Ain't nothing fo me to do back yonder. We'll nevah have our own place if we go back. Here it's different. I got a chance. A man can make it out here, no matter if he's white, Negro, Indian—or all three like me. He took her by the shoulders and forced her away from him, so he could look into her face. I'm gonna get us our own place, Mary, I swear it. But you got to give me some time. I know I'm only share-cropping, same as I was in Kentucky, but I been listenin. I been keepin a ear to the ground. There's ways, Mary, and I aim to work em.

She hadn't replied, but he didn't seem to notice that. As the months wore on and Mary asked again why they couldn't move back home, Tom's response was less gentle. I done tol you why.

When she brought it up a third time, he blew up at her, kicking the empty water bucket across the floor and ringing it off the wall. She never mentioned it again. That night she held Benjamen in her arms until he fell asleep.

Tom didn't come back in til nearly dawn. Mary woke as he lifted Ben's heavy warmth from her lap. Startled, she looked up at him, and Tom saw that her face, so round and apple-cheeked only last year, had become drawn and grey, her dark eyes full of pain. He laid Ben down in his cot and turned back to her.

Come on to bed, baby, he said, taking both her hands in his. It's gonna be okay. I'm gonna get us a right. He walked her over to the bed, talking all the while in a bright, whiskey-scented tone. Me and Sax been over at Joe Elliott's tonight. Joe's gonna represent me fo a land claim.

She looked at him, uncomprehending, still far away. Joe Elliott was a white neighbor of Sax's, married to a Creek woman named Anna. When they had first met the Elliotts, Mary had hoped for some female companionship from her, but she soon saw that Anna preferred male company. Toward Mary she behaved with a faintly mocking coolness. Lately it had become Mary's private opinion that Sax and Anna were spending too much time together when Joe Elliott wasn't around.

And often of an evening, the three men would go over to Stroud, where they had a wide selection of saloons to choose from. Once when Joe and Sax had come by to collect Tom for one of these outings, Mary had expressed her worry over the reputation Stroud had for fights, and sometimes even murders. Why y'all always got to go to Stroud? It ain't safe over there from what I hears.

Sax had laughed and said to Tom in his nasal voice, Watch out, now, Tom. Them little shy ones, they might start out quiet, but they always ends up tellin ya where ya can go and where ya cain't.

Tom had climbed up into the wagon bed without looking at her, but Joe had smiled. It was a cool, condescending dismissal, and she had watched through a film of standing tears as the wagon bumped down the track.

Now she watched as Tom went to the mirror and slicked his hair down with Morgan's Hair Refiner Cream, then pulled his stocking cap on over it. He had been careful to use his hair-straightening method regularly since they had come west. After wiping his hands on the towel, he checked to see that the cap was pulled down at the back. Then he came and lay beside her, taking her face in his fragrant hands.

A land claim, baby, jes think of it. Our own place, won fo us by my Indian blood. Tom's blue-green eyes shone, even in that dim room. Ever since 18 and 89, when I seen that piece in the paper about the Land Rush, I understood that this here's the land of milk and honey fo the likes of us, Mary. Ain't no use to even try back home. I ain't nevah gonna be nobody there, no matter how strong or smart I am. No matter how hard I's to work. But out here, Mary, out here we gonna have us our own land.

After Tom fell asleep, Mary lay awake, thinking about what it meant to be somebody. Tom thought it was all tied up with claims and rights and ownership papers. But they'd neither one ever lived on land they owned. Neither had their parents. That didn't signify. They could walk into a gathering of folks back home and hear their names called out in jubilant greeting, Hey there, Mary! Git on over here and set with us, gal!

Here no one ever called out her name that way. She had learned early that society in Indian Territory was, to say the least, complicated. Shortly after their arrival, she and the children had gone into Okmulgee for supplies one day with Sax and Tom. She had been waiting for the men on a bench outside the dry goods store with Ben and Alma when she saw a Negro woman about her own age coming along the plank walk. Mary fought back her natural shyness and called out a hello. The woman nodded and stopped, looking Mary up and down. Then she said, You ain't from around here, ain't that right?

Mary shook her head. My husband and me, we jes moved to a place tween here and Stroud. Ovah close to Smith. We from Kentucky.

The woman said, That's about what I thought, and walked on. It had been a painful first lesson about freedmen, descendants of the black slaves who had been driven west with their Indian masters. Most freedmen did not welcome newer black immigrants from the south. After that Mary rarely went into town. She grew more and more isolated, absorbing herself completely in the housework and in her children. Then little Alma had taken sick and died.

Now she looked up at the rough plank ceiling as Tom snored beside her. Already, with no trees to block it, the early sun was pouring its punishing white light into the tiny house. Why'd we evah come here? she wondered bitterly. But she knew well....

Tom's uncle, Saxton Johnson, had joined the exodus of colored people from Kentucky to Oklahoma in 1896. He had started writing letters home immediately, saying that Tom and Richard ought to come out and join him. They could live in their own place on his rented property and help him work his land while they saved up for their own. Sax was living on the banks of Smoke Creek, and the very name was enough to set Tom dreaming. Smoke Creek, he'd say. Sound like music, don't it, Mary? Richard, who had a girlfriend, and a good job as a wagon mender, wasn't interested; but Tom fancied the idea, and as soon as Alma was old enough, they had set off.

As the train slipped along the rails out of Kentucky and into Arkansas, Tom had bounced little Benjamen on his knees and chanted over and over in time to the train's clacking, Hush little boy now, don't say a word. Papa gonna buy you a mockin bird...

Mary had smiled fondly at them over baby Alma, pleased at the way Tom pointed out the Mississippi River to Ben, and the Ozark Mountains. She had looked out at them in some awe herself. But when they finally came to it, she was shocked by Oklahoma Territory—shocked and dismayed. The land looked so bare. And she had been led to believe there would be very few white people out here. This was Indian Territory after all—the place to which the Indian tribes had been force-marched on the Trail of Tears. Now they were all out here together, one big area for the Cherokees, one for the Senecas, one for the Chickasaws of western Kentucky and Tennessee, and so on. And ever since Reconstruction, Negroes had been moving here in search of a fresh start. She had even heard talk of the possibility of a Negro State. But Mary could see from the train window, as they ground to a stop in Muskogee, that there were plenty of white people out here as well. Why? If they weren't interested in this brown land, why were they here? She felt as disappointed as a child at seeing so many of them in their buggies and along the sidewalks and platform.

But there in the crowd, grinning from ear to ear, was Sax Slayden, as he had begun calling himself out here. Vess Johnson's youngest half-brother, he was thirty-five years old, only seven years older than Tom. He had always behaved more like a friend to Tom and Richard than an uncle, teasing them into pool halls and moonshine parties before they were old enough to make their own mistakes. At least this was how Clara told it, and Mary was leery of Sax as a result of those stories. She could see that Oklahoma Territory hadn't matured him any. He had added a few pounds to his short frame, and he winked and laughed when he saw them, like a boy ready for a party.

Saxophone! Tom had cried, hustling down from the train and embracing him. Their enthusiastic reunion had been almost exclusive; she and the children had rated only a comment for Tom: And look at all a this—a family man now, I see. Then Sax had taken some of the baggage and set off, still talking, and Tom had followed him eagerly through the wide, windy streets of the town, carrying the rest of their things. She and the children had trailed behind Tom, struggling to keep up.

With Sax's encouragement, one of the first things Tom acquired was a gun. All the men in the Territory seemed to carry one, and there was almost daily talk of murders and fights. The wild west, Mary thought ruefully, her babies soft against her as she tried to adjust to this new place.

For her, the worst thing about living in Wills County had been Third Mondays. It was trade day on the Greenberry court square, and farmers came in from all over the county. Every few months or so, some of the white men would get 'all likkered up' and go looking for what they called some fun in the black neighborhoods. They would sometimes venture as far out as Slayden's Crossing and stand shouting in front of a Negro household chosen at random. When no one came out they would shoot right into the windows. In a while they'd go on off, but only after the people inside had been on the back porch of hell.

They had come to Mary's family, the Pryors, three or four times, and she would never forget the sound of the horses and wagons coming up the gravel road that led to the farm her father share-cropped. Always a light sleeper, she would awaken on the pallet she shared with two of her sisters. By the time her father whispered to those in the beds to get down on the floor and keep still, she would already be crying silently. They would turn their wagons into the yard, light from their lanterns sloshing in through the window. Drunken voices calling, Come on out here, niggahs! Her father would never answer, though he gripped the rifle he kept under the bed. He would shake his head furiously at her older brothers, who clenched their jaws in anger. The sound of people jumping down from the wagons would be followed by more taunts, then by a gunshot or two as the raiders shot out the upper panes of the window. Glass showered the Pryors where they lay, but no one moved. After a few minutes the drunken hooting would die down. In the ensuing silence, the only sound was the hounds' low growling from under the house. Eventually they would fire a shot or two into the air, get back into the wagons and drive off. The Pryors never knew when they would be targeted again.

Third Mondays had been one of the reasons Mary had left Slayden's Crossing willingly. But out here it was no better. The color barriers were not as high or as strong, but violence was also less occasional. Mary failed to see how Tom's carrying a gun made that any better; however, as was her custom, she held her tongue. She was beginning to see that Tom's enthusiasm was at one and the same time his best virtue and his worst vice. But it was him, and it was an important part of why she had fallen in love with him in the first place.

One night when they were still courting, they had been sitting on Clara and Vess's front porch, Tom's family all around them. Suddenly he had taken her two hands in his, pulled her to her feet and, walking backwards, had towed her out to the road for a ramble. When several of his sisters jumped up and tried to follow after them, it had been his father Vess who'd called them back, saying, You kids come on back here now and let them two have some time alone. I'll tell you a story, but only if you come on right now.

Thrilled with this sanctioned and unaccustomed privacy, Tom and Mary had wandered down the road to the field beside the church, where a great expanse of sky sparkled above them. Tom sat down on the ground and motioned her to sit between his knees, and rest her back against him. He drew her head against his chest. Encircled by his warmth and strength, she felt completely safe. Completely happy.

Jes look a there at that, Mary. Look at all a them stars.

Yeah, they mighty pretty.

You b'lieve what they say bout our fate bein written out up yonder, in the stars?

I don't know nothin bout that, but I do believe what they say about God having a plan fo each one of us.

Yeah? Do you? Well maybe it's the same thing. 'Cept I think you gotta help God out a little by figurin what that plan is. He spread his two hands in front of her, palms out across the night sky. Maybe this is a great big map made out of fire, and we got to find our way across it, you know?

She had begun to giggle a little. Tom Johnson, you crazy.

Naw, Mary Pryor, I ain't crazy. That is one thing I ain't.

Well then, suppose you right about it. What happens if you read the map wrong, and go the wrong way?

I reckon that happens all time to people. We most of us on the wrong road most of the time, don't you think?

Sho seem like it.

Well, I b'lieve we jes keep gettin signs to put us back onto the right road, but we got to keep watchin fo em. When you watchin out and you get a sign, you can feel it. Evah'thing in ya heats up—member this is fire we talkin about here, gal. Me, I plans to travel right across that big ol map til I find my way. They's a big plan marked out in them stars fo me—I jes knows they is.

A big plan, huh? she echoed in a lightly mocking tone.

Hey, now don't you go makin fun, gal. Why else would God have made me so strong and handsome? She was laughing now and shaking her head. Why would he, Mary Pryor, if he didn't have some big plan fo me?

Preacher say it's wrong to be prideful, Tom.

Well I say it's wrong to be too scared to try and do the best you can in this world. You got to look around you and read the signs, and then you got to follow em. You see what I mean?

Yeah I do. I see what you mean.

Tom began stroking her arm, and they were silent for a while. He rested his face against her hair and inhaled deeply. Finally he spoke again, more quietly, almost shyly. You one of the stars along my road, Mary. I can feel it.

That had been early in their time together, but she had never forgotten. Now she lay beside him in a little shack far from that field beside the church where they'd gotten married. Tom was still on fire with all his notions, but she wasn't so sure he was choosing the right road.

He woke again an hour later, saw that she was awake, and said in a raspy voice, There's my pretty woman, getting me my breakfus. I'm gonna need the best one you can make, Mary, if I'm gonna go out and rassle us up a farm, now ain't I?

As she built a fire in the stove, Ben padded sleepily over and put his two arms around her legs. Mornin' my mama, he said.

CHAPTER FOUR

The day Axley came to town with his big news, Benjamen Tyree Johnson was hard at work down in the clay pit between Greenberry and Slayden's Crossing. He didn't hear about it until the walk back to Greenberry along the railroad tracks had taken him to within a block of his home on Walnut Street. When he saw his wife Nema waving and running towards him he knew something was up.

Ben! Ben! she cried. Yo daddy's done got word he's rich. They's sayin he's a millionaire!

Ben steadied himself to receive her as she ran at him full tilt, but her words caused him to lose concentration, and he staggered backwards, dropping his lunch bucket, when she jumped into his arms and wrapped her legs around him. What in the world you talkin bout, woman? he asked, laughing.

She swung back down, grabbed his lunch bucket, and hung off his shoulder as they walked. I am talkin bout oil, honey. Oil! Oceans of it. They done struck oil on some ol piece of prop'ty your folks had when they's out in Oklahoma back when you's a baby! Now they's rich!

She couldn't stop dancing beside him as they walked down the street, drawing a little following of children which included their two daughters Rosa Mae and Adella. As she told him about the white lawyer from Tulsa, Ben listened in silence. He had no memories of Oklahoma. His mother had brought him back to Kentucky when he was barely five years old, and he knew nothing about any land his parents had owned out there. He'd always understood that they had lived on a farm his Uncle Sax rented. His mother hated the very word Oklahoma, and all Ben knew about it was that it was where his baby sister had died, and where his father had gotten in trouble with the law.

Tom Johnson had been in Fort Leavenworth Prison for almost twenty years. Ben had grown up without him. When his father went to jail, he and his mother had returned from the Territories to the home of his grandparents, Vess and Clara. Every Christmas they sent his father a box containing things like razors, a cake, and some pipe tobacco. Sometimes his mother sent his father a book or a jar of Morgan's Hair Refiner Cream. Over the years she wrote and received many letters marked Leavenworth Federal

Penitentiary. The name alone sent a chill up the boy's spine. His father had been a story that he preferred not to think about.

For a few years, when he was an adolescent, there had been another man in his mother's life, Rollie. He and his mother had moved into Rollie's small rented house in Greenberry. After a year or so, Ben had taken a job with the clay mine at Slayden's Crossing and moved back in with his grandparents. It was closer to work, of course, but it also suited Ben to get away from Rollie. He didn't like seeing him with his mother. Didn't like the way he tried to pretend he was his father either, giving Ben orders or advice. He knew his moving out had hurt his mother, and he had visited her whenever he could, which meant whenever he knew Rollie wouldn't be around.

Then suddenly, in January of 1920, six months after Ben's marriage to Nema, a letter came to Mary from Ben's father saying that he was being released on good behavior; he didn't yet know the exact date of his arrival, but he would send word as soon as he could. Different members of the family received the news with varying emotions, but they were all shocked. They had assumed his life sentence had meant they would never see him again. Rollie moved off to Ohio somewhere, and Mary came back to Slayden's Crossing to get ready for Tom's arrival.

Ben, a man of slight build and copper complexion, was apprehensive about his father's return. He had been his mother's emotional mainstay all his life, and was extremely protective of her. What sort of man would his father be? How would he treat his mother after twenty years in Leavenworth Penitentiary? 'Good behavior.' What did that mean for Mary?

Vess Johnson had died during Tom's prison term, and Benjamen had never spoken with his grandfather about his father. But Clara spoke often of Tom, always with a sort of defensive pride. The fact that he was a murderer, a prisoner, these things seemed to make no difference to her; she still idolized him. Everybody understood that Clara was on Tom's side, no matter what.

Much as Ben loved his grandmother, he couldn't help but think of her as Clara the Unquestionable, dealing out pennies to all the children from her huge battered brown leather purse. The pennies always came with a stern little lecture. You can spend this or you can save it up fo a rainy day. That decision is fo you to make. But you got to stand by it once you done made up yo mind.

Mary, like Ben, was quiet by nature. Ben watched her closely during this time of waiting for his father's return. He thought she seemed a little apprehensive too, though she would never have said so to him or anyone. An intense person, she had remained quietly loyal to her husband. In preparation for his return she had moved back in with Clara. Hers had been a hard life, but she didn't complain. Even though she took in sewing and laundry, Mary had never had pennies to give out for treats. Rollie was often out of work, and whatever she could earn was needed to pay bills. Now that he was gone, and Mary was back in Clara's house, she was still powerless, waiting. Still living in someone else's home. Ben kept his watch over her, filling with sadness once when he caught sight of her thin, green change-purse. But he had his own responsibilities now. Nema was expecting their first child.

In August they had finally received a letter from Kansas City, where Tom had been working under his parole officer, a preacher by the name of Parsons. He had written to Mary that it was usual to have a 'readjustment period' of living and working in a neutral place under supervision, before returning home. This latest letter explained that he had injured his hand in a packing house, and couldn't work until it healed. He would be home on the eleven o'clock train on September first. Mary and Clara began counting the hours.

So did Ben.

When Tom's train arrived that warm morning, Ben noted Mary's compressed excitement, her painful shyness. Finally a handsome man with cafe au lait skin and a handlebar mustache, peacock-blue eyes and powerful shoulders stepped down from the second car of the train. His left hand was bandaged.

He scanned the crowd and his eyes landed on Mary. They looked at each other for a moment. Then, shaking his head slowly, he walked toward her. Ben saw that both of his parents had tears in their eyes. They only had a moment to embrace amid a background of approving noises, before the rest of the family crowded around in a riot of welcome. Ben's grandmother was next, then his aunts, his Uncle Richard and all his cousins. Ben stayed back.

Tom's favorite sister, Etta, had died of tuberculosis while he was in prison, and now her fifteen-year-old daughter, Gladys, stepped forward. Tom held her by the shoulders and looked at her carefully. So this is Gladys, he said. You look like her, too. I loved yo Mama so much, gal. I reckon she lef you here to take her place. More tears and hugging.

Ben stood at the edge of the crowd watching closely, hardly breathing. Finally Tom said, Why, Mary, where's our boy? Where's Ben? Ain't he here?

Tom followed everyone's gaze as they looked over at Ben. He stared for a moment, frowning a little, as if deciding whether or not this small, quiet man could be his son—his firstborn and only progeny—and then he cried out, Ben! Son! and made his way to him. Ben felt himself swallowed up in his father's embrace, swallowed by sensations—the rough fabric of the suit jacket, the mustache against his neck, strong scents of aftershave and pomade, the larger-than-life presence of a rumor become real.

When Ben presented his young, pregnant wife, Tom's charm expanded yet again, and yet again Benjamen was free to retreat into the background and observe the phenomenon of his father's unexpected return from a life sentence in prison.

In the seven years since that reunion, he and his father had maintained a cordial, if somewhat cool relationship. Ben always showed what he considered proper filial respect, but he found that his first impression of his father held. Tom Johnson was larger than life, domineering and proud. Not humility, but dignity was his answer to his chequered past. Though he was only guessing in the absence of real conversation on the topic, Ben couldn't help imagining that he himself was something of a disappointment to his father. A slight, shy man who liked to cook, and who had sired only daughters.

For his part, Ben watched his father carefully and saw that Tom treated Mary well. That was enough for him; the rest didn't matter. Within a year of his return, Tom had built her a fine house in Slayden's Crossing. He worked hard at his prison trade of plastering and was sometimes sought for jobs from as far away as Indiana and Ohio. The restoration job in Frankfort had been a real feather in his cap. And in his spare time he made things out of wood or clay for Mary, with all the tender enthusiasm of a young husband. And Mary showed these things off with an answering tenderness. Over the years, Ben had adjusted along with the rest of the community to his parents' resurrected marriage. They seemed settled and genuinely happy.

But oil wells? A millionaire?

As he and Nema arrived at their front steps a few neighbors who had been waiting sprang towards them in great excitement. One handed him a copy of *The Greenberry Daily Leaf*. There it was in bold letters: LOCAL NEGRO TO GET IMMENSE FORTUNE. A photograph of his parents' home was featured right in the middle of the front page. Ben's mouth fell open slightly as he looked at it. He shook his head. Once again, his father was larger than life. Once again he was becoming more rumor than flesh-and-blood man.

CHAPTER FIVE

That night Tom and Mary lay in bed exhausted, but unable to sleep. Gladys, along with Richard and his wife Parmalee, had been the last to go, finally leaving when the clock struck ten.

When's Rev'ren Parsons comin?

Said he'd get the train down tomorra.

Reckon we won't see him fo Satiddy then.

Naw, that's right.

The wind blew up and a redbud branch scraped at the window. After a while they heard the midnight train blast through Slayden's Crossing, leaving the silence deeper in its wake. In that silence Tom turned over and began stroking Mary's stomach. She put her hand on his and followed it down and soon they were making love, writing again the wordless declarations that are the real certificates of a marriage. Negotiating the balance of power. In this they took turns being compliant or demanding, and thereby understood each other whole.

Afterward they slept.

* * *

Reverend James Parsons sat back in his upholstered seat on the train and sighed. He had made it. It was Friday, January 27th, 1928, and he would arrive that night in Greenberry, Kentucky, as he had promised Tom he would. Now he was eager to read through the thick file of papers on his lap, labelled in flowing script:

> Prisoner # 3283
> Tom Johnson
> alias Sam Ford

Parsons had not read Tom's file carefully for a number of years, and he'd seen so many cases that he couldn't recall many of the early details of this one. From the first page the startlingly handsome face of the thirty-year-old man Tom had been when he was sentenced, engaged him. Mug shots were usually tragic or repulsive. This one showed a face blessed with generous, regular features, a sweeping mustache and a pair of piercing, confident eyes—the eyes of a good-natured, charming man, not afraid, even in this circumstance, to look the camera directly in the eye. There was even the faintest suggestion of a smile.

Parsons glanced through the description: light mulatto, 155 pounds, five feet, eight inches tall, a scar on the second joint of the left little finger, a mole above the right elbow. But it was the phrase listed on the line for eye color that was the most unusual thing here: Greenish Slate Blue. Amazing, thought Rev. Parsons. It was as if they couldn't decide what to put down. He did remember that Tom's eyes were a remarkable color, not only because he had expected brown in a Negro, but because he had never seen eyes he would classify as that color on anyone, not even a white person.

The Reverend's own blue eyes smarted slightly from the cloud of tobacco smoke that hung in the crowded passenger coach. It didn't help that the man who sat facing him was enjoying a rather potent cigar. He thought of opening the window a crack, but decided against it, since it would mean shifting the papers in his lap and causing a bit of a stir. He had little enough privacy without drawing more attention to himself.

He turned to the next sheet and read on. Tom had been sentenced in January of 1903, after having spent some time in the Muskogee jail awaiting trial. In the end his trial was only a short hearing, because Tom had pleaded guilty to the charge of having murdered Joe Elliott, a white man. There was no mention of why.... Ah, here, a few pages on, was a letter from the Warden to the Judge. It had been written in December of 1903, nearly a year after Tom arrived at Fort Leavenworth:

> I beg to make inquiry of you regarding Tom Johnson, a light mulatto who was sentenced for life from your court in January of 1903. He has behaved himself well thus far and has a clear record, but he begins to act in a manner that indicates either an aberration of mind, or else is an attempt to feign insanity. He claims he remembers nothing of his trial at Muskogee, nor anything about the crime with which he is charged. He claims only to remember disposing of some liquor and being told by the officer who arrested him that he was brought to jail for that offense. I would be grateful if you could give me your opinion of his guilt or innocence, and of his mental responsibility.

Parsons turned eagerly to the next page of the file to read the Judge's reply.

U.S. Marshal's Office
Western District
Indian Territory

December 10, 1903

Dear Warden McLeod,

    In reply to your letter re prisoner No. 3283, Tom Johnson, alias-Sam Ford, I beg to say that in my opinion Johnson was hired to kill Elliott. Elliott was a white man and a fellow by the name of Saxton Slayden was intimate with Elliott's wife, who was an Indian. It is my private opinion that Mrs. Elliott and this Saxton Slayden hired your prisoner No. 3283, but the case never went to trial because of the prisoner's confession. That is all this office can tell you.

Parsons clearly remembered that when he became Tom's parole officer, Tom had owned up to him repeatedly that he had done a terrible thing, and that he regretted it and resolved to set his life straight, if only he could ever get back to his wife and family and start over. Now, as he read through the file, Parsons could see that Tom had, in the first few years of his sentence, tried a number of things to free himself. First he had pretended a sort of amnesia, as evidenced by these entries. Then, a few years later he had been even more daring, as the next entry showed.

Muskogee, Indian Territory   Oct. 18, 1906

    Dear Warden, Your prisoner #3283, Tom Johnson, escaped from my deputy by jumping from the Frisco train running at 40 to 45 m.p.h. He was subsequently recaptured and brought to jail at Muskogee. This is for your information.

Reverend Parsons rested his head against the antimacassar on the high-backed seat and looked out the train window at the landscape that seemed to flow past like a white-churned river. How would it feel, he wondered, to jump from a train moving at 45 miles per hour? How desperate would you have to be to do such a thing?

He reread the letter. The Frisco train… Why was Tom on the Frisco train with a deputy in 1906? He flipped through the file, but it provided no enlightenment on this point. There were long lists of Johnson's correspondents, mostly family members, as well as records of his health and prison work over the years. In June of 1904 he had been put on bread and water for 'not closing up in line when he was about fifteen feet behind. I told him the second time and nearly touched him with my cane. When back in cell he said, "Pidsadny, you can speak to me, but I want you to understand you cannot punch me with that stick, and I expect to see the Deputy about it".'

Parsons shook his head, admiration welling up in him at Tom's dignified response to the prison guard. This backward look was building in his mind a picture of Tom Johnson as a millionaire by character. Whether the first time he read it he had thought the prisoner's rebuke of the guard noble, or impudent and stiff-necked, he could not now recall. It was a question, in fact, which he did not ask himself.

A 1910 letter from the Department of Justice surfaced. Perhaps this might explain the trip outside Leavenworth in 1906. He skimmed it eagerly and saw that people had been searching since 1906 for Sam Ford, to verify his land claim with the Creek Nation. Sam Ford? Parsons thought. But that was just Tom's alias. He realized then that he had always assumed Tom had taken an alias when he was arrested for murder, in order to protect his family's name and privacy. But, flipping back to the beginning, he saw that he had been tried and convicted as Tom Johnson. So the alias had to be connected to some other aspect of his life. This letter said the Department of Justice was seeking to verify Sam Ford's land claim.

Suddenly Parsons looked up, straight into the burning butt end of his fellow passenger's cigar, and recalled the tone of Tom's voice over the telephone the night before. Reflecting on it now, the parole officer realized that Tom had not sounded overwhelmed by good fortune, so much as cornered. Run to ground.

CHAPTER SIX

The train seat was hard and he felt pains in his stomach. He could tell by the intermittent smells that Deputy Reed's bowl of chili wasn't settling all that well either.

Let's go, said the guard, jerking at the cuffs.

Only when they were standing beside the stalls did Reed unlock the handcuffs that bound them together. When he finished first and pulled the chain, he heard Reed shout out, You set right where you're at, boy!

I's jes washin my hands; don't get all worked up. Then he was on the bucking floor between the cars more quickly than he'd have thought possible with the shackles, and had the outer door wrenched open. Assaulted by moving air and liquid landscape, he didn't take time to think. He coiled the entire length of his energy and leapt into solid, brown noise, rolling in his chains through an explosion of his own making. Leaping like a demented kangaroo across the brown plain, his mouth full of phantom grit, he always woke up to the screech of the braking train, the sound an incision without anesthetic.

Though it had been many years, the dream returned to him the night Ben Axley came to town with his satchel of papers. That Friday morning he jerked awake with a groan that also woke Mary.

She put her hand on his arm and could feel tightly clenched muscle. What's a matta Tom?

Damn nightmares back again.

She moved her hand over his heart, murmuring soothingly, as if to a frightened child. Slowly, he released his pent breath. He reached for her then, and held her against him.

Mebbe I oughta come with ya, Tom.

Hell no, Mary. I cain't have you out there in all this business. It's cutthroat, I tell you. It's gonna be hard enough fo me to watch out fo myself, let alone you too. They wouldn't stop at usin you someway to get at this money. Sides, if they's to jail me, you'd jes have to come back alone....He was about to say 'again', but stopped himself.

Why don't you jes tell em you ain't Sam Ford? Tell em bout them Creek brothers that helped you out in Oklahoma—the...the Washin'ton brothers.

Tell about them. The only reason they want you is cause of that oil money, and it ain't got nothin to do with you, really.

They already know about that, Mary.

Huh?

Axley knows the land claim was false. He don't care. Tol me he knows the ropes on land claims, and he can make this one pay—'fo both of us'. Tom gave a short, bitter laugh.

Mary said no more, but neither one of them fell back to sleep.

CHAPTER SEVEN

True to his word, Axley was back in Slayden's Crossing, satchel in hand, by ten the next morning. To his and Tom's dismay, Judge Wingate was there as well, having insisted on driving Axley out to the Johnson place.

Look, Tommie, it's this way, Axley explained. The state of Oklahoma is a writhing snake pit of legal cases to do with Indian oil claims. The governor wants them dealt with so we can free up the courts for other matters. Yours is one of the biggest, and believe me, everybody and his half-brother's trying to get a piece of it. I looked at this case ten years ago and said to myself, if I can solve this one I'll be doing myself, the government *and* the rightful owner a big favor. I have made a study of this case and come to a conclusion that'd make Solomon himself proud. You, Tommie, are the rightful owner, and I aim to see that proved in court. Now, what it means is that we're up against nothing less than the United States Government itself—that's who we got to prove our case to. But I believe we can do it.

The judge had grown restless during his long, unaccustomed silence, and had stood up. He lifted a wooden statue of a bird from the mantlepiece. Turning it over, he saw the initials on the bottom. You carve this thing, Tommie?

Tom nodded.

Hm. Well I'll say one thing... He set the bird back in place without further comment, and proceeded to break his promise. Your quiet ways'll do us good when it comes to the courtroom. All you have to do is be there, in your Sunday-go-to-meetin clothes, and leave the talking to Axley and me. Ben, lemme see those papers...those deeds...

Axley, his lips pressed to a white line, handed over an envelope. Judge Arch is right about your staying qui...

Do you have either birth certificate?

Axley sighed at the judge's interruption. There is no birth certificate for Sam Ford, he began. You see...

Ah, of course. Yes. I forgot. But still... you leave that part to me, Ben.

As Judge Arch is your lawyer, Tommie...

Seeing Tom's mouth open slightly and his frown deepen, the judge jumped in once again. I am your legal counsel as of yesterday, Tommie.

Not a bad thing to have a judge in your corner, if I do say so myself. And I am prepared to work without remuneration until such time as the case is resolved.

What if we lose? asked Tom.

Oh if we lose, you won't have to pay either of us, said Judge Arch grandly. There is absolutely no financial risk to you at all in settling this claim. The risk, and the responsibility, lies entirely with us.

That is customary in these cases, Tommie, Axley added. But we won't lose, never you fear.

And if we... or, *when* we win, what's y'all's take gonna be?

The two lawyers looked at each other quickly. It was Axley who answered. Twenty percent is customary in these cases.

Twenty percent each?

Well, yes, of course... but you'll hardly miss that much with what you're going to realize.

That's right, Tommie. Remember, you'll get the other sixty percent! said the judge, adding breathlessly, Why you'll have so much money you won't be able to spend it in your lifetime. If you shared it evenly with us and we each took a third—which we certainly would not do—but even if we did take as much as you, none of us'll see the end of it before our earthly term is over. I don't know if you fully grasp just how much money you stand to gain here. And don't forget, Tommie, you'll never see a penny of it without our help.

CHAPTER EIGHT

Maddie Wingate stood in front of the three-way vanity mirror pinning her new hat into place. She was getting ready for Friday night Benediction. Her husband Ted, who was not a Catholic and who in fact scorned Catholicism in general, often spent Friday evenings in a derisive sulk because of Maddie's inflexibility about attending Benediction. Tonight, however, he had been in a good mood through dinner, and right now she could hear him in his study across the hall rustling papers and actually whistling.

Although she was relieved by his mood, Maddie didn't dare to presume on it. Her determination to practice her faith in the face of his increasing contempt throughout these thirty-two years had used up the whole of her store of defiance. That and having married him in the first place, of course.

Madeleine Florentine Coyne was the sixth of nine children born to a well-to-do family in Harvest, Kentucky. Harvest, population six hundred, was an almost uniformly Catholic community twelve miles west of Greenberry. Maddie was descended on both sides from the founding families of Harvest, and the Coynes were at the financial and social heart of the little town. From their position as wealthy farmers, her father and eldest brother had started the Harvest Dry Goods Store, and then the Bank of Harvest, both of which had prospered mightily.

From her early childhood, Maddie had been her father's favorite. She had just returned from the Nashville finishing school where he had sent her to be groomed for a career as the wife of some suitable gentleman of business and society, when she broke his heart by eloping with Ted Wingate.

Now, on February 3rd, 1928, having completed her primping, she crossed the hall to Ted's study and leaned down to kiss him on the cheek. Good-bye, dear. I'm leaving now. Oh, I see you're going over the house plans again. It's too late to change anything at this point you know.

I don't want to change a thing, he said, I'm just gloating. Everything should be ready by the first of May. And then we'll move into the finest house in the whole county.

It's going to be beautiful.

Beautiful! he thundered. It'll be more than beautiful. It's a house fit for a millionaire. It's gonna be a god-damned showplace!

Maddie stood upright and stiffened. She could not abide blasphemy, and Ted rarely slipped in her presence. Tonight his buoyant mood enabled him to slide fairly quickly back into the teasing tone that could usually smooth her bristles. Oh, come on now—you know I just get carried away. He reached up and took her gloved hand into both of his. For heaven's sake, you're on your way to pray for me this very minute. Surely that little black mark'll be off my soul before you even get back home... which better be soon. I cain't stand this house without you in it.

She smiled tightly.

Which reminds me... he continued, I been thinkin about what to name the new house. How about 'Wincoyne'?

A real smile this time, a thoughtful one that lingered. 'Wincoyne.' Hmm. Yes, I think I like that.

Good, good. Go on then and do your prayin. You better not keep the congregation waiting. You know they'd never start a service without you.

She said nothing in reply, but sighed hard as she descended the stairs. Emmett Lewis stood at the door ready to drive her to church. He was their chauffeur and doubled as butler, gardener and general factotum. Except for Rachel Slayden, who did the cooking and housekeeping, he was the only person the Wingates trusted with their personal needs. Emmett's been with us for years, Maddie often said when people referred to him as their servant. There is no word for what he is to us—I don't know what we'd do without him. But he is not a servant. That's a presumptuous word and I loathe it. Ted and I don't have servants.

St. Joseph's was not nearly as grand a church as St. Isidore's of Harvest, and though this pained Maddie, she supposed it couldn't be helped. The Catholic population of Greenberry was neither as numerous nor as well-heeled, per capita, as that of the smaller town. Father Deroche had begun a building fund almost as soon as he had arrived the year before last. His plan was to replace the little white clapboard building with a solid red brick church. It would never measure up to the Spanish mission-style beauty of St. Isidore's, but Maddie would do all she could for the building fund.

The reality was that she would be as generous as Ted would let her be, but she never thought of it in such bald terms as that. Thirty-two years ago her mother had said with cold exasperation, Well Maddie, you have made your bed and now you must lie in it. Being a lady had helped her to lie in it because she understood clearly that being a lady means keeping still, and Maddie's marriage had turned out to be, not the hard cot of privation her parents had predicted, but as opulently exquisite a bed of nails as ever a lady lay down upon.

In the summer of 1896, Maddie had been a saucy, green-eyed eighteen-year-old with the perfect features of a Renaissance madonna. She had never known anything but comfort and admiration. Like all the Coynes, she took her religion very seriously, but she saw no reason to fret about the eyes of needles. If the Catholic Church loved the poor, it also loved the rich, and Maddie had been raised to believe that God would reward a lady who did her duty. When she sat in the fine church of St. Isidore, which happened to be next door to her father's big house, she felt completely at home, happy to be back from boarding school. She looked from the crystal rosary in her hands to the crown of stars encircling the head of the statue of Our Lady. In terms of her small farming community, Madeleine Florentine Coyne was to the manor born; but she was simultaneously to the altar born, and therein lay the essence of the woman she would become.

Walter Benedict Coyne, whose name had been shortened to W.B., always hired only the very best. He and Louisa had agreed over the winter that it was time to give their Victorian house a new coat of paint. And they had also agreed that the only outfit for the job was the one that had painted the new Wills County Courthouse nine years before.

The old courthouse had burned to the ground early in 1887 when a clerk—who was either very dedicated or very crooked, depending on who was telling it—was working late and fell asleep with his candle still alight. The clerk escaped with his life, and nothing else. With the slate of county records wiped clean a new era had begun, and many had taken advantage of the opportunity.

Ted Wingate had profited from the burning of the old courthouse in the simplest sense. He was eighteen years old at the time, and living alone in the little wooden house on East Broadway where his father had died several years before. Ted was the oldest of four boys, and Arch the youngest. When his mother had remarried, she took three of her sons with her to her new home out in the county, and Ted—who refused unequivocally to move—was delighted to find himself all but free of adult supervision. He had left school after the eighth grade, as most students did, and embarked on a career of odd jobs which included house-painting. He craved nothing so much as independence, and he had quickly developed a reputation as a hard-drinking loner.

When Charlie Reynolds took him on as part of his painting crew he found him to be a good worker—whenever he showed up. About once a week young Wingate simply wouldn't appear, but Reynolds never fired him, for two reasons: Ted never wasted time on the job, and he wasn't afraid of heights. The other men were full of talk and horseplay, but when it came to the most dangerous jobs, the third story work, the twinkle in their eyes would dim, only to reappear in Ted's. Without a word of bravado, he would climb straight up the ladder, and lay into the peeling paint with his scraper. Then back down for a can of paint, and he would scamper to the top again, holding on with one hand. Fearlessly, he would hang the can from the top rung with a meat hook, not seeming to notice its slight swinging over open space, and begin the job.

The new courthouse steeple was visible for miles above the trees around Greenberry. It was higher than any of the churches, higher, indeed, than anything except the twin black smokestacks of The Woolen Mills. The whole town had looked on in awe as humorless young Ted Wingate painted the white trim of the red brick spire in the summer of 1887, and the result, as everyone agreed, was a credit to Wills County.

The first time they saw each other, Maddie was washing her face in the pretty flowered basin in her bedroom. Her long, black hair, tied back with a blue ribbon, fell over the shoulder of her white robe as Ted watched, transfixed, from the ladder outside her window. When she looked directly at him over a dainty pink towel, Ted all but lost his balance. But his dizziness was completely internal, because to Maddie's eye, he stood still as a statue, brazenly staring at her.

She folded the towel deliberately, hung it back on its brass rack, and walked straight toward the window. Ted's hands gripped the ladder and his heart began to hammer. When she was face to face with him she reached up, so that the sleeve of her robe fell about her elbow and exposed a perfect, white arm. Suddenly, like a vision, she was gone in the tearing sound of the shade being lowered, and Ted was left staring at his own rapt reflection. He was twenty-six years old, and for the first time in his life, he knew what he wanted for his future.

The Coynes' house took two weeks to paint, and neither Maddie's family nor Ted's workmates appeared to notice what happened between them during that time. For the first week, theirs was an intensely compressed and private courtship of the eyes. Initially she regarded him with cool disdain for having seen her in her bedroom. But he returned her coolness with warmth, a challenging, appreciative, male warmth. Try as she might to ignore him, she found herself intensely aware of him.

During the second week they discovered their tongues, hers sharp at first. But his unfazed determination, his obvious and knowing fascination with her, threw her off balance. He was, after all, no boy. Finally Ted mentioned that he liked to eat lunch alone, in the little garden he'd found behind St. Isidore's. Against her better judgement, Maddie took the bait and followed him there, trying to pretend it was a surprise to see him. She found herself thinking about him all the time—his level, blue stare. Then the night before his indirect invitation, she'd had a most disturbing dream.

So they met. That day, and every day thereafter. By the last day of the job he had kissed her and told her that she had to be his wife. No one else. He had their elopement planned. It involved a ladder at her window, and the promise of a church wedding. Afterward. When her parents couldn't refuse.

W.B. and Louisa Coyne were more bitterly angry than Maddie had imagined they ever could be, when she and her bridegroom sat in the parlor and confessed their marriage. Her mother stared in dry-eyed shock, and her father erupted into wounded outrage. Several jagged fragments of Coyne's tirade, Ted never forgot: 'I did not raise you to marry a nobody of a housepainter!' and 'You have cut yourself off from all hope of a decent life!'

Maddie was haunted by their insistence that there could be no white church wedding, only a guilty official registry affair in the parish office to keep her 'in the Church'. But she found Ted's response even more chilling than that of her parents. When they said he must, of course, become a Catholic, he stood up and said, Maddie, I have heard enough. We're leaving.

That was when her mother had cried and so had she, but Ted had remained coldly unmoved. Louisa put her arm around Maddie and then drew her aside for a quiet, resigned bit of motherly advice. You have made your bed and you must lie in it.

W.B., finally unable to see his favorite daughter part from him, offered Ted a share of the family business as a wedding present, and the use of a converted creamery for their home, that she might not have to leave Harvest just yet.

That first night in their plain, new home, Ted stood looking across the field to the Coynes' capacious Victorian house. Someday, he vowed tightly, I am gonna own everything your old man does—and more. I'll show him who's a nobody.

Maddie's heart sank at his words. It was clear they did not involve a promise to her. In fact, they had nothing to do with her at all, in any positive sense. She, too, walked over to the window and looked across the field at her parents' house. It might have been a ship, separated from their tiny boat by an angry sea, and moving away from her. She looked at Ted's set mouth and wondered what sort of man she had bound herself to.

CHAPTER NINE

Ben Axley and his satchel of papers was bringing it all back to the surface of Tom's memory. The old dream. That drive he'd had as a young man when he'd first set out for Oklahoma.

He'd thought at first that he would get a farm for himself and Mary and their growing family, with his bare hands. He had imagined that if he just worked hard enough, and saved every penny, he would eventually achieve this dream of his. Talking to Sax and to Joe Elliott and others showed him he'd been wrong. Oklahoma Territory was no different for a colored man than Kentucky, or anywhere else in the country it seemed. The way it differed from everywhere else involved the Indian population. Sax and Joe assured him that there were ways, if you played your cards right. And so a different dream took shape. Or a different path to the old one.

Throughout the summer of 1901, Tom spent his spare time planning strategies with Joe Elliott and the Washington brothers. His natural animation seemed heightened as he moved closer to making his dream a reality.

The Washingtons, full-blooded Creek Indians, were 'Town Kings', as Tom told Mary—the town kings of Ketchapataka. Ketchapataka was the Creek community closest to the farm Sax was working. She imagined this meant they were something like a cross between a chief and a mayor. Tom himself wasn't much clearer about what it meant, but he was sufficiently impressed by the phrase to be a little in awe of them as he entered into the process of getting a land claim. They provided him with a new name, a new identity. He was to use it to register with the Dawes Commission in order to be granted the one hundred and sixty acres to which each person of Indian blood was said to be entitled.

Sam Ford.

Why you got to have a new name? Mary asked. Why cain't you register under yo own name?

Because I ain't got the papers to prove my Indian blood. This Sam Ford, he was one quarter Creek, and the Creek Nation's got papers on him.

Then why don't he register fo the land hisself?

Fo one, simple reason, Tom answered with a satisfied smile. He's done been dead two years. He can't use his right no mo, so the Washin'ton brothers is givin me a chance.

B-but... you said the Creek Nation keeps records. Won't they have a record of his death?

Naw. They don't keep no records on deaths out here. Only states bothers with that stuff. This here's Indian Territory. New rules, baby. We playing by new rules now.

But, Tom, you'll be lyin.

Tom put his pipe down on the table and walked over to the window. After a moment he turned and faced his wife. Look at me, Mary. Look me in the eye now, he said, beginning softly. The rules ain't never been fair fo the likes of us—now ain't that so? I am part Indian, part white and part Negro. I can do well enough as a Negro, if any Negro can be said to do well enough in America. But I can't never make no claim on my white blood to have me any rights. The 'one drop law' takes care a that. Here, in Indian Territory, right now, I got a chance to make a claim on my Indian blood. This man Sam Ford is dead. I ain't stealin nothin from him. You tell me why I shouldn't get us our own place if I can do it. Go on now. You say it. You tell me it's because I oughta play by the rules. Rules that are set up to keep me from makin it no matter how hard I work. Rules that're set up to keep our boy Ben from makin it, no matter how hard he works all his life. Tell me that I got to play by them rules, Mary.

He spoke like a preacher, his eyes blazing with passionate conviction, his voice building. Mary was silent. What could she say to that? She had no answers. She looked over at Ben playing with spools on the floor, and nodded her head slowly, giving her silent assent to the plan. Tom had laughed then, and had taken her in his arms. That's my gal, he said. Oh Mary, jes wait'll you see how things is gonna change fo us now.

That October when the Dawes Commission met at the Creek Nation Headquarters at Okmulgee, Tom went off to register Sam Ford's land claim. Joe Elliott went with him, and so did Elliott's wife, Anna. Anna later said she thought it was just a shopping trip.

Sax was already in Okmulgee. He had said he was going on business, but Mary suspected he had gone because Anna was going to be there. She had come across them one day a few weeks before in the live oak copse near Alma's grave. It was as she had suspected; they were lovers. They hadn't seen her and she never mentioned it to Tom, but one day in December Tom brought Sax into the house with a bleeding lip.

Mary, get some cold water fo Sax's mouth!

What happen? she asked, going for the bucket.

Him and Joe done had a fight's all.

Mary fetched the water and sponged Sax's lip with a cool rag, thinking all the while, I know what this is about.

That night in bed she pulled Tom to her in a way she hadn't in months. With a sharp intake of breath, she brought her right nipple upwards along his ribcage, striking a flame in both of them. This is *my* man, she thought, and I aim to keep him.

*   *   *

On January 22nd, 1902 it was official. Sam Ford was granted one hundred and sixty acres near the Cimarron River. Mary had heard it said that the Cimarron was a quicksand river, and could swallow a horse and buggy whole. But Tom laughed, and promised her they wouldn't lose so much as a shoe to it.

Let's go see it, baby! Let's go see our land, he said. He'd been given a survey map by the Dawes Commission, and so, as soon as the snow had melted in late February, they borrowed Sax's horse and wagon and set off to cover the twenty miles to their land. When they started over the bridge that spanned the Cimarron, Tom teased Mary mercilessly. She laughed, but held tightly to Ben all the same. The road went to within three or four miles of the claim, and then they travelled overland, using old buffalo trails whenever possible, bumping along and laughing.

Okay, said Tom as they came upon a creek, I reckon we almost home. He pulled on the reins and looked closely at his map, tracing a meandering line on it with a forefinger. This here is Tiger Creek. It cuts right through our place.

They tigers here, Daddy? asked Ben, taking hold of his mother's hand.

Naw, honey. I asked em that when I looked at the map, and you know what they said? They said this creek was called after a Town King name of James Tiger, and that *he* was named fo his black grandaddy who had killed a tiger back in Africa, where he come from. So don't you worry, Benjamen, he said, lifting first the boy and then his mother down from the wagon. Our creek is named fo brave men, not fo wild animals. Ain't no tiger nowhere round here.

The land was hilly and there were many trees, which pleased Mary deeply. It reminded her more of Slayden's Crossing than any place she'd seen since they had come west. Tiger Creek wandered prettily through its meadows and around its hills.

Oh Tom, she said, it's beautiful!

Yes it is, he said, shaking his head in wonder. Look like they done give us the prettiest place they had.

When can we move here?

Tom was radiant. Well, I done promised Sax I'd help him with the spring plantin. But come June we be free, and soon's we can after that, we'll move. And Ben, guess what I'm gonna take you to see soon as we get settled in here?

What, Daddy? The child had been tugging on his mother's arm, trying to get her to go exploring with him. Now he turned and gave his father his full attention. Tom squatted down to hold that attention.

Well, I tell ya... not very far west a here is the Shawnee Trail.

What's the Shawnee Trail?

What's the Shawnee *Trail*?! he echoed, as if stunned. Why, Ben, ain't you never heard tell of the big cattle drives?

The little boy shook his head solemnly, his eyes wide.

The Shawnee Trail is one of the biggest cattle roads in the whole of the wild west. You and me, son, we'll ride over to a great big ol bluff I know bout, where it seem like all the Territories is spread out right in front a ya. And then we gonna wait. We gonna wait til we can start to feel the earth jes arumblin underneath our feet. Then the next sign'll be a big ol cloud a dust comin up out of the south. And once we see that, we'll make sure we're on good high ground up out of the way. Cause then here they'll come, thunderin right below us. A million head of cattle, all colors, jes arunnin across them plains. And herdin em, mebbe a dozen cowboys...

Cowboys?

That's right, Ben, cowboys. Real ones, in big stetson hats ridin they hosses fast as the wind and keepin all them long-horned steers goin right where they want em to—like makin a river go where you say. Oh I tell ya son, it's gonna be a sight to see!

When, Daddy? When can we see it? Can we go today?

He put his hand on the boy's head and gave it a little wobble. Not today, Ben. After we move here to our own place, that's when we'll go. Tom looked over at Mary and saw how pleased she was to be watching her husband and son together like this. He stood up and put his arm around her shoulders. Smell it, Mary. Jes *smell* this land a ours.

CHAPTER TEN

Tom and Mary were happy that spring, and worked purposefully and hard. Sax's temperament, however, grew increasingly sour. His obsession with Anna seemed to be eating him up from the inside, and he began to hate Joe Elliott with as much passion as he longed for Anna. Tom and Mary's obvious happiness only added to his jealousy.

It seemed to him that for his whole life, he'd been looking in from the outside. He had been what was known as 'an outside child'. His half brother was Tom's father Sylvester, who was always called Vess. Everyone just thought of Sax as 'Vess Johnson's illegitimate half-brother'. Ten years after Vess's father died, his mother, Maria, had borne Sax, not telling anybody who his father was. Though Sax's pedigree was a matter of conjecture, Maria herself had been three-quarters Indian and one-quarter Negro. She had married Alf Johnson, a man of mixed race, and had six children with him, Sylvester being the fourth. Then when Vess and the others were grown, and Alf Johnson dead, along came Sax, whose dark brown skin caused people to assume he had been sired by a Negro. Saxton was given his mother's legal name of Johnson, but he wondered all his life what it should have been.

His mother died in 1896. Three years later the Oklahoma Land Rush had fired the imagination of the entire country, but it was of particularly keen inspiration for people like Sax Johnson. With nothing to hold Sax in Kentucky, he set out for Indian Territory as soon as he could get the cash together for the journey.

He liked the Indians for their directness, and for their easy acceptance of each day's unfolding. They were unconcerned with time, and not bothered by rules—notions with which whites seemed to be obsessed. He had settled down to his farming and to his new society with great satisfaction. Both men and women were easy to get to know out here. After Tom came, life was even better. Anna Elliott had provided the only flame to Sax's complacency, and now, in the spring of 1902, his feelings for her threatened to burn his body down to ashes. At first it had been enough that he could have her at all. Gradually he wanted more and more. Finally he couldn't bear the thought that her husband should have any of her, and he began to seek ways to be rid of Joe Elliott.

Everybody in the neighborhood was aware that Joe plowed his land with a stolen horse. He had bought it from a known horse thief, as many another man around there had. But Sax's obsession led him to give the Marshal's office an anonymous tip as to the origin of Joe's horse.

When the Marshal's deputies arrested Joe and took him off to Bristow for a hearing, Anna came over to Sax's place as soon as they left. He got up from the table to put his arms around her, but she pushed him away.

We got to get Joe out of this, Sax, she said.

For a moment Sax was shocked, then angry. What you talking about, 'get him out of it'?

Just what I said. They won't take my word for it, I'm his wife. But they would take the word of a neighbor. You got to go and say he bought the horse fair and square and didn't know nothin about it being stolen.

But, Anna, why should we help that old coot out? You know we don't need him around here anyway. He smiled slyly and moved back up against her, but she pushed him away again.

This ain't no time for that stuff, Sax. What're you thinkin? Joe may be an old coot, but he's my husband, and as long as he's alive I got to do what I can for him, if only for my boys' sakes. Besides, what good is he to me in jail right here at plantin time?

You let me take care of yo plantin, sugar, Sax murmured, moving against her again.

Anna gave a little half laugh. Only if you promise to go up to Bristow in the morning and testify for Joe at his hearing, she said, not pushing him away this time.

Alright, Anna, he breathed into her long black hair. Whatever you say. I'll go up and help him out—only cause you ax me to. But that's tomorra's job. Right now we got us some other bidness...

So it was that, having gotten Joe arrested, Sax went up to Bristow and got him set free. But one phrase of Anna's played over and over in his head: 'as long as he's alive'. Now Sax began to fantasize about Joe Elliott's death. He imagined him falling from his wagon, cutting himself on some sharp implement, being kicked in the head by his horse. A Ketchapataka man had been struck and killed by lightning last year. Another had shot himself while cleaning his rifle. And of course the barroom brawl had furnished many a funeral with its guest of honor. Sax was almost enjoying the inventory of possibilities; but unfortunately, Joe Elliott continued in perfect health.

He knew he couldn't simply kill Joe himself; Anna's surprising response to her husband's arrest had shown him that much. Finally he approached Tom. They were rebuilding a fence out back of the barn around the middle of April. The wind was up and there was talk of tornadoes.

Look, Tom, I got a proposition for you, he said suddenly, as if Tom hadn't been talking nervously about twisters.

The younger man looked at him quizzically, his hammer halted in mid-air. You ain't been listenin to me, have ya?

Never mind all a that. You listen here to me. He propped the plank he'd been holding against the fencepost and squatted down beside his nephew. You gonna be needin you some cash to start y'own place over yonder. I done got three thousand dollahs saved up and I'll give it to you... jes plain hand it over to you... if you'll do something fo me.

Hell. Tom laughed the word. I'd do a whole lot fo three thousand dollahs, Sax. What in the world is it you wantin me to do that's worth that kind of money?

I want you to kill Joe Elliott.

Tom's mouth went slack. Then he smiled, testing, but Sax remained tense. You... you jes foolin with me now, ain't ya Saxton? he said at last.

I ain't foolin. Never been more serious in my life. Anna and me, we need to get rid of him... fo good. He sniffed and looked off at the horizon.

Anna's in on this?

She don't know nothin bout this part of it. She's leavin ever'thing up to me. Anna, she jes takes things as things comes.

But... look a here. Even if I *could* do it—which I cain't—you need your three thousand dollahs to get you a place started. Tom realized as he spoke that they had both begun to whisper, though they were completely alone in the wide stormy landscape.

Naw, don't you see? If Joe was out of the way, I'd move in with Anna—on her place. I won't never be needin nothin again once Joe Elliott's gone. And neither'll you. Ev'body's problems be solved.

Tom blew a long, thin whistle through his teeth and shook his head. I... I cain't believe yo askin me this, man. I ain't no killer.

Ain't nobody gonna miss Joe Elliott once he's gone from this world, said Sax coldly. I'd do it myself, 'cep fo I's afraid Anna wouldn't like it. She wants him dead, too—I know she does—but she wouldn't never be easy with me again if I done it. I cain't take that chance. Look, Tom, you got nothin to lose and ev'thing to gain. Ain't nobody gonna suspect you. Soon's it's done, you take Mary and go on off to yo land—with three-thousand dollahs cash in yo pocket. Me and Anna, we be here happy as can be, and that'd be the end of it. Men dies ev'day—specially out here. Ain't nothin to it...

Shut up! Goddamn it, Sax, shut up!

But, you see what...

Jes shut up, you hear me? I cain't think! Tom went back to working on the fence, but there was a deep furrow between his eyebrows.

After a few minutes Sax couldn't resist asking, You gon do it, Tom?

Shut up I said!

They worked on in silence as the sky darkened. Then the wind blew up stronger and raindrops began to splat down on them. Without a word, they picked up their tools and ran for shelter.

* * *

Tom refused to discuss the matter any further with Sax, but he found himself unable to sleep for thinking about the three thousand dollars. What Sax had said about needing seed money was right. The Washington brothers had charged him a hundred dollars for putting his land claim through. That had cleaned him out. He had figured they would just struggle for the first few years, using whatever came to hand, growing what they could, and borrowing for the rest. But three thousand dollars in cash would make all the difference. It would mean a good house, a horse and wagon, mules and a plow, a milk cow and no debt.

He told himself he was only fantasizing. Thinking about the money didn't make him a murderer. Besides he couldn't stop thinking about it, even when he tried; but there was no joy in it. The trouble was, now that he had envisioned starting out with the money, starting out with nothing seemed impossible.

Tom became more and more touchy and irritable over the next week. He hardly slept at all. Two weeks later, as he sat on in silence after the noon meal, stroking his mustache over and over, Mary asked him what was the matter. He looked at her as if he hadn't even been aware she was there.

What you say? he asked sharply.

Nothin, she replied. She reached for Ben's hand and said, Come on, honey. Let's you and me go put some flowers on Alma's grave. You want to?

It was the second of May. The weather had cleared up with the nearest tornado touching down about thirty miles away. Tom was grateful to be alone. He got up from the table and took down the bottle of whiskey from the top of the press. Half filling the water glass, he recorked it and put it back up, out of harm's way. I need somethin to knock me upside the head, he told himself as he drank it down.

When the glass was empty he sat staring at it. He knew he should get back to the field, but instead he sat on, running the tip of his forefinger up and down an old knife mark in the table. Eventually he got himself another glass of whiskey, then a third. Flies drowsed in and out through the open door, their humming harmonizing with the ringing in his ears.

Tom would never remember how, but the next thing he knew, he found himself outside, walking aimlessly and muttering to himself about Sax's offer. Kill Joe Elliott... hellfire.

The gun he had bought two years before rode heavily in his pocket. Outside of target practice, he had used it only twice: once to kill a snake, and another time to shoot at a coyote. He preferred using traps to catch small game for the table, the way he had back in Kentucky; but he'd gotten used to the gun's weight in his pocket, and usually forgot it was there. Now, as he paced between the house and the windmill, he became keenly aware of it, almost afraid it would go off on its own and rend his leg with a hot bullet. He looked up and thought of testing his aim on the windmill. Shit, he thought, waste of a bullet. What the hell'm I...?

Before he knew it, he was walking towards the field where Joe Elliott was plowing.

I ain't gonna shoot him, he muttered aloud. Hellfire and damnation. Ain't shootin nobody.

He went the long way, so as not to be seen by Mary or Sax. By the time he came within sight of Elliott's field he had broken out in a sweat. As he got closer and closer to the figure behind the horse and plow, his monologue became more insistent. Ain't gonna shoot him; don't give a damn bout Joe Elliott. I jes wanna look at him, that's all. Cain't go the rest of my damn life avoidin the sight of him, can I?

He felt light-headed, but kept on walking. Ain't gonna shoot him, he muttered, unaware that he was talking out loud. He held onto the gun in his pocket, gripping the handle to stop his hand from trembling.

Joe's back had been to him as Tom approached from across the fields. It was only when he turned the horse at the end of the row that he saw Tom coming, and lifted his chin in greeting. He was just about to call out something when Tom raised his gun and fired. Joe was hit full in the chest, and the horse bolted, dragging the fallen man for a few paces along the furrow, the reins still wrapped around the dead man's wrists.

Tom was running like he had never run in his life, jumping furrows and fences, trying to get away from the moment, the gunshot ringing in his head, the fact of what he had just done. In his panic he had thrown the gun as far as he could into the next field. Now, as he ran, he realized he didn't have it. It was neither in his hand nor in his pocket.

He was running towards Sax's house. He couldn't go to Mary. Couldn't see her or Ben. Not yet. He ran blindly, not understanding this moment or his own actions. It took him years to understand that in his flight he'd been trying to run away from himself.

GLADYS: II

It was over that land out in Oklahoma; that was all they evah tol us—all they evah tol to me anyhow—bout why Uncle Tom'd ended up in trouble and done time in the Penitentiary.

Could I imagine him killin a man? Well, he wasn't much for church-goin and he had a temper on him. He wasn't nobody to fool with, if you know what I mean. He was strong. Confident. Didn't have no doubts bout what he wanted. If I's to weigh it out—bout whether he was the murderin kind or not—I could put them things on one side of the scales. But I'd have lots to put on the other side, too.

When I got married the first time I's real young and ignorant. Hadn't never been courted befo. The boy was a no-good, but I couldn't see that at first. Uncle Tom, he could. The first time me and my new husband come back from Paducah to Slayden's Crossin fo a visit, he—I don't never call his name—he made a joke about me. Somethin like, Gladys here ain't good for much, but leastways she can cook. Somethin mean—and wrong too. I could do anything I turned my hand to from the time I's a chile. He's jes tryin on bein a husband—the kind his daddy'd been maybe.

Anyway, when he said that, ever'body laughed a little, kinda surprised. Tryin be polite, you know. But Uncle Tom he didn't laugh. He jumped up an said, What you say, boy?

Things got real quiet, and I was so ashamed. I spect I thought it woulda been better fo evah'body jes to laugh and let it pass. I figured it was jes his way of tryin to be funny. Wasn't til later I understood that Uncle Tom had his number right off. I had picked myself a rotten apple.

My husband, he jes mumbled somethin, but Uncle Tom come across that porch, his eyes blazin, and got right up in his face. If I evah hear you disrespect my niece again boy, I will come lookin fo you, and you will be sorry you's evah born, you hear me?

He stared into Uncle Tom's face and we could all see he was mad, but he was more scared than mad, so he nodded his head yes. Then Uncle Tom made him pay me a pology—which was as hard on me as it was on him—but he said he's sorry. Then one of my aunts started talkin and things got on back to normal.

What I mean to say is that I never did see Uncle Tom lose his temper without he had him a good reason. And he didn't rare back and crack that boy's jaw, which I had cause later to wish he had've. If he'd a run off that day, it woulda saved me puttin up with him fo the few months I did.

Anybody ask me to try and explain Uncle Tom, all I can tell em is he was always good to me. And he was always good to Mary, and to his mama. Good to all of us, really. He was a man of strong will when I knew him. But that was after he come out of the Pen. Maybe when he was young he wouldn't've been able to get that angry and not crack somebody's jaw. I don't know. I didn't know him then—wasn't alive to know him then. I only knew the man that come out of Leavenworth Prison after near twenty year. That was the Uncle Tom I knew.

He was good at that plasterin—good with his hands, like me. He built that fine house for Mary, and had him some other houses in town too, in Greenberry, that he kept fixed up and rented out. He bought em with the money he saved from his plasterin work. As a investment, he said.

He knew he's good lookin and he'd act that part with the ladies, young and old, but they wasn't nothin to it. Not like with a lot of men. One thing couldn't nobody say—leastways not when I knew him—was that he run around on Mary. He fo sho did not.

CHAPTER ELEVEN

When Maddie Wingate returned from Benediction that Friday night, her fox collared coat redolent of incense, she found that Ted had visitors. This was an unusual enough occurrence to leave her slightly flustered. Hearing voices in the rarely used parlor, she handed her coat to Emmett Lewis, whispering, Who's in there?

Emmett hung the coat up and said, It's Judge Arch, ma'am, and another gen'man I don't reco'nize.

Arch was saying something about how easily both the legal and the financial aspects could be taken care of when Ted interrupted him. Maddie, is that you? Come on in here, Maddie, and meet Mr. Axley of Tulsa, Oklahoma. He's staying over at the Greenberry Hotel, and we persuaded him to have a little visit. Emmett, would you be kind enough to see about getting some coffee for us? We've gone ahead and built a fire ourselves, as the room was a mite chilly.

Yes suh, Mr. Wingate, Emmett replied, hurrying off to the kitchen.

She placed her hat on the hall table, brushed at her dress and moved tentatively into the living room.

Axley jumped up, walked over to Maddie and shook her hand. He was not much taller than she was, his manner excited but strained. Still, he seemed distracted, and she sensed he was longing to go back to his hotel room and was just being polite, as was she.

How do you do, Mrs. Wingate. Lovely home you have here.

She returned his handshake, but didn't have a chance to reply before Arch said loudly, Oh, if you think this one's nice, Ben, you just wait'll next spring when Ted and Maddie's new house is finished. It's shaping up to be a regular mansion.

Is that right? said Axley. Well, how nice. He turned back to Maddie. I guess you must have a big family then?

She blushed and looked away. No, we don't... w-we don't have any children. The faltering lull seemed to suck them in, and all three men stammered some inanity at the same time. It was Ted who resumed control.

Come on over and sit down by the fire, my dear. Was it cold in the church? Then, without waiting for her reply, he continued. My wife is of the Catholic persuasion, Mr. Axley, and she has just been to one of her weekly services.

Maddie sat perched on the edge of the couch in a reverie until Ted touched her on the arm. I asked you a question, Maddie. Was it cold in the church?

Oh, no it was... well, actually it was a little cool, but I kept my coat on.

Good, good, he said, trying for some sort of jovial atmosphere. But after a few dead-end remarks about weather from Axley, she stood up.

I don't really want any coffee at this hour, Ted; it would only keep me awake. I think I'll go up and see to the fire in the bedroom, if you'll please excuse me. Y'all'll want to talk business. It was nice meeting you, Mr. Axley. Arch.

After she left the room Axley opened his mouth to apologize for upsetting Mrs. Wingate, but Ted anticipated the comment and forestalled it, shaking his head and giving a slight wave of his hand. Tell me more about the Johnson case then, Mr. Axley, he said with a starchy politeness that meant business. You were saying before my wife came in that the Oklahoma courts are full of land claim suits like this one.

Yes, they are, and I am confident that we—that Johnson—can make a successful bid for the oil lease on his land. Axley was surprised to find himself feeling a little nervous in the presence of this small-town banker whom he had only just met. But Ted's eyes were fixed on him expectantly, so he carried on. You see, he's part Indian, and these Indian land grants under the Dawes Commission included the mineral rights. That isn't generally the case. White people with oil strikes on their land don't always have it so lucky.

Ain't that just the way? Arch said, pursing his lips and shaking his head.

Axley couldn't help but notice how different the brothers looked. The judge, who was tall, had dark eyes and a long, rather potato-shaped head with the face of an English butler. The banker, however, was a short, blue-eyed man with a small, round face, more like an English lord.

Well I had one of my girls at the bank do a little search on Johnson this afternoon, and it seems he is one of our county's finer colored citizens. As you know, he's a plasterer by trade. A hard worker. Not only does he own his own home, but he owns several more as well, here in Greenberry, which he rents out to other coloreds.

Axley made noises of surprised approval, but frowned slightly, until Ted added, However, there is the small matter of his prison record, which, handled correctly, may actually give us some leverage.

Arch raised his long eyebrows inquiringly. He had been too tied up with Johnson all day to research his history. Axley let an inaudible sigh escape. He could see that the Wingates—a plural now—were absolutely not going to be shaken, and he resigned himself to a reduction of the profit he had hoped to reap from the case.

CHAPTER TWELVE

Rachel Slayden didn't trust her boss, Ted Wingate. She was always on her guard, watching for him the way you watch for spiders in an outhouse. It wasn't that he ever yelled at her as some of her friends' bosses did; it was more the quality of his silence, the contempt he seemed to feel for the world in general, excepting only his wife. But not even his wife could make him do anything he didn't want to do.

She hadn't been there as long as Emmett Lewis had. She had come to work for the Wingates five years ago. But even at the age of nineteen—the age she'd been when she started the job—Rachel knew that most people were intimidated by the Wingates. They were especially afraid of him. As the bank president, Ted Wingate had a reputation for inflexibility. They said he handled all the mortgages himself. He never approved or renewed one until he'd had Emmett Lewis drive him past the place in question. And he preferred to do his surveying after dark so he could tell how frivolous the inhabitants were with lamps and candles. Mr. Wingate liked to see a plainly kept, dimly lit place. The way he figured it, any extra money ought to be saved to go toward the mortgage. If he heard music, or saw evidence of festivity or frivolity of any sort, he would immediately draw a red line through the papers on his lap.

Rachel had been half afraid of going for the interview when her mother first told her the Wingates were looking for a girl to cook and clean for them. But the chance of living in town and having her own room was too tempting to pass up. To Rachel's relief, Mrs. Wingate alone had interviewed her, and had taken her on for a month's trial.

Now when people asked her how it was, working for the Wingates, she would just say the work was steady and it did her fine. If pressed for more, she might mention that she had her own private room off the kitchen and kept her clothes in a white chifforobe with flowers painted on the drawers. She never mentioned the beveled mirror that put rainbows across the walls in the late afternoon. And she never named the other reason, which was that she stayed for Mrs. Wingate's sake.

Maybe Mrs. Wingate could be a little high and mighty at times, but that was to be expected from a lady of her position. She was always fair with

Rachel, and even gave her some of her cast-off dresses and coats. Though they were a little short for her, Rachel treasured these, sharing the ones she absolutely couldn't wear with her mother and sisters out at Slayden's Crossing.

But the real secret to the bond between them was that, for all the distance and formality of Mrs. Wingate's bearing, Rachel detected a terrible vulnerability in her. Perhaps it was her childlessness, or the fact that she was a devout Christian married to a man of no religion. Though it had never been spoken, Rachel sensed that Mrs. Wingate needed her presence in the big, fancy house. And she felt sure she would need her even more when they moved into their new mansion next May.

Rachel knew, in fact, a great deal about Mr. and Mrs. Wingate's private relationship just from fixing and serving them their meals. She cooked them the same series of suppers every week, from the fried chicken on Sunday, to the pork chops and fried apples on Saturday. Rachel had made up the menu herself, after consulting with Mrs. Wingate. The only meal Mrs. Wingate had ordered specifically was Friday's, when she had salmon croquettes, while he ate steak. Rachel ate a portion of what was left over each day, and Emmett Lewis carried the rest home to share with his wife. The Wingates ate at 5:30 sharp, almost without fail.

They didn't entertain, despite their money, except on rare occasions when Mr. Wingate's business required it. And these affairs were always painfully strained, preceded by an explanation to Rachel by Mrs. Wingate that they would have to serve alcohol. Though plenty of well-to-do Greenberry people served wine at their tables on formal occasions, Prohibition or no Prohibition, Mrs. Wingate was uncomfortable with it. She was a confirmed teetotaler, mostly because of her husband's former, but never mentioned, reputation for heavy drinking. See that you have two pitchers of lemon water on the table as well as the wine, Rachel, and keep the water glasses filled, you hear?

Except for one niece who came over sometimes to learn sewing from Mrs. Wingate, this policy of never having guests unless it was absolutely necessary extended to Mrs. Wingate's large family of brothers and sisters as well. I won't have em prayin over me at my own dinner table, now, that's all there is to it, Rachel had heard Mr. Wingate pronounce on two different occasions. Nor was his wife to give them any money. Once that starts, it'll never be done with, he'd said. They'll be lining up by the front door with their cups out!

He never said much more to Rachel than a terse, That's enough, or Close that window before you take the platter out to the kitchen. But she wouldn't have been surprised if he had suddenly slapped her face or fired her. She had observed that he was capable of sudden cruelty.

One day several years ago Rachel had overheard young Mrs. Bradshaw sobbing her heart out to Mrs. Wingate when Mr. Wingate was at work. The Bradshaws lived around the corner in a stucco house with a red tiled roof which Rachel had often admired as she passed it.

You gotta do something, Miz Maddie. It says here we have to move out, and it's signed 'Ted Wingate'. I... I just don't understand.

Mrs. Wingate had taken the letter from the young woman's trembling hand and read it, her own face registering concern and confusion. Verena, my dear, I don't understand this either. Have you and Randall not been making your mortgage payments?

We *have* been making em, evah single month. And, it's our dream house. We designed it ourselves in honor of Daddy's bringing the Spanish contract to the Greenberry tobacco market. Evah'body knows that. How can Mr. Wingate take away our home? Why would he do this to us?

I'll talk to him, Verena, she had said, patting Mrs. Bradshaw's hand. Surely there's been some mistake.

Oh, thank you, Miz Maddie. I just knew I could count on you.

That night at supper, Mr. Wingate had been stunned when his wife brought the matter up to him. He put his knife and fork down, knitted his fingers together, and spoke over them in cold, measured phrases. You must understand, Maddie, business is business. It is not supper-table conversation. I will explain this to you—just this once—the best way I can. Then we will never speak of it again. That house is worth a good deal more now than it was two years ago when they built it. Whoever holds the mortgage on a property owns it. In this case that is the bank. Now that mortgage is too much for a young couple. I am doing them a favor, while earning the bank money. That is my job, and the law upholds my decision. That is all the explanation you or anybody else is going to get. But you need to understand something here. That girl had no business talking to you... coming into my house and talking to my wife... about a *bank* matter. He shoved his plate away and stared ahead in inarticulate rage. I tell you, I've got a good mind to...

Ted, please, Maddie had said, alarmed almost to tears at his expression. Please forget I ever brought it up. I... I just... I won't...

Oh calm down, Maddie, he said contemptuously. Pull yourself together. Just never attempt to interfere in business matters again, and we'll drop the subject.

They had finished the meal in silence and within a month the Bradshaws had moved out of their beloved Spanish bungalow.

Now, when Rachel heard someone rattling around in the kitchen, she got up from the chair where she had been leafing through one of Mrs. Wingate's old *Saturday Evening Post* magazines, and opened her bedroom door a crack.

Emmett? she said quietly. Ev'thing okay?

I's lookin fo that fancy coffee pot. Mr. Wingate's got him some visitors out yonder he wants me to serve coffee to.

She went to the pantry and brought the silver service out for him while he got the percolator going. How many of em is there?

Fo, countin him and Miz Wingate. It's Judge Arch and that lawyer from Oklahoma that says Tom Johnson's a oil millionaire.

Well I'll be. I never heard a thing. She wiped out the little pitcher, poured cream into it and, with the sugar shell, began breaking up the hardened sugar in the silver bowl. What you think about this Tom Johnson business, Emmett?

They don't nobody pays me to think round here, gal. Jes rinse me out that fancy coffee pot. He dropped his voice to a hissing whisper. They's in there awaitin!

Rachel sighed and did as she was told. When Emmett carried the tray through the swinging door, his elbows high, she went back into her room, closed the door and picked up her magazine. It seemed she was likely to get more out of last summer's news than she could ever get out of Emmett Lewis.

CHAPTER THIRTEEN

When the neighbor's rooster woke Tom and Mary Saturday morning, each felt heavy and reluctant to face whatever the day would bring.

Mary had been dreaming of the farm they'd worked with Sax out in Indian Territory. She was walking beside Smoke Creek with Benjamen, a tiny boy again, toddling along in front of her. Suddenly the bank beside them crumbled. As they slid down it Ben began to scream. When Mary crawled to him in the mud, she saw that the slide had exposed Alma's coffin and torn the side off it. Ben was staring at his baby sister's partly decomposed body. Mary's own strangled cry in the dream morphed into the rooster's crow, and she woke up staring at Tom in horror.

He stared back dully for a moment, then pulled her to him. It's okay, Mary, he said. I done made up my mind I ain't goin back out there. All Axley and Judge Arch wants is the money. I'll jes sign whatever papers they want me to and they can go to the courts with it. If they's any money to be had they can have it. Ain't no way fo me to win this. If I tell the truth I could wind up back in prison fo makin a false claim. If I go after that oil money I'll have to lie on the stand and I'll end up back in prison again. It jes ain't worth it. I'll give em what they's aftah and get em off my back, but I ain't goin back out there. Not evah again.

Mary went limp with relief at his words, but relief vanished with the return of Axley, the newspaper reporter, and—it being Saturday—an even bigger crowd of curious well-wishers. Tom found himself forced to relate, over and over again, the fictitious details of his Indian land claim. The story Joe Elliott and Sax and he had cooked up back in 1901 involved a man named Doc Ford who had visited Slayden's Crossing when Tom was a boy.

He was a friend a my parents, just passin through, Tom would say. I hadn't nevah laid eyes on him befo, and I nevah did again. The only one time I seen him was when I's about thirteen, fourteen year old. We's at a church picnic and he pulled me aside, put his arm around my shoulders, and tol me he was my real daddy. Said Vess and Clara was raisin me fo him, but that my real family lived out in Indian Territory, and that we was members of the Creek tribe. Said when I's old enough I should go out there and look him up. But he also said I shouldn't nevah tell a soul what he tol me, in case Vess and Clara'd take it unkindly aftah all they'd done fo me. So I nevah did, and I nevah laid eyes on him again. When I's growed up I made my way out there to Creek Territory first chance I had. But by that time him and my real mama, and my brother Walter that I hadn't never knowed, they was all of em dead. So I filed me a claim fo my rightful land.

When people heard the story they were always impressed by the mystery of it, and full of questions. Today was no different.

Why'd yo real daddy leave you in Kentucky to be raised?

Didn't say, Aunt Sook. Reckon I must've been a handful as a youngun. He grinned.

Why didn't ya stay on yo land out yonder after you got it, Tom? someone else asked. What made you come back here?

Well now, I did stay fo a spell, he'd say. But Mary, she's wantin to come back to Slayden's Crossin, and I am not a man to ignore his woman's wishes. Then everyone laughed, and those who knew about Tom's prison sentence—mostly family members—kept that part of the story to themselves. In the small, sharecropping community of Slayden's Crossing, there was a tacit understanding that dignity was hard enough to come by without betraying one another's unpleasant secrets, especially with white people listening. And Tom Johnson's sudden, gaudy fortune promised to spread a little glamor over them all.

For her part his mother Clara kept silent on the subject. When the writer from *The Daily Leaf* had addressed her the previous day, her only comment had been, I don't talk to no reporters. When pressed in private by some of her friends, she changed the subject in a loud voice that left no doubt of her intentions. Look like this winter ain't nevah gonna end, don't it? Lawd, Lawd. Here it is only January...

Even Mary, who never dared raise it with her, had no idea what Clara's feelings were about Tom's story of his 'real family'. She only knew that Clara adored him, and would do absolutely anything for Tom.

At about ten that morning, when Tom and Mary were busy with yet another bunch of visitors, a buggy pulled up out front and released a tall, thin white man with graying hair. He wore a black coat over a black suit with a minister's collar, and knocked somewhat hesitantly at the door. Tom was standing in front of his mantelpiece entertaining the crowd with stories of Indian Territory and didn't hear the knock. The Creek Nation got em a gov'ment as grand as any white gov'ment, he was saying. It's made up of the House of Kings and the House of Warriors. Naw, now I ain't lyin. Almost sound English or something don't it, but that's what they call em—the House of Kings and the House of Warriors. They council house is fancy as any courthouse you ever seen. The Creeks is one of the Five Civilized Tribes, as they refers to em out yonder. And when I went befo the Creek Council back in 1902, they was all settin around a...

Rev'ren Parsons? Mary said warmly, opening the door. Though she had never met James Parsons, she guessed who he was immediately. We been expectin you. Tom will be so happy to see you. Please, come in.

You must be Mrs. Johnson, he said, leaning down to shake her hand. Then he looked at the crowd in the living room and said, Oh dear, I'm afraid I've come at an awkward time. Perhaps...

But the room had gone quiet by now, for Tom had seen him and was striding toward him eagerly. Rev'ren Parsons! he called, grasping the shy man by the hand with both of his. Rev'ren Parsons, it's so good to see you. Thank you fo comin.

At a lift of the chin from Tom, his brother Richard began leading people outside. The crowd of friends and relatives filed past them, nodding towards Mary and the white minister as they went. When the living room was cleared out, Tom led their new guest to the best chair.

How was yo trip, Rev'ren? I suppose you got into town last night?

Yes, I did, and it was fine, thank you, Tom. I took a room at the hotel in Greenberry. I have it until tomorrow morning.

Can I offer you a cup a coffee, Rev'ren? Mary asked.

No, thank you, Mrs. Johnson. I just had some at the hotel.

There was a moment of awkward silence, while Mary tried to decide whether to sit down or not. I'll be back in a minute, she said finally. Y'all got lots to talk about. Then she went outside where she had left Richard and Gladys and her sister Elizabeth to fend off more visitors.

Tom, I was so happy to hear of your good fortune. Tell me, what can I do for you? the minister asked, leaning forward with kindly interest.

Tom was caught between his storytelling mood, and his humility before Reverend Parsons. Well, Rev'ren, it's hard to explain the fix I's in here in jes a few words, but I know we ain't got long befo this Tulsa lawyer Mr. Axley'll be comin back. I reckon I's needin what you call moral support.

Well, I hope I can offer that to you, he said, smiling nervously.

It's jes that... well, you know my record. They's lots round here that don't know about my time in the Pen, and that's fine with me.

Parsons nodded his understanding.

And you also know how I turned my life around since I got out. He glanced around at his surroundings, as proof of his claim. I worked hard... and me and Mary, well... we was able to make a fresh start with one another.

Evah'thing was going along real good til this Mr. Axley come to town tellin evah'body I's a oil millionaire.

But... I don't understand, Tom. If you've had an oil strike on your land out in Oklahoma... what's the problem with that? I should think it would feel like God's blessing on you for all that you've done to right the wrongs of the past. Indeed I should think it would feel like a... like a well-deserved reward.

Tom smiled uncertainly, his mind awhirl with the stories he had been repeating all morning—the old lies—and the thought of abruptly telling the truth. If he told Reverend Parsons the truth now, would he be jeopardizing what might be a real chance to carry off the old ruse? Maybe he didn't need to confess, after all. If someone like Reverend Parsons could see an oil strike as God's favor, maybe the issue of the false claim wasn't as important as he had thought. If there was a chance he would get the money, or even some of it, should he let that one detail go?

The minister regarded Tom with respectful compassion. Though he was used to being a witness to silent struggle, he still wasn't sure what Tom's struggle entailed, and was therefore unsure what was required of him here. He decided patience was required, and sat quietly, waiting for Tom to speak again.

Tom laid his forehead into the palm of his left hand, rubbing his thigh with his right. It, it ain't simple, you see, Rev'ren. I ain't sure I can trust this lawyer, and I'm even less sure about Judge Wingate.

Judge Wingate?

Yes suh. Not only have I got this Oklahoma lawyer here all time tellin me what to do, but a Greenberry judge is onto this business like a fly on sticky paper, and it look like to me they jes in it fo the money.

Is it that you want to try to handle this without lawyers, Tom?

Just then they heard a car door slam, and voices out front. That's them back again, said Tom, then he added in an urgent whisper, Look, Rev'ren, I got reason to believe this oil business is dangerous.

I'm afraid I have to leave in the morning, Tom, on the nine o'clock train. I'm sorry. The door opened. Can we talk privately...?

Judge Arch pushed into the room just ahead of Axley, calling out in his loud voice, Ah, I see you've got company. Looks like you've always got company, but then I guess that's no surprise, given your big news. He had taken the white man for another lawyer who was looking to get in on the deal. His voice moderated slightly when he saw the minister's collar. Oh, I uh...

Mary, who had tried without success to delay their entrance, shrugged her apology to Tom, then took her coat from the peg beside the door and went back outside to sit with Gladys and Richard. Her sister had left. Mary had no stomach for the judge and the lawyer. In fact, she was longing to walk into Greenberry to visit Ben and Nema. She knew Ben would avoid his father's present limelight for as long as he could. But she denied her own wishes in favor of what she knew without a doubt: that she should stay near Tom in case he needed her.

CHAPTER FOURTEEN

Tom introduced Reverend Parsons as his 'friend and spiritual advisor'.

After the white men had shaken hands, Judge Arch quipped, Why on earth did you need to import a 'spiritual advisor' all the way from Kansas City, Tommie? I'd've thought old Uncle George Pryor over at the A.M.E. Church across the field here would be spiritual advisor enough for you. Looks to me like you're gettin used to being a big wig mighty quick.

The judge laughed at his own words, and Tom replied in as pleasant a tone as he could muster, I'm surprised, Judge. I didn't know you knew Brother Pryor. He is, like you say, a fine man. He's my wife's uncle. But Rev'ren Parsons and me, we've knowed one nother for some years.

The judge raised one eyebrow and swept Tom and the reverend together in a glance of vague contempt, but said nothing further. At Tom's invitation they all sat down.

Parsons, sensing the discomfort, moved to pacify things, as was his wont. I've never travelled to this part of Kentucky before, have you Mr... Mr....? Forgive me, I've forgotten your name.

Axley, Ben Axley. No, this is my first visit as well, but I hope it won't be my last. Very pretty part of the country, isn't it?

Yes. The countryside is a balm to my spirit after so many years in the city.

How is it you came to know Tommie here if you've lived in Kansas City so long? asked Judge Arch pointedly.

Our paths crossed out west, and we've stayed in correspondence ever since, said Parsons.

Correspondence? Really?

That's right.

Hm. Let's just say I wouldn't've taken Tommie here for much of a letter writer, let alone....Oh never mind. We'd better get down to business if you gentlemen don't mind. My wife'll be expecting me home to dinner before long. Is your 'spiritual advisor' going to be staying for our meeting, Tommie?

I would like him to be here, yes.

Parsons glanced at the others. The judge regarded him condescendingly while Axley smiled with obvious discomfort.

When're you planning to head back to Oklahoma, Ben? Wingate asked. And how soon will you be needing me and Tommie to come out there?

Well I'm planning to get the train out of here on Monday night, which will put me back in Tulsa on Tuesday. This case has been hanging fire for years, what with various neighbors and oil companies all trying to get the legal rights to the property. Of course, you know nothing of all that, Tommie, since you've been out of the Territory from 1903 on.

Tom's heart skipped a beat at this reference to his murder charge, but Axley said no more about Tom's history. They're hot to trot on this case. You've been the missing piece of the puzzle, and now that I've found you we'll get a court date inside the month, I can guarantee it.

Grand, said Judge Arch. As soon as you've got that date Tommie and me'll be out there, loaded for bear.

What if I don't wanna go?

What? cried Wingate and Axley simultaneously.

What in the hell are you saying, boy? Wingate asked, anger evident in his tone.

I'm sayin I don't wanna go. I done seen all I care to of Oklahoma. It's a dangerous place, especially where a oil claim's concerned. I ain't young no mo. I got all I want right here. He sighed deeply in the silence his statement had engendered. I'll sign whatever papers y'all want me to, but I ain't goin out there again.

Why, of all the damned... Wingate began, but Axley cut him off.

Wait a second, Judge Arch. Let me try to explain to him just why it's in his interest to fight this case. But first, don't you think we ought to take him up on his offer to sign whatever we need him to sign? Because there are a few details...

Wingate closed his mouth, shook his head with exasperation, then opened his briefcase and rummaged around. He produced a long, typewritten form that said 'Warranty Deed' across the top. Jist sign this deed right here... and Ben, you sign here. And maybe you, Reverend Parsons...We might as well put you to work seein's you're handy. You can sign as a witness. Otherwise we'll have to call in one of the neighbors. All it is is a record of your land out in Oklahoma, Tommy. Proof for the courts. Just sign right there.

But... this is in Sam Ford's name.

Naturally. How else are we to prove that you are Sam Ford, for purposes of the land claim in question?

I'm a notary public, Tommie, so I'll notarize that this is your signature of course, said Axley.

My signature maybe, but who am I?

I'd have thought you figured your way around that little contradiction back when you first applied for this land.

Axley placed a hand on Wingate's arm. It's all above board, Tommie. The court's just asking for more documentation. We're lawyers. That's what we provide. Don't disturb yourself over it. Just remember, as far as this land is concerned, Sam Ford is your name. You are the man who was granted this piece of property; there's no doubt about that. Sam Ford was the name you went by then, so that is the name you must sign now concerning your land claim.

May I see it, please? asked Reverend Parsons.

Certainly, said Axley. We've got nothin to hide, and naturally you'll want to read it if you're gonna be a witness; but, bear in mind, your signature will simply mean that you saw your friend here sign this paper.

Reverend Parsons read through the deed with a frown. When he finished, he looked at Tom, who took the paper from him. Axley snapped a pen toward Tom, offering his briefcase as a desk. Here you are.

Still hoping he could sign his way out of returning to Oklahoma, Tom took the pen and signed his alias. Axley then wrote his name below, where it said Witnesses. As soon as he had done so, he lifted the briefcase and deed over to Reverend Parson's lap. There you go, Reverend. Just sign right there below me.

Parsons swallowed, obviously plagued with doubt.

You ain't gotta sign it if you don't want to, Rev'ren, said Tom.

The minister looked over at him. After a moment he said, I've seen you go through a lot, Tom. If I can help you to this reward... I'm glad to do it. With that, he signed the paper and handed it into Judge Wingate's outstretched hands.

Now listen, Tommie, said Axley with renewed energy. As for going back out to Oklahoma: first of all, you don't have a choice in the matter, don't you see? This is a federal case. The United States Government is looking for you. They are going to subpoena you, and if you don't go, you'll soon be back in prison.

The last three words, which Axley had let slip inadvertently, altered the atmosphere in the room. All of them had known about Tom's life term, but now it was clear to Tom that they all knew about it. He began to shake his head slowly. Axley and Wingate looked at Reverend Parsons, and saw that the minister's face registered sadness, but not surprise.

After a beat, Axley continued. Second of all—and this is the real point to keep in mind—twenty million dollars is within our grasp here. Twenty million dollars, Tommie. It's not just about a piece of land to farm anymore. It's about a locked treasure chest containing more money than you've ever dreamed of. And you are the key.

CHAPTER FIFTEEN

The lawyers offered Reverend Parsons a ride back to town, but Tom also invited him to stay to dinner, his invitation stilted by the presence of Wingate in particular.

Axley and Wingate looked at each other with silent mirth before Wingate said, Obviously the Reverend would be better off returning to the hotel with Mr. Axley—surely you can see that?

Parsons was paralyzed by the social discomfort he sensed in Tom and Mary. She remained silent, but smiled her worried smile. If only the lawyers hadn't been there, he could've seen the proper way to proceed. I... I don't want to put you to any trouble, Tom...

Good. It's settled then. Come on, Reverend. You'll find the Greenberry Hotel puts on a fine meal, isn't that right, Ben? He had started down the walk, but turned to wait for Parsons to follow him. Parsons glanced at Tom, but Tom was silent, as hamstrung as the others by the unusual social dilemma.

As soon as the judge's car disappeared down the track, Richard and Gladys drew nearer the front porch, and they all began talking at once:

What you gonna do, Tom?

Why they got to go and take him over that away?

You got to get into town and talk to Rev'ren Parsons, Tom. This last was Mary.

Tom stared at her a moment, then nodded. As soon as he got into his hat and coat, he set off walking. By the time he reached the Greenberry Hotel, the noon meal was over and the desk clerk said Reverend Parsons had gone out. Tom crossed the court square and ordered himself a barbeque sandwich and an orange soda from the colored window of Waller's Grill and Restaurant. He sat on the courthouse curbing under Tom Tinker's tree, unwrapped the waxed paper and ate, wondering where Reverend Parsons could've gone. From here he could keep an eye on the hotel, as well as the bank and the drugstore. After half an hour or so, Tom spotted the tall, grey-haired minister coming around the corner of Broadway and 7th Street.

Rev'ren Parsons! he called, hurrying across the street to catch him. He thrust the empty bottle and wrapper at a little boy, who threw the paper to the ground and ran off rejoicing, to redeem the bottle at the Piggly Wiggly just down the block.

Oh. Tom! Good! I was just having a look around the town, I'm glad you caught me. Is there anywhere private we can talk?

Yeah, long as you don't mind keepin yo coat on. Tom had given the matter some thought as he walked into town. The court square was too busy for privacy, as was the hotel lobby. He led Parsons towards Boxtown, past the house one of his sisters lived in, to the back of a rambling tobacco warehouse which wasn't currently in use. Aint nobody gonna notice us here, he said, entering the long, low open shed behind the brick warehouse. The other warehouses were windowless, and there were only two houses in sight across an empty lot, both inhabited by the Sherrills, black families Tom knew well and could trust.

He turned over a couple of crates in the most sheltered corner of the shed. Do you chew, Rev'ren? he asked, holding out a twist.

Thank you, no, though I must say the wonderful fragrance in here is almost enough to turn me into a user of tobacco! He took in a slow lungful and shook his head with pleasure. But you go ahead, Tom.

Tom cut himself a chaw from the plug and tucked it into his jaw. You get too cold I'll make us up a fire.

Won't that draw attention?

Naw. Ain't nobody gonna pay us no mind back here. Long as you ain't too particular, Rev'ren, I've found you can usually git you some privacy even in a place like Greenberry. Fo a little while anyway.

Well then, it is kind of chilly after all. Let's have that fire—and then we'll get right down to business. Parsons smiled at Tom in anticipation, and they began gathering up scraps of wood, broken planks and bits of tobacco baskets that were strewn about the packed mud floor. Comforted by the fire, the two men talked over the complicated situation until dusk. Tom explained his fears about the land claim, though he still withheld from Reverend Parsons the fact that the claim had been false in the first place.

They tell me I ain't got no choice but to go out there, but like I said, I don't want to. I got all I want right here...Looking around at the ramshackle shed, Tom laughed a little at the absurdity of this statement, and Parsons smiled.

No, I think I know what you're saying. You have a fine home, meaningful work, and a loving family. The fact that you are satisfied is... well, I admire you for it, Tom. How many men can honestly say they're happy with what they have? That's a state of grace anyone would envy you for.

Well, the truth is, Rev'ren, it ain't that I'd mind bein a millionaire. He laughed again with that note of self-deprecation. I wouldn't mind bein one at all if it wasn't for that very thing you jes said—envy. I'd a whole lot rather be envied fo bein happy with the life I got now, than fo twenty million dollahs. Ain't nobody likely to come after me over what I got now.

Parsons nodded. Yes, I see your logic, but Tom, have you thought of this: what if this is a test of some kind? What if you are meant to use the money to help others? Or to set an example? An oil strike is hardly the result of greed or ambition—it's an act of God. I believe it happened on your land for a reason, Tom. It's made you visible, given you power. The kind of power that could do your people a great deal of good, if it's used wisely.

Tom chewed in silence, close to a full confession. But he was unable, finally, to bring himself to forfeit the Reverend's respect by admitting that he was connected to the oil strike precisely because of ambition, let alone fraud. So they talked around the subject until the fire was only a necklace of golden embers glowing on the dark mud floor. After stamping it out, Tom led his guest back to the hotel with a promise to see him off at the depot in the morning.

Late that night, he paced the small bedroom in his union suit. He was wearing the stocking cap he still used at night to keep his wavy hair straight.

Tom, we have got to get us some sleep tonight, else we gonna get sick, said Mary, sitting up to pull the covers open for him. Tell me right now, what're you gonna do? If you make up yo mind, then maybe we can get us some rest.

He came over and sat down beside her on the bed. Alright then, here's my thinkin. If I *got* to go back out there—if I ain't got no say ovah that part of it—then I'm gonna carry this thing through to the end.

She found herself rocking slightly as he spoke.

You know, Mary, it's a funny thing. They was a time I couldn't sleep fo wantin three thousand dollahs. Now I cain't sleep fo wishin away twenty million. But I been thinkin on it. I been thinkin on it, and I can remember Mr. Ford's face. I can see it jes like it was yestiddy. He had him a hawk nose and reddish skin like a Indian, but his hair was nappy, on account of one of his grandmothers was a Negro. And his eyes, why they was blue-green—the color of jewels. Jes like mine.

*   *   *

That Sunday morning, while Mary poured out her soul in prayer at Saint James A.M.E., Tom set out once more to walk the three miles along the railroad tracks to the Greenberry depot to see Reverend Parsons off on the nine o'clock train. It was sunny with a light wind, not too cold for late January. A small group of people waited at the north end of the platform, ready to board the colored cars up at the front of the train. Others were strung out loosely, alone or in pairs, waiting for the white carriages.

Tom could make out the Reverend's tall, thin frame well before he arrived at the platform. When he got closer, he saw that the minister was reading from a worn Bible, his grip at his feet. He looked up when Tom called his name, and closed the book, smiling and frowning at the same time.

Ah Tom, here you are. I was hoping to have another word with you before the train came. Just then they heard it blow its whistle at the edge of town.

I wanna thank you fo makin the trip, Rev'ren Parsons. I know we didn't get much time together, but it's meant a lot to me to see you again. It's meant a lot to me that you come when I called on you.

And to me that you *did* call on me, Tom. He slipped the Bible into his bag, then straightened back up and looked Tom in the eye. I can see you're in an awkward spot. I only wish I knew how to help. I'm worried about you, you know.

The train was in sight now, rounding the curve beside Ben and Nema's neighborhood, just west of Fairview Baptist. Tom smiled away Parsons' worry as if it didn't matter to him anymore. Naw suh, you helped me jes by comin and I won't fo'get it. The train's churning had swallowed the town now. Then its mournful whistle sounded again, warning them all to clear the tracks.

Tom, you may telephone or write me any time you need to, you know that. Here's another of my cards, in case you need it. And of course you must keep up your regular reports, as you always have. He was shouting now as the hissing, metal giant chugged slowly past the Planing Mills. Having drowned out the hymns at Fairview Baptist, it now challenged the choir at St. Joseph's, where Maddie Wingate knelt at High Mass. As it hissed into place two yards away from them, Parsons said loudly, But I just want to say one thing more to you, Tom.... He looked intently into Tom's drawn face and said, All you have to do is tell the truth.

Tom looked down for a moment. Is it, Rev'ren?

It had become less necessary to shout as the train came to a halt, and both were grateful for that. Both were feeling an emotion more intense than they had expected.

Lawyers can be difficult to deal with, Tom. I know that. They can try to... bend people to their own ends. But no matter what else, you have the right—you have the duty—to tell the truth. If you hold to that, I don't see how you can go wrong.

Well. Thank you, Rev'ren, he said, but he was thinking, Like you and me both told the truth yesterday with my alias on that deed?

Would you want me to try and find you a different lawyer to handle your affairs? I know of several who are men of good character and I could...

I appreciate the offer, Rev'ren, but I ain't nevah gonna be able to shake them two off my back now. They done took control.

The minister put his hand on Tom's shoulder and nodded his head several times. I expect you're right. Well, what I wanted to say to you was just what I've said. The... the truth is your best friend.

Best friend. First friend. Tom stared at him for an instant before he smiled and nodded. Would it have been better if he had told this man the truth? His advice probably wouldn't have been any different. No. No, there was nobody in the wide world who could help him now. He would have to do the best he could by himself.

The conductor began calling, All aboard! They shook hands, and Tom reached down for Reverend Parsons' bag. He handed it to him as the minister climbed aboard the nearest passenger car. Parsons held up his hand to Tom, then disappeared into the business of finding himself a seat.

Tom took a step backward and stood staring at the train as if in a solemn trance. After a moment, the engineer gave the two-whistle blast to signal departure, and Tom turned and began the walk back to Slayden's Crossing. Above him, puffs of white smoke rose into the air and dissolved as the train moved away to the north. He reached into his pocket where he had put Reverend Parson's card. The Society For The Friendless. He tore it neatly into two pieces, dissecting the phrase First Friend. Then he tore those in half, and so on, until he had a flurry of little pieces to scatter along the railroad track behind him.

GLADYS: III

I was a outside chile. My name was called Gladys Johnson. My mama was Tom Johnson's sister, Phoebe Etta. She was always called Etta. After I was borned she lost her teachin job and had to go to workin for Miz Appleby, so my grandparents raised me. But evah Sunday mornin during the spring and summer Miz Appleby would let Mama gimme a bath in her kitchen, put me into my meetin dress and set me out on they front steps. I had me a penny bank and all them Appleby's'd walk by and put in a penny as they went off to church.

I knew who my daddy was; his name was Labe Galbraith. Same man as fathered Emmett Lewis's wife and quite a few other outside chilren round there. He courted my mother when he was a porter on the train. She used to teach school in Covington, Tennessee and ride the train back and forth. I only seen my daddy two three times when I's a chile, but I knew who he was alright, cause my grandmother pointed him out to me one time at the depot. What I didn't know was if he knew who I was. Did he even know my name? The second time I seen him I was standin behind a tree when he come walkin down the street. I studied and studied on him, and when he passed by me I reached one finger way out. I jes wanted to touch him, that was all—but I missed. Later on he settled down with a nice lady; she was a cook at the Greenberry Hotel. She sent for me once by cab and bought me some clothes, but he wasn't nowhere around. When he passed—I's married by then—he lef me and all his outside chilren a little money each.

Both my grandparents that raised me had Indian blood in em. My grandfather, Vess Johnson, he was high yellow—three-quarter white and a quarter Indian on his daddy's side, and three-quarter Indian and a quarter black on his mama's side—and his Indian blood showed mo in him. But Clara, my grandmother, for all that she was dark-skinned, she always said she was part Indian too, and the way you could tell her Indian blood was by her straight hair, and by the things she knew about. She was a root doctor—knew exactly what plant to turn to when folks was sick. If she didn't cure em, at least she could soothe em. She'd started out as a wet nurse, givin her milk to white babies. She would go and stay with them white folks for three weeks at a time once her own baby was old enough.

From that she went to makin soup for sick folks and washin em and such like, til finally she was good as a doctor and people called on her when they needed em a healer.

And from the time I's eight year old I went with her. She was a tough woman. 'Gladys!' she'd say, 'come on', and I wouldn't ask no questions. But the touch of her hand was like balm to a sufferin person. And she wasn't jes called to sick folks. She laid dead folks out, too.

I come to be her apprentice the night John Smith was run over by a train. He was the son of Clara's best friend. He'd hitched him a ride home from Paducah on a freight train, and they said when he went to jump off, he got caught under it. It was going fast since it didn't have to make a stop in Slayden's Crossing, and it cut him all to pieces.

Soon's my grandmother heard about it she went over to Miz Smith's place, and I tagged along. Adolphus Taylor, the colored doctor, and Avery Dowdy, the colored undertaker, had done been called and were on their way out from Greenberry. So when Clara went to wash the cinders and blood off a poor John I's right there, and I wasn't a bit afraid or sick like all the others. I jes stood real close and watched.

When she went to working on his face she was havin trouble, so I jes reached up and helt open his gashes where she could wash em out good. She stopped her washin a minute and looked at me real hard. Then she went on, without a word. After she'd cleaned in all them wounds, I helt his head together while she washed his face. When Dr. Taylor come in he give a big, loud gasp to see a little chile doin such work. He was shocked, but Clara tol him to leave me be, that I was doin a good job. And that's when I become her apprentice. I was happy as I could be fo her praise. After that I went evah'where she went and learnt all I could. I wasn't afraid. I liked it. Wanted to learn evah'thing about it.

When that terrible flu epidemic hit in 1918, Clara and me was nearly the only ones who would go and do fo people in Slayden's Crossin, white and colored both. They's all scared they'd get it. We would go and we'd wash the people and comb they hair and clean they houses and make em a big pot a chicken soup and spoon it into em. Most of em got better and lived, and me and Clara, didn't neither one of us catch it. Fact, I nevah have had the flu in my whole life, and I'm 92 years ol now.

We looked aftah so many people... family too. My mother's younger sister was poisoned by her boyfriend. She'd been married to a Greenberry man, but they done split up, and Nannie (that was her name), she took up then with Jerry John Holmes. He was the one taught me to drive, in the Slayden-Covington's blue Lincoln car. Anyway, when Nannie told Jerry John she was goin back with her husband, Jerry John said he'd rather see her dead. He bought her a quart of ice cream at Evans's Drugstore and poisoned it. She done turned black and swelled up so they had to pump her stomach at the undertaker's. He give her the ice cream on a Friday and she was dead by Satiddy—jaws locked, bowels blocked, couldn't breathe. That night when she lay sufferin so, I asked her was they anything she wanted. Said she wanted some strawberry soda pop. I set off to go to the nickle pop box that was outside a little grocery sto on the corner a 8th and Water Street. It was so dark you couldn't see yo hand, but I got it fo her and tried to feed it to her with a teaspoon; but she couldn't drink none of it. She passed not long aftah that.

Mostly evah'body dies at night. Mama had the TB for three and a half years and she knew she wasn't gonna get well. She'd have what she called a 'smotherin spell' evah day long about lebem o'clock. We done evah'thing we could to help her, but she died hard fo all that we tried to save her. That was at nighttime, too. Still, I often wonder how would it be if you didn't even try to help people when they's down sick. They's some comfort—a lot, really—in knowin you done evah'thing you could fo em.

I wanted to be a doctor or a undertaker when I's growed, but they wasn't nobody to help me. I hadn't had but fo years a education at Dunbar School in Greenberry, plus Sunday School where we learned to print with Sunday School cards. Us colored kids from Slayden's Crossin, we used to catch the train into town to go to Dunbar, so we's always late. But I had to leave school altogether when I's still jes a youngun, and go to workin for Miz Willie Clarence. She had sent word fo a girl to play with her daughter, cause her daughter had a elephant foot and couldn't go outside. She paid me fifty cents a week.

From that job I went to cookin and cleanin fo different people around Greenberry. I've worked hard all a my life and I ain't nevah been fired off a job. Been drivin a car since 19 and 19, and I nevah got but one fifty cent ticket. As a kid I walked behind the mules on the farm my grandfather share-cropped out at Slayden's Crossin, and helped pull corn behind them wagons. After I left Miz Clarence's, I went to cookin and cleanin fo Dr. Al-bright's's family. I worked the elevators at Bright's Store in Paducah, and cleaned hallways and steps at the Bank Buildin—from seven a.m. on the top floor, to five p.m. on the bottom. Then I went to work tendin bar at Pug Low's place over on 7th St. at Paducah—beer and smoke evah'where.

That's where I met my first husband. He was a Louisville man. But that marriage didn't last cause he hit me, and I wasn't about to stay with no-body who hit me. I left him and found me a job at the Chinese laundry in Paducah. Oh, I could press ruffles with the best of em, don't you doubt it. I's good at that fancy launderin.

My second husband, Ernest, he was blind from the age of nine with glau-coma. He went to blind school fo awhile in Louisville. Ernest was good to me, not like the first one, but he couldn't earn a livin on account a his eyesight. So I opened my own restaurant fo awhile. And oh, I farmed pigs, and I kep house fo white folks, and I even got to work fo a spell as a nurses' aide at the Greenberry Hospital. Naturally I liked that the best of all the jobs I evah had.

When Uncle Tom left fo Oklahoma in 1928, that was when I's workin at a Paducah restaurant on Tennessee Street. They was a cold rain fallin the day he rode the train ovah to tell me goodbye. I's his favorite niece, because my Mama had been his favorite sister. She had died in l913 when he was in prison, and Uncle Tom sort of had a special place fo me in his heart on account a that. You my pick, Gladys, he'd say. You my pick outa all of em.

We stood out on the back porch of the restaurant lookin at the rain comin down, and he said, Mama don't want me to go, and neither does Mary, but I got to. Uncle Sam done sent me a telegram sayin I got to go settle up about them oil wells. So I ain't got no choice in the matter.

I could tell it, too, that he didn't wanna go. His hands fairly hung in the pockets of them white overalls. He'd jes come home from Frankfort, where he'd been repairin ceilings in them gov'ment buildins up there. Fancy work, that was his specialty. Things was goin real good fo him and Aunt Mary at that time.

But you a millionaire now, Uncle Tom, I says to him. You can do what-ever you want, cain't ya?

He didn't laugh, just shook his head. It ain't as simple as that, Gladys, he said to me. I hope I do get the money. But you don't know what it's like out there in Oklahoma. People'll kill over a thing like this. I'm gonna have to be watchin out fo myself evah minute. He got quiet then and fiddled with his cold pipe. Anyhow... ain't no use worryin you with all a that; it's my load to carry. I jes come ovah here tell you goodbye. Then he gimme a hug and I went on back inside to my work.

CHAPTER SIXTEEN

As promised, Ben Axley wasted no time in getting a court date. Tom was summoned by the U.S. Government to appear at McAlester, Oklahoma on February 10th, 1928. Axley sent a telegram advising him to get out to McAlester as soon as possible. So it was that on February 2nd, only about a week after Axley had arrived in Slayden's Crossing with his fabulous news, Tom stood beside the train bidding his family good-bye.

Mary cried, but Clara remained dry-eyed. Giving him a fierce hug, she said, Tom, I didn't raise you to play the fool. You watch yo'self out there. Most especially you watch what's put in front of you to eat and drink.

He nodded earnestly and replied, I know. I'll be careful, Mama, and I'll be back jes soon as I can get here.

Nema and her little girls reached up to hug him. Ben shook his hand and wished him luck. Mary turned away to blow her nose and Tom looked at Ben, but he had already moved to put an arm around his mother's shoulders.

As the train began to roll off slowly, the family group backed away and Tom jumped aboard with his cloth bag. He stood waving in the doorway until he could no longer see them, then he found himself a seat in the first passenger car of the train. Cinders blew in and the noise from the engine was deafening, but it was less crowded than the next car back, which was the only other choice for colored passengers.

Tom had hardly settled himself into an aisle seat, his fedora on one knee, when the train pulled up beside the Greenberry depot. Judge Arch had a crowd of interested spectators to see him off, and of course his wife, Lexie, and their two young sons. Ted Wingate was not there. It being business hours, he was ensconced in his office over at the Greenberry Bank. He had held a conference with his younger brother over breakfast that morning, and he would keep in close touch with the proceedings by telephone and telegraph.

A reporter from *The Greenberry Daily Leaf* hovered about the platform trying to catch the judge's attention. How soon do you expect to be back, Judge Arch? he asked, pencil poised over his notebook.

Oh, I imagine it'll take a few weeks. This is a very important case, you understand. But it's in good hands, if I do say so myself.

He stepped up into the door of the car on a wave of appreciative laughter, and flourished his derby at the people on the platform. Good-bye now. Lexie, don't worry about me. You just look after our boys. Good-bye everybody! I'll see you in the funny papers!

They all laughed again. Judge Arch was generally regarded as a wit, except when he was pronouncing sentence, and sometimes even then. *The Daily Leaf* often carried anecdotes from his bench, such as the time he was presiding over a dispute between two young Negro 'muleskinners' as he called them. He sentenced one to the county jail and let the other go, saying, If I put them both in jail—which is where they no doubt belong—they'd only kill each other. This way at least we'll have a few weeks before old Uncle Avery will have to pretty one of them up for burial.

Now the train chugged in a steady rhythm toward Memphis, where they would change trains for Little Rock and points west. Judge Wingate often travelled to Tennessee on business. He settled back and thought about the whiskey he would have the waiter slip him at a certain restaurant near the Memphis train depot. There was nothing like a whiskey with your last cigar of the day. The deeper they moved into cotton country, the freer he felt.

They only spoke to each other once during the eighteen hour journey. Shortly after the train crossed into Oklahoma, Judge Arch left the dining car and moved up toward the front of the train. There he waited in the vestibule between the last white car and the first black one while the porter fetched Tom for him.

The porter was black, and the oldest one of the three of them. He waited humbly for his tip, not daring to look the imposing white man in the eye. However, he sensed that the man he had just fetched from the colored section was not the white man's servant. As he palmed his coin and left the vestibule, the porter couldn't resist glancing back, and was surprised to see Tom looking directly at the white man with a mildly challenging expression.

Yeah, Judge? You wanted to see me?

You been enjoyin the trip so far, Tommie?

I have. You?

Oh, I've been as comfortable as one can be in these tiny compartments.

Tom, who had had to sleep all night in his upright seat, made no answer and waited for the judge to drop the 'civilities' and get to the real point.

Axley wired me that he'll meet our train this mornin, and that he's arranged rooms for us and all that. He has also rented a law office for us to conduct our business in.

Tom still said nothing, though he nodded slightly.

Now. I just want to assure you, Tommie my boy, that we'll look after everything for you. Between us, Axley and myself will have the courts eating out of our hand. The less *you* say, the better. There are some delicate areas here to be negotiated around, but we can handle anything, as long as you do what we tell you to. No talking about the case to *any*one apart from me and Axley, either inside or outside the courtroom. Do you understand?

Tom's temper was inflamed by Wingate's suffocating authoritarianism, but he knew he must bide his time and play his role carefully. So he choked back the resentment and replied with dignity, Yes.

The judge felt very unsure of Johnson's cooperation and had not looked forward to dealing with him without Axley. Now, relieved, he became expansive and patted Tom on the back. Good, good. That's just fine. As long as you maintain that attitude, and we all do our part—because, don't forget, you wouldn't get one mile along this rocky road ahead without me and Axley—but if we all work together…I have a feeling we are on the pig's back.

*   *   *

Some of the towns in the Territories were built on a grand scale, as if to accommodate the great metropolis each was sure to become, with streets as wide as a Manhattan boulevard separating a handful of buildings. McAlester, Oklahoma was a small, hilly town with a spanking new ten-story red brick hotel on the same street as the depot. The only other building to rival the hotel in size and style was the courthouse, which sported an Italianate, tiled, open porch, where lawyers and their clients often stood consulting in groups. The two buildings were within a block and a half of each other, on opposite sides of the capacious street, and formed the locus of the little town's purpose.

Ben Axley was there to greet them as they made their way toward him from their separate cars. Hello! Welcome! he called with rather manic enthusiasm, then whispered as they walked towards the hotel, No business talk until we're alone. There are ears everywhere. So… have a good trip?

Tom saw what he guessed were reporters here and there, looking around as if for a story, and assumed that was what Axley was referring to. Three blanketed Indian men sat on an empty luggage cart, passing a bottle around. Tom was slightly behind the lawyers as they walked by an open doorway that spurted piano music and lively talk. The word BEER was painted on the window in large letters and for a moment Tom wondered whether prohibition was not officially in effect out here. Then he saw the word Ginger painted above it in smaller lettering. He turned to see a Negro boy of thirteen or fourteen, dressed all in white, cross the wide street carrying an empty silver tea service from the courthouse to the hotel. Cowboys mixed with men in suits. A native couple dressed in expensive, stylish hats and coats looked haughtily down from a yellow carriage drawn by matched bays. A middle-aged black woman in a red felt hat passed them with two girls in tow. The girls were perhaps seventeen or eighteen and wore fringed flapper dresses under thin coats, their hair crimped into shiny black caps.

To his surprise, and despite his dark memories, Tom felt invigorated by this first taste of the west after so many years. He had the sudden feeling that anything might happen. As if to illustrate this, a white bull wandered up a side street toward them, meandering around two parked cars.

Good God, said Wingate, also spotting the animal. You know, I've never been out here before. I see now what a sheltered life I've lived back in the more civilized region of the country.

Axley slit his eyes up at the judge. Things are different out here, that's for sure. But we do have our virtues. I've rented rooms for all of us here in the hotel, he said, as a man in a top hat opened the door for them.

Well, touché, said Wingate, indicating the doorman.

Oh, that's nothing, Axley continued. That's just imitation east. Wait'll you see your first oil derrick. Now that's virtue, western style.

We saw some from the train...

Ah, but they're different up close, Judge Arch. You can smell the oil.

The lobby of the Hotel McAlester was bustling with guests of every race; there were even a few Chinese busboys thrown in at no extra cost. Tom stood on the patterned carpet and looked up at the chandelier hanging from its nest of plasterwork. He was impressed despite himself. He had never been inside a hotel in his life, let alone as fancy a one as this. It was almost as grand as the Capitol building at Frankfort. The massive elk's head mounted behind the desk stirred something long forgotten in him.

Wingate and Axley had rooms on the second floor; his was on the tenth. You better hope the elevator keeps working, Tommie boy, Wingate remarked, lighting a cigar as they ascended to their rooms. When they got off, Axley said, Meet us back in the lobby in one hour, and we'll have dinner. And remember, speak no evil. Axley put a finger to his lips.

As the doors closed, Tom asked the elevator operator, an old black man, what time it was.

'Lebem o'clock, suh. Dey's a clock on evah flo.

Thanks.

Yes suh.

Tom was feeling strange at being treated with such deference. If he actually did end up with the oil money, this would probably become the usual manner with which he'd be treated by everyone around him. I reckon

I could get used to it, he thought. He didn't realize he had shrugged until he saw the elevator operator looking at him.

Dis here's yo flo, suh.

He came to then, and feeling awkward, handed the man a nickel, as he'd seen everyone else do when they got off the elevator. The old man acknowledged the tip with a nod and a smile as the doors closed.

Tom looked at the key in his hand. Room number 1016. He started down the hallway to the left, passing a Negro couple, the man in a suit and overcoat, the woman in a fur. They were too busy cuddling to notice Tom walking past. He began to wish he hadn't insisted that Mary not come with him. For one thing she might enjoy staying in a fancy hotel once in her life.

His room was simple, a double bed with a maroon spread that matched the drapes, a basin and pitcher, with soap and towels. There were buttons beside the door and over the bed for the electric lights. Indoor toilet just down the hall. He opened the drapes and saw that he had a view of the main street. Far below he could make out the roof of the courthouse, tiny cars, buggies and people moving like toys along the street. Like play pretties, he said aloud. The little town spread out over the hills before him until, abruptly, the fields began. In the distance, oil derricks dotted the countryside, like the spires of churches dedicated to Mammon.

CHAPTER SEVENTEEN

The court business turned out to be a lot of time-consuming emptiness for Tom. Axley and Wingate were forever holding conferences with him in their 'office', which was a small bedroom at the back of the first floor of the McAlester Hotel. Like the court sessions themselves, these were long boring meetings in which the lawyers talked strategy in legal terminology, while Tom mostly sat on the edge of the bed whittling or day-dreaming, and ended up with a stiff back and a crick in his neck.

The day after their arrival, Judge Wingate suddenly turned around from the desk. Tom had been studying an ornate brass letter holder, running his finger over and over the petals of its design, his mind somewhere in the highest corners of the Frankfort Capitol. Okay, Tommie, gimme the name of one of your fellow inmates from Leavenworth. Somebody you got along with.

Tom leaned over and spat into the trashcan. Didn't get along with none of em.

Wingate sighed. Aw come on now, Tommie. I didn't think you sent em Christmas cards, but there's gotta be somebody from all those years that you remember... if not fondly, then at...

Um, mind if I try to explain it to him, Judge Arch? Thanks. What we need to set up here, Tommie, is a witness who can verify that you told him about your land out in Oklahoma, and about how you were an Indian and all that. First of all, *was* there anybody in Leavenworth—a cellmate perhaps—that you told all that stuff to?

Wasn't no talkin allowed.

The lawyers cut an exasperated glance at each other.

Just give us a name of somebody you knew in prison, and we'll take it from there, said Wingate.

Abner Butts.

Is he colored or white?

Why you wanna know that?

Just wonderin.

He's white.

Wingate smiled and nodded. What was he in for?

Larceny.

Any idea where he'd be now? Axley asked, writing the name down in his notebook.

Tom pushed his lower lip up into a cynical inverted smile and laughed through his nose. No idee in the world.

Where was he from? Wingate asked in a more encouraging tone.

Tom shrugged.

Listen, Tommie boy, Wingate said, dropping the new tone. You can make this thing run a whole lot quicker if you play ball with us. Or... don't you care about a measly twenty million dollars? Maybe you don't need any more money—is that it?

Jes don't know where he lives, Judge. Mebbe Flah'da.

Okay, that's a start, said Axley. Why do you say Florida?

He got out before me. Said he might go down yonder lookin to get him a fresh start.

Get Leavenworth on the telephone, said Wingate, and Axley picked up the receiver.

Leavenworth. That closed, iron world of rules and walls that he'd hurled himself against until it had entered his soul. *You!* Number 3283! I saw that. I saw you talking to 7220. You're comin with me. That had been his first time in solitary—what they called 'the blind cell' in Leavenworth. The tiny, windowless room. The reeking bucket at the end of his bunk. The echo that sharpened every footfall to a blade, every voice.

The others had started looking for him only a few years after he had been locked up. That was back when he was still fighting it, still falling into the blank space he'd seen on his form after 'Date of Release'. The Bennetts, neighbors of the Sam Ford land grant, had been the first to stir things up. They wanted the Dawes Commission to grant their son this land that was lying fallow. If Sam Ford didn't have any use for it, they did. So he was brought before Warden McLeod. Tom was always distracted by the fact that the warden's geometric, white beard followed stiffly along whenever he moved his head or spoke.

Your alias is Sam Ford. And the trail for the owner of this land in Oklahoma leads to our prisoner Number 3283. Do you own this property?

My name's Tom Johnson.

The warden had waited. When Tom still had no more to say, he came to the point. Well, I have a subpoena here for Sam Ford, the owner of a hundred and sixty acres in Creek County, Oklahoma. And Sam Ford is your alias. But it seems you'd rather not talk about it. The warden raised his eyebrows. Looks like you might be in even more trouble than you've already been caught for. Could that be it?

Tom had stared back at the warden with silent hatred until McLeod looked away, the beard pointing to the guard at the door. McRae, I want you to accompany Number 3283 to the depot at five o'clock this evening. There you'll turn him over to the United States Marshals—they're sending a Deputy... Reed for him. He's to attend a hearing at Muskogee. They're scheduled to leave on the Frisco train at 6:11 this evening. Make the arrangements for his transport to and from the depot. And McRae... advise them as to the prisoner's character. Without further ceremony, McLeod dipped his pen and signed the paper on his desk, then turned away from Tom to reach for his telephone.

At the Muskogee hearing, Tom had been brought before a panel of white men and Creek Nation officials to testify as to his land claim. The panel was chaired by Commissioner Benvenuti, a distinguished looking white man whom Sax Slayden had pointed to the day before when asked to describe Tom Johnson. Look sump'in like him. None of the others being questioned at the hearing were present for Tom's examination. In fact, Tom didn't know until later that Sax, Anna, the Washington brothers, and others had already been questioned here, one at a time, about his land claim.

Sitting in the small room while a storm sought entry at the windows, Tom had told the Creek Nation and Dawes Commission officials that his real name was Sam Ford, but that he'd been raised by the Johnson family in Wills County, Kentucky. Once again he told the story. He said he had always considered himself to be the eldest of the children of Sylvester and Clara Johnson, until a mysterious man came up to him at a picnic when he was about fourteen years old and told him the truth. When he grew up he'd wasted no time in getting out to the Territory to look up his real family. Upon discovering they were all dead, he enrolled himself as a Creek citizen and was granted land by the Commission at Okmulgee.

He even added that he had been approached there by unscrupulous men who wanted to enroll someone else under his dead brother's name, and explained how he had refused to take part in such a ruse, since he knew the man in question was not Walter Ford. Asked how he knew it wasn't Walter Ford, since he had already admitted to never having met his 'real mother and brother', Tom replied that he knew who the man was who wanted to *call* himself Walter Ford.

Very interesting, said one of the Commissioners. And who was this man who wanted to make a false claim before the Creek Nation?

Jes somebody I met when I first got out to the Territory. I can't call his name to mind no mo, but I did know at that time that he wasn't my brother. My brother was already dead.

Several times during his testimony, thunder had made it necessary for Tom to repeat what he had just said. For a while it became dark enough for lamps to be lit, but by the time they finished with him, the light of the lamps—so influential a moment before—was rendered completely ineffectual by sunshine. So much so that no one remembered to blow them out as Tom was led from the room.

Since the panel was unable to make contact with several key officials, including the Attorney General for the Western District of Indian Territory, the hearing was continued, and the question of ownership left open. However the Commissioners recommended that Sam Ford's name be stricken from the roll, and the Bennett family be allowed to farm his allotment, given that Sam Ford was, in any case, serving a life term in the penitentiary under the name of Tom Johnson.

Deputy Reed had a way of moving and walking that wore Tom's wrists raw. He led him along the dark, shining halls of the Muskogee Courthouse, down the back steps and over to the jail, Tom's chains ringing like a holiday harness. But even the deputy's punishing pace couldn't quite eclipse the pleasure he took in the smell of the newly rinsed air, the sliding cloud shelves, the bright clothes of the people going about their ordinary business in the Muskogee streets.

He had relished the time outside of Leavenworth's walls, despite what had occasioned it. His appetite for freedom, dulled somewhat by the years, was whetted again. He was thirty-four years old. The thought of going back seemed intolerable as he looked at the broad fields and sky outside the train. Then a bad bowl of chili had given him a chance to escape, and he had seized it blindly, ready to suffer any injury, in fact half-hoping to be shot in the back rather than be returned to Leavenworth Penitentiary. But the attempt had only gained him two weeks in solitary confinement, and refusal of tobacco privileges for a month.

The day he was returned to his normal cell, the guard had taken him first to the showers, then to the admissions room, where incoming prisoners were processed. Tom was puzzled, but refrained from speaking lest he be returned to 'the blind cell'. The guard made no explanation.

Behind the desk sat the warden's son, E.P. McLeod, a records clerk for the prison. The younger McLeod had a boyish face and wore his sandy hair parted in the middle. He was dressed in a belted woolen jacket of the latest style and looked up at Tom with unbridled enthusiasm.

Ah, good! Another man for the cause. Bring him on over. He indicated the chair across from his own.

The guard led him over and stood hovering nearby. You need me to remove the cuffs?

It's not strictly necessary. That's one of the beauties of this new method if you ask me. The guard was attentive, and several other clerks drew near, obviously in some awe of the young man and what he was doing. McLeod looked up at the guard, smiling. I'd have thought the novelty would've worn off a little. You must've brought me at least two dozen men by now.

Guards were encouraged to speak as little as possible, to support the prison's policy of silence for the inmates. So out of habit, Tom's guard didn't answer at first. But the atmosphere here was different; conversation seemed to be tolerated. I still cain't hardly believe in it, the guard said finally.

McLeod gave a proprietary laugh. Oh you may believe in it, alright. It was the hit of the World's Fair. Everyone was talking about it. But it wasn't in St. Louis, it was in Europe that I learned the finer details of the science. Paris, Berlin, Amsterdam... they're using it everywhere now. It was in London, at Scotland Yard itself, that I perfected the system we're implementing here at Leavenworth. And I can assert with some pride, gentlemen, that my methods are second to none in the world. Addressing Tom almost as an afterthought he asked, Name, please.

Tom Johnson.

Are you right handed, or left handed?

Tom lifted his right hand up slightly.

McLeod made notes at the top of the page. Then, resuming his expla-nation to the guard and the clerks, the warden's son grasped Tom by the right hand, somewhat methodically, and pulled it towards him. You can take it from me, I've studied thousands of sets of them, and no two men have the exact same fingerprints. McLeod ran his hand under Tom's palm, saying, Open it out flat... That's it. Then he pressed Tom's thumb onto an ink pad, lifted it again and said, Now spread your fingers wide. That's right. You see, gentlemen, you must take the prints one finger at a time to get a good impression. He was rolling Tom's broad fingertips one by one onto the paper as if in illustration. Our prisoner Number... He peered up at the label stitched onto Tom's shirtfront. ...Number 3283 here, has very clear prints.

He took hold of Tom's left hand to repeat the procedure. He began with the thumb again, and laughed with delight as he lifted Tom's hand from the paper. *Ah*, look at this, he said to the watching men. Look at this left thumb print! It's a relatively rare double whorl. Tom was as amazed as the others. He had never before noticed the two sets of concentric circles on his left thumb.

Suddenly McLeod directed his boyish gaze at Tom's face. What are you in for, 3283? No wait! Let me guess. You have moderate-sized, but ex-tremely well-shaped hands. Muscular. Almost an artisan's hands. I would say you've left these fingerprints all over a... printing press somewhere, making counterfeit bills. Am I right?

Tom stared coldly at the smiling, self-satisfied face before him.

Answer Mr. McLeod, boy! What're ya in for? the guard barked.

His own voice sounding foreign and rusty to him, Tom rasped, Murder.

Murder? McLeod echoed. Really? Well.... How did you do it? How did you carry out this murder of yours?

Pistol.

McLeod made a face of distasteful surprise at the others. *Hm.* He grasped Tom's left hand again, turning it over to show the men a small scar at the base of his little finger. You see this scar? he asked rhetorically. A little thing like that can also help identify a perpetrator. The men nodded, totally absorbed in this new aspect of criminology.

When McLeod had completed the fingerprinting, he wiped at Tom's hands with a rag. You'll want to give these a good washing right away, and even with that it'll take a few days for the ink to wear off completely. But then I doubt you're any Lady Macbeth, so that probably won't bother you much.

One of the clerks laughed, and McLeod directed his next remarks to him. You see, if this man's trial were to take place today and his gun were submitted as evidence, we now know his fingerprints would be all over it, leaving no questions as to the murderer's identity right from the start. He had dipped his pen into a pot of ink and was writing Tom's number and some other symbols at the top of the sheet bearing his fingerprints.

Are they permanent then? On... on, on the gun I mean? another clerk asked.

Well no, they can be wiped off. But what murderer would bother wiping them off? What murderer would ever have suspected he was leaving his signature all over the weapon, just as I am leaving mine on this pen?

The guard was pulling him to his feet now, but, despite himself, Tom wanted to hear more. And it seemed the guard, too, was reluctant to leave, moving slowly. He leaned over the desk, Tom's arm firmly in his grip, to squint at the ink pen. How can you see em? I don't see nothin on that pen.

Ah, said McLeod, raising his index finger, on the tip of which Tom now noticed, a faint oval whorl was engraved. He opened a drawer and took out a small bottle containing white powder. Then he looked at Tom, who was watching intently. Uh... tell you what. Why don't you take this man back to his cell, and stop by a bit later for the demonstration. What do you say? He winked.

I got ya, said the guard, and Tom was yanked to the door and out of the room, tripping over his fetters.

CHAPTER EIGHTEEN

The episode involving the land claims trial and Tom's fingerprinting had taken place in1906. These things punched that year out a little from the usual flat round of prison routine. Another such memorable year was 1910, when two important events in the history of Leavenworth took place.

One morning in April, as he loaded bricks onto a wheelbarrow for the building of the new cellblock, Tom heard the train whistle signal its exit through the west gate. Shortly afterward there was a splintering crash, as the train broke through the closed gate from inside the prison. Sirens split the air almost instantly and, as shots were fired from the guardhouse, Tom threw down his bricks and hit the ground.

In the confusion that followed, the men in the brickyard were left unguarded for a few minutes. Tom rose tentatively into a crouch, as did several others. They looked at one another, scenting the air for an opportunity to join the escape that was obviously in progress. But before they could think which way to run, two of their guards ran back into the yard wild-eyed, their clubs drawn. Of the six prisoners who escaped that day, all were recaptured except one, Frank Grigware, who'd been imprisoned for train robbery. Against all the odds, Grigware escaped to Canada, where he lived for the rest of his life, eventually even becoming the mayor of a small town in Alberta. However his successful escape did nothing to help the inmates of Leavenworth.

For the next few months everyone paid for Grigware's freedom by a constriction of the rules and an atmosphere of heightened mistrust. Then in June, Congress passed the Parole Bill, establishing new hope for federal prisoners. For the first time even those serving a life sentence—the ten percent of the prison population to which Tom belonged—now had a chance of being released on good behavior.

Tom first heard this news from Butts, who was immediately behind him while his cell block marched in lock-step to breakfast. He didn't dare turn around, but, heart pounding, whispered the word to the man ahead of him. At supper that night, Warden McLeod made an unusual appearance. He stood in front of the prisoners, roughly a thousand men all facing one way at closely packed tables.

Let me begin with a warning, said McLeod with his precise diction. Any vocal response whatsoever to what I have to say will be punished immediately by a lock-down of the entire prison. You are to maintain the code of silence, as usual. Now. I have an announcement to make. As some of you may already have heard, Congress has passed the Federal Parole Bill.

Some shifting in posture, some collective intake of air tuned the atmosphere in the hall to a new key. Though it seemed to roar in Tom's ears like a stadium cheer, in fact the silence in the hall remained unbroken.

You must understand that it will be months before the bill can be implemented, but even so, this is good news for all of us here at Leavenworth. No one can say who will be the first to become eligible for parole, except that of course a clean prison record is required. This will eliminate those, for example, whose behavior has incurred extra penalties, such as solitary confinement. Consequences, men. That word should guide your every step—especially now.

Once again, Tom felt the body blow of his leap from the train four years before. A split second after that, at least in memory, he was chained in the Blind Cell. Consequences.

However, the possibility of parole offers each and every one of you an excellent incentive to begin building a clean record from this day forward. And for those who are paroled, any infringement of the rules of parole—which is, do not forget, not a full release, but a monitored release... I say, any infringement of the rules of parole will be subject to the strictest punishment. Let us pray that this new hope which the government has seen fit to hold out to you will result in a better and more disciplined life for us all.

When the warden left, Tom closed his eyes. He was shaking all over at this official confirmation. Desire moved through him like an illness. His first spoonful of beans trembled as he brought it to his mouth. Everything he took part in or observed at Leavenworth—writing letters home, working in the brickyard, going to the prison dentist, lying on his bunk, attending the weekly religious services—all of it had been shot through with the weight of the bars that surrounded him. Here was a lightening of that weight, the first in seven and a half years. He finished eating and marched back to his cell in an altered state.

After that announcement in 1910, Tom's behavior changed. Now he had something to lose. He began trying to look after his teeth. Signed up for courses when they were offered, and eventually asked to be moved to plastering detail. From that day on, he had only one more setback in his entire prison career. In February of 1914, the guard he hated the most, Pidsadny, jabbed him with his stick to hurry him along to his cell. Instinctively Tom caught the end of the stick and thrust it back towards Pidsadny with a half-strangled oath. Behind him, Butts had cleared his throat, so Tom would see him lift his chin in silent solidarity. The stick only grazed the guard's stomach lightly, but the incident was enough to land Tom four days in solitary confinement.

This time the silence and the tiny cell had caused him to redefine space and time. I can blow up from the inside here, he said to himself somewhere between the first and second day, or I can work on Good Behavior. Work on it! Work on it! Work on it! What he couldn't afford to think about were the years ahead. This infringement would mean starting all over again to build a clean record. He'd have years to go before he would become eligible for parole. If he just didn't count the months and years, if he took it a day at a time and set himself on Good Behavior, maybe he could make it. He vowed to concentrate on the positives. He actually liked going to work and learning about plastering. They no longer chained you to the wall in the Blind Cell like in the old days. This meant not only that you could move around more easily, but also that you could sit facing the door, which helped abate the claustrophobia that the windowless cell inspired. There was talk of abolishing lock-step. But most of all, there was the possibility of parole. He might one day actually get out!

For the rest of his confinement he filled the hours with activities which included physical exercise—whatever he could manage within the limited space—and singing through every song he could remember. He had to do this quietly, so as not to be heard by the guard that came down to check on him occasionally, but he didn't have the voice he'd once had anyway, due to years of using it so rarely. He found, to his surprise, that he knew more hymns than anything else, but he was grateful for them. He sang his favorites, like Rock My Soul, Joshua Fit the Battle of Jericho, and Swing Low Sweet Chariot, over and over again. Their images of river and sky had a way of making the cinderblock cell disappear for a while. And when he sang 'The battle is in my hands' he was filled with inspiration. Another method he used to steel himself was to compose a letter to everyone he knew, repeating in each one his resolve. Since he wasn't allowed any paper or pencils in solitary, his family and friends never received these fervent vows that took on almost a tone of prayer.

First, Mary. His mother had written to him recently that she had moved to town and taken up with another man, Rollie Sharps, a distant cousin on Clara's side. At first the thought had chewed him up, blunt teeth gnawing at his vitals. Now he said to himself, She believes I ain't nevah gettin outta here. She believes she ain't nevah gonna see me again. She needs somebody to look after her til I get freed. He closed his eyes on the filthy cell and visualized Mary, the way she sometimes gazed into the distance. With a groan he thought of her breasts. The way her pear-shaped bottom swelled under her clothes, the way it felt under his hands. No one could ever know Mary as he had. It seemed to him then that she'd never done him a wrong of any kind, and if he couldn't imagine her taking him back again, there truly would be no reason to struggle on. Nothing to go for. Without Mary to return to, the amputation of his life would be complete; the life sentence might as well have been a death sentence. He had to believe they would be able to forgive each other everything and start over. Together.

Angling all the love and all the power he had left into an imaginary pencil point, he composed his letter to his wife, weeping through each sentence.

Feb. 23, 1914. Dear Mary. I love you. I love you so much. I regret, more than I can tell you, all I done to mess up our life. All mistakes are mine. You have been a good wife and a good mother and if I ever get the chance I aim to make it up to you. If I start to think on how much I miss you, I won't be able to go on. Our Benjamen is lucky to have you with him while he grows up. Maybe he's better off not knowin me. And little Alma is better off where she is too. Any comfort you can get while I am in this fix is okay with me. But if I get the chance I'll come back to you and make a home for you and try to make up for what I done. I sit lookin at these brick walls and wish I could undo everything and start over, and that wishin just burns and burns in my stomach. But I ain't gonna let it get me, Mary. I aim to beat the system and come out of it stronger than ever for you and me both. But especially for you. I will see you again, I promise. And if you'll have me back, I will make us a good, clean life. The life you deserve. Love, your husband Tom.

He composed similar letters to his mother, his brother, to each one of his sisters, nieces, nephews, cousins, neighbors. Going through them all helped pass the time, helped exercise his mind. Through these letters he began to see who he had been in relation to each one, and—more importantly to him now—who he could be. He even composed one to Sax, and it was the last.

Dear Sax, It is hard for me to know what to say to you now that I have put in eleven years in the pen over killing that man you wanted to be shed of. I could say that I wish I hadn't never laid eyes on you or him neither one, and to be truthful I have had them thoughts lots of times during these years. But I done bucked against these walls all I can. I have set with my tongue in the place where my front tooth used to be that the law man busted out when they captured me, and I have let regret make me feel like I got a bad fever that ain't never going to lift til it takes my life. But then I open my eyes and I'm still here. I have tried to get away ever way I know of and all it does is to make things worse. I am writin you from solitary, but this is the last time that will ever happen. I got your letter sayin that

that woman married somebody else. Lord, what the hell? Lord God. But I am writin to tell you that I am through with all of that now. I am settin my face forward and I intend to take myself in hand and get out of here on Good Behavior. That is the only good thing I can make happen in the wreck I made of my life. I don't hold you to account for what happened back in Oklahoma. I fired that gun my own self. I just want you to know that from now on I aim to do what I want to and not what nobody else wants me to. So let's let the past die between us. Don't never make no mention of it to me again. I am movin on.

Your nephew, Tom

When two guards came to take him back up to his cell at the end of the fourth day, they were surprised to find him peaceful, with even the faint suggestion of a smile.

Hoooo-wee, one said. Good thing they got you down for the showers. Your cell mate'd have to go off to the Infirmary if we was to take you back to your home sweet home smellin like this.

Tom replied, I'm right happy about it myself. The two guards looked at each other, incredulous, and laughed.

CHAPTER NINETEEN

The courtroom was always crowded. There were almost enough lawyers involved in this case alone to populate an average graduating class in most American law schools. No fewer than nine oil companies had registered claims on the Sam Ford land, as well as the Bennetts who, as neighbors, had originally wanted it for their eldest son to farm.

Axley said the Bennetts, a mostly white family, except for a quarter of Creek blood on the mother's side, were the most determined of all the claimants, as they felt they were the most entitled. Back in 1906 old man Bennett had initiated the search for Sam Ford in order to clear the title for his son, Earl. Now over twenty years later, Earl and several of his brothers were bound by an oath to carry out their father's dying wish never to give up on the land claim. They had promised him to hold onto the land, come hell or high water. Unkempt and stone faced, three or four of them sat and stared malevolently at Tom every day, moving only to chew their tobacco, or to spit into the cans they carried inside the courtroom for the purpose.

One of the points of contention was whether Tom had been served his 1906 subpoena when the Bennetts were first trying to get title to the property. It seemed the records were scanty and unclear. The alias further confused the issue. There was a letter on record at Leavenworth from the now dead Warden McLeod to the effect that Tom Johnson had evaded the issue by stating that Sam Ford was just an alias and not his true identity. The Bennetts had stirred a little and looked at each other when the letter was read out. However, the court held that this issue had to be made clearer, and that records from the 1906 case would have to be produced before a judgement on the matter could be reached.

The case had been delayed while lawyers from all sides descended upon Leavenworth. Though Tom's mugshot was available to all comers, and subsequently began showing up in newspapers to titillate an already fascinated public, the warden claimed there were 'some 32,000 jackets on file' and that, though the location of the prison records had been moved several times in its history, anyone wishing to go through the files was welcome. No one was successful at finding the papers. The lawyers for the defense, however, produced Abner Butts.

Mr. Butts, Wingate asked, how did you meet Thomas Johnson?

In Leavenworth Federal Prison. We was inmates together.

Butts was a short man with red hair and a chronic expression of intense determination. His tattooed arms were folded across his chest. He had agreed to wear a dress shirt, but insisted on rolling the sleeves to the elbow in order, Wingate now assumed, to show off the stars and stripes, the snakes and hearts that decorated his forearms.

For the record, tell us when you entered Leavenworth, and on what charge.

1906. Grand larceny.

And you were released...?

1916.

So you knew Mr. Johnson for ten years?

Yes.

Did he ever speak to you about his life outside of prison?

Yes sir. He said he was part Creek Indian and had him some land out in Oklahoma.

Was there anything else?

Yes. I met his parents.

You met his parents? What were their names?

Doc and Molly Ford.

The names acted like smelling salts on the drowsing courtroom.

Now let us proceed carefully, Mr. Butts. You knew the defendant in Leavenworth under what name?

Number 3283. The assembled audience burst into laughter, and Wingate smiled. Clearly they were beginning to enjoy this witness. That was good, very good.

Yes, but what name did you know the prisoner by, Mr. Butts?

He was called Johnson, but he told me that was his Kentucky name. His other name, his Oklahoma name, was Sam Ford.

Did he explain to you why he had two names?

He did, but lots of guys at Leavenworth had two names. Another round of laughter, even longer this time. One reporter doubled over with delight, and people began whispering to each other, until the judge banged his gavel for order. Butts grinned at the response, but maintained his bearing of compact erectness.

And will you tell the court what he said about his having two names?

He said he always thought he was Tom Johnson from Kentucky up until he was fourteen years old. Then, at a church picnic, a man come up to him—a Indian man he'd never seen before—name of Doc Ford. The man told him he was his real father, and that the Johnsons'd been rearin him as a favor to him and his wife, but that, soon as he was grown, Ford wanted him to come on out to Oklahoma and meet his mother and brother, and live out there with them.

Go on.

Well sir, when he told me who his real parents was, I come near to pitchin a fit, because I knew em!

You knew Doc and Molly Ford?

Yes sir, I did.

Are you from Oklahoma?

No sir, I'm from Michigan, but I have cousins out there...

Cousins in Oklahoma?

Yes sir. Cousins in Stroud, Oklahoma. At least I did then; they're dead now. But I had visited them in Stroud when I was a youngster, when it was jist called Oklahoma Territory and Indian Territory. They was—my cousins, I mean—they was friends of Doc and Molly Ford and their son Walter—Sam's brother that he hadn't never met. But you see, I *had* met him; Walter Ford was about my age. So me and Sam, we had lots to talk about. He wanted to hear all about his little brother and his mother and all, since he hadn't never got to meet any of em. They died before the turn of the century, you see, all three of the Fords. So that, by the time T... Sam went out there to meet em, they was already dead.

Alright, Mr. Butts, I'll recap for the benefit of the court, and you correct me if I'm wrong about any of the details. You met Tom Johnson—whose told you his real name is Sam Ford—in Fort Leavenworth Federal Prison, where you knew him for ten years. He told you he was born in Oklahoma of Creek Indian parents, Doc and Molly Ford, and you realized you had met the Fords as a child, while visiting your cousins in Stroud, Oklahoma.

That's right. Butts nodded deeply.

The defendant explained to you that he had been raised by the Johnson family in Kentucky, and didn't know his true identity until he was fourteen years old. At that time, Doc Ford came up to him at a church picnic in Slayden's Crossing, Kentucky, and told him he was his true father, and that he wanted him to come out to Oklahoma and live with the Ford family upon reaching manhood. Am I incorrect in any of these details, Mr. Butts?

Butts, who had been nodding like a pump jack as Wingate spoke, answered, No sir, that's correct. Ever bit of it.

Did he ever mention to you that oil had been struck on his land in Oklahoma?

No sir. I don't believe he knew anything about that while he was in Leavenworth.

Thank you, Mr. Butts. I have no further questions.

The cross-examination was intense.

Mr. Butts, it is my understanding that Leavenworth had a rule of silence, is that not correct?

Yes sir, they did use to have one.

So when, exactly, did you and Mr. Johnson conduct your warm and intimate conver...

Objection, your honor!

Objection sustained. Just state your question, Mr. Ward.

When did you and Mr. Johnson manage to talk?

In 1914 yard privilege was allowed, and prisoners could talk to one another as much as they wanted during it. That's when we talked the most, and after that I begun calling him Sam, at his request.

What were your cousins' names who lived in Oklahoma?

Butts. More laughter from the audience.

Their first names, please?

Ethel and Ronald. And little Marion.

Did the little girl die, too?

It was a little boy, sir, and yes he did. The typhoid took em all.

How old were you when you visited the Territories?

Twelve.

What year was it?

1890.

How old are you now?"

Fifty.

Describe Doc Ford.

He looked like a Indian.

More laughter.

Can you do any better than that, Mr. Butts?

No.

A wave of hilarity swept up even the judge. Ward sighed.

When you told Mr. Johnson about his mother and brother, what did you say?

Jist that his mother was nice to me, and me and Walt played catch together sometimes. He had him a little bow and arrow and me and him shot a gopher with it once.

The two of you together shot one gopher?

Well really it was Walt shot the gopher. I just pulled the arrow out.

The courtroom was so convulsed by this time that Mr. Ward thought better of continuing the cross-examination.

By God, Butts, exclaimed Wingate when they were safely back in their hotel bedroom office, you certainly earned your money. Why you had the whole courtroom eating out of your hand! You've just got to stay for a little celebratory supper, though we can't talk about any of the courtroom business in public, of course. Will you join us?

Don't mind if I do, he replied, clapping Tom on the back. Man, if only we'd a known back at dear old 1300 Metropolitan Avenue we'd be having this much fun one day... huh, Tom?

Lots a fun, Tom replied flatly, and they repaired to their customary table at the Hotel McAlester, Butts and the lawyers laughing and chatting like old friends.

CHAPTER TWENTY

By late March the judge ordered a continuance. They were wrapping up in McAlester, and the case was to be moved to the Federal Court at Musk-ogee. They'd been given a date in mid-September, and all the oil and gas companies working the land were ordered to keep the court informed as to their earnings until then.

As soon as the judge retired from the courtroom, Wingate poured him-self a glass of water from the pitcher on their table. Axley did likewise and then pushed the pitcher over to Tom. Here, Tommie, help yourself, he said. There's plenty left.

Tom looked furtively into the pitcher, and filled the third glass on the tray. Seeing that Axley and Wingate were gathering their papers, shaking hands with other lawyers and talking with reporters—and seeing that neither one had taken a drink of the water—he lifted the glass to the light flowing in through the windows. Then he drank, sipping carefully at first to be sure there was no strange taste in it.

By the time he trailed Axley to the door of the courtroom only a handful of people were still there. The Bennetts, in an unsophisticated attempt to frighten them, always made it a point to sit and stare at Tom and his law-yers as they left. But today their attention was diverted as another figure rose from the rear bench. Hey, Tom! He turned to see Sax crab-walking between the narrow benches toward the aisle to greet them. Tom had seen his uncle only a few times since the old days. Sax had stayed in Oklahoma and did not often visit Kentucky. If he had been in regular attendance at the court proceedings Tom hadn't noticed him.

Wingate and Axley turned with proprietorial interest to watch as Tom shook the hand Sax extended. Sax was grinning. Hey man, you got the whole place hoppin, look like.

With a strained expression Tom said, Saxton, meet my lawyers: Mr. Ax-ley of Tulsa and Judge Wingate, who you'll remember from back in Wills County. Y'all, this is my uncle, Sax Slayden.

As they shook hands the judge studied Sax's face. Sax Slayden, he said thoughtfully. You're from Wills County? With a name like that I reckon you must be from Slayden's Crossing.

Sax, still grinning, pumped his head in affirmation.

If you've come all the way out here to watch what happens with Tommie's land claim, I'm afraid you've picked the wrong time for your trip. We've just been continued until the fall.

The judge was filibustering a little, while he tried to remember where he had seen Sax before. He was unable to place him, partly because when Sax had come before his bench some thirty years earlier, he had been a young brawler named Saxton Johnson. Sax had decided that his new life in the Territories merited a new name as well, and had chosen Slayden in honor of the town where he'd been born, and in honor of his mother, Maria Slayden Johnson.

Aw, naw suh, Sax said. I been livin out here fo most of my life. I's jes borned in Slayden's Crossing, 's all. Didn't have far to come to see the trile.

Axley, however, remembered the role Tom's uncle had played in the murder charge that put him in Leavenworth. He too reached over to shake Sax's hand. I'm very glad to know you, Mr. Slayden, he said. We were just leaving for the hotel. Would you care to come back and eat dinner with us?

Sax cocked an eye at Tom hoping for some direction, but Tom's face remained utterly non-committal.

Uhhh, well...He scratched his ear and looked at the ground.

The judge, meanwhile, glanced at Axley, who was signaling with an intense stare that this encounter might benefit them somehow. Yes, said Wingate. Why don't you join us?

The four men crossed the street, Wingate glancing back to assure himself the Bennetts weren't following as they entered the hotel. Axley led them in stilted conversation about neutral subjects such as the weather and travel. Where did you say you live again, Saxton?

I got me a little farm out from Beggs, a little calf and bull operation. It's small, but it does me.

I see. A cattle man.

Well... He made a deprecating gesture.

And... what about your family?

While Sax rattled on nervously about his carefree bachelor life, Tom watched in silence. He couldn't fathom what purpose Sax could serve to Axley and Wingate, but he knew they must have some plan for him. If they were thinking of using him as a witness, they clearly did not grasp the nature of Sax's character. He was not only prone to running off at the mouth, but he had been part of the false land claim, and Tom knew he couldn't be trusted to be discreet under pressure from the other lawyers, or from reporters.

Who you got lookin aftah yo animals while you's away? Tom asked.

Oh they bein took care of, no need to worry bout that.

At the door of the hotel Wingate stopped. I've got to send a few telegrams. Our newspaper back home has been following Tommie's case with interest, and my wife will also want to know of my early return.

Well now, Judge Arch, don't be too hasty. We'll need a few more days to plan our next move before you all go back to Kentucky.

Of course, of course. What do you take me for, Ben? I thought we'd wait'll Friday to leave. Will that give you enough time? He put a hand on Axley's shoulder and squeezed hard, smiling.

Friday should do. Axley moved away, rubbing his shoulder. We'll be at our table.

They sat at what had become their usual place, in the back corner. A large potted plant was all that hid them from the kitchen door, which swung back and forth with the steady traffic of the black waiters in their crisp white uniforms, and the Chinese busboys. At the tables were white couples, black couples, native couples, and racially mixed groups of men in business suits. Only one table was close enough for its occupant to overhear their conversation, but as the only person seated at it was a nondescript, middle-aged white woman, they felt no need to censor their remarks.

I don't know as I can afford to eat in a place like this, said Sax. This place is jes for the quality, look like.

Oh, don't worry, Axley assured him, throwing his hands open. I'll put the bill on my account. Expenses. You know.

Well, well, well. In that case look like I ought to've come sooner. He forced a laugh.

What did make you decide to come?

Why, shoot, Tom. You been all ovah the newspapers. They say this is the biggest oil strike since Glen Pool. I jes thought I'd come and see whether a shiny new millionaire might not remember his ol Uncle Sax. He laughed again and fired a playful punch in Tom's direction, then cleared his throat. Naw. I's just figurin on visitin with you awhile's all. Didn't think they was fixin to close on down like this.

Oh these things take time, said Axley, especially when the stakes are high. But we'll see it through.

The waiter had just finished taking their orders when Judge Arch joined them. While Wingate was busy placing his order, Sax leaned conspiratori-ally toward Tom. This seem like a real nice place, but if you was evah of a mind to have a drink with yo meal, I could hep you, you know...make the connections. He winked, bobbing his head rapidly sideways.

Wingate rapped a closed menu against his palm and handed it to the waiter with an air of satisfaction. What's that you say about a drink?

Sax shot an expression of alarm at Tom. Wingate had jailed him for drinking when he was a resident of Wills County, and he hadn't meant his remark for the judge's ears. Tom remained impassive.

Aw nothin. I's jes makin small talk, like they say.

Didn't you say you knew where we could get a drink with our meal? Tom asked.

Axley interrupted Sax's gestures of denial. That's right. That's what I heard.

Well, that's fine then, said the judge. Maybe you could get us a bottle of whiskey for after the meal.

W-Well... I c-could, sho nuff... but... uhh...

But I sense some hesitation here. Is anything the matter?

Naw. Naw, ain't nothin the mattah, Judge. I jes thought, what with you bein a judge and all... why, I jes thought m-mebbe you wasn't a drinkin man.

Wingate laughed heartily. Prohibition is a fine thing in its place, don't get me wrong. But this ain't its place, if you see what I mean. He laughed again, Sax joining in nervously.

Well, if y'all got the budget, I got the product! said Sax, and the three of them laughed again.

The waiter brought iced tea and rolls, reaching across Tom and cutting him off for a moment from the others. The white linen of the waiter's jacket brought to mind his lost world of plaster and white duck overalls. The precision and elegance of smooth surfaces, or of complicated ornamentation. The crew of laborers around him. The control. A new man would be getting worked up over a batch of plaster of paris setting too fast, and Tom'd pinch up a little cream of tartar. When he had shown the man the bit of white powder between his fingers, he'd throw it into the bucket, a king showering gold coins over the mob. Mix that in and it'll hold back that compound for hours. Power and control. He could do whatever he wanted with a little lime, sand and water, and it made people respect him. It gave him something nothing else ever had.

I don't know, I'd say it's more likely he's thinking about getting back to his wife, Wingate was saying. Tom frowned at the judge.

Go on, Tommie, said Axley. Tell em. You were counting your millions, now weren't you?

Tom smiled slightly. Yeah, that's right, Mr. Axley. That's jes what I's doin.

Axley raised his glass of tea. I knew it. I could tell by the look on his face. Here's to me for being right, as usual. He gave Wingate a smug look.

Even though this is nothing but iced tea I guess I'll drink to that, said the judge, and I'll drink to Tommie's millions no matter what the beverage.

Tom held up his glass, studying it intently while the others clinked theirs against it, then he lowered it and took his customary cautious first sip.

Here, said Sax, offering him the sugar bowl.

No thanks.

What the hell? You mean to tell me you done give up sugah? Why you's always the sugah-eatin'est man I evah did see! What's got into you, Tom?

I reckon I'm just a clean liver now, Sax. For one thing I ain't got the teeth I once had. The bridge that had been meant to replace the front tooth he had lost during his arrest had been badly done, and did not match his other teeth. He looked pointedly at Sax, who stopped smiling and looked away. Don't fret yourself over it; I ain't tellin you not to have none.

You mean Tommie here wasn't always a man of plain tastes? asked Axley. Why, I haven't seen him kick back and enjoy himself once since I made his acquaintance. Eats like a hermit. Won't touch alcohol.

As far as I can tell he's even true to his wife, Wingate added, laughing.

The waiter returned with their meals, setting trout in cream sauce before Axley, beefsteak and onions in front of Wingate and Sax, and a half portion of unsauced fish before Tom. The others had fried potatoes while Tom ate his baked, with no butter.

See what I mean? Like a hermit. So when did all this clean living start, that's what I wanna know? It's hard to represent a man properly when you don't know him. Which is why I'm glad you happened along, Uncle Sax. I'm hoping you can solve a few mysteries for us.

Sax gave Axley a rather sickly smile. The white lawyers and Tom were looking intently at him. He had stabbed the knife and fork into his meat, then paused during Axley's little speech. Now he began sawing away busily. Aw, Tom... Tom's jes... Tom. He shrugged, and took a bite almost the size of a wallet, then went on trying to talk as he chewed. Tom began to laugh despite himself, but Axley shook his head with concern.

Um, you better not try to keep talking, Sax, he said, real alarm leveling his voice now. You're gonna choke yourself.

By this time Tom's fit of mirth was completely out of control. Scuse me, he said. I'll be back.

The two lawyers glanced at each other and watched to see which way Tom went. Axley leaned over to whisper something to Wingate, then said mock-casually, Listen Sax, can you stick around for a few days?

Sax's mouthful had been reduced enough by this time for him to reply and be understood. Don't see why not... long as they's some good reason fo me to.

Axley looked at Wingate, then took out his wallet and tucked a ten dollar bill under Sax's plate. Sax raised his eyebrows, stashed the bill hurriedly in his pocket and smiled.

Get yourself a room someplace close by. Oh—he pulled out another bill—and this ought to cover our little after-dinner treat. No rotgut, you hear?

CHAPTER TWENTY-ONE

During the last few days of their stay in McAlester, the lawyers told Tom they wouldn't be needing him to work through their plans for the next phase of the fight. You can take it easy, said Wingate, but watch out who you talk to. Speak to no one about the case. It's at a very delicate stage and loose talk could make it drag on even longer. In fact, maybe you'd better just stay in your room til we leave.

No thanks, Judge. I done done my time.

Wingate narrowed his eyes, but Axley interposed. Come on now, Tommie, you know what we're saying here. None of us wants this thing to go on any longer than it has to. Just refrain from discussing the case, or your land, with anybody—like Judge Arch says. Just use your head, boy.

Tom got up from the breakfast table without another word and left the dining room, narrowly missing the corner of a nearby table where a woman sat writing a letter. She shrank away from him, but said nothing. In the lobby, he made a decisive turn for the front doors of the hotel. He often found himself grateful for the education in self-control that Leavenworth had given him, but never more than when he was dealing with these lawyers. As he walked across the lobby the desk clerk called out to him.

Excuse me, Mr. Johnson, some mail just came for you, sir.

Much obliged, Curtis. Tom nodded his thanks at the pale clerk, walked to the counter and collected a bundle of letters, then carried them over to a chair beside the window. He read the one from Mary first, then his mother's. Both told of the death of an elderly neighbor in Slayden's Crossing. Both asked when he would be home again. Clara closed with her oft-repeated warning to be vigilant and to gag himself at the first sign of stomach pains.

The third letter was from the Muskogee firm of Carson, Carson & Able, offering to assist with his case should he find himself in need of their expert legal advice. Got all a that I can use, he muttered. Glancing up to see whether anyone was within earshot, Tom was surprised to see Sax coming through the hotel doors. His urge to call out was slowed by something in Sax's manner, a certain stealthy glance toward the elevator.

Tom held up the letter he had just opened to shield his face. Peeping around it he saw Sax enter the dining room, pause to study the scene, and then proceed forward with more confidence.

So. Ol Sax is still around, and he's holding private meetings with my lawyers, thought Tom, settling the letter onto his lap. It took him a moment to get to his fourth piece of mail, a printed, unsigned note from one of his many enemies: WE WILL GIT YOU YET

Tom immediately folded the note and stuffed it back inside the envelope, which he now noticed had been hand delivered. It was the third such note he had received. Although he'd broken into a heavy sweat, anger was the strongest of the emotions that coursed through him as he strode toward the hotel desk.

Curtis, who brung this note in here?

It was on the desk when I came back from... when I.... I was away from my post for just a moment, sir, and it was, just lying on the counter when I returned. The little man ran a hand through his scarce hair; his reddish mutton chop sideburns seemed ready to blaze up with the heat of his anxiety. Tom studied him hard. Curtis's face grew even redder.

I need to know who left this note.

I'm very sorry, Mr. Johnson. I... I wish I could tell you, but... he leaned closer, lowering his voice to a whisper. The truth is I had to go to the Gentlemen's Room and... well... I would be very grateful if you didn't let it be known, as there's a chance I might lose my job if it came to the manager's attention that I left my post. Standing erect again, he wrung his hands and looked pleadingly into Tom's eyes. I can assure you, sir, it won't happen again.

Tom looked at the man in cold silence, then turned toward the dining room, shoving his mail deep into his pocket. But his plan to surprise Sax in conversation with Wingate and Axley backfired. The table where he had breakfasted with the two lawyers, and where he now expected to see the three of them conferring secretly, was empty. A Chinese man was clearing it of their dishes. While Tom watched, he stripped away the dirty tablecloth, his pigtail swinging, and snapped over the table a fresh one, white as snow.

*　*　*

Just as the doorman reached to open the hotel door, a strong gust bowled the top hat from his head and sent him scurrying down the street after it, to the great glee of a group of children on their way to school. Tom caught the door as it was about to slam in his face, and stepped through it. He buttoned his jacket and braced himself as he looked up and down the street. There were plenty of people about, since the 9:15 train was due in a few minutes, but Sax and the lawyers were not among them. He went back up to his room for his hat and overcoat and then struck out.

After some aimless wandering, he spent the day in a small, dark restaurant about half a mile down the tracks. It was run by three Mexican brothers and most of its patrons were black. The brothers kept an armed watch on the door, and he was frisked as he entered.

What the hell?

You wan dreenk or not?

Tom closed his mouth and nodded. He found a place near a table in the back where a series of checker games progressed, minimal conversation required. Tom was just one of a dozen or more people floating free of context. An old white man pulled a concertina from the bag beside his chair and Tom's mood began to lighten. The middle-aged black man beside him invited him to a game of checkers. After winning four times in a row, he realized he'd have to keep on playing if he kept winning, so he deliberately lost the fifth. At the bar he ordered a beer and some tamales. By habit he lifted the glass to the light, then inhaled tentatively before taking a drink. He unfolded the cornhusk wrapping and examined the first savory tamale. All seemed well. Slipping the final notch into complete relaxation, Tom lifted it to his mouth and took a bite. Its spiciness pleased him enormously.

By late afternoon the clientele in the place had turned over somewhat, and several women were among the crowd. Tom had only had three beers, but he let one of the women sit close to him without telling her to move on, as some of the others had. He felt sorry for her; she wasn't all that bad looking. What harm could a little sweetness between strangers do?

The girl—for that's about all she was as far as he could tell—was too thin for her tight, red dress to be very exciting. Still she had a nice enough face. She was part black, and he guessed her other parent to be either Mexican or Indian. Before long she kicked off one shoe and began rubbing his leg with her bare foot. She smelled like flowers and didn't say a word. Tom bought her a beer and had another himself.

The door opened and the light showed that it was getting on for suppertime outside. If he didn't turn up, his 'keepers' would get restless. The old man had changed his lively music to something as mournful as a train whistle. The girl had turned his hand over and was slowly tracing the lines in his palm. Tom sighed deeply.

The door opened again and a silhouette was outlined against the lurid orange sky. The man stood there a moment before entering the restaurant, then nodded to the guard and was allowed in without being frisked. Tom closed his eyes. When he opened them again, Sax was standing in front of him.

Well well. Look like you done foun yo'self a good time!

The girl immediately sat up straight. Tom stared up at Sax in silence.

Mind if I join ya?

Yeah I do, matter of fact, Tom said, putting his foot on the chair Sax'd drawn up.

Aw now. Don't be like that. Sax was grinning, refusing to take Tom seriously. I jes come by to see if you's wanting to accompany me to the picture show tonight. They ain't got nothin like the Lincoln out here, but up the street from the hotel, at the shed they call the Cherokee Palace, they's playin a Zane Grey picture called Under the Tonto Rim. He said the title in as dramatic a voice as he could, like an announcer. Don't that sound fine? A western. He stood there grinning.

How'd you know where to find me?

I didn't. Fact, this here place was gonna be my last try fo I give up and headed on back to the hotel fo supper.

Tom's foot was still on the chair, but he removed it. Just as Sax sat down, he stood up. Let's go then.

Out on the path, Sax offered Tom a chaw of tobacco, saying, I done seen you hand that gal a dollah in there. Now, Tom, I think it's only fair I should warn you about these Oklahoma street gals, cause I knows all about em. Fact I might've knowed that gal there even—she seem familiar to me someway...

Tom had waved away the tobacco and now he stopped walking. Listen Sax, the less you say to me about women the better, you got that?

Alright, alright! Sax threw his hands up and they resumed walking. If you don't want the benefit of my superior age and experience, that's yo bidness. That's jes fine. But I've heard tell of more'n one oil baron who got took by a pretty young wench from offa these Oklahoma streets. That's all I's wanting to say about it. I mean, after all, I am yo uncle and I got me a duty to...

Tom stopped again. Sax, if you don't shut up I got a duty to warn you that my fist is likely to meet with yo...

Whoa cowboy! Sax said, still grinning. I git ya, I git ya.

The words of the unsigned note he had received that morning came back to him then and he wondered, not for the first time, just how dangerous Sax was to him in this oil game.

*   *   *

On Friday they caught the ten p.m. train and Sax came with Axley to see them off at the depot. His chummy manner with the two lawyers irked Tom.

Well, I suppose you'll be getting back to your little ranch now, ain't that right, Sax? the judge asked.

I sho will. I didn't nevah aim to be away this long. I jes got caught up in this bidness of Tom's an...

Yes, there's nothing like a good legal battle to draw a man in and hold his attention—right, Tommie? said Wingate.

Tom didn't reply, but busied himself with his pipe, tamping down tobacco from a freshly opened packet.

Well, I know you're both eager to get back home, but keep in touch, said Axley. Judge, I'll be expecting those documents as soon as you can manage them.

I'll get right on it, Ben, and you keep up your end, too.

Of course, of course.

Tell Mary and all of em I said hello, Sax called as Tom swung himself up the steps into the first passenger car, pretending not to see his uncle's outstretched hand. Once he was out of reach he glanced back and nodded, including all three men in his cursory farewell.

The car was almost full. He carried his grip past noisy families and exhausted laborers, a throng of young men setting up a card game, a preacher and an old woman. At the back he found a seat beside a one-armed man with a distorted face. The man dabbed at the side of his mouth with a handkerchief. Tom soon realized this was a constant occupation, as the man's mouth couldn't close, and dripped incessantly.

'Hu *wah*, he said.

Tom nodded.

Yerm'ny.

He nodded again and reached to shake the man's left hand with his own left. Name's Tom Johnson.

He put down the handkerchief for a moment and accepted Tom's hand. Red Ames.

Nice to meet you, Red.

Red. H-red.

Hred. Oh, you mean Fred?

At's it, at's it, at's it. He bobbed his head in evident pleasure over being understood. You in a wah?

Tom shook his head. I's too ol. He saw no need to go into the irony that he had been imprisoned for murder at the time, and was therefore safe from being sent to war, no matter what his age.

Good. How ol?

How old am I now? Fred nodded. Be fifty-seven come July. Tom could hardly believe his own words as the train clacked along through the spring night. How bout you?

Wenny-nine.

Tom looked into the ruined face beside him, hoping he didn't betray any of the shock he felt upon learning that Fred Ames was the same age as his Benjamen. They settled back and let their conversation give way to the lulling rhythm of the train. Eventually the regular flight of the white handkerchief ceased, and Tom saw that Fred had tucked it under his chin and fallen asleep.

He closed his own eyes, but sleep wouldn't come. A waking dream with all the elements of a nightmare took him deep into Arkansas. Death threats and 'friendly' advice blocked his every turn. Earl Bennett and his brothers stared at him with murderous intent. Judges loomed above him, lawyers crowding him on both sides. Cringing, red-faced clerks held out scrawled threats, as dead animals lunged from the walls. And always, lurking in the background, was the grinning face of his own Uncle Sax.

CHAPTER TWENTY-TWO

Rachel was almost as thrilled with the Wingates' new mansion as they were. Her room here had three windows. Three! From them she could see the northwest corner of the seven-and-a-half-acre grounds with its park-like arrangement of trees. The window beside the bed had a view of the little white arbor and beyond that the wishing well. The other two windows faced the garage, but to the east she could just see beyond the patio, which the Wingates were calling their 'outdoor living room', to the pond and bridge. As in the old house, her room was right off the kitchen, where boxes and crates were being stacked. Time enough to fuss over my room later, she thought with satisfaction.

She worked tirelessly, nesting silver cutlery into segmented drawers, arranging crystal and china into glass cabinets, hanging curtains and pictures as Mrs. Wingate directed. The floors were mostly covered with beige carpeting that went all the way to the high walnut baseboards, but the Wingates had ordered special rugs as 'accents'. They had been custom woven by French nuns and when they arrived, Rachel and Mrs. Wingate ran their hands in wonder over the velvety nap.

My, my, my, said her mother on Rachel's Sunday visit home. Tell me the colors.

Well they's all of em got lots of different colors—like jewels, like sapphire and ruby and emerald—all in these patterns yo eye cain't hardly follow. But they each one got one main color. So the one in the hall and goin up the stairs, that un's mostly red, and the one by the livin room fireplace is mostly blue, and the one in they bedroom is mostly purple...

What color rug you got in yo room, Rachel? asked her ten-year-old sister, Hallie.

Aw now, my room ain't got no fancy rug in it. I jes got me a old rag rug side the bed, same's I had in the other house. But I likes it fine to step down onto of a mornin.

Hallie, who sat along the edge of a bed crowded with siblings, rubbed a bare foot on the plank floor. I'd like it, too. When I get growed I aim to have me fine rugs all over my flo. The others laughed and carried on at this, but Hallie reached over to where Rachel sat on the other bed and pulled

Mrs. Wingate's cast-off scarf of sky blue from around her big sister's neck. It fluttered through the air, no one minding its one little moth-hole right in the middle. Hallie jumped up and caught it, winding it around her head dramatically. She turned in circles in the narrow space between the beds. I am Miz Wingate and I ride my golden hoss round the court square and buy an'thing I want.

Rachel laughed with the others. Don't be silly, chile. Miz Wingate ain't got her no hoss. Emmett Lewis drives her around in they Ford car.

Two of her brothers began to snatch at the scarf and Rachel barely got it back in one piece. Gimme that! she said. I swear ya'll could tear up an anvil!

But they kept up their noisy teasing about living in the Wingate mansion until Mrs. Slayden resumed control. Y'all hush up! Get down on yo knees, ever one a ya, and ax God A'mighty to forgive ya! Her children did as they were told. Dear Lawd, she intoned, fo'give these chirren for they scrappin and messin. But most of all, Lawd, fo'give em fo hankerin after the false idols of this world. Lawd, let em not make money into they mastah. Let em not want what it ain't fittin and proper fo em to want. In Jesus's name we ax it, Lawd. Amen. They all echoed her 'amen', even Rachel.

That evening when Brother Price drove her up to 'Wincoyne's' gleaming new gates, Rachel tried to integrate the thrill she felt with her mother's fervent prayer. It was difficult. She wanted to be righteous, yet as she waved to Brother Price and pushed open the heavy gate, she couldn't help but be conscious of the pride that straightened her back and lent grace to her carriage.

The only light that had been left on was the ornate fixture of marbled glass and wrought iron that was suspended above the elegantly winding handrail of the central staircase. The back hallway was in darkness. Rachel moved slowly, not yet familiar enough with the house to move more quickly without light. Feeling her way around the small table in the kitchen and along the tiled wall, she came to the door of her bedroom, and entered it. The open windows admitted the brightening nearness of a dogwood in full bloom. Its sweetness mingled with the smell of new wood and varnish, which she paused to inhale. Knowing how Mr. Wingate wished to conserve electricity, she left the light off, letting the lamp-like dogwood do for now. Rachel laid her bag and sweater on the chair and glided quietly back through the kitchen and the lighted main hallway to clear the supper dishes from the dining room. To her surprise, the shining table was bare. Could Emmett have cleared it all away for her? He never had before.

As she stood wondering, she heard a sound and moved in its direction. The breakfast room was in darkness, but if she had come this way before, Rachel would've seen that Mrs. Wingate was in the sunroom. The radio, which looked like a toy church to her, was on, its voice announcing a waltz played by The Palm Court Orchestra. Through the partly open doorway Rachel could see that Mrs. Wingate sat alone on the cane settee, leaning slightly toward the music. She was wearing a white dress, and white, open-toed shoes. Looking at her, Rachel felt that she sat at the heart of the fashionable world among the ferns and fronds on her spanking new sunporch which was all windows on two sides. Wherever that music was coming from, surely this was the vessel it was meant to pour into.

The remains of the cold chicken plate Rachel had prepared for their supper lay on the rattan table in front of Mrs. Wingate. Mr. Wingate's portion was untouched. Rachel cleared her throat, knocking softly at the doorframe. The older woman jumped slightly.

Evenin, Miz Wingate. Sorry to disturb ya. I's jes wantin to clear away them dishes fo ya.

No, no, Rachel. You didn't disturb me a bit. How was your visit home?

Real nice, ma'am.

Mrs. Wingate sat looking at her, as if she wanted to hear more. Uncomfortable with the silence, Rachel added, My... my mother's rose bushes've come into blossom, and the crops is comin up jes fine. It's promisin to be a good year fo growin things.

What sort of roses does your mother grow?

Well, ma'am, she's got her some red ones and some white ones... jes bout ever color I spect. She's even got her a orange rosebush. That... that un's my favorite.

You mean coral, I suppose. Yes, I've seen those; they are lovely. Maybe I ought to have Emmett put in a coral bush down by the stone basket just along the path there. That's where I'm planning to have my rose garden. I've already started a red American Beauty and an Abraham Darby in the greenhouse. And of course my yellow climber over by the arbor. But a coral would look nice with the others.

I'm sho Mama'd be glad to let you have a cuttin from hers, Rachel offered.

Why thank you. Yes, I would like that color, and if it takes, then you could keep a rose or two from it in your room.

Rachel smiled at the thought. I'll ask er bout it next week. She began placing the dishes back on the tray, but hesitated at the full plate. M... Mr. Wingate be wantin this later, ma'am?

No. He's gone over to visit with his brother's family. I had one of my headaches this afternoon...She tapered off vaguely for a moment. I'm sure he's taken his meal with them by now.

Rachel waited a moment, but Mrs. Wingate said no more and stared away at nothing, as radio listeners do.

Is they an'thing else I can get fo ya, Miz Wingate?

Her gaze swung back again as if she'd already forgotten about her. No, thank you, Rachel. You go on. I'm glad you're back. The house feels so big when nobody else is here.

Rachel stood for a moment longer with the tray. She meant to ask about the headache, but Mrs. Wingate sat so quietly, her empty hands on her lap. The center of the fashionable world.

Night then, ma'am.

Goodnight.

CHAPTER TWENTY-THREE

Though Tom was happy to be home again, he found himself somewhat lost among everyone's expectations. As the court case was still unsettled, he had no more money than before, yet everyone thought of him as a millionaire. When he announced he was going back to work in Frankfort, there was a great reaction among his neighbors and family in Slayden's Crossing.

You cain't jes go off workin like nothin's happened, said his sister, Loretta. What's ev'body sposed to think?

Lola's right, Richard added. Hell, even them lawyers might get the wrong idea bout fightin yo case if you's to give up on it yo own self.

Tom snorted. Believe me, them lawyers'd keep on if I's dead. They ain't nevah givin up on this much money. They like buzzards that smells rotten meat. Ain't nothin'd make em give up this case.

That's the gospel truth, Clara said. Case don't take up again til Septembah anyways. A man cain't lay around all summer long at they biddin. Tom's got him a talent fo that fancywork, and he's got a right and a duty to exercise it.

Mary smiled at Tom as his mother gave her fervent testimony. Though she agreed with Clara about his plan to go back to Frankfort, Mary was happier than anybody to have him back. He knew how to sweeten the nights. Made her feel like a bride again the way he came home to her. But he was getting restless after almost three months. He had run out of things to do around the house. The other night he'd gone out with Richard and several others and had come in late, smelling of Uncle Jerry Cruickshank's home brew. She didn't much care for that. Besides, they needed the money to pay their bills. So the next morning she got his work clothes ready and saw him off on the 8:25 to Frankfort.

After the train rounded the corner, Mary said goodbye to Clara and turned for home, thinking about herself and Tom and their unusual marriage. She had no worry at all that Tom might seek out the company of other women while he was in Frankfort, or even when he travelled as far away as Oklahoma. At this point in their lives they were completely sure of each other for reasons that had nothing to do with aging. Though they'd been married for over thirty years, they had spent only twelve of those years together. Since he had returned from prison, their life as a couple had been further punctuated by his out-of-town work, and now by the trial in Oklahoma. Was its intermittent nature what kept their marriage so fresh and strong? Absence, that made their hearts grow fonder? She smiled to herself, happy enough to ponder the mystery of it, and praying it would last.

Back inside the house, Mary went into the bedroom and opened the drawer where she kept the letters Tom had written her over the years. He had not brought her letters back with him when he was released from prison, perhaps thinking he wouldn't need them if they were together. She hadn't re-read his letters to her since he'd been released, but today she was in the mood. Today, with Tom's farewell kiss still on her mouth, she felt protected against the hex of that round date-stamp marked Leavenworth Federal Penitentiary.

Carrying the bundles into the living room, Mary sat in her chair—the chair Tom had built for her. She had long ago put the letters in chronological order, and so she opened the first one, the one dated Jan. 8, 1903. Tom's large, sprawling handwriting on the unlined paper plunged downward on the page.

Dear Mary:

They tole me I can rite letters many as I want. They have give me a tablet and pensil. Wont let me seal it, so they can read what we rite. I had to sine a paper anyway saying they can. Mail come ever Sat. I am countin on you to rite me Mary. Days here all same. They wake you up and march you to brekfus. No talking. Then they march you to work. I am in the brikyard. It is hard but lease it is outside. I thank of you all time. Rite me Mary. I am very low.

Yore loveing husban Tom

Mary had written Tom as soon as she got word he had been sent to prison. But he had not received her letter for a few weeks, and she had not gotten his until after she had returned with little Benjamen to Kentucky. These first letters were among the hardest to read.

Jan. 10, 1903

Dear Mary:
No letter from you. Did you get the 1 I rote. I sent it to Sax where I rekkond you was. I rote Mama to. She rote me you plans to take Ben back to Ky. I dont blame you but then I wont never see you agin. Mama say yall can live with them. They will look after you for me.

I cant rite more today. Pleese rite me.

Yore loveing husban Tom

Mary had begun to cry. Perhaps she couldn't read them, after all. The feelings were stored in them it seemed, and waiting to engulf her with their old power, despite all that she and Tom had regained. Despite the healing of these past seven years.

She blew her nose, and gazed out the window. No, she couldn't read them all—maybe no one ever would—but there were a few she needed to read again. The next letter was one of these.

Jan. 24, 1903

Dear Mary:

You letters come today. It was mitey good to here from you. I new you would rite me. If you did not rite me I dont think I cood go on. I am glad you back home, even tho I cant see you. Mama an Daddy will take good care a you an Benjamen. But I do wish I cood see you sometimes. That is the worse thing about this place.

In the brikyard we bilding a big new part on the prison. They call it a wing. Not the kine a wing that will help us tho.

You will be glad to lern I go to church here ever Sun. A colored preecher name of Brother Noah comes in the afternoon. He makes us to know we are siners. He dont have a hard job.

I thank of you all time Mary. I miss you an Ben. Thank you for the letters. Plees rite more.

Your loveing husban Tom

Mary felt better after reading the letter that established the communication as two-way. She and Tom had written each other every week for the seventeen years he had been in prison. She had written with the understanding that he would never get out. That he would die there, and that she would likely never even see him again. But she knew that he needed her letters in order to keep from going crazy. And so she had never stopped writing them, even after taking up with Rollie. It was a promise she had made to both Tom and herself, and she had kept it.

The period with Rollie was something she deeply regretted. If only she had known Tom would come back she never would have taken up with him. But Rollie was there, and he was flattering and insistent. And she was lonely. She reached a point when she didn't think she could stand to go on living with Tom's parents, not if Tom himself was never coming home. She felt it was only right that she move out and try to live her own life. Rollie had been easy—or so she had thought at the time. What she now knew was that there is no such thing as easy where intimate relationships are concerned. And, for her at least, without the underpinning of passionate love, the inevitable sacrifices and compromises simply weren't worth it.

Mary looked through the stack until she found the letter Tom had written her on Christmas Day 1915.

Dear Mary:

I wanna thank you for the pakage you sent. I et some a the cake after dinner an I give a slice to Kranz, my cell mate but I am savin me some for tomarra if the mice don get it. It is fine. An the tobacca is real good to have to. And the sox. My others was wore out. I wish I cood sent you sumthin.

Try and not worry about Ben. He is a big boy now I rekkon, an will be ok now he has a job. I jes hope the wars over for he is the age to go. If a war had of been on when I was his age, wooda nothin stop me from goin.

It is quite here today. A lot of the men are at prayer serviss or have compny. I am here lookin throo my pakages—yours an Mamas an eatin yore cake an thankin about you all. Riting to you is close as I can get to bein with you.

Mary I love you. I will allways love you. I hope to make it up to you one day all that I have done.

Tom

She had received this letter before the end of December, but it only confirmed something she had already come to understand about her marriage to Tom. That it was still a marriage, despite distance and prison walls. Despite any other life she might try to live.

Mary held the letter to her heart and shook her head, thinking about Christmas Day 1915. She remembered it very well. It was the second Christmas after she had moved into Greenberry to live with Rollie. Tom had stopped signing his letters 'your loving husband' when Clara told him about herself and Rollie. But, though Rollie was never mentioned between them, both Mary and Tom kept writing.

It was a cold, rainy Christmas in Greenberry that year. She and Rollie had planned to get a ride out to Slayden's Crossing with a man Tom's sister—the one they always called Sis—had taken up with who had a horse and buggy; but the rain made it unlikely they would be going. Mary was especially blue about this because Ben had moved back to Clara's to work at the Clay Pit. She and Benjamen had never been apart at Christmas.

She had put up a little cedar tree and made a star for the top. She fixed a good chicken dinner, and tried to hide her sadness. And she thought she must've succeeded, because Rollie didn't seem to be particularly aware of her feelings. Christmas wasn't important to him. He had suggested they not waste money on gifts for each other. His current job as a freight loader at the depot didn't pay much, but Rollie wasn't one to worry about the future. He took things as they came.

After they ate, he went into the bedroom to take a nap while she washed the dishes, and Mary felt oddly relieved. She didn't have to cover up her feelings for a while. She dried her hands and looked around. The little Christmas tree somehow made the place look bleaker than before. Slipping on her coat, she took her writing tablet outside onto the tiny half-porch of the duplex they rented.

No one was out at all and the only proof that she and Rollie weren't the last people left on earth were the muffled thumps and shouts emanating from the other half of the duplex. Rain sheeted over the porch roof. Feeling like she was failing everyone no matter what she did, Mary did what her heart called her to do. She began a letter to Tom. She wrote slowly, letting it lift her out of this rainy day, this tiny house where she still felt like a guest. In fact, Mary had felt like a guest at Clara's too. She sought a place of belonging, and found it, strangely, writing to her imprisoned husband, whom she hadn't seen in almost thirteen years and would probably never see again.

Dec. 25, 1915

Dear Tom,

It is rainin here today, so it dont look like we will get out to Slayden's Crossing. I hope Ben is haveing a good time with the folks out there. I made him a shirt but will have to give it to him next time I see him.

I wonder what you are doing today. I went to church this mornin and the singin was fine. Brother Willett had the chilren do a play about Christmas. Minky Dellard's youngest boy was the Baby Jesus. He is so sweet they was sho he'd behave but he wanted Mary's halo. Mary was Videy Lewis. And he did not stop till he pulled it off and cut her ear and she hollered real lowd and he begun to cry. It was...

At that point Rollie opened the door behind her and startled Mary so much that she almost dropped the letter. She turned the paper over as she reached down for the pencil.

What you doin out here, gal? 'S too cole be settin outside.

I got my coat on; I'm okay. Jes wanted some fresh air, 's all.

He looked at the tablet on her lap. Well, come on in why don't you and we'll get us up a game of gin rummy or sump'n. I don't wanna be all by my lonesome on Christmas.

Mary had laughed a little. Alright, Rollie. She'd put the letter in her coat pocket and had not been able to finish it until the next day when he was back at work. But she had never forgotten that long wet Christmas. How she felt that every choice she made was a betrayal.

Rollie was not a bad man. He was just not her man. Not the way Tom had been. He never would be that to her. She understood that on Christmas Day 1915, when writing a letter to Tom was the only place she could turn to find comfort in her deep loneliness. From then until Tom was released some four years later, Mary and Rollie just limped along, making the best of things. When she got the letter that told her Tom was coming home, she sat on that little half porch in shock until Rollie got back from work.

Hey gal, what you doin settin there like a rock or sump'n stead of making me my supper? She handed him the letter. It was the first, the only letter from Tom she ever let him read.

Jan. 29, 1920

Dear Mary:

I am comin home. The Parole Bord is releesin me on good behavyer. What I have worked for so long is gonna happen. I am comin home. I have to spend some time in Kansas City working first till I get use to bein free. They call it a reajussmunt period. I will go there in April so I will likely get home in the summer sumtime. I will let you know soon as I can. I wanted to tell you first. Now I will get my chance to make evah'thang up to you like I promised. Rite an tell me how you feel about this Mary.

Love, Tom

After reading it Rollie sat down on the porch step with his back to her.

Rollie, I...

Yeah, I know. You ain't gotta say it. Ain't gotta say *noth*in.

Mary had started to cry, but neither of them spoke. After a while, still carrying her letter, he went into the house and began throwing his clothes into a flour sack. She sat there, frozen into silence, her only thought being how to get the letter back without him tearing it up. No words came to her, just regret. Searing regret.

Rollie came back out with the sack over his shoulder and the letter in his hand, and said, You'n Tom have yo'seff a nice life. You never was the woman I thought you was anyway. He let the letter fall onto the porch floor, then stepped on it as he left. He started whistling as soon as he reached the sidewalk.

Mary's tears had dried instantly.

CHAPTER TWENTY-FOUR

Dampness had split and crumbled some of the moldings in the rotunda of the Capitol building. Laden with bucket and brushes, Tom climbed up the scaffolding at the edge of the dome a little more slowly than he had in former days. Feel like dampness done split my left knee, he thought. Still, it was good to be back at work. He set to scraping away the damaged plaster, his hand finding the right tools in his various pockets exactly when he needed them, as if he'd never been away at all.

During the first stage of the work, the fine plaster dust sifted over him like a new skin, making him distractingly aware of his short, curly eyelashes, the slopes of his nose. He could hardly wait for the sanding phase to be over, so he could dip his handkerchief in the still-clean water and wipe the white dust from his face and arms.

It was the wet work he loved. Sculpting and shaping the heavy, sensuous clay, hurling each tool into the water bucket with a musical plop and reaching for the next. Once he got into a rhythm he robbed his hawk of its compound as gracefully as a butterfly moving between flowers. He would flip the wet plaster several times, then apply it with pretty flourishes in a seamless and rhythmic series of motions. Gradually the stepped cornice and baroque moldings were rebuilt to perfection.

Sometimes when he was cleaning his tools, especially the hawk, he would find his left thumbprint in the edge of the dried plaster. Two whorls angling towards each other, like wings just unfolding from some creature's back, preparing to lift it skyward. The birds that sometimes soared around inside public buildings came to his mind then. They would often mistake the high ceilings for the freedom they were used to. You had to be very careful they didn't cause you to topple from your scaffolding, prone as they were to panic at finding themselves trapped indoors. You could not afford to mind their soaring and fluttering. Images of these birds came to him often at the end of a workday, as he sloshed the tools in his pail of water and wiped them clean.

Tom spent the summer engrossed in his silent artistry, no longer an idle pawn in a dangerous game, but a man in charge of his gifts. The long hours of quiet were just what he was looking for and he rarely entered into conversation with the other workmen. It didn't bother him that he had a reputation for cool overweening pride. Grateful for solitude, he lost himself for a while in the restoration of leafy architraves, scrolled capitals, cartouches and medallions in the loftiest reaches of the rotunda. Below him, the self-important men of law and government crisscrossed in their own insect-like patterns, all but unaware of how his skill added grandeur to their lives.

Weekends he went home to Mary, on the very trains that carried Sergei Rachmaninoff on his endless and tortured concert tours, the trains that carried King Oliver on the wane, and a young, waxing Louis Armstrong. Tom was as oblivious of the other people on the trains—be they on great journeys or ordinary ones—as he had been back in Leavenworth when Robert Stroud had experimented with birds in the next cell block. Tom had been experimenting with his own character back then, striving for Good Behavior. Now he pursued his work as a plasterer with some of that same zeal, if not an artist, a craftsman. What was the word McLeod Jr. had used when he fingerprinted him? Artisan? Perhaps that's what he was. But the art of plastering was only part of the work he was trying to perfect. Once again he was deeply preoccupied, restoring his spirit as much as damaged plaster.

Gladys Morse, Tom Johnson's niece, on her 90th birthday.

L to R: Rosa Mae Robinson, Tom's granddaughter; Delores Blackmon Bradley, Tom's great granddaughter; and Derek Blackmon, Tom's great great grandson, circa 1995.

Georgia Ruth Jackson, Tom Johnson's cousin

Clara, Tom's mother.

Creek Capitol - Okmulgee, Oklahoma

The Creek Capitol Building; Postcard from the 1990s.

UNITED STATES PENITENTIARY,
LEAVENWORTH, KANSAS

Name Thomas Johnson ..... Reg. No. 3283
Alias ... Sa m Ford R.N. ....

Color. Lt. Mul. ....
Age 29 .. Height 5 .. ft. 8 .. in. Weight 155
Build M. Stout .. Complexion Lt. Mul.
Hair Blk. .... Beard ....
Eyes Greenish Slate Blue
Nose ....
Sentenced Jan. 3rd 1903 ..... 192..
Sentence ... Life ....
Crime Murder..
Date of Release.. Paroled Jan. 10.
........................1920. ....
Marks, Scars, Etc. ....
Upper Rim of both Ears dented
Scar Obliq of ¼ at 2nd Jt
Lft little Finger rear.
Mole of ¾ above Rt Elb rear

St. James A.M.E., Slayden's Crossing (Pryorsburg), Ky as it looked in 2022.

Mary & Tom Johnson, 1920s.

House Where Tom Johnson
Received Word of Riches

Tom Johnson, the negro, who last week was notified he was worth from ten to twenty million dollars in oil properties in Oklahome, lives at Pryorsburg, and the above is a picture of his home. While the house is very ordinary looking, it is expected that in due time, and after certain legal proceedings, he will be able to build one much finer.

Johnson is now at Tulsa, Okla., conferring with his lawyer and other advisors who were here last week.

The house Tom built for Mary, Slayden's Crossing (Pryorsburg) Ky., January 26th, 1928.

Edana Locus, the house that inspired 'Wincoyne,' 'Greenberry' (Mayfield) Ky. 2022.

Foyer of 'Wincoyne'.

Faris's Clothing Store as it looked in the 1920s, 'Greenberry' (Mayfield) Ky.

GLADYS: IV

The Eighth of August was always a special day fo us, what some white folks used to call 'Nigger Day'. Others call it Emancipation Day, but that ain't right neither. Emancipation Day comes in January and it's the day Lincoln signed the paper that freed the slaves. The Eighth of August is the day the word got down to the slaves in Paducah, and from them on to the rest of the slaves round these parts. It took that long, and it wasn't no small thing when it finally happened.

Evah year they'd be a great big picnic and celebration over at the Paducah fairgrounds, endin up in a parade. Thousands would come from all the states around. They'd come from Memphis, St. Louis, Chicago, and naturally from all ovah Kentucky. But they was sometimes fights broke out and it could get outta hand. So different communities started havin they own Eighth a August picnics, and we'd have ours out at the Greenberry Fairgrounds. When I married Ernest we went to live in Hickman, and we'd hold it in our big stock barn and get the town to donate bus service out to it and Christmas lights and all like that. Yeah, we had us good bands and sho nuff dances back when we run it; but now the church people's done taken it ovah.

Anyhow, fo a few years I helped run the one at Greenberry. Lawd we'd cook up a storm fo that picnic, but we had us a good time. Fo days ahead, we'd be bakin cakes and pies, makin potato salad and smokin barbeque.

In the summer of 1928 I was still livin over in Paducah, but I come home to Wills County fo the Eighth a August. I was in between husbands at that time. I'd done lef my first one and hadn't yet married Ernest. I'd of been twenty-two or -three, and about as pretty as I was ever gonna get, but I wasn't on the look-out fo no husband. I was kind of sour on men in general fo a little while aftah what I'd been through. If I'd of known that summer that I was gonna marry me a second husband that was as gentle as my Grandaddy Vess, I'd a been a whole lot happier.

So there I was workin with Clara and Mary and a gang of my aunts to make the picnic, and I reckon I must've been quieter than was usual fo me. The talk was all about Tin Cup Alley, a kind of a rough neighborhood, as you might say, down by the Greenberry tracks behind the Post Office. One of my aunts—the only one livin that wasn't there with us that day—had used to live on Tin Cup Alley. Minnie her name was, but she was always called Sis. Eventually Uncle Tom let her move into one of his houses over in Boxtown. Sis wasn't too much older'n me and she was the black sheep of the family—her skin all tallowy bright, nasty yellow stringy hair on her that she didn't nevah wash, no teeth. She was what they call loose. Had her five chilren by five men, and them babies all died young. Couldn't nobody, not even Clara, talk sense to her.

But it wasn't Sis they was discussin at that point, it was Fred Ailesworth, who was settin ovah in the Greenberry jail right that minute charged with murder, and look like if they didn't hang him, he'd be goin to the pen fo the rest of his borned days. He'd done shot Bill Brakes, who lived right beside of him ovah yonder on Tin Cup. Shot him fo puttin a curse on his wife. Leastways that's why he said he done it. They was fond of Fred Ailsworth, and it had em in a uproar. I was jes settin there shuckin ears of corn and listenin to the talk, when my Aunt Loretta says to me, Gladys, what's eatin you? You ain't said a word all day and that jes ain't yo style. Aunt Loretta was a glamorous sorta person—fixy, you know. Had her lots a boyfriends and liked a good time. But she wasn't trashy with it like Sis was.

While I's thinkin on what to answer her, Clara said, Let her alone, Lola. Ev'body has em down times. She'll come out the other side. Gladys is made a strong stuff. I'll always remember the way she said that, and how it made me feel, cause my grandmother wasn't much given to handin out compliments; but that is jes what she said: Gladys is made a strong stuff.

Then Mary piped up and said she'd seen Pete Cross that mornin, and that set ev'body to askin questions all at the same time. She was jes tryin to get the limelight offa me, I reckon, cause she could see it was makin me squirm. Pete Cross was a boy about Ben's age who had gone off to the War in 1917 and nevah come back. The army wouldn't take Ben cause a his eyesight. But Pete Cross, like most of them boys his age, he'd gone off to the war. He hadn't been killed, nor even wounded far as anybody knew of. He jes liked the way he got treated in France so much he nevah come home again. He used to write to his brother at first, but hadn't nobody heard from him fo a couple years, and he'd become a sorta legend, like. He could always play anything had strings on it and they said he'd made himself a life ovah there outta music someway or other.

Pete Cross's name was enough to turn any conversation. Then, after gettin ev'body all worked up, Mary says, Turned out it wasn't Pete Cross at all, but jes some boy from Tennessee who's the spit and image of him.

They was all yellin at her for windin em up that away when in walks another legend, Uncle Tom. He was still wearin his white work clothes with plaster all over em and soot from the train. But even with all a that he could stop evah'thing right in its tracks. Mary jumped up like she was seein a ghost.

Why Tom! What're you doin here? I thought you's comin in on the late train at Slayden's Crossing.

He could see how pleased she was and he laughed a low satisfied laugh that he had. I jes decided to surprise y'all and take the early train instead. I knew y'all'd all be over here at the fairgrounds, so I got off at the Greenberry stop, and here you all is. Do I know my women or don't I? He walked all around our shuckin circle and kissed ev'one of us on the cheek. Oh, that Uncle Tom, he might've been a man of moods, but he could sho be charmin when he took a mind to.

I remember as well as anything the way he was that year of 1928 at the Eighth a August picnic. Seemed like they wasn't nothin he couldn't do. He played darts, horseshoes and checkers with the men. Even sung with the St. James A.M.E. choir, though his church attendance was irregular whether he's in town or not; but he had him a good singin voice, so I don't reckon they minded him joinin in. He helped out with the mule pullin, danced with all the women. Lawd yes, he ate, drank and he was merry. I do believe he was the handsomest man in the world that day and he treated Mary jes like she was a queen.

When I look back on it, I cain't help but wonder if he didn't know, way down deep inside hisself, what was comin, and didn't wanna miss a single minute of a good time.

CHAPTER TWENTY-FIVE

Rachel Slayden wasn't much given to snooping and gossip, or she would never have lasted with the Wingates. But neither was she as devoted an employee as Emmett Lewis, who wouldn't hear a word spoken against them and seemed never to be off duty, even when he was at home with his wife over in the Bottom. So it wasn't in character for Rachel to do what she did that Saturday afternoon in September, and she never spoke of it to a soul. But in some way it changed her life.

Mrs. Wingate was at a meeting of the Altar Society at St. Joseph's Church, and Rachel, a white cloth knotted around her head, was dusting the foyer. She knew that Mr. Wingate was with his brother in what he called his office. The judge had come in by the side door about half an hour earlier. His Model T was parked under the porte cochère and a double bouquet of cigar smoke festooned the side door hallway.

The judge had a carrying sort of voice, but she couldn't make out the details of what he was saying, nor was she paying particular attention, being busy with the statue that stood on the table in the middle of the entrance hall. It was a bronze Indian aiming his bow and arrow, and she had just wiped a spider web from the inside of the bow when she distinctly heard her name, 'Slayden', spoken by Judge Arch. Rachel's head came up involuntarily. She felt her face grow warm. It hadn't been a summons; they hadn't called for her. So what were they doing talking about her?

Taking no time to think, she moved quietly into the living room. The dust rag was her excuse, and with it she worked her way over to the doorway that opened into the side hall, the doorway closest to Mr. Wingate's office. The judge was still talking.

...easy to get to the people in charge; but Slayden's made it possible for us to get to some of the lower men on the totem pole. It's perfect. *He's* perfect.

Ah, so it wasn't her. But what Slayden could they be talking about? Rachel knew she'd be able to hear them more clearly from the other side of the doorway; besides there was only an upholstered chair on this side. The corner beside the mantelpiece, with its lamp and two tables offered a much more likely reason for her to be there dusting. Though it seemed enormously risky, she peeped around the doorframe. Only a corner of Mr.

Wingate's desk—which he had made it clear she was never to go near– was in her sightline, but she could see the judge's foot propped up on his knee as he sat opposite his brother. With her heart in her mouth, she crossed over. Yes, she could hear more clearly from this side, though she could hardly trust her trembling hands with the knick-knacks on the first little table. Mr. Wingate was talking now.

...convince *me*. That's precisely the sort of thing it would be damned difficult, if not impossible, for us to work unless you were out there in a hands-on position.

Yes, exactly. I...

Now look. Mitchell has offered to help any way he can on his end. Johnson's prison records show he kept in touch on a regular basis with a woman in California, a...hold on, here it is... a Miss Vidalia Connors of Halcyon, California. Look at this.

Hmmm...

I'll tell Mitchell to check that angle. She's probably just one of those women who write to men in prison as part of her religion... or for other reasons. Who knows, but she may be of some use to us.

Whatever you wanna do, Ted, but if you ask me we have all the help we need with good ol Uncle Sax.

Rachel stopped all pretense of dusting. She knew Tom Johnson had an uncle out in Oklahoma, but his name was Sax Johnson. Sax was hardly a common name; he must be the one they were talking about. But why were they calling him Sax Slayden? She could hear her own breathing like a trapped wind inside her.

Honest to God, Ted, I wish you could meet this guy. He's the dumbest damn darky you ever saw. I have it from one of the Muskogee marshals that it was Slayden who hired Johnson to carry out the murder that landed him in Leavenworth. And what's more, it was all over some squaw! So we got ol Uncle Sax right where we want him.

Fine, fine, but I seem to recall you thinking the last time we were on this subject that Earl Bennett would take care of the matter for you. One thing we've learned is that we cannot just drift along letting things take their course. Timing is the key here, Arch. Do not forget that. And do not forget how important it is to keep the Leavenworth man on our side.

Oh it don't take much to keep Butts happy.

They lowered their voices then and Rachel lost the thread. By leaning forward she could catch a snippet here and there from the judge, with stretches of long low mumblings in between. Our man in Washington... The hell they will! ...Oklahoma assholes.... Easy Street.

The side door opened like an explosion in Rachel's brain, and immediately Mrs. Wingate was right there on the other side of the wall calling goodbye and thank you to the niece who had driven her home. Rachel dropped the dust-rag to the floor and, stooping to pick it up, found herself unable to rise from her squatting position. She heard the two men come forward to greet Mrs. Wingate in the hallway beside her. Turning to lean against the wall, the better to be hidden from view, Rachel waited for the end. The three stood talking casually near the doorway not five feet away from her. When they came into the living room she stood to lose more than just her job. For a wild second she considered trying to hide behind the window curtain two feet to her right. But before she had time to think or move, she heard the judge say no to a cup of coffee, that he must be leaving to pick Lexie up from her sister's. The side door clattered open again and their voices shrank as all three moved to the threshold of the outside door.

Mr. Wingate was saying that he would see Arch before he left for Oklahoma next week, but Rachel wasn't listening anymore. Almost blinded by the blood pounding inside her head, she stared down at her long thin hands around the dust cloth, and couldn't think whether to try for the curtain, or leave the room altogether under cover of the judge's exit. No matter which way she left the living room, she was afraid Mr. Wingate would realize she had been nearby during their conference. The only hope, she decided, was to hurry back toward the entrance hall, and from there, pretend she'd been cleaning at the other end of the room, near the foyer. Still, there was a good chance one of them might turn and see her through the doorway as she crossed the living room. Half paralyzed with indecision, she straightened her back, ready to rise.

Well, I need a cup of coffee anyway, Mrs. Wingate said as they closed the door and re-entered the side hallway. These meetings are enough to parch a fish!

I'll join you in a minute, Maddie, said Mr. Wingate. I just need to put some papers away. You be on the sunporch?

Oh, let's sit in our outdoor living room; it's too nice a day to be cooped up inside.

Alright. Be right there.

Rachel waited, suspended in agony, as Mrs. Wingate's steps carried her toward the kitchen, where, thank the Lord, she had left a pot of coffee on the stove. She remained frozen, listening intently as Mr. Wingate shuffled his papers. There was one final moment of silence. She looked up to her left, expecting to see him staring at her from the doorway. But he wasn't there. Then, mercifully, she heard his footsteps as he also walked off toward the kitchen. When she was sure they were outside the house and safely sitting on the patio, Rachel crept shakily back to the front foyer, ready to pretend she'd been there all along.

CHAPTER TWENTY-SIX

The new starched collar and pleated shirtfront chafed his skin as Tom sat in the Muskogee courtroom. He pulled at the knot of his pale blue and yellow patterned silk tie, too conscious of his clothes for comfort, even in his summer-weight grey suit. It wasn't that he minded the lawyers' insistence that he dress up. Oh no, Tom Johnson had always prided himself on his looks. The shapeless prison pyjamas he had been made to wear for so long had hurt his vanity. But it was hot. Everyone's clothes wilted in the crowded room. The overhead fan only seemed to push more smothering air down onto them. The windows were open, but all that came through them was the noise of street traffic below, the drone of motors punctuated by Klaxon horns and the clopping of horses' hooves.

He glanced at Judge Arch beside him, whose striated wings of thinning hair shone on either side of a straight side-part, as if designed to match his highly polished shoes; his signature silver-headed cane was propped against the half wall behind him. He wore a cream-colored suit which emphasized his girth. The occasional bead of sweat at his temple gleamed like an ornament before it ran down his face. Axley, beyond, was less glamorously attired, his olive green suit clean and pressed, but merely able, as opposed to the opulent styles Tom and Judge Arch sported.

An old, bearded patriarch of a man entered from a side door and the court clerk bawled everyone in the courtroom to their feet. His honor, Judge Ambrose Potts, who wore a suit of questionable age and laundering under his black gown, nodded pleasantly to Judge Arch and began the latest round in what promised—or so it seemed to Tom—to go on forever: The United States of America versus Tommie Johnson, the sensational case in which, as one reporter had phrased it, 'The defendant is being asked to prove whether he is a millionaire Negro-Indian, or just a colored plasterer's helper from Kentucky.'

The room was full to capacity with Creeks and freedmen, oil company executives and reporters. Tom glanced about until he spotted Sax, who was also looking around the room, his head wobbling slightly in a manner that told Tom he had been drinking. The loose wave Sax began when he saw Tom was aborted by something which caused his mouth to drop open slightly. A woman had craned her head over her shoulder to look at Sax.

When she turned and followed Sax's gaze to Tom, he saw that it was Anna Elliott, Sax's former lover. Heavier now, her hair streaked with white, she stared at him, unsmiling, until Tom turned away. Beside her sat a native man of imposing build, presumably her husband. Hellfire, thought Tom.

Judge Potts was explaining that it was the defense's responsibility to prove that this man—he pointed at Tom almost indifferently—was in fact Sam Ford, a half blood of the Creek tribe and the rightful owner of Section this, Township that, Range this, of Creek County in what is now the State of Oklahoma.

Suddenly Wingate was leaning towards him. What the hell's the matter with you, boy? he whispered. You're bout to kick my goddamn leg off.

Don't look around, Tom answered through clenched teeth. The wife of the man I shot is here. She was around the whole time we's plannin the land claim business.

Shit.... I'll get us a recess soon as I can. Don't talk to her. Don't even look at her, you hear me?

As soon as it could be managed, Wingate and Axley were locked in an antechamber with Sax and Tom.

I don't even wanna imagine what she could do here. She can put me back in prison if she wants to, Tom said. She knows evah'thing.

We should've thought of her, said Axley. I figured it was enough the Washington brothers were dead.

Okay, okay look, said Wingate. We got two things on our side here: she's female and she's Indian. In other words, she's a squaw and she's a squaw.

Right, Axley agreed. Shouldn't be hard to take her down if we can establish the point that her character is, shall we say, not all that pure and upstanding.

Wingate and Axley looked simultaneously at Sax. You willin to testify, Sax? asked Wingate.

Why me? What do I gotta do with it?

Aw, come on, Wingate sneered. Come on, Sax. You got plenty to do with it, as I'm sure you can see if you'll just think about it a minute.

But...

'But' hell. You're either with us or you're not.

That's right, Axley added. We understood you were in. On the winning side, so to speak.

Well... I...

Tommie needs your help here, Uncle Sax, said Wingate. If she gets up on that stand and starts tellin about how Tommie went before the Creek Nation with a plan to impersonate a dead Indian, we're going to need you to tell the people all about how she was... how shall we put it... enjoyin your company all during those years.

But... I.... I ain't...

Listen, said Axley, you're not even married. What possible harm can it do for you to speak out about a dalliance you conducted over twenty-five years ago, can you tell me that?

Tom could well imagine that Sax's worries were tied up with Anna's present husband.

It won't harm a thing. But it'll help Tommie and our little team here a considerable amount, said Wingate, who had leaned close to Sax in an effort to strike a conspiratorial pose. Wait a minute....He sniffed at Sax's breath. Damn it to hell, Slayden, have you been drinkin?

Sax's denials were somewhat confused and Wingate grabbed him by the lapels, lifted him off his chair and shook him.

Tom had sat through this needling of Sax in silence, studying the uneven plastering job at the corner of the small room. Now he was up from his chair before Wingate knew it and grabbed the judge's arms.

You let go a him!

The men froze in deadlocked silence until Axley jumped to his feet and intervened. He's right, Judge Arch. It won't help matters to get physical. Tommie, let go of Judge Arch.

I let go when he does.

The judge turned his dark, angry eyes from Sax to Axley. He let Sax go with a shove, his mouth flat as a split tire, and Tom released the judge, then walked over to the window and stood with his back to them.

Listen, Sax, we can't use you if you're going to be drinking at ten o'clock in the morning. It just ain't smart on your part. You have got to stay sober, at least between midnight and six p.m. Now if that's asking too much maybe you'd better just go on back to the farm, huh? What do you say? If you work with us you'll have all the whiskey you want once we win this case. Anybody who helps us is gonna be well rewarded, isn't that right, Tommie? You'll have twenty million dollars; you can find a little for your Uncle Sax who played a part in keeping you from gettin trampled by the herd on this thing, isn't that right? Well? Isn't it? Isn't that *right*, Tommie? Axley's voice was becoming manic.

Tom turned and looked at the little lawyer in sullen silence.

Axley rattled on then, as if Tom had agreed. Course it is. We all need each other here; not a one of us got a hope of winning this case on his own. Now I'm going to go find me somebody to run out and get us a pot of coffee. We still got...He pulled out his watch and looked at it. It may as well have been a hypnotist's watch the way the others stared at it. We got better'n forty-five minutes before we resume. Now let's everybody sit down here at this table and work on a plan to deal with our surprise guest out there.

CHAPTER TWENTY-SEVEN

The Prosecution wishes to call Anna Brightleaf Elliott Bearcat to the stand.

Murmurs simmered as Anna sailed slowly up to the witness box. Resplendent in doeskin, beadwork and feathers, she had gotten herself up to be nothing less than the Creek Nation itself. She took her time getting settled with a minimum of motion, made the solemn vow to tell the truth, then looked in regal stillness upon the prosecuting lawyer, Mr. Ward.

Mrs. Bearcat, do you know that man sitting there?

She nodded, and Ward said, We need you to speak your answers, for the record.

I know him.

Can you tell the court his name?

Tom Johnson.

Are you sure his name is Tom Johnson, and not Sam Ford?

His name is Tom Johnson. He took the name Sam Ford to get land from the Dawes Commission.

Tom's muscles were rigid as she spoke. His neck began to ache. He'd stopped breathing. To avoid looking her in the eye, he focused his gaze on the brass eagle nailed to the front of the judge's bench.

Mrs. Ell… Mrs. Bearcat, please tell the court how you know all this.

He came here some years ago and introduced himself as Tom Johnson from Kentucky. Had a wife and two babies with him. I was in Okmulgee on a certain occasion when he and his uncle, Sax Slayden, who is also from Kentucky, came there on business. He and the Washington brothers started talking to my husband, Joe Elliott, about how they were going to get Tom Johnson enrolled in the Creek Nation as Sam Ford, so he could get a land grant from the Dawes Commission. I overheard the Washington brothers say they would have him take the name of Sam Ford, a dead man of Creek blood, because that name was easy and he'd be able to remember it. They wrote it on a piece of paper for him, and said, 'Practice on this until you get it by heart.'

How did this scheme make you feel, Mrs. Bearcat?

It made me angry and I told em so.

You told *who* that it made you angry?

I told all of them: my husband, the Washington brothers, Sax Slayden and Tom Johnson hisself.

What did they say?

They didn't answer me. But when we got back home, I told my husband again. And the next night, when Sax Slayden and Tom Johnson come back over to our house to drink and talk about their plans, I told them again. My husband said, 'Well, it's too late now. Tom has filed as Sam Ford with the Creek Nation, and from now on he has changed his name and we will call him Sam Ford.' I said, 'He did not file, you're joking.' But my husband said, 'Yes, he did and now he's Sam Ford.'

Ward asked her to continue.

It made me madder than ever. I said, 'I don't see how you, a state Negro, can file for land as a Creek Indian when you have no right.' Then he started to get mad, too, and he said, 'I have filed and that's the end of it.' Then my husband said, 'I already represented him before the Commission. It's done.' I said they might get into trouble if they didn't mind, and my husband repeated, 'It's done,' and he went outdoors to draw a bucket of water. While he was outside nobody said nothing. But when he come back in, I said, I don't think it's right for state Negroes to come in here and get our rights and our land. But Tom Johnson said, 'By God, somebody else'll jes get it if I don't!' and Sax Slayden said, 'That's right. He may as well have it as anybody else.'

So you know for sure that Tom Johnson, a Kentucky Negro, assumed the identity of a dead Indian, Sam Ford, in order to enroll with the Creek Nation and be granted land under the Dawes Commission.

Yes, that's what I know.

And he was granted the land in Creek County?

Yes. Right before he shot and murdered my husband that had helped him get the land.

As she began this last sentence, Mr. Ward held up his hands to make her stop, but she continued to the end, swinging a piercing gaze at Tom. Ward sighed. Your honor, the Prosecution asks that that final statement be stricken from the record.

As you wish, Mr. Ward.

Thank you. Mrs. Bearcat, please confine your comments to the questions I ask. What can you tell us about the Sam Ford claim?

I can tell you that the name of Sam Ford was stricken from the roll in 1906 while Tom Johnson was in Leavenworth Prison.

Stricken from the roll of the Creek Nation in 1906?

Yes.

Do you know why?

Because they knew by then the claim was false, made by a Kentucky Negro in the name of a dead Indian named Sam Ford.

Objection!

Can you prove that last statement? Judge Potts asked.

Judge, we present this document as exhibit A. Mr. Ward went to his desk for a piece of paper which he then presented to the judge, who looked it over with a great show of attention, then put it to one side without further comment. After a moment Ward said pointedly, For the benefit of the court, your honor, I will explain that Exhibit A is the order from the Creek Nation, dated December 8th, 1906, to the effect that the 1902 enrollment of Sam Ford be stricken from the record and cancelled.

Judge Potts cleared his throat and mumbled, Uh, yes, yes. Um-hm.

There was another moment of silence. I have no further questions, your honor.

As Ward resumed his seat, Wingate rose with a deliberate air of relaxation, and strolled towards the witness stand. Mrs.... Bearcat. They stared at each other for a moment, as the court waited. What year did you marry Joe Elliott?

Objection, your honor. What possible bearing can this question have on the case?

Overruled. We'll see. There was a ripple of laughter.

Around 1890.

Around 1890? Not precisely 1890?

No. It was 1890.

Can your hesitation as to the date of your own first marriage be because the Indian people aren't as concerned with matters of time and date as we are?

Anna stared at him without answering, her face devoid of expression.

Well, perhaps you're not sure about that either. No matter.

Objection! He's badgering the witness.

Sustained. Carry on, Judge Wingate. Without badgering.

Wingate nodded at Potts. What year did you meet Tommie Johnson?

Anna hesitated, barely flickering her eyes. About 1900 or 1901.

Wingate smiled tolerantly. 'About.' Thank you. Now, your husband... that is, your first husband...Joe Elliott *was* your first husband I assume?

Yes.

Right. Your first husband, Joe Elliott, is dead, is that right?

Yes.

How did he die?

Objection! That issue has no bearing on this case!

Overruled, Mr. Ward.

I repeat, how did your first husband die?

He was murdered by Tom Johnson.

Why did Tom Johnson kill your first husband, Mrs. Bearcat?

She looked down, saying after a moment, I don't know why. I only know he did it.

This is the crime for which the defendant served a life term in Fort Leavenworth Federal Prison, correct?

Yes.

Having been thoroughly punished, then, by the authorities of the United States Criminal Justice System, he was released after seventeen years on good behavior. He was returned to society with a clean slate, reformed, and the matter before the court today, as Mr. Ward has so insistently reminded us, is that of his land claim in Oklahoma to which you referred in your testimony before Mr. Ward. Correct?

Y-yes, she answered hesitantly.

Let me ask you then, Mrs. Bearcat: have you forgiven the man who killed your first husband?

Objection!

Did you agree to be a witness in this case in order to further punish...

Objection!!

The judge's gavel finally drowned out the two lawyers. Silence! Objection sustained. Judge Wingate, you will not proceed any further with this line of questioning.

Very well, your honor, we've got plenty of other questions. Smiling at his audience, he paused for the laughter. Mrs. Bearcat, you say that Sam Ford was a Creek Indian who died before 1902, is that right?

Yes.

Did you know this Sam Ford of whom you speak?

No.

You yourself never met such a person?

No, but...

Please, Mrs. Bearcat. I will have to make the same request of you as Mr. Ward did: confine your answers to the questions I ask. So, Mrs. Bearcat, you did not know any Sam Ford before you were told by your husband that this man sitting here was Sam Ford.

Objection! She said she was told by her husband to call the defendant Sam Ford, not that he...

Objection sustained.

Well then, let me rephrase myself. You did not know the Sam Ford who supposedly died before 1902, never met him. Correct?

Yes.

But you mention knowing the defendant's uncle, Mr. Saxton Slayden, isn't that right?

Yes.

How well did you know Mr. Slayden?

Anna looked down and remained silent.

Mrs. Bearcat, let me repeat the question. How well did you know Mr. Saxton Slayden?

He was a neighbor.

A neighbor. Anything else?

She was silent, refusing to look at him.

Would you say he was a friend of your husband's?

Yes.

Alright, he was a friend of your husband's. Good. Now, was he also a friend of yours?

She was quiet for a moment, then said, No.

He was not a friend of yours? Was he anything more to you than your neighbor?

He ain't nothin to me.

He may be nothing to you now, Mrs. Bearcat, but that is not what I am asking. Wingate was not deterred by the fact that she made no answer, nor that she simply stared ahead at nothing. Indeed, he let the silence stand as her discomfort grew.

Frowning slightly, Tom glanced back at Sax, who, stilled at last, was watching Anna in stricken silence.

I am asking whether Sax Slayden was ever anything more to you than a neighbor, Mrs. Bearcat.

She remained silent. Finally, Wingate broke the tension. Well, we won't push the point. That will do for now, Mrs. Bearcat. You may return to your seat.

CHAPTER TWENTY-EIGHT

The Defense wishes to call Saxton Slayden to the stand.

Sax came forward with a nervous smile, looking erratically around the room. He took the oath in a quick, offhand manner and sat down, bobbing his head slightly and twiddling his thumbs.

Mr. Slayden, said Judge Wingate, you are from Wills County, in Kentucky, is that correct?

Yes suh, it is.

And you have been referred to as the defendant's uncle, correct?

Yeah, that is I's the half-brother of Vess Johnson—Sylvester Johnson—the man that raised Tom, or, or, Sam there.

Your hesitation concerning the defendant's name is understandable, Mr. Slayden. Please explain it to the court.

Well, you see, I been callin him Tom all his life, up til he come out to Oklahoma to...

What year was that, Mr. Slayden?

1901 it was, when he come out here to...

Thank you. Let's take matters one step at a time. Why did he come to Oklahoma in 1901?

He come... said he come to meet his real, true family, the Fords. But they's all dead time he got out here, and he took up with me then, til he could get his land and all.

Of course, he knew you were out here as well, isn't that right?

Why sho. I done wrote and tol him to...

To look you up when he came out?

Objection! Council for the Defense is leading the witness.

Objection sustained.

Alright then. Mr. Slayden, said Wingate, rolling his eyes at Ward and crisping the words in an exaggerated show of tried patience. Tom Johnson came out to Oklahoma from Kentucky in 1901 for the purpose of meeting his real family, and filing for land, is that correct?

That's right.

And this was the first you knew about his real identity?

Yes suh, first I ever knowed bout it.

Can you explain to the court why you, his uncle, would not have been aware of it before then?

Well you see, I's a lot younger'n my brother Vess. I's his half-brother, and a lot closer to Tom's age than Vess's. So I wasn't much more'n a kid myself when Mr. Ford come through town that time and tol Tom who he really was and all. I's a young man then, and all taken up with my own life and plans.

Did you meet Tom's father, Mr. Ford, at that time, when he came through Slayden's Crossing?

Well I seen him. We's havin a picnic in the fiel' out back of the church there, and I seen him alright. Ev'body was all excited on account of they bein a full blood Indian at the picnic. He was dressed like a full blood Indian too. That was unusual roun Slayden's Crossin. He didn't have no truck with me nor nothin, but I sho nuff seen him.

After you moved to Oklahoma... what year was that, by the way, that you moved out here yourself?

18 and 96.

When you moved to Oklahoma, did you ever meet any of the Ford family?

Naw, never did come acrost none of em. Mebbe they's all dead by that time, I don't rightly know.

Thank you, Mr. Slayden. Now, I would like to turn to a more delicate matter as far as you yourself are concerned. Sax drew himself in and began biting at his lip. As Mrs. Elli... Mrs. Bearcat stated during her testimony, you were a near neighbor of Joe and Anna Elliott's, is that correct?

He nodded, and had to be asked to state his answer. Yes suh.

Tom slid down a notch in his chair. He couldn't look at Sax, and he certainly couldn't turn to see how Anna was taking this.

Now remember, Mr. Slayden, you are under oath to tell the truth. Wingate allowed another dramatic pause. What was the nature of your relationship with Mrs. Elliott, as she was known then?

Well, we was neighbors, and we was friens...

Is that all you were to each other, Mr. Slayden?

Objection!

Objection overruled, Mr. Ward. Carry on, Judge Wingate.

Were you and Anna Elliott ever more than just friends, Mr. Slayden?

He nodded, and again Wingate asked him to state his answer in words. We's more'n friends, yes suh.

Were you lovers?

Yes suh.

A palpable interest tightened the atmosphere. People sat forward slightly, or simply stilled themselves.

When, Mr. Slayden? During what period were you and Mrs. Elliott lovers?

He scratched his head and looked to the side with a small shamefaced smile. Fo some years, I reckon. The assembled crowd showed its appreciation to the extent that Judge Potts had to resort to his gavel again.

You say you and Mrs. Elliott were lovers 'for some years'. Would those years include the period before she was widowed?

Yes suh.

I see. This makes the relationship an adulterous one if her husband was still alive while you and she were lovers, isn't that correct?

I reckon it does. His answer came in such a low voice that he had to be asked to repeat it. Then he shrugged.

Wingate eventually cut off the laughter with his next question. Did Mrs. Elliott have any children?

Sax looked up at Wingate with a frown. Scuse me?

I asked whether Mrs. Elliott had any children.

Objection, your honor!

Judge Wingate, what is your intention in asking about Mrs. Elliott's children?

Judge Potts, I am attempting to demonstrate the character of the prosecution's key witness.

The witness is not on trial, Judge Potts!

That's true, Mr. Ward, and yet her character is of sufficient relevance in this matter for me to overrule your objection. Carry on, Judge Wingate.

Thank you, Judge Potts. Now then, Mr. Slayden, did Mrs. Elliott have any children at the time of your affair with her?

She didn't nevah bear no chile a mine, if that's what you mean.

No, that is not what I'm asking, though I can see why you may've gotten that impression...under the circumstances. Wingate turned and mugged his incredulity to his audience as general hilarity broke out again. When the laughter subsided, he said, Did she already have children—presumably by her white husband—when you—a 'Kentucky Negro', to use her own phrase... Wingate appeared to have trouble suppressing a grin,...when, when you and she began your affair? Is the question clear to you now, Mr. Slayden?

Yeah. She did.

How many were there, and approximately what ages? Children, I mean, not lovers. The ensuing laughter was punctuated by Ward's cries of 'Objection!' and the tattoo of the judge's gavel. Wingate apologized merrily and reiterated the question unembellished.

Had her two boys, round mebbe four or five, or mebbe six or seben.

Fairly young then... say, between four and seven years old?

Yeah, sump'n like at.

And where were they?

What? Sax asked, frowning.

Where were the children when you and Mrs. Elliott would meet for the purposes of conducting your... intimacies?

Sax was visibly squirming. Why, I don't rightly know, Judge. I... I... They jes aroun somewheres I reckon.

With the last few questions, Wingate had reinstated an atmosphere of sobriety by becoming more and more grave of face and manner. Now he turned away from Sax to look directly at Anna, who sat slumped in the chair, her long hair partly obscuring her face. Her husband sat grimly still beside her. Wingate allowed the silence to stand for a moment, then said, Thank you, Mr. Slayden. That will be all.

CHAPTER TWENTY-NINE

Sax was leaning forward in the witness chair, pulling at his lower lip.

Mr. Slayden, said Ward, his close-set eyes fixed in a squint. Let me bring you and the court back to the matter of your knowledge of the defendant, Tom Johnson. You have stated that you are his uncle... his step-uncle or half-uncle... that he is the child of your half-brother... Vess, was it? Vess Johnson? Is that correct?

Yes suh.

Do you know for certain that he is the child of your half-brother?

Well... I cain't say fo certain, I guess, but I b'lieved fo some years he was.

What do you mean, you 'can't say for certain', Mr. Slayden? We don't want anything that you 'can't say for certain'. What can you say for certain about this man's ancestry?

Well, that is... I mean, I know my half-brother was married to his wife, Clara Johnson, at the time he was borned, but beyond that, I cain't say nothin cept that they was raisin up a youngun we all called Tom Johnson roun that time, and this here's the person they raised up.

When was Tom Johnson born?

Borned in 1872, in the summertime.

In Kentucky?

Yes suh, back in Wills County there.

So, you say his parents were Doc and Molly Ford, from Oklahoma. Yet they were in Wills County Kentucky when Tom Johnson, or Sam Ford, was born?

Yes suh.

Why were they in Kentucky in 1872?

I-I's jes a kid at that time. I don't have no idee bout any a that.

I see. Yet you state that this man here, your nephew, was born in Kentucky, and that Doc and Molly Ford were his parents.

Yes suh. Far as I can know it, that's the truth.

When were you born, Mr. Slayden?

Well now, my record is guesswork. I's borned sometime aroun mebbe the first year a the wah.

I assume you're referring to the War Between the States?

Yes suh.

So, around 1861 then?

Yes suh, roun then.

In Kentucky?

Yes suh.

Where, exactly?

In Wills County. Slayden's Crossin. My mother was Maria Slayden John-son. But from the time I's six year ol I's raised in my grandmother's house, same as Vess was. Raised right there in Wills County by my grandmother.

What was her name?

Adella.

Adella what?

She went by Slayden...mastah's name.

Your grandmother was a slave?

Yes suh, and my mother too.

Who was your father?

She didn't nevah say.

Who was the father of Vess Johnson?

Name was Johnson. I cain't call his Christian name. Didn't nevah meet him, a course. He was dead time I was borned. He wasn't *my* daddy, jes Vess's. But Vess was half-white and went by the name of Johnson. That's all I can tell ya bout him.

Now, how do you account for this man—Tom Johnson—how do you account for his claim of being Indian or part Indian?

I cain't account fo it, only to go by what he says, and by his looks.

Did your grandmother Adella also claim to be part Indian?

Yes suh. And my mother. And Clara Johnson, the one who raised Tom up, she say she got Indian blood, too.

Clara Johnson, too? Ward repeated, shaking his head.

Say she does.

Who were Clara Johnson's parents?

Don't know.

You don't know, or she doesn't know?

I don't know. I imagine she'd know, but she ain't never talked about it to me, ceptin jes to say she's part Indian, like Vess.

So, just to be clear, Vess and Clara Johnson, your mother Maria, and your grandmother Adella, they all claimed to be part Indian?

Yes suh.

Well. Are there any Negroes or mulattoes in this part of Kentucky that don't claim to be part Indian? This time the loudest laughter came from the Indians in the courtroom.

I couldn't say.

More laughter.

Um, let us come down from the defendant's family tree, if I may put it that way.... Once again the judge had to restore order with his gavel, this time primarily because of appreciation from the white contingent. Mr. Slayden, I wish to return to the issue of your relationship with the defendant. You say you were raised by your grandmother, Adella Slayden. How far was her home from that of Vess and Clara, where the defendant was raised?

Wadn't no mo'n a few mile.

Few is not a very specific term. Can you be more exact?

Bout mebbe three-fo mile.

So you lived, for many years, three or four miles apart?

Well, and part of the time I lived right with Vess and Clara. That was after my grandmother passed.

You lived in the same house with them?

Yes suh. I's jes a chile when my grandmother passed and Vess got married, so I lived with them fo a time.

Right in the same house.

Wingate and Axley were both groaning inwardly. They dared to glance in each other's direction for a second.

Very interesting. That's... that's very interesting, Mr. Slayden. Can you explain then how you remained unaware of Tom Johnson's 'real identity' living so close to him? Indeed, living in the very same house?

Jes never did hear nothin bout it. Didn't never come up.

Thank you, Mr. Slayden. You may step down. I have no further questions.

* * *

Good God A'mighty, said Tom to Judge Arch as the court recessed for the day. Is they anything you won't do fo money?

That's an interesting question coming from you, Tommie.

Please, Axley cautioned between clenched teeth. People are watching. Tommie, let's discuss this in our office and not out on the public street.

Axley had fended off the gaggle of reporters that accosted them at the door of the courtroom, but several were still trailing them. Sax was craning his head around nervously in search of Anna, or in fear of her husband, but Axley stayed close beside him. We'd better go on up to the office and wait a little while before we go to supper.

In that case I'll jes go get us a little refreshment and bring it on up....

Wingate cut him off. I don't think that'd be wise just now, Sax, unless you have a disguise handy. No, I think we'd all better stick together for awhile, like Ben says. He smiled and tipped his hat to two white ladies driving by in an automobile. I know there's no one else I'd rather consort with this evening. And I couldn't help but notice that Mrs. Bearcat made a fast getaway, so, if you were hoping to renew...

You done said enough on all that, Judge, Tom said, causing Axley to repeat his plea for quiet from all of them until they had some privacy.

As they crossed the lobby of the Muskogee Grand, a tall white man was turning away from the front desk, hat in hand. His brown hair was severely parted, the teeth-marks of the comb visible in his pomade. He looked pointedly at Tom with a friendly smile, then made for the front doors. Tom recognized him from the court-room. Both courtrooms.

Isn't that one of our competitors? Isn't that Cooper, of Cooper Oil and Gas? Wingate asked Axley.

Sure is. His is one of the smaller outfits with an interest in Tommie's land. Chooses to represent himself. The two lawyers smiled contemptuously at the idea.

You watch, he'll be claiming to be a lawyer next.

The clerk handed Tom his messages last, and among them was one, hastily scribbled, from Cooper. Dear Mr. Johnson, Would like to meet with you privately on a matter of your interest. I'm staying in Room 233 at the Arrowhead Hotel on Chisholm St. W.L. Cooper P.S. Urgent

They were all glancing through their messages, but Tom could see that the lawyers were more interested in the ones to him than in their own. He had only read Cooper's, but quickly tucked them all into his inside breast pocket as they moved toward the elevator.

At the Muskogee Grand their office was a step up from the cramped converted bedroom at the McAlester Hotel. It was a meeting room on the second floor with a conference desk and plenty of chairs. Axley went to the telephone and ordered sandwiches, coffee and cake from room service and they all took cigars from the humidor in the middle of the table. All except Tom, who took out his pipe and the pack of tobacco he kept in his pocket.

Tommie, look. I can see you're a bit testy, Wingate began. I don't think you understand what all it's gonna take to win this case. We've reached a very delicate stage...

'Delicate stage, delicate stage...' Tom was thinking, as he shook his head in silence and tried to tamp down his anger.

He's right, Tommie, Axley added, starting to outline, once again, their strategy for establishing this and discrediting that. But Tom was watching Sax, who had propped his feet on an empty chair and seemed to have no thought for anything but puffing his fat cigar to life. He put the pipe and tobacco away again.

You right, he said, rising from his chair. All I un'erstan is that I am sick a the sight a the three a you.

The door closed behind him on the rising pitch of their voices, ordering or cajoling. When Sax scampered up behind him, emitting cigar smoke like a smokestack, he said, I mean it, Sax. Get the hell outta my sight.

But Tom, come on, man...

Tom spun around suddenly and grabbed Sax by the collar. You done made the choice to sell yo soul fo money. Me? I ain't got no choices left. But I *can* say I won't set in there another minute, and I won't be chaperoned by you neither. So git on back to yo keepers and leave me the hell alone.

As Tom got onto the elevator, a young black waiter squeezed carefully past him with a silver tray. Sax took the stairs and left by the back door.

CHAPTER THIRTY

Tom walked out into the warm evening with no thought of where he was going. The air was already cooler, the streets emptying for the supper hour. He felt his stomach rumble as he turned away from the busier part of town. A train cried off to the west and he moved in that direction, toward the ripening sky. Broadway gave onto Osage, which turned onto 38th, each street becoming smaller and darker. He knew Chisholm was near the depot because he had noticed the Arrowhead when they arrived in Muskogee—a small wooden hotel in need of paint. Now he stood across the street from it, weighing the prospects of going in.

It was the smell of fry grease from the bar and grill behind him that made up his mind. Hell with all of it, he thought. I'm hungry.

Gimme one of them hamburgers you done got cooked, he said to the girl behind the counter. She was a mulatto, a white term Tom hated and never used out loud. She swept back her frizzy reddish hair, glancing up nervously. And turn around here so I can see what you doin.

Now she looked quizzically at him, but did as she was told, still saying nothing. She reached for the ketchup bottle.

Don't want nothin on it.

Placing the burger on a dry bun, she handed him the plate and wiped her hands on her scrofulous apron. That be all?

And a Co'Cola.

They're in the box yonder.

This suited Tom fine. No middle man. He fished a Coke out of the cold water, inserted the lid carefully into the dull silver opener on the side, and flipped the cap off. Chink-hssssssss-clink. Satisfying as music. He could already taste the sweet cold burn in his throat.

The place was nearly empty, a family of skinny whites by the front window, and one or two lone men here and there. Absorbed in selecting his place, he started toward a table near the back, but the girl said, That'll be thirty-five cents, mister. He looked at his food for a moment, then carried it back over to the till with him while he paid.

Having returned to his chosen table, Tom studied the salt and pepper in their glass shakers before sprinkling them over the patty. Within minutes he had finished eating. Why hadn't he ordered two while he was at it?

Damn, he muttered.

Scuse me? said a broad, hawk nosed man two tables away. Tom looked over. Long hair that clumped in strings hung past the shoulders of his dirty red shirt. Probably half Indian, half white. You talkin to me?

Nope.

What you doin in here, dressed up so fine? Huh Mr. President? Look like you own the railroad or sump'in. His laugh might've been friendly or it might've been mocking, Tom couldn't tell, but the odds favored the latter. He looked down at his own clothes. He had forgotten he was still dressed for court. Or maybe you done struck oil.

Said I wasn't talkin to you.

The man's jaw ceased chewing; he stopped his root beer halfway to his mouth. Placing the bottle down on the table with elaborate care, he gave Tom a look. Think you too good talk to me, zat it?

Tom rose to leave. I'm too good, *and* I got a meetin to go to.

He was almost through the door when his shoulders were forced down and he was dragged back inside the restaurant. To sounds of females screaming and chairs scraping, Tom was whirled around and punched in the face. He fell amid the tobacco juice and crud of the floor, his pipe skittering into a table leg. But scrambling back to his feet, he unleashed the full strength of his fury. Blood from the man's nose squirted over them both, sliding their punches askew. By the time the police arrived Tom's front teeth were broken out, cheap bridge and all. The elegant clothes were in ruins. But his assailant's face was unrecognizable, his right arm dangling from him like a broken toy.

Goddamn it, Tommie, Wingate scolded as they left the police station. You jist won't listen, will you? You'd think the prospect of twenty million dollars'd keep you out of trouble, but no. I guess that wouldn't ever be excitement enough for you.

How ya fhind me, Yudge? I ain't nevah ast fo you.

Sax coughed nervously, and Wingate said, Ain't too much gets by me, Tommie, and you oughta be thanking your lucky stars for my connections. Because the next thing I'll have to do after I get you out of this mess is to get us another trial delay. You can't go into a courtroom now til you get some new teeth.

He's right, Tommie, Axley chimed in. You want to be a millionaire, you gotta look the part.

Hell, you got to act the part, too.

While Tom lay in his hotel bed, Sax running in and out with fresh ice, Wingate replaced his good clothes, and Axley found him a dentist.

Dr. Wolfe was a youngish man, the son and grandson of freedmen. He made no conversation with his patients. His office was over an undertaker's parlor, and Tom wasn't sure he wasn't about to be embalmed as Dr. Wolfe settled the cone of ether over his nose and mouth. He awoke to wavering cracks on the ceiling, and a mouth like a catcher's mitt. Every last one of his teeth was gone and his gums felt like they were full of live bees. After a while the dentist came in and trickled water down Tom's throat. He began to choke, then fainted, as Dr. Wolfe rolled him onto his side and gave him a needle. The next time he came to, the window was dark and Sax sat, lamplit, beside him. Tom tried to speak but found he couldn't.

Here you go, man, open up. Sax sealed the drinking straw with a finger as he'd been shown by Dr. Wolfe, and dribbled water into Tom's wound of a mouth. Shooo-weee, but yo' mouth's...

Tom reared up on an elbow and vomited into an enamel basin the dentist had left on the cot beside him. He shoved the water glass from Sax's hand and lay back down. Dr. Wolfe heard the glass smash on the floor and hurried in. Tom woke, crying, an hour later.

It was two weeks before he could be fitted with dentures, but he was pleased the first time he saw his gleaming new smile in the mirror. Though he was less pleased as he tried to learn to talk and eat with false teeth, Dr. Wolfe assured him that by Christmas the blisters would be gone and he would be completely accustomed to them.

CHAPTER THIRTY-ONE

Wingate and Axley had told Sax he'd be cut from the budget if he didn't keep a constant watch on Tom during the period of his recovery, but Sax saw no reason to sit around the hotel every afternoon while Tom napped. After all, the two of *them* were out doing whatever they wanted to. The afternoon was the best time to scare up some distraction from the dull routine imposed on him by the lawyers. And so it was that Sax was sauntering happily down Broadway on his way to the Chisholm Trail Pool Hall a week or so after Tom had gotten his teeth pulled.

A tall white gentleman tipped his hat to him. Lovely sky today, isn't it? the man said.

Sax glanced up with a smile, though he kept on walking. Yes suh. Ol shepherd wind done movin them flocks again, look like.

The man paused at the doors of the Muskogee Grand, watching until Sax rounded the corner; only then did he nod to the doorman and pass on into the lobby. At the desk he asked if Mr. Tom Johnson were in. A few moments later, the elevator doors opened and a bellboy led Tom over to the tall man in the houndstooth suit, who rose from one of the leather wingbacks.

Well, well. Mr. Cooper, said Tom, touching his tongue to his sore gums. His mouth was as wrinkled as his clothes and it was obvious to Cooper that he had interrupted a much needed nap.

Why, Mr. Johnson, I'm pleased to see you know who I am. Wellington Lyman Cooper, to give you the entire moniker. He offered his hand and Tom shook it. What's... um. You, you haven't been well, I take it? The voice rose and fell with the lilting accent of the southern gentry.

Tom shook his head, unwilling to speak more than was absolutely necessary.

I'm so sorry. Can I get you a drink in the hotel's soda bar?

Tom indicated that he would accept such an offer, and they passed through frosted glass doors into the smokey pocket of a room the hotel had named 'The Western Arms' in the days before prohibition. The name was still painted on its doors, which were propped open. Shelves behind the lustrous mahogany bar were lined with various innocuous choices of soda pop and juice. Whiskey, Tom said in answer to Cooper's deferential gesture. When the barman brought a half-full bottle up from under the counter, Tom mumbled a protest and demanded an unopened one. Cooper watched Tom watch the barman carefully as he opened a new bottle and poured the drink.

Ice, sir? Tom shook his head no.

And, just a lime soda for me, thank you, said Cooper; then to Tom, Religious reasons... but, I have no quarrel with those who do partake. Howevah, fo'give me, but I must ask, have you tried takin headache powders? They are quite efficacious, I must say.

Again Tom shook his head no. Religious reasons, he muttered.

They sat in a little nook at the end of the bar and Tom noticed that Cooper kept an eye on the door. For his part, he welcomed the effect the whiskey had on his aching mouth, and waited for Cooper to offer whatever deal he had in mind.

Mr. Johnson, I presume you are aware that I am the founder and president of Cooper Oil & Gas.

Tom nodded, his expression passive to bored.

I thought so. You're obviously quite astute. Well, our company first struck oil on the Creek County land along the banks of Tiger Creek in 1905. We were among the first to discover what a rich deposit it is. Now I have personally been associated with every hearing and trial in the case, from that date forward, and I believe—though of course I wouldn't state it this way to anyone else...He leaned toward Tom and whispered the sentence: I believe that you are the rightful ownah. As far as I can see, the evidence shows that your claim deserves to be honored before the many others, even including my own.

Tom continued to stare at the man, careful not to betray his surprise at Cooper's confession.

Now then, Mr. Johnson, as that's my feelin on the mattah, naturally I want to know more about you. Your family, your home, etcetera. Can you, um, can you speak at the present time, Mr. Johnson? Or does it pain you too dreadfully?

Hurts.

Cooper nodded deeply, with great empathy. Well then... perhaps I might just tell you a little bit about myself, and then I could ask you a few questions about yourself. Would that be alright, Mr. Johnson?

Tom shrugged, and looked at his empty whiskey glass.

Another? Yes, yes, I'm sure it helps ease the pain. Um, say, waiter? Another whiskey over here, please. Perhaps, perhaps you'd just leave us the bottle.

Un-open, said Tom, and when a new bottle was brought, he relaxed visibly.

I must ask you gentlemen please to keep this wrapped, the barman said after opening it. He had some sort of European accent. Polish? And, should there be any... um... how could I say...? He pronounced the last word with two vowels: sai-ee. Tom was pondering what made this two-syllable 'say' different from the way Cooper would pronounce it.

I will accept full responsibility in the event of a raid, Cooper said with the utmost gentility. Ray-eed. Perhaps the only difference was speed.

They settled into a companionable lull in the semi-darkness of the empty bar, the bartender twitching his great mustache over a newspaper, which he occasionally folded and used to swat a fly.

Cooper told Tom about his life as a cotton planter's son in Mississippi, his dreams of going west, his eventual apprenticeship as a wildcatter. My daddy died believing I'd wasted my life, he said with a sad smile, but he'd've been proud of the black plume I raised out here on the banks of Tiger Creek, I just know he would. I think you're about to win this case, Mr. Johnson, I really do, and what I'd like to propose to you is that you put me in charge of the oil wells on your property. I'm prepared to guarantee you proper administration of your resources with none of the shenanigans which are unfortunately so common in the oil business. I recognized in you the inherent qualities of a gentleman the very first time I saw you, and I dare to hope that the same qualities are evident when you look at me.

Tom looked up into the watery blue eyes of Wellington Lyman Cooper and shaped his mouth into a wistful smile as he reached for the bottle and refilled his glass.

After a short period of silence, Cooper spoke again. There's... there's no need to give me an answer right now, Mr. Johnson. You'll want to take some time to think it over, naturally. Here's my card; you may contact me any time. I stand ready to serve your interests as soon as you call upon me. He threw up ten long fingers to illustrate his sincerity and a change of subject, sighing deeply. If I may ask, Mr. Johnson, how is your wife taking all this? I mean you bein gone from home so much and all?

Tom shrugged. She be fine.

Yes, of course. I myself never had the good fortune to take a wife, and at this point I hardly think it likely I evah will. I am what they call a 'confirmed bachelor' I suppose, which suits me well. But, back to your wife... Mary, I believe her name is? Right, Mary. Lovely name. Is she staying with relatives during your trips to Oklahoma?

Tom shook his head lazily. Home.

She stays in your home? But not all alone, surely. All alone? I see. Well...
He swallowed. No doubt Slayden's Corners is a safe and respectable community.

Crossin.

Beg your pardon? Oh. Slayden's Crossin, of course. That's... I... that's
what I meant to say. It's a small town a few miles south of the county seat of
Greenberry, as I understand? Yes, I thought so. No doubt I've been through
it many times myself on the train. You see I do make regular visits home
to Mi'ssippi. I'll have to watch out for it on my next journey. He sipped at
his drink. And, um, your son...what does he make of your good fortune?

Ben don't worry hisself bout this stuff.

You mean, he's not followin the case with much interest?

Tom laughed sleepily. Naw.

Oh. A rare attitude, given the circumstances. And a mark of character I
might add, not to be caught up in the greed so common to our times. What
does your son do for a living?

Clay pit.

Ah. There in Slayden's Crossing?

Uh-huh.

And how old would your Ben be now?

Thirty, round there.

Cooper had slipped a small tablet and a pencil out of his pocket and
was making notes under the table on his lap. He carried on asking Tom
harmlessly phrased questions about his extended family, their names,
where they lived, how each felt about the case, etc. until the whiskeys and
Cooper's mellifluous voice had all but cast a spell. Even the bartender sat
half dozing over his newspaper until a flurry of arriving guests out in the
lobby caused him to sit up straight. Cooper consulted his watch, then he,
too, straightened his posture.

Mr. Johnson, one more thing I wanted to say, and then I suppose I
really had better let you get back up to your room and rest. Um, pardon
me... Mr. Johnson?

Tom opened his eyes and frowned.

Mr. Johnson, I must let you get some rest, I never meant to keep you so
long, but I've enjoyed our little visit a good deal. Cooper reached out and
touched Tom's arm in an effort to rouse him from his doze and regain his
attention. I do hope you'll give my offer to manage your oil wells serious
consideration. But, uh, there's just one more thing, Mr. Johnson—the most
important thing of all, the way I see it. Do you remembah the message I
sent you a week or two back?

I do.

Yes, well in that message, you may recall, I alluded to somethin I had to tell you that it was in your vital interest to hear. Part of what I was referrin to was my bein appointed your oil man, which, as I say, I hope you won't forget when you 'come into your kingdom' as it were. He smiled for a moment, then let his face fall back into lines of concern. But the other thing I was referrin to is not so pleasant, Mr. Johnson. Mr. Johnson, I have reason to suspect that your lawyers do not have your best interests at heart.

Tom had been holding lightly to this ribbon of talk as he balanced at the lip of a canyon of dreams. Cooper's last comment gave the ribbon a little jerk. Tom smirked, eyes still half closed.

I have no doubt that you are an astute man, Mr. Johnson, a natural judge of character. This is one of the gentlemanly qualities I have noted in you from the courtroom alone, and now that I have had the pleasure of meeting with you face to face, you have confirmed it for me. Tom's eyes began to droop again, and Cooper, who was whispering now, laced his tone with some urgency. Mr. Johnson, *please*. I've been wantin to tell you somethin fo weeks now. I have reason to believe your lawyers are plannin to... remove you from the picture, if you take my meanin.

Tom's eyes opened suddenly and tried to focus. Cooper nodded like one who has finally struck home.

Kill me, you mean?

Cooper glanced at the bartender. He was wiping glasses at the far end of the bar. I fear that may be the case, he whispered.

What'd make you say that?

I overheard them talkin. I was in the readin room at the courthouse one day—just before I sent you the message. By sheer luck, I was behind the shelves near the back when your two lawyers came in. They thought they were alone you see, and the shorter one...

Axley.

Yes, Axley. Axley was sayin somethin about killin rats. It might've been harmless enough, but then Judge Wingate said he had heard that 'it' was 'best masked in coffee'. And Axley said, 'That's good. At least he drinks coffee.' They went on talkin, and I heard your name several times. But then again, it might not've been you they meant, because they kept sayin Tommie instead of Tom.

Wearily, Tom leaned his head against his left hand. Oh, it was me alright.

CHAPTER THIRTY-TWO

By the third week of December Tom was fully recovered. With some reluctance he presented himself at the door of the room they used as their office. He understood the lawyers wanted a final meeting before he and the judge returned to Kentucky for Christmas.

So! You decided to turn up after all, said Wingate. We'd just about given up on you, and you the guest of honor!

Surprise! said Axley, grinning, and a ragged chorus echoed the word without much energy.

Sax twisted around in his chair, beaming. The room was half full, with men Tom had most definitely not been expecting to see there. Men Sax had taken up with during the early years and who formed the nucleus of his circle of Oklahoma friends. Kenny Prettyboy was a full blood Choctaw, who had been a ranch hand back then. He had evolved into a depot Indian, one who hung around doing odd jobs for tips and whiskey. Howard Buckman and Sonny Day were mulattoes from Tennessee who sometimes worked for Sax on his ranch. All Tom knew about Solomon—who was rumored to have a rising career as a hired gun—was that he was a half breed who'd been found on the steps of an orphanage in Tulsa. He still wore the medicine bundle that had been placed around his infant neck, presumably by his mother, before he'd been abandoned.

He noted them one by one, and the last person in the circle was Abner Butts. Hello there, Tom. They done scraped the barrel for your party, bringin me out here, wouldn't you say? Butts laughed, exposing yellow teeth.

Tom looked from the men to the decanter and glasses on the conference table. He remained near the door, silent, mouth slightly open, waiting for an explanation.

Come in, Tommie, come on in! said Axley, rising to take his elbow and lead him into the room. Tom pulled away. What's the matter, never had a surprise party thrown for you before?

It ain't my birthday.

The men's laughter played itself out in a minor key, as if pushed back down and smothered by the blue cumulus of cigar smoke.

Tommie, we got reason to celebrate, said Wingate leaning forward in his chair. Judge Potts is an old friend of mine as you know. He has agreed to a continuance 'til next spring. That's good for a number of reasons we don't have to go into right now, but it means we continue the trial here in Muskogee where the atmosphere is more... shall we say, pleasant. And furthermore, it means we'll have time to 'git our shit together'—as Sax here likes to put it—before the final battle.

Look to me like our shit's all in one place already. Tom looked around the circle of faces.

The two lawyers laughed uproariously, as Axley pulled out a chair beside Sax and motioned Tom toward it.

Set on down here beside me, said Sax, grinning. They done ordered us a great big platter a oysters to help get this awful whiskey down, heh heh. Set yo'sef down right here, Tom.

Tom sat. Sax held out a cigar, but Tom reached past it to select one for himself, from the far side of the humidor. Aware of their eyes, he rolled it under his nose, from end to end, inhaling the flavors of rum and vanilla, running a finger along the tightly folded leaves. Then he drew out his pocket knife and cut off the end, flipping it into an ashtray. The men continued to watch his every move. With a sudden tongue thrust he pushed his dentures forward. It was a trick he'd practiced in front of the mirror in his hotel room, thinking to make his granddaughters laugh. He couldn't quite gauge the reactions here.

After a beat, Wingate said, Oh, I get it. Why I thought you were gettin mighty persnickety on us, Tommie, trimming your cigar with a knife.

They seized the opportunity for conversational fuel, and rattled on about teeth and dentures until the oysters arrived, held earnestly aloft by the boy who reminded Tom vaguely of himself at thirteen or fourteen. If for no other reason than the way the boy carried himself, Tom imagined he had dreams of taking control of his life someday, in whatever situation or job he settled into. He had looks, health, youth, energy, and something more—the secret ingredient of pride, like the pinch of cream of tartar that held the plastering compound until it was needed. Axley handed him a bill. There you go, Silas.

After the boy left Tom sat serenely smoking while they fussed over the oysters, filling little gold trimmed plates that were thinner than a child's front tooth, and refilling their cut-glass tumblers with the amber nectar they loved. He let them shove his portions in front of him. Let them exclaim over the taste of the oysters, the fresh salt crispness of the crackers, the sweet bite of the whiskey. He let them carry on and offer and urge, while he sat without comment, his only motion the cigar to mouth, smoke to air, ashes to ashtray ritual of smoking. It was a calming ritual, and it helped him as he retreated from his enemies without moving.

Axley offered to order some coffee, but Tom shook his head no.

Exasperated by his resistance, Wingate tried for a tone of concern. What's wrong? You not feelin good, Tommie?

Nevah better, Judge. Preciate yo concern.

Why, help yourself, then. After all, all of this is for you.

Tom smiled, took another drag on his cigar, and made no answer.

CHAPTER THIRTY-THREE

Two days before Christmas, Mary sat on the edge of the bed to draw on her stockings, arrowing her toes carefully so as not to snag the silk. She clipped each stocking onto the garter belt, pulled her slip and her orange wool dress down and smoothed them out with practiced motions. Using the hand mirror, she twisted to check whether her stocking seams were straight. On the vanity table, the blue evening window curved over the pear-shaped bottle of scent Tom had brought her from Louisville five years before. She reached for it, removed the heavy stopper, and dabbed a little of the flowery liquid at her temples. Though Mary had never been one for luxuries, a woman had to keep herself up, even at fifty-three. Even if her man had no teeth. She pinned on her hat, frowning slightly into the mirror.

Ever since she had gotten Tom's letter about his false teeth, she had been concerned. It wasn't so much the dentures themselves she fretted about, but how he would look at night when he took them out. She had seen a good many people with no teeth, their mouths reduced to a drawstring purse, their profile collapsed until nose and chin nearly met. How would it be to kiss such a mouth? Her handsome Tom had always been such a good kisser, his lips tractable and knowing.

She sighed, slipped into her shoes and walked toward the front door. The train was due in twenty minutes and would make a stop at Slayden's Crossing. Though their house was right beside the tracks, Mary always went over to the platform to meet Tom. Clara was having them for supper tonight, so there was no cooking to fuss with. She'd be doing plenty of that tomorrow anyway, what with roasting the turkey, making sweet potato croquettes and baking a coconut cake. They would be sixteen for dinner on Christmas Day. The turkey was plucked, and the others would bring the dressing, vegetables and pies, but still Mary liked to get as much of it done as she could on Christmas Eve.

She pinned on her hat, swung her flared beige coat around her shoulders, and looked with satisfaction at the living room. The house she had no doubts about, though it was getting a bit chilly since she'd let the fire go out an hour or so ago. But it shone with a welcoming gleam that she was sure Tom couldn't help but be proud to come home to. Ben and the girls had come out last weekend and cut her a tree, which sparkled in the corner with tinsel and ornaments. Beside it was Tom's beautiful mantelpiece, dressed with a red felt cloth edged in gold ribbon; she had been careful not to cover up the fruit and flower swag. That was the work of his own hands, and prettier than all the rest. His pride would never stand seeing it covered up.

Pulling the door to behind her, Mary found the path beside the tracks in the failing light. The Emerson children were outside playing and called greetings to her; otherwise Slayden's Crossing was busy indoors and looking forward to supper. The air felt clean and dangerous, slightly metallic, as if this early winter evening were a boy with a half-hidden pocket-knife he was eager to try out for the first time. The cold air made her aware of the moist warmth under her arms. There hadn't been any snow yet of course, but there might be a flurry soon, Mary thought. Be nice if they had one for Christmas.

Several of the family were already gathered on the platform. Gladys was there, Richard and his wife Parmalee, his sisters Nettie and Loretta. Clara would see Tom back at her house, and Ben and Nema wouldn't bring the girls out until Christmas dinner.

Hey there, Mary! Nettie cried. Get on over here and warm us up! We done been standin out in this cold air fo ten minutes and we are about to die!

Yeah! the others chorused. Come on! Lawdy, we need more people to huddle up against! Richard put out his free arm and drew her in. They were stamping impatiently and laughing.

I'd light me a cigarette, said Loretta, but it's too col to smoke! Now that's the truth. It is too cold to smoke! And you know if I say that, it be *cold*!

Mary laughed. Well, it's winter. What y'all spect?

Tell you what *I* spect, said Parmalee. I spect fo it to be seventy-five degrees and sunshiney evah day of the world. Now why cain't it be like that? You tell me one good reason!

They kept up this distracting ruckus until they heard the first faint train whistle, which lifted a cheer from them that was only partly given in welcome for Tom. They all agreed that, mm, mm, *mmm*! it was *the* most beautiful sound in the world, and that's how Tom found them when he stepped off the train a few minutes later—loud and excited. A committee of high spirits.

Mary's first worry was instantly put to rest. His face looked as handsome as ever, and the new teeth gleamed evenly –an improvement, if anything, over the discolored smile he had brought home from prison. But there was something else. She watched him closely throughout supper. He had been gone for four months this time, hardly long enough for his hair to be appreciably grayer, yet she thought it was. He'd lost a little weight. His manner was slightly different as well. When he laughed, it was not for as long nor as freely as before. He seemed to want them to do the talking.

Here, son, have some mo a this ham. Clara nudged the plate against Tom's folded hands. You ain't et hardly any.

Naw, Mama. I done had enough. Tasted real good.

You tellin me I stood over that stove all day fo you to take one measly little helpin?

When Tom didn't look up, Richard grabbed the plate from her. Here, I'll have some more, Mama. Ain't no need to worry bout food goin to waste with me here. You know that. They laughed.

Yeah, Mama, what a*bout* that? Loretta added. Sound like you only cooked fo Tom and don't even care bout the rest of us!

Gladys asked for someone to pass her the field peas, and they all began reloading their plates. But Clara didn't smile until Tom asked what was for dessert. He took a huge slice of pumpkin pie—just to please his mother, as Mary observed, for he ate it at a dull pace. Maybe it was the new dentures, but she thought it was more than that.

They walked home in near silence, which was lifted momentarily when she lit the small lamp in the living room. Well now, he said, smiling at the decorations, you done been busy roun here. Place lookin real pretty, Mary. *Real* pretty.

She smiled and bit her lip. It's cold in here, but I didn't like to leave a fire burnin while we's out. Ben and the girls cut me the tree. Christmas jes day after tomorra, ya know. You better have some surprises hidden inside of that new suitcase you carryin.

He looked at the suitcase in his hand as if he'd forgotten all about it. Oh yeah. I bought it cause of all this travellin.... Tell ya what I'm aimin to get you fo Christmas, Mary. I'm gonna have em put us in a telephone. What you think bout that?

She smiled, a little uncertainly. Well now... wouldn't that be somethin? Our own telephone.

You know, I jes thought... with you here alone so much...

She nodded. By now he would usually have tossed his bag down and taken her in his arms, but they stood on in the cold living room.

How much longer you figure it's gonna take out there?

He shook his head slowly. Reckon I'm jes gonna have to see how it goes.

To cover another awkward silence, Mary picked up the lamp. You ready go on to bed? Me, I'm bout to fall ovah. He nodded and followed her into the bedroom. Leaving her clothes draped over the trunk at the end of the bed, she wasted no time getting under the covers in the unheated house.

Tom opened his bag, removed the jar of Morgan's and performed his usual bedtime ritual, applying the salve and then the cap to his hair. He turned and left the room without a word. She saw that he lit a candle in the kitchen, then heard him go out to the privy. Then he came back in, and she heard him at the water jug. When he returned to her, the dentures were floating in a glass of water, which he placed on the windowsill beside the bed. She saw his face only briefly as he leaned to blow out the candle, then to put out the kerosene lamp. She saw new lines and shadows, the diminished mouth she'd been dreading. Mary waited, nervous as a bride, while the bed squeaked and jostled under his weight, but he only murmured goodnight and settled himself with his back to her.

For a moment her eyes pricked with tears. Then a small, familiar sound relieved the tension a little. The room gathered all it could of the distant train, collecting more and more noise and vibration, until noise and vibration seemed to be the only thing the room held. It was a freight train; after the engine no lights strobed the walls. In the time it took to pass by and then out of their hearing, Mary made up her mind what to do.

Tom?

No answer.

Tom.

Um hmm?

Ain't you gon kiss me g'night? Still no answer. Tell the truth, Tom, I been wonderin what it'd feel like. He made no move. You been wonderin, too? Silence. She scooted over next to him. His knees were drawn up and she fitted herself against him, spoon-fashion. She reached up to stroke his arm, but the undulant muscle-scape she loved was less defined than usual, loose and deflated by his mood. She ended by resting her arm along his thigh. Tom? He put a hand over hers. You *better* been wonderin. You better not already know. He laughed a little, despite himself. Put em back in if that's what it's gonna take, but either way, I want you to kiss me.

After a moment he rose up on one elbow. He started to stretch towards the glass on the windowsill, but stopped in mid-reach and turned to her instead.

CHAPTER THIRTY-FOUR

Judge Arch sat in the sunroom of his brother's new mansion. He tossed a cigar butt onto an already full ashtray somewhat harder than necessary and ashes spilled onto the end table. Ted Wingate looked pointedly at the mess, blinking. Arch cleared his throat nervously, but said nothing.

Taking an apple from the bowl on the coffee table, Ted made a precise incision near the stem with the fruit knife. Slowly he circled the edge of the blade just under the peeling, lifting it away. The red skin, shot through with green and yellow markings, hung between his knees, curling in a longer and longer ribbon as the banker pared with a steady hand.

It's just not as easy as you'd think. Grey ash streaked the white linen handkerchief which Arch folded and pushed back into a pocket. You're not out there. I'm tellin you Ted, we've got the court eating out of our hands. We've got all the paperwork under control. We've got the people we need ready and in place. I don't think you realize what all we *have* done.

Um-hum. Ted rewound the peeling into its original shape and set it on top of the others in the bowl, before cutting a wedge from the naked apple in his left hand. He popped the bite into his mouth and chewed, looking with satisfaction at the 'empty' apple.

I tell you we've tried, but the bastard keeps eluding us every time with his damned suspicions about food and drink.

Ted cut himself a second slice, and said, Oh I'm sure he thinks he's one smart nigger, but he won't outsmart us. He chewed for a moment. Maybe it's just as well he's still around; the court case needs to be all but finished anyway before you all... take care of the matter. In the end you may have to use force. Simple as that. He raised his eyebrows at his brother and popped the second wedge into his mouth.

I suppose it will come to that. Arch sighed, drawing out another cigar from his breast pocket. It'd be a whole lot easier if we could just get him drunk. He stood up to throw the cigar band into the ashtray, lit the smoke, then stood looking out at the garden through the generous expanse of windows.

You ought to know from me that once a man makes up his mind to go off the drink...

The day was muted, purple and grey. Leafless trees waved feebly in a damp breeze. An aborted snow squall whitened the margins and corners, melting almost as he watched. Lexie and Maddie were walking toward the house along the flagstone path in their high-heeled galoshes, each one hugging herself against the cold. Maddie was thin as a rail, Lexie more shapely. Arch always measured what was his against what was his brother's, not even conscious anymore of the lifelong habit.

Maddie was looking down, concerned with her own passage over the wet, uneven stones. Lexie's face was turned away; she was calling something to Archie and David, who were running beside the small 'lake' in matching houndstooth coats. David, who tended to be sickly, was struggling to keep up with his robust older brother, whose tweed cap flew off and landed upside down in a petticoat of icy snow beneath the shrubbery. When Lexie turned back around, she saw her husband in the window and waved with a forced smile that seemed to say, My. Isn't this fun. He lifted his cigar to her and returned to the cane settee. Here they come.

Ted nodded. You'll do it, Arch. You'll figure out a way.

Damn right I will.

Yes, well, just make it a priority at the end of the next round out there. And remember, use force if it becomes necessary. Cover yourself, of course. Now. No more of that. The new hospital is coming along well. You been over to see it?

Only in passing, but I spoke with Bradley after church this morning. He seems real pleased. Says it ought to be open for business just in time for the malaria season.

Ted laughed as the women came in through the door off the kitchen. I guess it takes a doctor to get excited about malaria.

Ye-heah, said Arch, stapling a laugh into the word. Made it sound like golf or somethin.

Lexie padded into the sunroom in her stocking feet. Who makes what sound like golf? she asked, sitting down beside Arch and putting her feet into his lap. They're cold. They need a rub. She tilted her head prettily. He gave her a look, but began rubbing her feet, as directed.

His question about where the boys were collided with Ted's voice and trailed off. We were talking about Bradley Scott. He's excited about the prospects of the malaria season for his new hospital.

Maddie came in and put her hands to the radiator. Lexie, what about the boys? I don't want them falling into the lake. Only when she saw her sister-in-law's stockinged feet did she realize she hadn't removed her galoshes, and began pulling the elastic cord off each button as Lexie answered her.

They'll be right in; I told them to. She turned to look out and saw that Archie had tackled David and was rolling on the ground with him. She immediately withdrew her feet from her husband's lap and tucked them under the curve of her hip. Oh Arch, you go and get em; they never do what I say. Davie shouldn't be rolling on that damp ground. Arch got up and went out, using the door right off the sunroom. Ted have you got anything like a cigarette around here? I mean, after all, where are we, Kentucky or Cuba? Y'all ought to smoke cigarettes anyway, if only for the sake of the local economy. She ran a hand through her crimped blonde hair, mussing it slightly.

He forced a laugh and opened the drawer of the end table, offering her a pack of Chesterfields. I do plenty for the local economy.

She took one and, placing it between her lips, leaned toward the flame her brother-in-law had ready.

I must say, it'll be strange going to the hospital in our old home, said Maddie, observing Lexie's casual confidence with equal measures of envy and judgement.

Lexie inhaled deeply and blew smoke from her nose and mouth with relish. I wondered if you'd thought of that. I can't imagine going into the hospital under such a circumstance... my very own former kitchen smelling of rubbin alcohol and ether, my bedrooms full of sick people. She shook her head as if to repel the distasteful images.

Well, I, I don't know. It's...

Maddie and me talked it all over before we made the decision, Lexie. It just made good sound financial sense to renovate a building that was already standing instead of constructing a new one from scratch. And besides, we both wanted to do something for the people of Greenberry, isn't that right, Maddie? This is our contribution.

I suppose, but let's just hope you neither one have to go to the hospital for any long-term period. Short visits won't be so bad. Maybe you'll just be in the new part of the buildin. She wrinkled up her nose and nodded her head with a condescending smile.

We're both as healthy as horses, aren't we, my dear?

Just then, Arch bustled into the room with David in his arms. I'm gonna let Archie play outside a little while longer. Maddie, would it be too much trouble to ask you for some sassafras tea? Davie's sort of chilled. I'll just take him into the bathroom and dry him off some. The slight, pale, eight-year-old huddled against his father's shoulder and said nothing.

Arch, I don't think it's safe to leave Archie out there with no supervision—not with the lake and all. Do you, Ted? Maddie asked.

Not really, no. I can see him from here, but if he was to cross over the bridge...

Arch lifted his chin at his wife in an unspoken command and carried David out of the room. Since it was Rachel's afternoon off, Maddie stood up to go out to the kitchen and make the hot tea. I imagine a cup of sassafras tea'd do all of us some good.

Lexie sighed and rolled her eyes. She rose from the settee, opened the patio door and bellowed into the winter afternoon at her firstborn son. When she sat back down, Ted held the fruit bowl out to her. Would you like an apple?

She was about to decline, then noticed the carefully propped peeling. Oh Ted, you clever thing. I suppose it was you that did that, and not Arch.

Old Indian trick.

Well I would say, 'how Biblical,' to be offered an apple, except that it's the wrong way around. And besides, you aren't really offering me anything, are you?

Depends on which one you take. He smiled. Neither of them noticed Archie running from tree to tree, engrossed in a private game of hide and seek, as he drew closer and closer to the glass room that housed the adults.

CHAPTER THIRTY-FIVE

What's got into you here lately, gal? asked Mrs. Slayden in her best dog calling pitch. She was a small-boned woman whose cotton dress of faded green hung from her shoulders as if from a coat hanger. Ain't enough yo brothers got to worry me half to death runnin off to them Satiddy night dances. Hangin around with the likes of them Cruickshankses. You was always a good Christian chile and now here's half the congregation tellin me how you's dancin with this un and that un and makin a spectacle out of yo'self over yonder at Carmody's last night. What you got to say fo yo'self, gal?

Rachel had barely had time to hand her mother the money she brought her every week. Had barely registered the smell of cabbage over the kerosene and wood-smoke. She froze in her hat and coat, pursed her lips and turned to leave again. But Hallie and the younger children ran up and grabbed her arms, pawing at her pockets and begging for the treats she always brought. Uncharacteristically she smacked at their hands and joined in the general shouting until they backed away. In the sudden silence Rachel's behavior caused in the children, her mother stood staring at her from beneath a thunderous frown.

I got me a right to some fun, ain't I?

Fun. The word might've been a chaw of tobacco the way she spat it out.

I ain't done a thing wrong, Mama. Not one single, solitary thing.

And jes what you call dancin with a whole passel of different men?

I call it fun! she said, in a slightly louder voice. Then, sighing, she added more gently, Wasn't no harm in it, Mama.

Mrs. Slayden answered with an articulate noise of contempt.

Ain't you nevah gone dancin when you's young?

Naw I ain't, and I's proud to own it. But we ain't talkin bout my behaviour here, gal. We talkin bout you. And what's mo, I hear tell you been goin to that picture show in Greenberry stead of goin to church of a Winsdy night.

Oh, Mama. Rachel's voice was freighted with sudden sadness. She took a step back into the room. How'd you and Daddy meet?

Knowed him all a my life. We's chirren on the same farm.

I know that. I... I mean... how'd y'all come together? You must've done some courtin, sho'ly.

Mrs. Slayden blinked her eyes. Who's axin the questions here? You courtin some man? Z'at what's goin on with you, gal?

Rachel was still for a moment, looking down at her gloves, as if considering whether or not it was worthwhile to remove them. The children watched both women with intense curiosity, not making a move lest they be sent outside.

I... I ain't courtin no particular man, Mama. I jes wanted to have me some fun fo I gets too old. Fo it's too late. When I come to think about it, seem like all I ever do is work and go to church.

What kinda talk is that, gal? Only one thing that sorta thinkin'll lead to and that's trouble. You listen to your Mama, Rachel. I ain't never looked for this class of trouble out of you! If it's a husband you's wantin, you'll find a better one in church than at that Lincoln Theatre in the Greenberry Bottom, let alone over at that Carmody dance hall!

Well maybe it ain't a husband I's lookin fo...

Then you is lookin for trouble, sho's I'm borned! Her voice grew even louder and more shrill. You hear me, gal? Huh? Cause I'm here to tell you that's what you gone find if you go...

How in the name of all that's holy is a man s'pposed to get any peace in his own place? And on the Lawd's Day, what's mo! Rachel's father stood in the doorway of the back room in his underwear, red eyed. His hair was flattened on one side from where he'd been napping. Rachel noticed that the chest hair visible above his undershirt was turning white.

Folks is sayin Rachel done been actin like a tramp roun town...

Now, Mama, that ain't fair! Rachel fought back tears.

Don't lemme hear you back-talkin yo mama, gal, her father said, his voice now ominously quiet.

Jes tell me what has got into you to make you start behavin trashy this away. You's always the best chile.... You got you a good job, and here you is ready to throw evah'thing onto the garbage heap...

Rachel had her gloved hands over her face now and was crying uncontrollably. You... you don't know nothin, Mama. You don't know...

Mr. Slayden stepped across the room and grabbed her by her coat collar. She covered her ears with her hands, crouching low as he began to strike her across the head and shoulders. His righteous curses were like something overheard from another room, something that had nothing to do with her. It was the strongest resistance she could offer.

Out of breath, he finally stood up and backed off. Rachel reached to the floor for her hat and slowly got to her feet without another word. She looked at no one, didn't see that her mother had turned away. She barely heard her sisters whimpering in a corner, her brothers snickering nervously. Halfway across the yard she remembered and took the candies from her pockets. With trembling hands she put them onto the well cover, shaping them into a little mound. Then she wiped her face, blew her nose, and began the long walk back to Greenberry.

CHAPTER THIRTY-SIX

Tom measured his stride to the ties in the rail bed, his good shoes, which were still fairly new, rubbing at his heels. Corn stumps in the fields sheltered the last of the snow. A flock of birds swooped and somersaulted above, their turning beginning at one end and taking a moment to move through the body of the flock. Tom stopped walking to watch. The motion reminded him of helping his mother turn feather mattresses. She had always insisted that turning the mattress was part of changing the sheets. Then every year in the early spring—about now, Tom reflected—the mattresses were removed from the frames altogether, and the bed ropes retied.

Mama, why we got to do this? he had asked once, complaining.

Don't ack stupid with me, Tom, cause I knows you ain't, she had answered, sweeping vigorously at the bed-frame as she spoke. Ev'body always sayin 'sleep tight, sleep tight' and don't half of em even know what they's sayin. You ain't never gonna 'sleep tight' without you retie them ropes evah year. All these folks goin around gettin down in they backs and it ain't on account of nothin but lazy housekeepin. That's all in the world it's down to. She had thrown the broom onto the floor and squatted across the bed-frame from him. Now you pull on yo side. Pull *hard*. And don't go botherin me with foolish questions.

The birds settled into a copse of trees like filaments to a magnet. Tom lit his pipe before walking on, sheltering the flame with his hand until the tobacco caught. The bowl of it would do nicely to warm his hands on, one at a time. Maybe some of these days he'd get around to buying himself another pair of gloves. Maybe today. Hell, why not? Might go by Faris's Store this very day and get himself a pair of gloves to replace the ones he'd left on the train last year. Though consciously he resisted the whole Oklahoma adventure, the idea of himself as a millionaire was becoming an insidious player in the small choices of his daily life.

The plastering job at Frankfort finished, he had decided to do what he liked with the time he had left before returning to Oklahoma. Today what he liked was walking into town to visit with Mose Galbraith over at the courthouse and catch up on the news. Kate Ailesworth had died soon after her son Fred was sent to the Eddyville Penitentiary. Everybody said she died of plain heartache and shame, but she was so big she had to be buried in a piano crate. Tom knew Mose had been a pall-bearer and he wanted to hear all about it. But first he had to go over to Boxtown and check on Sis. She rented one of his houses, just paying him whenever she could talk some money out of one of the men that hung around her. It was actually Mary who felt sorry for Sis, and had insisted they let her live in one of the rental houses. There was a broken window that needed fixing and the Lord knew what else. He preferred not to think about Sis when he didn't have to.

It was a fresh Friday morning in late February. He was determined to enjoy himself, determined to put Oklahoma out of his mind for as long as he could. After the Clay Pit, the tracks were bordered only by bare trees and fields for a while. Richard Creek sang a subdued chant of late winter beneath its little trestle bridge, then the road angled through the landscape to run parallel with the tracks and Tom had the company of the odd vehicle. A truck rumbled past with a boy huddled and bouncing in its open bed. He raised a hand in greeting and the boy waved back. Tom he couldn't be sure who it was. He didn't recognize the truck at all, nor its white driver.

The first indication he was nearing town were the twin smokestacks of The Woolen Mills, sailing like a riverboat beyond the trees. Then the courthouse spire. These disappeared again as he drew closer. The low whitewashed buildings of the stockyards were quiet today, but he could smell the animals that weren't there. After these came the grain mill. Before long he was in the neighborhood that clustered around Dunbar School and along the south fork of Red Duck Creek. This was Ben and Nema's neighborhood, but he knew they would all be at work or at school. The tracks curved slightly at Mrs. Wilson's tidy white frame house. She was standing in her doorway and waved to him.

Mighty cold fo walkin this mo'nin! she called through the screen.

It's cold alright, til ya get warmed up!

She laughed. Yeah. You lookin like a train engine yo'self what with that pipe-smoke atrailin out behind you, you sho nuff do.

Tom trotted for a few steps, working his arms like the coupling rods on train wheels as he puffed on his pipe. He could tell Mrs. Wilson appreciated it, but it was murder on his sore heels. Around Water Street he began to pass people on the tracks, lifting his hat if they were white, pausing to talk if they were black. Reverend Ellegood was out front of Fairview Baptist picking up litter from behind the shrubs. He called Tom over to ask how the case was progressing, then seeing his limp he insisted on bringing him into the parsonage.

My wife'll fix you up good as new. You can't be walking all the way back to Slayden's Crossin like that.

Knocking his pipe out on a tree, he stowed it in his breast pocket and followed the minister into the little brick house behind the church. Tom was embarrassed by the way his socks stuck to his heels as he tried to peel them off at Mrs. Ellegood's command. Then as if that hadn't been bad enough, he had to sit there in front of the Ellegoods in his bare feet.

Great heavens! You lemme have them socks. I'll wash the blood out of em and you can take a pair of Reverend Ellegood's...

No. No. No thank you. I preciate the offer, Miz Ellegood, but these'll do me fine til I get on back home. Why Mary'd die a shame if I let you wash my socks.

They tussled it out for a few minutes, but Tom prevailed, pulling his own socks back up over the bandaged heels. He could barely fit the shoes on again, but pretended there was no problem at all. Out of embarrassment he refused the cup of coffee he would've dearly loved.

Next he ran into Richard and Lily Smith, who were in town for supplies. He hadn't seen their newest baby, and of course he had to ask how old Mrs. Flowers, Lily's grandmother, was doing after her gall bladder operation. And so, another long conversation later, he left the tracks just past the depot at Broadway, and turned into Rule's Meat Market. There he bought a jar of applesauce, two cans of pork and beans, a pound of sliced ham, a tub of potato salad, and a gallon of milk. Mr. Rule seemed surprised and pleased when he paid cash.

A grocery sack in each arm, Tom turned onto North 13th Street. The tobacco market was all but finished for the year for white farmers, but there were still some wagons and one dusty old truck as the colored farmers waited their turn at the chute. The scent of cured tobacco perfumed the whole area, and Tom inhaled with deep appreciation, noticing here and there a leaf or two of 'weed' on the brick street, where it had fallen from someone's load. The bricks gave way to dirt down past the creek where Sis lived. He stepped up onto the little porch, calling out to her. There was no answer so he opened the door and walked in, quickly kicking it closed behind him to keep out the chill.

The smell of unwashed bodies pricked his eyes. Sis lay sprawled under a thin blanket on the stained ticking of the bed in the front room, lice moving in her hair. One child was asleep beside her and the other crawled across the bare floor to him, whining hunger like a cat. Both children were the pale olive-brown of grocery sacks. Empty grocery sacks. Their skin had a waxy sheen. He sighed, put the groceries on the table, and bent down to pick up his nephew. The house was cold, no fire in the grate. Coal. He hadn't thought to buy any coal. No matter what you did for Sis, it seemed you could never do enough to make yourself feel better.

Okay Jody, he said, tucking the child inside his coat. S'okay. He tore off part of the sack and wiped the boy's nose with it, throwing the heavy scrap onto the grate. Sis, he said, walking over to the bed to shake his sister's arm. His foot came into contact with something on the floor and sent it skittering under the bed. He knew without looking it was an empty whiskey bottle. Goddamn it! he muttered. Sis, wake *up*! It's me, Tom.

She snored on and didn't move. He could smell the whiskey on her breath.

The baby still whimpering against him, he walked through the filthy empty kitchen and out into the backyard. As he gathered up branches, he remembered a hand of tobacco not too far up the street, and went around to get that for a starter. Once he had a fire going, he got a cup and spoon from the kitchen, and pulled the only chair nearer the fire. The milk bottle came out of the sack like something so clean, so pure. The child gazed at it through crusted lashes as Tom prised the pleated paper cap off and poured a little into the cup. Fighting his nephew's insistent grasp, he fed him the milk a little at a time. Then he wrenched the lid from the jar of applesauce and fed Jody some of that with a slice of the ham and bread. Warmed and fed at last, he fell asleep in the crook of Tom's arm, his head lolling down like rotten fruit. Laying Jody beside his brother, Tom began to shake Sis in earnest. Eventually she stirred and rolled her eyes open. They were red and blank. He had to resist a sudden urge to smack her.

Wake up, Sis!

She began coughing. Her dress was unbuttoned from when she had been nursing the baby and now one breast swung into view. Goddamn it, Sis! Cover y'self up. Ain't you got no pride nor decency left at all?

She rolled to a sitting position on the side of the bed, scrambling ineffectually at the buttons. What the hell? Do I got to do that for ya too, long with evah'thing else? He pushed her hands away and did up the buttons with rough motions. She continued trying to clear her throat, then bent over, holding her head in her hands. The infant woke and set up a thin, tearless whining.

Why won't you let Mama take these chillen? You ain't fit to care fo em.

She made no answer, but fixed him sideways with a cold grey eye. He turned in anger and looked away. After a moment he said, Better put that food someplace safe when you done eatin. Member them rat holes I had to close up last year? I don't wanna hear tell of all this food bein carried off by rats.

Sis looked over at the groceries. You brung me any coffee or tobacca? Smell like tobacca...

He swung back around to face her. I brung you milk and meat, you s... With a great effort he dammed the river of curses that pushed up from inside him. Then he emptied one of the grocery sacks and carried it out to the kitchen. The hole in the kitchen window looked like it had been made with a fist—or maybe a ball, but he doubted that. On the shelf over the stove was a small sack of flour. He poured a little into a saucer; it was running with bugs. There was no cover on the rain barrel beside the back steps, and it too was buggy, but Tom didn't care. He mixed up a paste in the saucer, tore off part of the sack and pasted it over the hole. Thinking to himself that he would come back and fix it right before he left for Oklahoma, he let himself out the back way without saying goodbye.

CHAPTER THIRTY-SEVEN

Tom walked along North 7th Street toward the square, trying to shake off the images of Sis's sorry life. He was passing The Greenberry Bank when a sharp rapping close by on his left startled him. He looked involuntarily toward the noise. The filmy curtain at one of the windows was pulled aside and a white knuckle was knocking at the glass. As soon as he looked up, the hand beckoned to him imperiously. Wingate the banker. Several people on the sidewalk looked at him. Mr. Wingate often summoned people in this manner, but it was a first for Tom. The passers-by didn't appear to realize who he was; they looked at him as if he held a bad debt. Then as he stopped at the corner of 7th and Broadway he heard one woman say to her companion, Ain't that that nigra millionaire?

Oh. She swung the word upwards. Why... I b'lieve you're right!

Tom was prepared to cross over to the courthouse, ignoring the summons, but he heard a young woman call out to him from the doorway of the bank as he waited to cross the street. Excuse me, Mr. Johnson? Mr. Wingate would like to see you. She smiled invitingly and motioned him back toward the bank's Art Deco entrance. He turned with a frown, but followed her inside. She indicated that he should turn to the left, but he stopped and stared a moment, never having been inside the Greenberry Bank before.

It smelled of paper and metal. Money. Tom removed his hat and hesitated before the row of tellers and customers as he took in the monumental style of the bank, with its marbled floor and columns, the high ceiling with its graded stepped coving. Then he heard Wingate call out to him from an office on the left, In here Tommie! Everyone looked up. The door was ajar, a rainbow of gold letters on its frosted window announcing that this was the office of Ted Wingate, Bank President. Wingate beamed at him from behind his big oak desk.

Come on in. Shut the door. Sit down, sit down. I been wanting to talk to you.

How'd you reco'nize me so fast, Mr. Wingate?

Oh come now, Tommie. Ever'body in the county—hell, ever'body in two states knows who you are. It was just my luck to be looking out the window as you came along. Of course, you know who *I* am, Judge Wingate's brother. He reached across the desk to shake Tom's hand.

Yes suh, I know who you are.

Well, he may or may not have told you that we here at The Greenberry Bank are part of your, how shall I put it?... support group. We are backing you like a racehorse! He laughed and offered Tom a cigar from a box on his desk.

No thanks.

Wingate bit the end off of one for himself, spat it into the trashcan and struck a match. Tom noticed that for a small man the banker had rather large hands.

So, I hear you and my brother'll soon be off to Oklahoma once again.

Tom nodded, still on the edge of his chair, and only making sporadic eye-contact.

Sit back. Relax! I just thought it was about time we met. Arch talks about you and your oil case quite often.

Tom gave the perfunctory smile, but held to a strong instinct to say as little as possible.

So, I understand this next round of hearings should wind things up very nicely for you.

This time Wingate let the silence stand a moment.

Tom shrugged slightly. We jes have to see what happens. Wingate smiled at him, holding the eye contact and saying nothing. Tom felt the discomfort of his own refusal to speak. Well... he said, starting to rise.

No no. You don't need to go yet. You just got here! The banker was on the edge of his chair now. I'd like to hear about the case from your perspective. Are you confident it will go your way?

Tom laughed a little and shook his head. You a religious man, Mr. Wingate?

Clearly Wingate was unpleasantly surprised. He was not accustomed to such direct, personal questions, though he asked them of other people on a regular basis. He wrinkled his nose with a sort of grin, searching Tom's face for a clue. Well... I... I am interested in the question of God, if I may put it that way.

But you not a believer.

Tom was delighted to see the banker actually blush a little and flick his cigar at the ashtray several times in rapid succession. He had also stopped staring into Tom's eyes so intently. I... Frankly I'm surprised at the question. What about you?

I asked you first. This time Tom's smile was real.

Well, but you must tell me why you want to know.

Tom had posed the question simply as a preliminary to saying that the outcome of the case was all in God's hands. It had been a ploy to keep the conversation general. However, he could see he had unwittingly struck a nerve, and was not anxious to let Wingate off the hook where he was squirming so nicely. Now Tom sighed, as if from some pulpit of the heart. I jes b'lieve it's a question that tells you somethin bout who a person is.... Don't you?

Wingate studied his cigar a moment, nodding deeply. Then he met Tom's gaze again and said, You're right, of course. And... yes, I am a believer, like yourself. And I trust the Lord will reward you richly, Tommie.

Tom stood up, pretending to be moved. Well, I got to be goin, Mr. Wingate. Good to meet you.

Well, I'm sorry you're so determined to leave. I, uh, I just wanted to assure you that my brother has the matter under control. Just put your trust in him. Let him handle everything and it'll all work out in... in everyone's best interests.

Tom smiled. Good-bye, Mr. Wingate.

CHAPTER THIRTY-EIGHT

Except for grocery stores, Faris's Clothing was one of the few businesses in town where both black and white people shopped. Big signs inside and out boasted that it was the 'Cheapest Store in Greenberry'. The bell on the door brought Sam Faris out from behind a display of overalls.

Well now, he said, smiling. If it ain't our millionaire. What can I do for you, Mr. Johnson? I'm proud to see that the cheapest store in Greenberry ain't lost your bidness, spite of all your oil money. Mr. Faris was an extraordinarily pale man of about Tom's age.

Lookin fo a pair a gloves, Tom replied, removing his hat.

Pair a gloves, you say. Well sir, right back over here you'll find all the gloves you're ever gonna need.

Following the shopkeeper to the far end of one of the glass cases, Tom couldn't resist glancing into a round mirror that sat on top of it. He was happy with his hair today. It had just the right amount of wave. And the interview with Wingate, though it didn't change a thing, had lifted his spirits in a way nothing had for months. Mr. Faris, meanwhile, was scrutinizing Tom's hands. A bare bulb suspended from the tin ceiling shone off his balding head. After a moment he squinted his eyes and drew out a pair of black leather gloves. I reckon a medium ought to do you about right. You... you was wantin leather ones now and not cloth, am I right on that? He held onto the gloves, waiting for Tom's answer.

What do they cost?

Well, seein as how the season's almost over, I'll make it fifteen cents for cloth ones, and a dollar even for the leather. But now, your leather'll last you a sight longer'n your cloth will. And of course, you got your reputation to consider. You ain't gonna see too many millionaires wearin cloth gloves over their diamond rings, wouldn't you agree?

Tom laughed. Lemme have the leather.

For the first time, the clerk smiled. There you are then, Mr. Johnson. You want em in a sack or you wanna wear em?

Tom handed him the dollar bill. I'll jes wear em. He pulled the gloves on and flexed his fingers, nodded his approval at the shopkeeper, and turned to go. Much obliged, he called back over his shoulder, just in time to see Mrs. Faris peep out from behind a coat rack, her eyes wide.

Anytime! Maybe next time you be wantin somethin bigger, like a automobile or somethin.

I didn't know y'all sold cars in here.

If it's a car *you*'s wantin, we'll put in a order for it. He smiled. We don't want to lose *your* bidness, Mr. Johnson.

The door closed behind him with its hollow clash of bells, and Tom crossed over to the court square to find Mose Galbraith. He whistled as he walked, his shadow trailing out from him like a king's cloak.

Mose was cleaning the glass panel on the county clerk's door, an almost visible stench of vinegar around him. He dropped his rag into the bucket, wiped his hands on another rag he took from his back pocket, and reached for Tom's hand. Why looky here! Look what the cat done drug in!

The two men clasped hands and pumped, slapping each other on the back with the other hand and exchanging salutations for a good fifteen seconds. When they released their handshake, they stood grinning at one another.

Place look clean as a whistle, said Tom, admiring the hallway from floor to ceiling.

Yeah well, I try. Hey frien, you is jes in time fo my break. Come on downstairs with me... just lemme... here... Tom tried to take the bucket, but Mose insisted on carrying it himself. Naw now, I cain't have you come ovah here and do my work. How'd you like it if I's to come up to you one day when you's plasterin and try to carry yo things fo ya? Huh? You see what I mean?

Tom nodded. Well now, I jes might let you fetch and carry for me, Mose. Depend on how wore out I's feelin. Laughing, they walked across the shining linoleum floors to the staircase and went down to a doorway in the basement. Mose opened it and pulled a cord that hung down in the center of the ceiling.

Le'trit light. Now don't that beat all? Jes a minute here. Tom waited while Mose poured the dirty water from the bucket into a concrete sink. Then he pulled out a chair and gestured Tom toward it. This here is *my* office, Mr. Johnson. Why'n't you have y'self a seat? He broke into a fit of laughter and Tom sat down, smiling. I be right back. Tom looked around at the neat rows of mops, brooms, buckets and tools. He inhaled the closet's blended incense of cedar chips, floor-wax, oil, soap, and vinegar. Mose had always been consumed with tidiness, even as a child. Tom remembered the teasing he had taken over his discomfort with having his shirttail yanked out or his hat knocked off.

After a moment Mose came back with a second chair and two Coca-Colas. Here, have a dope on me, brother. Now then, I want you tell me all about it.

Bout what? I come here to get some news from you.

Mose gave him a half-frown. The oil bidness! What you think? I wanna hear all about it. He took a church-key from his toolbox and flipped the Cokes open, handing one to Tom, and tossing the caps into the trashcan.

Oh, that. Well...He paused. Tell you the truth, ain't nothin doin on all that right now. I's kinda hopin you'd tell me what's been goin on roun Greenberry. I hear tell you's a pallbearer at Kate Ailesworth's funeral.

What? What you mean, 'nothin doin on all that'? You done got bored with bein a millionaire? You tellin me you'd rather hear about Kate Ailesworth's funeral instead? Come on, man...what? They done got you underneath a code of silence you cain't even talk to your ol friens? He finished the sentence with a trailing laugh.

Tom sighed again, looking down at the bottle in his hand. Tell the truth, I *would* rather hear about Kate Ailesworth's funeral. Mose was staring at him with a smiling frown, so he continued talking. Well, it... I don't know... it ain't ovah yet.

Aw come on, Tom? Don't hold out on me like this. Why ol Judge Arch done been in here tellin ev'body how it's all in the bank!

Hell, Mose, that's jes hot air. That's Wingate bluffin; you know how he is. I ain't seen a penny of it yet. When Mose's eyebrows rose, Tom began to squirm. Nobody in the whole town seemed to want to talk to him about anything else. Somehow Mose made him feel that the outcome of the land claim trial wasn't just about himself. He seemed to take it so personally, as Tom's last words hung in the silence. But... it's... it's lookin like it'll all be ovah this spring when we go back out there. Mose's eyes brightened again. If evah'thing goes like it ought to, why—Mose was smiling broadly now—hell, I reckon I'll be comin back to town in a solid gold Bearcat throwin diamonds at the crowd.

Mose beamed at him like he'd just told him he was a millionaire himself, and Tom was doing his best to smile.

You jes be sho to aim one of them diamonds at me now, Tom. Ya hear?

Yeah, Mose. I will. Promise. He lifted his Coke up to the light, then put it to his mouth and drank a long gulp as if it were his last whiskey. I sho nuff will.

CHAPTER THIRTY-NINE

Tom slept spraddled in his chair, the newspaper open across his lap and chest, his hands palm down on either side of his legs. It was the attitude of one who has literally surrendered to sleep. Mary studied him from the kitchen doorway, her floury hands rolled in her apron. She had asked if he wanted a cup of coffee and gotten no response. She would've blamed his lethargy on the rain, but here lately he'd been taking afternoon naps no matter what the weather.

Mary had a headache. Her forehead was corrugated with worry. This was becoming so characteristic an expression that two of the frown lines between her eyebrows never quite went away anymore. With only a month to go before he was to leave again for Oklahoma, Tom showed no interest in anything; he hardly ever even left the house. His brother Richard had up and bought a car yesterday and it was the talk of Slayden's Crossing, but Tom had refused to walk over and see it with her. Now tonight he and Parmalee were coming by after supper to drive them into Greenberry to go to the show.

Richard's profession as a wagon mender had developed into that of an assistant automobile mechanic at Price's Garage, which is where he had found out about this car coming up for sale. It had belonged to Mr. Toy Armstrong, of Armstrong Hardware over at Wingo. When Mr. Armstrong announced he was selling it off in favor of a new Ford Coupe, Richard had been first out of the gate. But even Richard's job as a mechanic was due in part to Tom, who had sent him the book from the prison course he'd taken on automobiles back in 1916. Richard had always been the more practical of the brothers, less fussy about getting dirty for a good cause.

Yesterday the crowd around Richard's car had been boisterous, several of them shouting comments like, Which one of them Johnson brothers is the millionaire? Why, I heard tell it was Tom, but look mo like Richard's the one rollin in money if y'ax me! This had all been for Richard's benefit and not about Tom at all, but Mary knew he'd get his back up over it all the same if he heard that kind of talk. These days his mood soured with any reference to the oil money.

When the car horn brayed that evening she opened the front door and called brightly, We be right out! A crowd of excited children begging rides was already forming. She turned to see Tom rising from the chair with a grim face.

Let's go, she coaxed in a lilting tone. Our chauffeur has arrived.

Hmmmh.

He stood in front of the mirror angling his hat and she smiled. You lookin good, sugar.

No response.

I look okay?

Without even glancing at her he nodded, refusing to be drawn into words, which might break his reserve. Refusing to be rushed. Finally he followed her out to the gate, where she moved through the crowd and helped three little boys off the running board so she could open the back door. Eventually they were settled up high on the tufted upholstery, and Richard drove out into the road with much honking. There was a smell of oiled leather, scented with popcorn. Mary looked out the back window, laughing at the children who ran behind. Her headache had receded and she was thrilled to be an automobile passenger for the first time. It was a pity Tom wasn't in a better mood.

They turned the corner onto the highway a little too fast and Parmalee shouted at Richard. But it seemed nothing could dim his jubilation. He laughed back over his shoulder at Tom. What you think, big brother? Ain't this jes too much?

To Mary's relief, Tom gave a half-hearted laugh. It's alright, Richard. You done good.

Not bad fo a wagon mender, huh? And I owe it all to that book you sent me from....That book you gimme made me see I better move with the times!

We movin now, that's fo sho! Mary offered.

The need to shout over the noise meant that conversation wasn't much of an issue. And in any case, Richard was so pleased that Mary doubted he would even notice Tom's subdued state. She sat back and relaxed. She could just see the dogwood and redbud trees blossoming off in the woods and in people's yards. Flocks of March flowers ran down the slopes of roadside ditches. Mary felt grateful for every bit of beauty and wished Tom could be lifted so easily from his doldrums. Her pocketbook was between them on the seat, so she moved it to the floorboard and snuggled up against him. He put an arm around her and they flew along the road in their private darkness.

Rumbling through the streets of Greenberry, Richard took Broadway, turning at the court square for the sole purpose of driving at a stately pace all the way around it. Since the day had been wet few people were out, much to his disappointment; but those they passed, black or white, waved expansively, giving him a chance to honk his beloved horn. Finally he turned the car south onto 6th Street, then drove eastward into the neighborhood of the Bottom. He parked in front of the Wilsons' house, across from the Lincoln Theater. They were sitting out on the porch, and immediately rose from their chairs and ambled over to join the people who were congregating to have a look and ply Richard with questions.

How much this thing coss, Richard?

Can I have a ride in it?

How far she take ya on a tank of gasoline?

Eventually Parmalee said, Hey now! Y'all better let us get on out fo we miss the show! She pushed open the car door, and with her grocery sack full of popcorn, made her way through the crowd. Here! Take a handful of this popcorn now and y'all let us get on by, she said to the children.

As Tom climbed out of the car, Frank Wilson singled him out. Hey Tom, how you comin with that oil bid?

Oh, bout the same. How's Ellis doin? Still in Chicago?

Frank's son Ellis had left Greenberry to pursue a career in art while Tom was still in Leavenworth. Though Tom had never met him, Ellis Wilson's was another story the black community followed with keen interest.

Naw, he done moved on up to New Yawk City last year, but he's doin real good. You ought to see how that boy can paint now. Minnie and me went up to visit him last Novembah an...

Tom, you gonna make us late—Hello there, Frank—Tom, come on now. We got to go, y'all! said Parmalee, her voice rising in pitch when she saw Richard starting toward the other men to join in the conversation.

Catch ya later, Frank, said Tom.

The four of them left a curious swarm around the car and strolled across the street.

Don't y'all scratch my paintwork now! Richard called, walking backwards a moment.

The Lincoln ran movies after white viewers at the Dixie and the Legion were finished with them. A long narrow building of red brick, it was tucked between two ordinary houses, but performed the same magic on the other side of the door as any movie theater. The magic began in the foyer. The ticket table was just inside the door, 'womanned' as she liked to say, by Mose Galbraith's Aunt Rita Marie. A large woman both in figure and in presence, Rita Marie wore red everywhere she could, from her turbaned head to her twenty glistening nails.

Why land sakes alive! she shouted when she saw the Johnsons. If it ain't the closest thing we got to movie stars here in Wills County, and a sky *full* of em at that. Parmalee, I done heard yo man up and bought him a automobile!

That's right, said Parmalee, nodding and beaming at everyone around her. It's a Model T Ford and we done drove ovah here in it tonight.

Naw!

We did. We sho did. Go and have a look fo yo'self. It's parked right outside.

I'll look alright, soon's I take all a y'all's money. Rita Marie swung herself left and right as she laughed, then held out her hand to Richard. Come on now, Mister Ford, cross my palm with silvah or you don't get to go through them curtains yonder. She giggled as he paid her. Then she turned her attention to Tom and Mary. And jes looky here who's right behind Mr. Ford! Why if it ain't Mr. Moneybags hisself and Miz Moneybags with him! She jumped to her feet and enveloped Tom in an all-consuming hug, for which he engineered a big smile and much back-patting. You listen to Rita Marie, Tom Johnson. They gonna be showin a movie bout you in this theater fo too long, sho as I'm borned! Now, y'all mark my words! The idea set everyone nearby to shouting and laughing.

Except for her lingering cloud of perfume, they managed to leave Rita Marie eventually and get inside the theater where about seventy-five people were assembled for the showing of The Perils of A Poor Girl. Several people jumped up from their seats and ran over to greet the Johnsons, as others called out their names. Big Jerry Cruickshank cranked himself slowly around in the chair in front of Parmalee to say hello. Mary could see that Tom had lapsed into his smiling public persona. No one would guess how grim he had become at home these last few weeks. The excitement over Richard's car helped dilute the attention, until finally the lights were turned off and the screen flickered to life. In the corner young Shaddrack Smith started a big introductory roll on the piano and Mary felt Tom relax beside her.

For the best part of an hour and a half the spell held. But, just as a train bore down upon the heroine and angels hovered to lead her on to better things, Tom whispered to Mary that he'd meet them at the car, and slipped out of the theatre.

It took them a while to get outside, as it was the custom for people to stand talking after a picture, the way they did after church. By promising everyone rides on Sunday Richard was finally able to lead them out of the theater, and across the dark uneven street. The car, however, was empty.

Where'd Tom go? I thought you said...

I'm right here. He came walking out from between the Wilsons' yard and the Powells' next door. When he left the theatre early to avoid the crowd, Tom had been grateful to find the Wilson porch empty, Frank and Minnie having gone inside to bed. I had to see a man about a dog.

Yeah, Richard said. Bout a little bitty dog, huh?

Tom laughed tunelessly and climbed into the backseat, eager to get inside the sanctuary of his own home again. Richard started the engine and they set out for Slayden's Crossing, trusting to the headlamps for the few feet of vision they could muster against the enveloping night.

CHAPTER FORTY

On a map, Slayden's Crossing looked like a complicated Chinese character sketched off to the east side of the highway to Memphis. A graph of unpaved streets in which houses were outnumbered and dwarfed by shade trees, the town itself was like a cosy, crowded room at the center of a palace, the other rooms of the palace being the wide fields where the inhabitants spent most of their time.

Tom walked the three streets over to his mother's place in the late morning of his last full day in town. He was to leave for Oklahoma at 7:40 the next morning, for what he hoped would be the last time. It was the twentieth of April. The muddy roads were drying up, the air pregnant with the coming summer. As he passed the Boyd's place he slipped off his jacket and, making a hook of one finger, slung it over his shoulder, grateful that most of Slayden's Crossing seemed to be busy in their gardens or seedbeds. The smell of newly turned earth lifted his mood slightly. Surely all that jubilant birdsong was meant for someone else, but Tom eavesdropped anyway, absorbing what he could of the world's pleasures.

A stray alley cat was worrying a chicken head on the back doorstep of Clara's small, tarpaper house. The head still in its mouth, it backed away, flattened its ears and growled as Tom approached. Don't worry, pusscat, he said. I ain't after what you got.

Clara was up on a kitchen chair and turned as gracefully as an ornament on a rich woman's music box when he came in. She didn't smile with her mouth, but radiated satisfaction at seeing him.

They you is. I hope you's all set fo a big feed, cause I got ya one ready to go.

He could smell the green beans simmering in bacon grease and salt water on the back burner. Saw the jar of pickled beets. Knew well that biscuit dough waited under the cloth that draped the old striped crock. Still he said, A cup a coffee's all I want, Mama.

Suddenly stern, she turned back to her shelf. Well that ain't all you gonna get, son.

Mama, I don't eat like I used to. I...

A small, shapely woman, Clara wore her hair in shining coils on top of her head. It was still black, despite her years, and had always been silky straight. Now she stepped down from the chair with a skillet and two saucepans. Ain't no use a you tellin me what you want, Tom. You oughta know that. I aim to fix you a decent meal and that's all they is to it.

Tom sat down at the table beside the open window and sighed. That his mother was getting smaller in stature was undeniable, but in force of character, she was as commanding as ever. Mama, Mary done fix me a great big breakfast not three hours ago.

Mary is a fine woman, and a tolerable cook; I ain't sayin nothin bout Mary. But if you a mind to talk about her let me ask you this. Don't you think that if Benjamen was fixin to go off to some big ol battle away out west to where he couldn't trust a soul and had to watch evah bite he put into his mouth... why, don't you think Mary would want to cook him a good big meal fo he left? Huh? Don't you magine that fixin him a big meal and watchin him eat it would ease her pain ovah lettin him go?

Tom smiled and shook his head, defeated. She clattered the pans down onto the stove lid and set to work. In her hand was the knife his father had made, with its corncob handle. He hooked a foot under the chair she'd climbed up on and drew it back to the table out of her way. As his mother expertly chopped the chicken into pieces for frying, Tom drew out his pocket knife and reached around her for one of the pots on the stove.

Put that back. What you doin?

Nothin, Mama. I jes noticed this handle's worked itself loose is all.

Oh. That's alright then. Thought for a second there you'd taken a notion to peel them potatoes.

He tightened the handle and slid the pan back onto the stove. Now woman, don't you try that stuff on me.

You better watch yo mouth talkin to me thataway, son. Jes what stuff you be referrin to? She rolled the pieces of chicken in a plate of flour as she spoke.

Tryin get me to do yo work fo ya. You spectin me to cook them potatoes fo you, wasn't ya? Why shoot. You set me down here and tell me you don't care what I want, that you bound and determined to fix me a big old feed of fried chicken, and then you try and get me to do all the work!

Wasn't doin no such of a thing, she said, suppressed laughter pushing a stronger melody into her words. I's tryin to tell you them's new pota...

You think I's borned yesterday, now ain't that right, Miss Clara Ann?

She laid the pieces into the skillet as she spoke, and turned the potatoes on low. I happen to know jes zactly when you's borned, Tom Johnson. Fact I know a sight mo bout the day you come into this world than you know y'self.

Oh you think so, do you? You know more bout me than I do myself?

That's right, and you better watch that disrespectful way you's talkin or I'll have to turn you acrost my knee and teach you yo manners all ovah again. That's one right a mother don't nevah lose, no matter how big her babies gets.

Their voices had gotten progressively louder with the teasing, and now the chicken was starting to spit and hiss in the skillet, forcing them to speak even louder in competition.

Hey! Easy now. I ain't lookin fo no trouble here, woman.

You been lookin fo trouble right from the git-go, Tom Johnson. You commenced lookin fo trouble in the middle of the hottest night of a mighty hot summer fifty-seb'm years ago. I labored to give you birth fo nigh onto twenty-fo hours. She turned down the flame, covered the skillet with a large plate and turned around, spatula in hand, entering her story as if she had never told it before. We had us a little place out back of Obion Creek, way out past Heaven's Gate, workin for old man Tobias Pryor. It was our first home together, me and Vess, and it wasn't worth a hill of beans but we's as happy in it as if it was a palace. Havin you was as hard a job of work as I evah put in befo or since. The window frame was chock full a stars when it started and it was chock full a stars all ovah again by the time my mama finally laid you in my arms.

Clara was gazing over Tom's shoulder with a tender rapture most who knew her would have been amazed to see. Suddenly a sound at the window startled Tom halfway out of his chair and he rose to look outside. A small band of neighborhood boys ran through his mother's side yard. One shouted, This way! The smallest, tripping over his long pant legs, glanced back at the window wide-eyed with purpose, before getting his bearings. As the others had before him, he went veering around the outhouse and out of sight. The honeysuckle vine, livid with new leaves, swung a little where the boy had brushed it.

Them boys trample my garden all up? Busy with the chicken, she hadn't even looked out.

Tom shook his head. Naw. But I wonder if they wasn't listenin in on us. He leaned to see what was under the window that might have drawn their interest, but it was just an empty grass plot, bald in places. You ever had that happen befo, Mama—boys listenin in at yo windows? he asked as he sat back down.

Naw, not as I knows of, but you know what boys is like. They was prob'ly after that ol cat's been hangin around here. Unconcerned, Clara began shaping out biscuits, leaving him to stare at the plate of flour on the table, the bright red drops of blood at its rim already darkening.

*   *   *

Tom left his mother's house that afternoon with a heavy stomach and an even heavier spirit. The boys under her kitchen window were probably just playing, he told himself, and felt foolish even giving it that much thought. Yet the uneasiness lingered. The hum of the telephone wires seemed to vibrate inside his bones as he walked along the path at the side of the road.

It had taken him quite a while to convince his mother not to bother coming to see him off in the morning. He was weary of these dramas at the depot. When I get the money, why then y'all can all come and carry on ovah me. But til then I'd jes as soon come and go by myself. You can un'erstand that, can't you, Mama?

She looked up at him and back down quickly. If at's the way you want it, Tom. I ain't one to press myself on people.

Aw, now Mama...

But they's two things you better hear me out on. You write me while you's out there. I need to know from *you* what's goin on. I don't preciate hearin about you from other folks. And, like I done tol you befo, watch out fo yo'self out yonder. Don't trust nobody! Money is the root a all evil, like it says in the Good Book. Some people'd do anything fo a million dollars an...

I know it, Mama. He'd given her a long hug then and promised to do as she said. He called goodbye to her over the incoming whistle of the 3:45, which was taking on Slayden's Crossing's handful of passengers by the time he rounded the corner. He glanced idly along its length, not particularly anxious to talk to anybody. He didn't recognize any of the people the conductor and porters hurried up the steps, though he did look again at one white couple. The man, who had his hand on the woman's back as she mounted the steps in front of him, reminded him of Cooper, the oil and gas man from Mississippi. But Cooper had said he was a confirmed bachelor. Of course he had also said something about going through Slayden's Crossing on the train.

The resemblance was striking enough that Tom tried to see where the couple had seated themselves inside the car. He spotted the man settling down at a window and moved a little nearer. Suddenly it became clear that the man saw him as well. Just as the whistle blew again and the train began to churn slowly forward, he saw that the man had turned his face away and held up a newspaper. Recognition raised Tom's temperature. It was Cooper; he could almost swear it. But if so, why hadn't he waved? He knew the man had seen him, but instead of acknowledging him, he had tried to cover his face. Tom hurried closer, just catching sight of the long-fingered hand on the newspaper as the train rolled away.

Staring at the caboose, Tom felt foolish; he might've been wrong. He walked along the now empty track trying to remember the interview. It had been a few months ago now, right after he'd had his teeth out. Tom had hardly been at his sharpest that day. Still he remembered a lot about their meeting, especially Cooper's warning about his lawyers. The man had said he always passed through Slayden's Crossing on his trips to and from Oklahoma, and it would make sense. He'd be going back to Oklahoma for the April twenty-third court date, same as Tom and Judge Wingate would be in the morning. But why would he hide from him? Unless he was up to something....

Tom walked on toward his house through the lengthening shadows, head down, hands in his jacket pockets except to reach up to his hat in the intermittent breezes. What if Cooper had been in Slayden's Crossing spying on him? Maybe he had set those boys up to following him around and listening at windows. If so they'd done real damn good if they heard his mother talking about giving birth to him. But, surely that couldn't have been what they were doing. He was just letting his imagination run away with him. He glanced around to see whether anybody was paying any particular attention to him. No one was. He shook his head. He needed to watch himself or people would start to get the idea he was crazy. All those threats out there had him jumpy. For God's sake—reduced to chasing trains like a dog and scaring people into hiding behind their newspapers. He straightened his posture and cleared his throat. He even began to whistle half-heartedly, in an effort to improve his mood.

In mid-stride he stopped. Wait a minute, he thought. Oklahoma is to the southwest of Kentucky. Mississippi is dead south. Why would a man going from Mississippi to Oklahoma come as far north as Kentucky? If that was Cooper on the train—and Tom felt more and more sure that it had been—he was up to no good. He was well off his route. He walked on, but at a slower pace. His collar, one of the new-fangled ones sewn directly onto the shirt, suddenly felt too tight around his throat and he tugged at it, wishing he could take it off altogether, like the old style collars.

When he reached the little road his own house was on, Tom hesitated. He had some time before Mary would be expecting him. A couple of hours at least. He had visited his mother; perhaps he should pay his father a visit as well. Walking past his and Mary's turn, he ambled on up the highway to the edge of town where the fields began, all the way to where Heaven's Gate Cemetery crowned the hill overlooking Slayden's Crossing. The steep, rutted path into it stopped just at the crest where the graves began. Tom worked his way among the fenced plots of white people at the front and on to the last row of graves, just before a sheer drop down to Obion Creek. He surveyed the geography. The creek was slowly eroding the hill. Eventually, he reflected, this graveyard will be worn away, one row at a time, the bones of the dead sliding down into the creek all in a jumble with the headstones. His father was buried in the last row.

Sylvester Johnson

1850–1917

R.I.P.

Further along the row were the older graves of his sisters, Nannie and Etta, their inscriptions nearly illegible with moss and lichen. No one would know, to look at Nannie's, that she'd been murdered. Even if they had been an avenging family, every word cost money. Who could afford to remember their wrongs in stone? They were lucky to have headstones at all; many didn't, or had only homemade ones of concrete which cracked and split with the first hard winter, shattering the hand lettered inscriptions.

For the first time, he wondered about Joe Elliott's tombstone. Did he have one? And if so, did it proclaim his murder?

He put his jacket back on, sat down on a neighboring headstone and lit his pipe. The many trees in Heaven's Gate made it as private a place as a person could wish for, and Tom fervently wished for privacy. A light wind told secrets among the young leaves, while the fallen leaves of other years drifted across the ground, shoots of green grass growing up between them. Squirrels ran about. Tom watched them dig furiously for some half-remembered treasure, freeze at the slightest noise, listen intently, then flee into hiding.

He lit his pipe, took a deep draw on it, and studied his father's headstone. Vess had been sixty-seven years old when he died, only ten years older than he himself was now. Hmmm. The gap was closing. His father had been a gentle, self-effacing man, something like Ben. Tom had sometimes been secretly ashamed of his gentle ways, wishing he'd been stronger, more manly. It had always been Clara who laid down the law, and Clara who enforced it. She was the decisive, intimidating figure in the family, not his father.

Tom blew out a cornucopia of sweet-scented smoke and wondered what he and his father would think of each other if they were to meet now. Vess had died believing Tom would rot in Leavenworth Prison. They had never written letters to one another, but had only sent oblique 'regards' through Clara. What would his father have made of his life after Leavenworth? He'd have been proud of my plastering work, Tom thought. But what about this oil business, everybody making a big deal over him and his twenty million dollars? What would Vess do now in Tom's place? After trying to imagine it for a moment, he laughed at the thought and said aloud, Hell. You'd a never got y'self mixed up with this bunch of criminals in the first place, would ya, old man? That's my trouble. I keep lookin to good people to help me out of this mess. He laughed again and shook his head. That's a thought. Mebbe I ought to ask the devil hisself fo advice. Heh... yeah. That's what I oughta do, seek out the devil fo advice. Trouble is, only devils I know of is all in this thing with me.

The sun dropped so low that the long shadows blended and the light took on the quality of pond water. Slightly chilled, Tom rose and shook himself and made his way out of Heaven's Gate without a backward glance at his father's grave. He froze on the tilted path like a squirrel at the sound of an approaching car, and stepped behind a tree until it passed. Its red tail-lights peered like Satan's eyes through the dust it raised. He knocked his pipe out and put it back in his pocket, then absently ran his left thumb and forefinger outwards under his mustache.

Suddenly he was gripped by a new idea. Why not simply run away? What if he were just to go on down the highway all the way to Memphis? He could take on a new identity. Disappear. That image he had drawn for Mose of himself in a Stutz Bearcat, throwing gold and diamonds to the people of Wills County—he knew that wasn't likely, not without the Wingate brothers in the front seat driving him where they wanted to go and running the whole show. Their slit-eyed smiles would always be part of the picture. Not to mention Sax with his outstretched hand and big grin. And there would always be more Saxes and more Wingates. Nothing was free, and the bigger the prize, the bigger the price. No, he could never escape. They'd hunt him down no matter what it took. They needed him. They actually wanted the money more than he did. Everybody seemed to want the money more than he did.

Except Mary.

He hung his head at the thought of her. How could he ever think of leaving Mary to face the shame of it if he ran off? She was used to dealing with him being away. She had even had to face telling them all he'd been imprisoned for murder. Had had to make a new start and raise Ben under that cloud of shame. No, he couldn't run away and leave her now, no matter how much he wanted to escape.

Had anybody been looking, even in the dusky half-light, they would have seen his outline slacken, his shoulders droop, as he stepped onto the road and turned in the direction of home.

CHAPTER FORTY-ONE

Mary stood waiting with him as the train ground to its brief stop in Slayden's Crossing. He hadn't been able to ask *her* not to come; but they had done their kissing, their true parting, at home. You all right for money? he asked from inside the noise and steam of the huge engine that hissed beside them. She nodded.

I'll be callin you on the telephone. They smiled at each other.

Write when you can, too, she said. I like having yo letters.

I will, baby.

He gave her a quick, one-armed hug, kissing her on the head, then he nodded to the conductor, and climbed aboard. At the window he saw she was standing there like she always did, waiting to wave him out of sight, a small, shy woman in a white dress and sweater. She was biting her lips. Her vulnerability hit him like a fist as the train pulled away and left her behind.

When they changed trains at Memphis, Tom walked over to the big map of the tracks nailed above the wainscotting. The railroad looked like a stitched wound that branched all over the body of the country. The part of the scar that absorbed Tom ran east from Muskogee, through Arkansas and into Memphis. He ran his finger across it. From here anyone going to Mississippi—anywhere in Mississippi—would take the Natchez line south. Anyone going to Kentucky would turn north and take the Illinois Central. It was just as he had thought. A train trip through Slayden's Crossing would be considerably out of the way for Mr. Wellington Lyman Cooper.

Just then the floor creaked behind him and he turned to see Judge Wingate stretch his long, rubbery mouth into a smile. So, Tommie! I see you're becoming a student of the railroad. And after all our trips back and forth on the train I guess that's only natural. Or are you planning another trip?

Tom shrugged, eager to change the subject. You enjoyin this un so far?

Oh I wouldn't use the word enjoying. I've been busy. He held up his fat briefcase. Been going over every detail, just to be absolutely sure we haven't missed anything. Can't be too careful at this stage, you know. He lowered his voice and spoke behind his hand, But we'll be okay with Judge Potts. Him and me go way back. He winked.

I'll sho be glad when it's all ovah.

Well I have to say, it's been one of the more interesting cases I've ever worked on. But I'll be going back to the bench myself after this one. I may even look to new climes, as they say. Change of scene.

You mean you'd leave Greenberry?

Not for good I wouldn't. Family and all. You know how that goes. But I have my eye on something... cain't divulge just what yet. But something exotic, tropical. Why not? Feel like I've earned it after all I've done. I mean, think about it, I never had the kind of youthful adventures you did, Tommie, goin out to Indian Territory and all that. Hell, while you were off consortin with the savages and God knows what all, I was holed up in the Greenberry courthouse punishing petty thieves! We're about the same age, you know, you and me. But, you don't want to hear about my little life. I, on the other hand, have always thought I'd like to hear more about those early years of yours. I bet you were something else in your day, huh? Bet you could tell a...

The rest of the judge's sentence was swallowed up by a passing conductor bawling for all passengers to Little Rock and parts west to board the train on track number two. Between the noise of the crowd and that of the wheezing engine, only minimal conversation was possible before Tom and Wingate parted, each making his separate way to his section of the long train. Tom was just as happy.

But as they curved through the Ozarks he couldn't help thinking about the judge's strange remarks at the Memphis depot. He had gotten used to Wingate's transparent efforts to pretend they were on close, friendly terms. His patronizing inferences about Tom's life were always annoying; but this time the judge's attitude felt different in some way that Tom couldn't quite put his finger on. More final...was that it? And what was all that about his plans for moving to a tropical country? It could've been more empty chatter to lure him into some conversational trap; but it could also have meant the judge saw himself at some sort of crossroads... on the threshold of a new life. Just how was the The United States of America vs Tommie Johnson involved in the judge's personal plans? Were these simply the ramblings of a man who thought he was about to become very rich? Or was there something more?

* * *

At the Muskogee Grand Tom was given the same room he'd had the last time, on the 9th floor with a view of the neighborhood at the rear of the hotel. He had just taken off his shoes and stretched out on the bed for a short nap before lunch, when someone knocked at the door.

Who is it? he called, expecting a bellboy with a message from the lawyers.

To his amazement a key turned in the lock and the door opened slowly to reveal a woman in a shiny black dress cut all the way down to there. She was the color of milk chocolate, and as rounded and firm as the upholstered chairs in the lobby downstairs. She had adorned herself with bright red lipstick, long, glittery earrings and a silver scarf wound up into a turban. A shiny spit-curl spooled at the edge of each cheekbone. She stepped inside and closed the door and locked it, slipping the key into a tiny purse that was mostly swinging tassels. Hello there, Mr. Johnson, she said in a voice so deep and sweet it might've issued from a saxophone. Her mouth remained slightly open after she spoke.

Tom sat up, swung his feet to the floor and stood. Who... who are you?

I ain't nothin but a present from a frien a yours. She put her purse on the chair and turned to the mirror where she brought her hands slowly down the sides of her dress.

He sat staring, mesmerized. The woman was a feast for the senses. The smell of hot honey cakes came to him when she drew nearer. As he watched her he was being brought to near pain by the thought of how she would taste, how she would feel under his hands. She drew closer and closer to him. His mouth watered, but there was something else at work inside him.

What brought him out of his reverie was the key with which she had so simply opened his door. The key she had slipped into her purse. She put her hands on his shoulders saying, Wanna unwrap yo present, baby?

Who sent you in here? He barely enunciated the words.

She didn't answer, but, lips slightly parted, brought her face close to his. Tom closed his eyes to steady his head, then shoved as hard as he could. The woman went reeling backwards into the chair on which her purse sat. She stared at him, her bright, glistening mouth open but silent.

Who sent you to my room? he demanded, letting all his aroused passion turn to anger. The purse in her hand, the woman tried for the door, but Tom was faster and got there first. Splayed against her escape he repeated his question. I said, who sent you in here? As he clenched his dentures he became aware of a ridiculous gratitude that he hadn't removed them for his nap.

The woman's eyes darted around, dark and pinched now. If you don't want me I...

Oh I want you alright, Tom said, but that ain't the way this thing's gonna go. Naw. You gonna tell me who sent you, or you ain't gettin out of this room.

She stared at him, one eyebrow raised, lips trembling.

Okay. Look like it's gonna take awhile. That's alright with me. I got all the time in the world. But while you's waitin to tell me what I wanna know, you better do me one other little favor. Take that key out of yo pocketbook and throw it on the bed.

Her mouth pouted into a crooked line of pure hatred, but she opened the purse and threw the key, bouncing it off the window as hard as she could. By chance it didn't break the glass. It only ricocheted to the floor.

You are lucky you didn't break that glass, gal. Now all you got to do is tell me the name of the man that sent you up here, and you free to go.

Don't know his name.

What color is he?

Don't know.

How the hell could you...

It was all arranged through the telephone.

Then how'd you get that key?

It was in a envelope at the desk with my name on it.

That envelope in yo pocketbook?

She shook her head no.

Hand it to me.

She paused, then threw the purse into Tom's face so quickly he didn't catch it. The tassels stung his cheek lightly, but he didn't move from the door. He struggled to resist the urge to smack her.

Gal, you are playin with fire. That's two. Now. They better not be a three. If you don't want me to rearrange yo pretty face, you better do like I tell you and stop foolin aroun. Pick up that pocketbook and open it so's I can see what's inside it.

With erratic motions she plunged for the purse, opened the clasp and held it in front of Tom.

Wider.

She obliged. Except for a lipstick and handkerchief, it was empty.

A envelope with yo name on it you say. And jes what is yo name?

She lifted her chin. Cleopatra.

Tom smirked. After a moment he put the key in the lock, stepped aside and opened the door. Aw get on outta here. And don't come back, you hear me, cause I already owe ya for two, and I always pays my debts.

She bolted for the door, muttering Bastard! over her shoulder as she pushed the elevator button.

Now, now. I wouldn't start no name callin if I's you, he said as she disappeared into the wall.

Laughing despite himself, Tom relocked the door and leaned against it, shaking his head. When he had collected himself he took the key out of the lock and held it up. You are gonna remind me evah time I touch you, not to trust a livin soul out here. He slipped the key into his pocket and lay back down on the bed. After a moment, however, he opened his eyes and sat back up. Stepping into his shoes with a cursory glance in the mirror, he went down to the lobby, careful to take both keys, and to lock his door behind him.

In the lobby Cleopatra was nowhere to be seen. Two bellboys were flipping a coin and laughing near the door to the Western Arms, and a plain, middle-aged white woman sat reading a newspaper. The desk clerk was a bearded man whose honey colored eyes matched his hair. He watched without expression, as Tom moved around the lobby checking each trashcan and cuspidor.

Excuse me, Mr. Johnson, may I help you?

Tom walked over to the desk. You can hand me up yo trashcan.

May I ask what for?

You may not.

They engaged in a short staring battle which Tom won. The young man reached down, frowning, and placed a small wire mesh trash receptacle on the counter. Tom sifted through the twisted papers for a moment before he found what he wanted. A small envelope, torn jaggedly at one edge, with 'Cleopatra' scrawled across it in pencil. He didn't recognize the writing, but at least it was a clue. If only he could take fingerprints like good old McLeod Junior back at Leavenworth. He turned without a thank you and walked slowly away, studying the envelope. With a furtive glance at the clerk in the mirror beside the elevator, Tom saw him spit into the trashcan as he lifted it back down.

CHAPTER FORTY-TWO

Emmett Lewis piloted the 1923 Ford along the road to Memphis, grateful for the noise cover it provided. From the backseat Mr. Wingate surely wouldn't notice the way his stomach growled. They'd made several stops out in the county and were running late. To compound matters, it was pork chop night, his favorite. That Rachel gal might get on his nerves, but she was a fine cook; he had to give her that much.

She's trouble, he often complained to his wife. Won't come to no good, you mark my words. Keeps that room off the kitchen as good as the rest of the house. 'I jes be in my room if you need me.' Gettin herself up in Miz Wingate's ol clothes like she's borned to em.

Turn down here, Wingate suddenly barked.

Yes suh. Emmett straightened up behind the wheel.

Not here, for God's sake! I meant back there.

Yes suh. I-I's jes turnin round to go back. The road come up too sudden fo me. I...

Alright, alright. I want to have a look at the Johnson place, as long as we're out here. Go by it slowly and then turn around and come back past it again.

Yes suh, Emmett said aloud, but thought to himself, Hard to do anything else when the road don't go no place.

The sunset, which had spread itself so glamorously over the open fields a few moments before, was now a low fire in the woods beyond. A few chickens wandered around. The Johnsons lived in the third house, the largest and best kept of the handful lined up beside the tracks. While the others seemed to grow right out of the trees as shapelessly as evening shadows, the Johnson place was all straight lines and smartly fenced off with short palings. There was even a low gate flanked by brick pillars, each of which sported a small hand-shaped concrete lion.

Wingate, on the far side of the car, hunched down and peered at the property as they passed. No lights on, no sign of life about. The dirt road ended at a field that had been planted in tobacco. As Emmett spun the wheel and craned his head to execute a three point turn, a hound sprang out from beside the last house and set up a defensive racket. It waited to charge until they started moving again, but trailed off half-heartedly when they failed to build up any speed.

Pull over and let me get a closer look, Wingate ordered over the barking. As the banker silently pored over the details of the property, Emmett saw Mary Johnson walk around the corner. He could tell when she missed a beat in her gait that she noticed the car right away. Emmett nodded weakly in greeting, embarrassed to be caught spying. She did not return his nod.

Uh, Mr. Wingate, yonder come Miz Johnson. You want me go on now?

Hmmm. Tommie's wife, eh? No, just wait. I may as well have a look at her, too, while I'm at it.

Emmett shifted in his seat as she got closer. She was wearing a pale yellow dress and summer heels. He couldn't help but notice she had very shapely ankles. He pulled at his collar and scratched his neck. She made no eye contact, but frowned self-consciously down at the path. Emmett suddenly realized the car was in her way. I...I better reverse a little so she can get up to her gate. We's kindly blockin her way. Grateful for an excuse to look away from Mary, he flung his arm over the seat and backed the car up. As he did so he observed from the corner of his eye Wingate's open stare of appraisal. You better git on out of the way now, dog. I ain't aimin to run you down. Come on now... that's it. Good dog.

Stop! That's far enough, Emmett. You don't need to back up any further. She's inside the gate now.

Uh, sorry, Mr. Wingate. Sorry, suh.

She was up on the porch now, collecting her mail. With a minimum of motion, she got herself through the door, never looking back at them.

You ready now, Mr. Wingate?

I suppose I've seen all I can. Yes let's go on back. Rachel'll have supper ready. Actually, wait just a minute.

Emmett put the car back in neutral and sat frozen in place while Wingate peered at the house. Eventually, through the sheer curtains he saw the glow of an oil lamp flare into life.

Hm. Alright. Go on. Let's get on home.

As they drove back through the May evening, Emmett threw off his vague sense of shame at the encounter by thinking about the supper to come. Wingate, too, was quiet for a little while. Then, halfway to Greenberry, he said, What's Johnson's wife like? What sort of a person is she?

Don't know her, Mr. Wingate. He smiled nervously as he spoke.

Oh come on now, Emmett. You must know her. You knew who she was quick enough. Besides, I thought you people all knew each other.

Emmett paused uncertainly. N-naw suh, I ain't never met her—jes knows her to see. Mebbe you's fo'gettin, I-I's borned and raised over in Illinois.

Oh yes, I had forgotten that. So all these colored Lewises around here are no kin to you?

Naw suh, that's right.

But still, you've been living here for years. You must've run into her somewhere in your travels.

Naw suh, jes never have. You'd think I would've, sho nuff. I knows her to see, but that's all. Jes... jes knows her to see. In the rearview mirror he saw Wingate turn to look out the window, his mouth set in an expression of dissatisfaction Emmett was familiar with. She look like a nice person.

Look, you see what you can find out about her, Emmett. Ask your wife. Or ask Rachel. Of course, Rachel. She's from out here, isn't she? Never mind. I'll ask her myself.

The high black iron fence in front of Wincoyne had two gates, one at each end of its curved driveway. On each side of the gates were pillars topped with marble pineapples, symbols of welcome. Those had been Maddie's idea. As they turned in through the first entrance, Wingate noticed a young black man walking casually across the side lawn with his hands in his pockets, as if he were just leaving after paying a friendly call.

Who the hell is that? And don't tell me you don't know him either.

Look like Reggie Cruickshank, but it's hard to tell fo sho in this light.

Turn the headlamps on him then. Hurry up. Wingate lurched forward and hunched over Emmett's shoulder as he spoke.

Emmett swung the car sideways in the driveway and the man, thinking he was about to be run over, dove full length into a flowerbed. Wingate got out of the car as quickly as he could, but the intruder had gotten to his feet and fled through the gates, disappearing between two houses across the street.

Goddammit! said Wingate. I'm calling the police!

Emmett, one leg still inside the car, stood with his mouth open as Wingate marched toward the porte cochère muttering about niggers in his flowerbeds. At the door he turned and shouted, Don't stand there gawking! Put the car in the garage. And lock the gates. Both of them!

By the time Emmett got inside, Wingate had his wife and Rachel in the kitchen for questioning. The elusive pork chop dinner scented the air and Emmett's stomach growled quite distinctly as he entered the room. Mrs. Wingate stood gripping the back of a chair, her face pale. Rachel was beside the stove, looking down at the pot holder in her hand. She shook her head as Mr. Wingate fired questions at her.

Well, if he wasn't some boyfriend sniffin around here lookin to court you, and he wasn't a workman, and he wasn't tryin to sell us something or lookin for some other kind of handout, then he's a plain criminal up to no good as far as I can see. Why else would he have run from us like that?

Wingate was still in a state of cold rage when they heard a siren turn the corner and cut off abruptly. They waited, but no knock at the door followed.

Suddenly Emmett began turning his hat in his hands. Oh Lawdy, I done locked them gates. They cain't get in. He looked at his boss like a frightened child.

Well then, go *un*lock the gate, dammit!

Emmett turned and fumbled at the door, getting back outside as quickly as his frayed nerves would allow.

Maddie had been standing still as a statue. I'll... I'll go put a light on in the front room, Ted. Is that where you'll want to talk to them?

Yes, said Wingate to his wife, though he was still staring at Rachel, whom he suspected of knowing more than she was willing to admit. As soon as the two of them were alone in the kitchen, he looked her up and down. She blinked, but kept her eyes down and said nothing.

No boyfriends, you say. Never met Reggie Cruickshank.

Rachel shook her head, and after a moment they heard Emmett lead the policemen into the house through the side door. Heard Mrs. Wingate greet them. Wingate moved toward the door. When he was very close to Rachel, he stopped. She could smell the cigar smoke trapped in his wool suit, the oil he used on his hair. He was a compact man, a little shorter than she was. She held her breath, and kept her eyes on his shoulder as he stared into her face. When he finally spoke again, it was not his clipped tone that surprised her, but his words.

I will talk to you tomorrow, Rachel, right after breakfast. I have some questions to ask you. I hope you'll do a better job of answering them than you have tonight. In the meantime, lengthen your skirts.

*   *   *

Mary had been returning from Pryor's Grocery that evening, where she had paid off her bill and Clara's, as well as that of Aunt Sook, an elderly friend. The sight of the banker's car at her gate had wilted her mood instantly. At first she thought maybe they were bringing news of Tom, but it became clear when they remained inside the car, staring openly, that they were simply out snooping around, as was their habit. Mary had endured their stares with as much dignity as possible. Stepping over her newspaper so as not to have to bend down for it in front of the men, she took her mail from the box, a letter from Tom on top, and went inside, closing the door firmly behind her, though the evening was fresh and fragile. The house was a little dark, but she waited a moment, hoping the car would drive off.

The new telephone was on a table near the door. Tom had called the day he arrived, and it had been strange to hear his voice through the receiver. She was grateful he had also written to her. She preferred letters, perhaps because she could keep them and read them over and over again. One hand on the doorframe, Mary stepped out of her beige pumps and then walked over and lit the lamp on the table at the front window. By its new-kindled light she sat down to read Tom's letter, noting with relief when the car pulled away and drove off. The letter was postmarked the day before yesterday, April 30th.

> Dear Mary, cort started a week ago. Judge Arch an Axley say won't be long an I be roling in it. Hard to make you see the crazy people comeing at me day an nite wanting to cut deals or warn me about another one or saying they finnish me off if I don't quit the clame. I am wached all time case I run for it. Wich I won't on account of

> Write soon. Your lovein husban Tom

Mary refolded the letter and absently outlined the bottom of her lip with one corner of it. Her characteristic frown in place, she sat on in silence as evening filled the room. Rising, she carried the lamp into the bedroom. Tom kept his tools in a bucket on the floor. She squatted down and lifted one of his scrapers. The blue and yellow paint on the handle was nearly worn away. She gripped it for a moment, imagining how it would feel to be wielding it at the top of a scaffold in some fancy building. To know how to fix a ruined ceiling... Mary had always been mystified, and moved, by the mixture of man and boy in Tom. She laid it gently back with the other tools and said a silent prayer for him.

In the kitchen she tied a cherry printed apron over her yellow dress. She had left a bowl of crowder peas on the back of the stove, and there was butter and leftover cornbread. When Tom was away she often ate a cold supper; but she lit the flame under the coffeepot. Moments later, just as she was lifting it to pour herself a cup, a sudden knock at the door caused her to spill a little coffee onto the stove. What if that banker, or his driver, had come back?

She was hesitating at the edge of the circle of lamplight when she heard Ben's voice. Mama? Open up the door; it's me.

A flood of relief told Mary how tense she'd been and she almost ran to the door. Benjamen!

Whoa Mama! You better not hug me. I ain't got changed yet, and you don't wanna get clay all ovah yo clothes. Here's yo paper. I's jes wonderin how you was doin s'all. Cain't stay too long.

Well come in here and have some supper with me. It's jes some leftovers I was gonna eat cold, but fo you I'll even warm it up!

He smiled. Cain't stay that long, Mama, but much obliged. I better get on back to Nema. She didn't know I was comin out here and she'll be spectin me at the usual time. He had stepped inside and was following her into the kitchen. I will take me a cup of that coffee though, if you got it.

Sho do. It's warmin up.

They sat at the table.

You hear anything from Oklahoma?

I jes got through readin a letter from yo daddy. He says they been back at court fo a week now, and the lawyers're sayin it'll all be over with right quick this time.

Um hum. Course they said that last time too.

I know it. You wanna read the letter? Oh *sugar*!—there's the coffee boilin ovah! He laughed at her ladylike epithet. She went to clean up the mess and poured them each a cup, pushing the sugar bowl across the oilcloth. Bet I done scorched it.

It'll be fine. You go ahead and eat, Mama. I don't wanna hold up yo supper.

Why Benjamen, I cain't set here and eat if you ain't havin some. Why don't you have a piece of cornbread... jes to stay yo stomach for the walk home. That ain't gonna spoil yo appetite, you a workin man and all.

Okay... but I'm only doin it so you'll go ahead and eat, you un'erstan.

Mary smiled, so happy to have him all to herself for a visit. She cut him a generous pie-shaped slice and set it on a flowered plate, pushing the butter dish toward him. There now. I'm right glad you come by tonight, Ben. Tell the truth, I's feelin a little bit spooked. That banker, Wingate, he had his driver bring him by here this evenin.

What'd he want?

She shrugged. Don't know. They was settin out there in his car when I come in from the grocery sto. They gimme the creeps—even that driver a his.

Aw, I think Emmett Lewis ain't no harm. He... he's jes a step-n-fetch-it fo Wingate.

Well that don't exactly recommend him to me.

Ben laughed. Y'all got yo mortgage with his bank?

She shook her head no. Savin's and Loan. Mind you, this house done been paid off, but we still owin a little on one of the rentals.

Ben nodded. We'll be awhile with ours, but the payments is kep up with reg'lar.

That's all that mattahs.

This cornbread taste real good.

Don't try to talk while you's eatin it, now. Cornbread'll choke you quicker'n a snake.

Yes'm, Mama. You been tellin me my whole life I's goin to die eatin cornbread, but I notice you keep on feedin it to me. You ain't tryin a get rid of me nor nothin, is ya?

She beamed at him and patted his hand. They's one or two I wouldn't mind gettin rid of, but you sho ain't one of em.

Why Mama! That's the un-Christianest thing I evah heard you say!

She pulled her face straight, like a chastised child. I didn't mean nothin by it. I's jes teasin.

Oh I know you was, and so was I jes teasin. They sat on, chewing the cornbread, neither one needing to say much. When Ben finished he patted her hand. Well, I better get on home to Nema, no kiddin.

Her happiness evaporated in a sigh at his mention of going. He paused at the door. Mama, you sho you okay out here all by yo'self? You could come and stay wi...

No, no, Benjamen, I do fine. Jes fine. Anyhow, I done got used to it, and now I got the telephone case I need anything. He canted his head to one side and smiled tenderly. She knew he felt bad leaving her all alone. Anybody'd think I was a ol woman, the way you carry on. Shoot, if yo gran'mama can live by herself I sho oughta be able to. Sides, yo daddy say he be home soon this time.

If you was a old woman I might not worry so much.

Oh Ben, you always was the sweetest thing. I'm gonna give you a hug, clay or no clay.

He leaned into an a-frame embrace, trying to be careful of her clothes. On the wall behind her his father gave the world a challenging, level stare from inside a picture frame Tom himself had made.

CHAPTER FORTY-THREE

While Mary and Ben sat talking in the kitchen at Slayden's Crossing, Tom was caught up in a storm of unwelcome attention. The hearing had been postponed once again, this time until July, to give Johnson's lawyers time to present positive proof on paper of his identity as Sam Ford. The crowd had closed in on him as soon as Judge Potts left the courtroom. One reporter jumped the low balustrade and grabbed at his arm, even as Wingate hauled him up from his chair in an effort to get him around the table.

He could hear many voices at once, braided as if into a whip:

Come on, Tommie, we better move!

What kind of proof are you going to produce for the next round?

Mr. Johnson! Mr. Johnson! What're you planning to do with the money?

It ain't over yet, Johnson!

Cheatin thief!

Over here, Mr. Johnson...

This way, Tommie.

For God's sake, where's Sax?

Tom saw Cooper trying to catch his eye. The Bennett brothers had stood up from their customary seats, and were staring daggers at him. Ward, the prosecutor, was pushing his way through the crowd with a sober expression, followed by his two assistants.

Though it seemed interminable, it couldn't have been more than five minutes before, with the help of a court official, they finally made it into the hallway behind the judge's bench. Sax was still in the crowd, and this concerned Axley.

No tellin what he'll say if some reporter gets ahold of him.

I'm more worried about how the hell we're supposed to get out of here, said Wingate, looking down the hallway to the back door. They'll be coming around that way next. Axley tried the knob of the door nearest them. It opened onto the antechamber they had used during court recesses. Better get in here til they get bored and give up.

When the judge pushed at him from behind, Tom stopped like a wall and looked around at him coldly. I'm just trying to hurry us along, said Wingate, clearly exasperated. Look Tommie, I don't think you want anymore crowd scenes just now, do you? If we stand out here much longer somebody's going to see us through the window of that back door.

Come on in here, Tommie. Judge Arch is right. Hell, even Earl Bennett was showing signs of life near the end there. We better hole up. After awhile I'll scout out all the exits and we'll see about getting back to the hotel. For now we don't have much of a choice.

Wingate followed Tom into the room, but when he started toward a window both lawyers reacted. Stay back! called Wingate over Axley's, I wouldn't go near a window just now, in case they're watching to see where we went. Wingate removed his jacket, and pulled his collar and tie loose. As he sat down he looked over at Tom and pushed his outspread hands towards the floor a couple of times. Just sit down and wait it out a little while.

Tom leaned against the wall beside the door, unwilling to do exactly as Wingate directed. The two lawyers sat at the table in equal attitudes of weariness and self-congratulation.

Well, well well. Looks like we're nearly there, said Wingate, raring back to stretch out his long legs.

Axley exhaled a short laugh, then sighed. All that mob excitement must mean something alright. I'd say the others can feel it slipping right through their fingers. Must be awful.

Wingate smiled with satisfaction, then raised his eyebrows. Course it doesn't pay to get too cocky just yet. We still got some work to do... but not much. Not much at all. The smile became a grin.

No, by God. Now I know you all'll want to be getting out of here as fast as you can, but...

Yes, we'll go back to dear old Kentucky day after tomorrow, soon as you and I have gone over everything with a fine-toothed comb. You hear that, Tommie? Day after tomorrow we're back home. For nearly two months. Tom made no answer.

Yes, and we shouldn't have to leave the hotel at all tomorrow. I'll pay that scoundrel behind the desk, and one of the bellboys...

George. Be sure it's George. He's the best of em.

I agree. I'll pay George to keep a look-out for us, and we should be able to work in peace, undisturbed by the rabble. You know, Judge Arch, I must say, your connection with Potts has proved invaluable. I gotta hand it to you there.

Wingate compressed his lips and nodded slowly. Yeah, I thought he'd come through for us. You can't beat a little...

A sudden urgent knocking at the door caused them all to jump. Who is it? Axley and Wingate called in unison.

Open up, it's me! answered Sax in a strained stage whisper.

Axley jumped up to unlock the door and Sax came in, all out of breath, hat in hand, looking as if he'd just run a race.

Damn it to hell, y'all done lef me to the wolves out yonder!

Hell, boy, what do you think we could do about it? Wingate replied. We barely saved ourselves!

Where you been? It was the first thing Tom had said since he had been on the witness stand that afternoon.

Well first them damn Bennetts and their lawyer come at me—and they wasn't actin none too friendly. Then once I excaped from them I had me a couple of reporters on my tail fo a little while. But I got away through the backstairs and hid out in the janitor's closet til the place cleared out some.

Good for you, Sax, said Axley. You say anything to any of em?

Jes told them Bennetts they's jealous cause the prop'ty was goin back to its rightful owner. He winked in Tom's direction and laughed.

Wingate pulled the corners of his mouth down as if pleasantly surprised with Sax's performance. That's not bad, Sax. Not bad at all. What about the reporters? You speak to any of them?

Ya'll didn't want me to, did ya? I thought y'all done said...

Oh no, we didn't want you to. I just wondered whether you did. Wingate laughed.

Naw suh! he said, shaking his head broadly. I took off outa there like a calf from a brandin iron. Didn't talk to no reporters.

How'd you find out where we were?

Tip from Judge Potts. He jes leavin when I come back up from the basement.

Tom watched from beside the door, noting how Sax had pulled out a chair and sat down with the white lawyers. Axley was laughing and handing Sax a cigar as a prize for being a good boy. Why thank you, Lawyer Axley, he said, putting his feet up on the table and rolling the cigar under his nose. B'lieve I will.

Happy to be momentarily forgotten by all of them, Tom watched the sky redden over the buildings across the street. He knew when it became dark enough, they would make their way across to the Muskogee Grand, and soon enough he would be back home with Mary.

CHAPTER FORTY-FOUR

Tom spent most of the next day in his hotel room. He slept late since there was no court. He woke from a dream of Mary in bed beside him. As he lay there savoring the dream, he suddenly remembered a moment from his early days in Leavenworth.

Shortly after he got there, he was issued a tablet of paper and a pencil for writing letters. He had written several letters to Mary before he received any from her. Fear that she might never contact him was one of the strongest emotions he'd had to grapple with during that dark period. On the second Sunday of his incarceration—Sunday mornings being one of the few periods in the schedule prisoners were given any time to themselves—he was lying in his bunk preparing to write her another letter, when he was swept by an intense physical longing for her. The idea that he had lost her forever bore down upon him until he thought his heart would break in two.

Seizing the tablet he began to try to draw her naked body. It was a crude sketch, and he tried again on the next page. This time he got closer. Though he only drew the outline of her shape and private parts, every detail was coming back to him—the dimples in the small of her back, the plump and silky insides of her thighs, the aureoles of her nipples, the smooth shell that divided her collarbone, the elegant little column that appeared on her neck when she turned her head. He sat up and was deep in concentration when his cell mate—a man named Hitch—looked down from the top bunk and saw what he was doing. He started to hoot and holler. Tom told him to shut his mouth, and they began pushing at each other.

Guards came running, and Tom was sent to the blind cell for the first time. His tablet was confiscated, and they were slow to return it to him. When he finally got it back—two weeks after he had served his three days in solitary—the drawings had been torn out.

Now, in the luxury of his Oklahoma hotel room, he lay thinking about Mary for a while longer, trying to hold onto the spell of the dream. He was in no particular hurry to join his lawyers downstairs. However, despite his deliberate dawdling he found Wingate and Axley still waiting for him when he went down to breakfast and was immediately sorry he hadn't skipped the meal altogether.

Jes dry toast and black coffee, he told the waiter. Ever since Cooper's warning he had made a point of avoiding coffee completely; but he still ordered it, so the lawyers wouldn't guess he knew, and also to observe their reactions.

They fix eggs here just right, Tommie. Perfect every time, said Wingate.

The waiter hesitated, in case he should change his order. When Tom ordered two hard boiled eggs and looked away, the judge shrugged at the waiter, who returned his shrug and left for the kitchen.

What do you think of the coffee here, Tommy? Axley asked artfully.

Tom just shrugged, never touching his full cup.

The only other person still in the dining room was a middle aged white woman in a grey suit and hat, who seemed to be completely absorbed in the newspaper. When they left the room twenty minutes later she was still there.

She look familiar to you? Axley asked Wingate as they entered the lobby. It was a Friday and many people seemed to be checking in or out. There were line-ups at the desk.

That lady in the dining room? Maybe, answered Wingate. But then, women like her are a dime a dozen. You could line ten of em up in a row and have a hard time tellin em apart.

Axley laughed. Excuse *me*, he said, making his way around an Indian who stood at the end of the longest line and who did not move back to let them through. He was dressed in a suit, his braids descending from under a derby hat. Axley shook his head after they had squeezed past him. We know all about his kind in Tulsa, let me tell you.

Would you like him any better in feathers? Tom asked.

After a moment Wingate gave a hollow laugh and turned to slap Tom on the back. Seeing that Axley could not even feign amusement, the judge snapped his fingers at one of the bellboys who came hurrying over. It wasn't the one that reminded Tom of himself, the one he had heard the others call Silas. This boy was of the eager, grinning variety, his very eagerness making him seem less competent in Tom's eyes. George, today's your day to watch out for us—remember?

Yes suh, I 'memba.

Good. Now we told the desk that if we ring, you are the boy we want to see. If all goes well, you will receive a handsome tip at the end of the day.

The grin widened. Yes suh. I be the one suh, evah'time.

Oh, and George, stay closer to the desk. Anybody asks for any of us, we want to know who it is before we say whether or not we'll see em. You understand?

I unnah'stan, Mr. Wingate.

You are working for us today, Axley added. Don't let anyone else divert your attention.

Yes suh. Special duty.

The lawyers laughed. Special duty, that's right, said Wingate.

After Wingate and Axley got off on the third floor, the elevator operator handed Tom a note, then turned back to his panel of buttons without a word.

Tom unfolded the note, which was not in an envelope. You will never work that land. You will not see one dollar of that money. Uncomfortably aware of the two other elevator passengers, two black men who didn't seem to be together, Tom nevertheless asked the operator, Who give you this note?

Desk clerk, Mr. Johnson. Tom stared at the three men. The younger passenger seemed embarrassed and looked away. The other spat tobacco juice into the spittoon. Bad news? he said, his voice reedy from some ailment of the throat.

Tom fingered the key in his pocket. Trust nobody. Without answering, he handed the elevator man a nickel and got out on the 9th floor. Once inside his room he locked the door and stuck this warning into the envelope with the others. He washed his hands and face in the basin, then stretched himself to break his tension. What now? Wasn't worth writing any letters when he was so close to going home. He'd already filed his report for the previous month to Rev. Parsons, as he always did and always would, no matter what.

> Sir: I respectfully submit to you my report for the
> month of April 1929
> General conduct and associations during month? Good
> Name of employer? none Business?
> Employer's address
> My duties? none
> Number of days employed during month? none
> Number of days not employed during month? all
> Reason for not being employed? cort case
> Amount of money earned during month? none
> Amount of money received during month? none
> Amount of money expended during month? none
> I have been honest, industrious and temperate and
> have made a true report.
> Signed Tom Johnson

He walked over to the window. A locomotive attached to three cars was pulling slowly onto a sidetrack. He opened the window so he could hear the trains chugging in and out of the station. The crossed rails reminded him of the netting on a hat Mary sometimes wore to church. The parallel tracks shone like the strings on Estlin Krebbs's guitar and him singing The Cottonfield Blues. Two white horses in a row...Tom began humming it to himself as he gazed at the rails. They shot away in either direction as far as he could see. One more day. That's all he had to get through and he'd be free for a while.

If only he didn't have to come back out here in July. He sighed and shook his head, separating the wings of his mustache over and over again, distractedly. Finally he kicked off his shoes and flung himself across the bed, but sleep wouldn't come. He reached for the Bible on the bedside table, but couldn't concentrate enough to read.

The wind lifted his curtain and made it dance like Salome at the foot of the bed. A wind that strong could blow up into something terrible out here. Tom had seen twisters grow out of a boiling green sky that looked like a nest of vipers. Then suddenly one would strike at the ground, and start to move like a sucking mouth on a long, sinewy neck. There was nothing it couldn't suck up—buildings, trees, people. When it spat them out again they'd be all smashed and good for nothing. He sat up on the edge of the bed to look, but the sky was blue all the way to the horizon, bluer than a robin's egg, with white, scudding clouds.

When he didn't go down for lunch, they sent George up to get him.

Tell em I ain't hongry, Tom said through the locked door, though his stomach rumbled. But, George? ...You still there?

Yes suh.

Send me Silas up here.

But... them gen'men say I's the only...

George!

Yes suh?

Jes do like I say. It ain't no need to tell them gentlemen a thing about it. If you do you'll be in trouble with them. Don't do like I say, and you'll be in trouble with me. Send me Silas, and then you go and tell em I ain't comin down fo lunch.

Silence.

George?

Yes suh?

Go on now and do like I tol you to.

Yes suh.

Tom heard the boy scamper down the hall, and a few minutes later there was a knock. Mr. Johnson?

Who is it?

Silas suh.

He got up and unlocked the door. Silas stood in the hallway, unsmiling, businesslike. You call fo me, Mr. Johnson?

Come in here a minute. He pulled the boy inside his room, glanced up and down the hall and then locked the door. He could see by the way Silas cut his eyes that he was uncomfortable, braced. It's okay, Silas. I won't hurt ya. But I need you to do something fo me without nobody knowin you done it, you un'erstand?

Silas nodded slightly.

I don't wanna eat down in the dinin room, but I'm hongry, see? Now, they's a grocery sto aroun the corner—Cane's. You know it? Good. I want you to go aroun there and buy me some slices a ham, a pound's worth. And a bottle of milk and a loaf of bread. You got that?

Yes suh. Ham, milk, bread.

Good. Now listen Silas. Don't tell nobody, not even the man at the sto, who it you buyin it fo. Anybody sees ya, you tell em its fo the ol man on the tenth flo. In fact, *go* to the tenth flo, and then take the stairs back down here to me. Here's a fi' dollah bill and you can keep the change. He opened the door and Silas left, but Tom called him back. He handed the boy two quarters. Here, take this too, and get me a newspaper and a deck a playin cards. Take the stairs, remember, not the elevator. And once you got the food, use the back do. Don't be carryin it in through the lobby.

Silas hadn't moved while he spoke. Yes suh, he said, watching him closely. When he was sure Tom was finished, he nodded solemnly and walked away with an attitude of purpose.

While he awaited the boy's return, Tom stood at the window. None of the action below seemed to matter. The movements of the people, animals, and vehicles were like short sentences from the books of other lives, impossible for him to read. Finally he saw Silas coming down the back street carrying a grocery sack. He smiled, and was just about to leave the window, when someone else approached the hotel from the rear, the sight of whom wiped the smile away and caused Tom to break out in a sweat. He could've sworn it was Sax's friend Solomon. Solomon, the hired gun.

That evening at suppertime Sax knocked at his door and called out. Tom opened the door a little, having carefully concealed all traces of the food. He had even put the cards under his pillow, just in case they should arouse any suspicion. When he cracked the door he could see Sax shifting his weight from foot to foot, but he grew still and smiled when he saw Tom. Hey there! So you *is* still here after all. We jes about decided you up and lef town. Thought maybe you'd jumped a freight train, stead of waitin to use the ticket ol Judge Arch done bought for ya.

If you come to bring me down to supper, I ain't goin.

Tom was about to close the door, but Sax thrust an arm in.

Ho... wait, now. Hol on. Hol on here a minute. Why not? Why you ain't comin down to supper? Wha's a mattah th' you, Tom? He tried to move past him into the room, but Tom blocked him.

I didn't invite you in, Sax.

Aw now, come on, man! What you got gainst me all a sudden?

Nothin—all of a sudden.

Now jes what you mean by that? Sax was straining to see past Tom into the room. He gave a sly grin. I know what it is. Aw, you devil! You done got you a lady frien up here, ain't ya? One of them little Oklahoma street gals I done tried to warn you bout. Hmmm? Z'at it?

Sax, if you don't step back I'm gonna have to slam this door right on yo ugly face.

My ugly face! His grimace of wounded outrage almost set Tom to laughing, but he conquered the urge.

I ain't eatin with y'all. Now go on down and tell yo *friens* what I said.

Sax attempted to change tactics, taking on the role of concerned, solicitous uncle. Tom, you got to eat ya some supper. You cain't jes starve yo'self. They got beefsteak down there like y'ain't nevah tasted in yo life. Ordered it special to celebrate. Tom you jes got to come down. They's waitin on ya.

Tom stood his ground, staring close range at Sax. In the silence a new understanding between them grew. The muscles in Sax's jaw relaxed; his gaze became less intense.

Alright then. If at's way it's gotta be. After a moment, Sax stepped back and walked away. Behind him the door closed and a key turned in the lock.

CHAPTER FORTY-FIVE

Rachel woke the next morning feeling leaden. It took her a moment to remember why. Mr. Wingate wanted to see her right after breakfast, to ask her some questions. To which she had better have the answers. What was this all about? More about Reggie, she supposed. Whatever it was, she dreaded it.

As soon as he finished eating, he called her name. She came into the dining room to find Mrs. Wingate already gone.

Clear these dishes and then come back in here. You can wash them later. I want to talk to you first.

Yes suh. She stacked them and carried them into the kitchen, hoping he couldn't hear the way they clattered against each other with her trembling. She put them onto the draining board more noisily than she'd have wished, then wiped her hands on the cloth beside the sink. For just a moment she stood staring out the window over the dirty dishes, seeing nothing. Then she took a deep breath and walked back into the dining room.

Sit down right there, Rachel. He indicated an extra straight chair against the wall.

She sat, cloaking her legs carefully with her skirt—an old brown wool one too hot for the season, but which she had put on because it was the longest one she had. She angled her knees away from his chair, and sat awkwardly twisting back toward him.

Do you know Tommy Johnson and his wife? When she didn't answer right away, he added, The new 'millionaire'—you know who I mean. You know them?

This was not the line of questioning she had been expecting and it threw her into confusion for a moment. Yes suh, I knows em. She frowned as she spoke.

How do you know them?

They from Slayden's Crossin, same as me. Mary, she go to the same church my folks goes to.

Just Mary?

Mary and her kinfolk.

What about her husband Tommie?

No suh, he don't.

Tommie does not go to church with her?

He goes sometimes, but not all time like her.

I see. And why does he not attend?

I don't know, Mr. Wingate.

Could it be because he is not a believer?

Could be I reckon.

Wingate's mood soured even more as he recalled his exchange with Johnson at the bank. Is this unusual, would you say, among colored men?

Rachel frowned again. I... I don't rightly know, Mr. Wingate. Some goes to meetin, and some don't.

What sort of a man would you say Tommie Johnson is?

Well suh, I don't know him real well. He's always been right nice I reckon. He's a hard worker, and friendly like. Because Wingate sat staring at her in silence, she tried to think of something else to say. Folks say he a good family man.

How many children does he have?

Jes one, far as I knows.

What about his wife?

Suh?

What can you tell me about his wife?

She a good Christian woman. Always real nice to ev'body. Rachel could not think of another word to say. The Johnsons were her parents' age. Ben Johnson had been a few years older than Rachel and she knew him from school, though not well. But whatever the case, she was not about to volunteer any extra information about *any*one to Mr. Wingate.

I'm sure you know that Tommie Johnson killed a man out in Oklahoma and did almost twenty years in Leavenworth for it. Wingate tried to catch her eye as he said this, but she kept her face down, looking at her hands, which were in her lap. Rachel? Answer me.

Not having understood it as a question, she was slightly alarmed. I've heard tell he'd been in jail, but I's jes a youngun then.

So you're saying you did not know he was a murderer?

She shook her head, her eyes now on his highly polished shoes.

You must know that I don't believe you. He gave a little smiling shrug. But that doesn't matter. What did Mary Johnson do while her husband was in prison?

She jes waited fo him, I reckon.

You reckon. Let me be more specific then. How did she support herself and her son? Where did she live?

Rachel now felt Wingate's eyes on her ankles. Sh-she...live with her mother-in-law. Took in piecework and other kinds of sewin.

Well. So I see you do know a few things about her after all. Did she have boyfriends? Did she run with other men while her husband was in prison?

Now thoroughly flustered, Rachel kept her eyes down and shook her head. Naw suh, Mr. Wingate. Not as I know of.

Neither one of them spoke again and Wingate let the silence become extremely uncomfortable before he finally said, Go on then. Get back to your work. Maybe you can make yourself useful in the kitchen. And Rachel... you do not entertain guests—of any kind—on my property. Is that clear?

Yes suh.

When he said no more, she rose and went out to the kitchen, shaking like a sapling in a strong wind.

CHAPTER FORTY-SIX

A ball of butcher paper and an empty milk bottle were all that was left in the wardrobe of Tom's hotel room as he glanced around it to be sure he'd packed everything. George had called through the door that morning to say that Tom was to meet Wingate and the others by the front doors of the lobby at 2:30. They had tickets for the 3 o'clock train. It seemed they'd given up asking him to join them for meals.

At almost every floor, the elevator filled with people he couldn't recall having seen before. One woman wore a hat piled with ribbons and birds and fruit; it was so wide-brimmed she took up two places. He pushed in beside her, holding his suitcase close to his body and looked down into the creation as they descended. You could make a plaster mold of it, he thought absently, but who'd want to?

The cubed potpourri of close bodies and colognes left him light-headed as he detached himself from his elevator companions. The clock over the desk read 2:25. The clerk looked up at him, pointedly Tom thought, as he crossed the lobby. Wingate and Axley stood near the door, wreathed in cigar smoke. They, too, watched him, making little side-mouthed comments to each other as he approached. Then Wingate glanced at George, who abruptly left the room by the back way. The elevator people milled around him, their voices a distant ringing in his ears. Silas was nowhere to be seen.

Well, well, here you are! The judge blew out a little smoke along with his hearty, mock camaraderie. All ready to go then? He handed Tom his train ticket like a father. Tom slid it into his inside pocket. And here's a telegram I received this morning. Thought it might interest you. You can keep it as a reminder.

Tom put down his suitcase to open it and Axley said, Here, there's no need for you to fool with that. I'll send it on ahead with the judge's bag.

By the time he opened his mouth to protest, a porter was already carrying his suitcase away. Days of resisting their control had worn him down; Tom was suddenly overcome with a curious lack of energy.

The telegram was from the *Greenberry Daily Leaf*, telling the judge that they planned to run the story of their return on the front page, and asking for an interview as soon as possible. Tom stuck it in his pocket absent-mindedly. Wingate was instructing Tom not to get off the train in Slayden's Crossing tomorrow, as he usually did, but to take it on to Greenberry, so they could talk to the *Leaf* reporters.

Come on then, boys, said Axley. We may as well get on over to the depot. Look at the time.

Tom looked at the clock over the desk. It was only a few minutes past 2:30. They still had half an hour and the depot wasn't a five minute walk. But the two acted like they were late. Abandoning their cigars to an ashtray, they started forward briskly, glancing back often to be sure Tom was following. The doorman bowed slightly to the white men, the top of his hat shining for an instant like a phonograph record. He gave Tom a level stare from behind the glass.

The early afternoon sun felt like an arm across his shoulders. Passing cars dusted his wingtip shoes as he followed the lawyers on their diagonal march across the street. They moved purposefully along in front of him for a block or so. It had just struck him that they were uncharacteristically silent with one another, when he was blindsided and pulled into a narrow space between two buildings.

Something like a feed sack was thrown over his head. When he tried to thrash out against it he found it impossible to move his arms. The two close brick walls were coming at him bumping his shoulders and elbows, so eventually he became still, only to find that his arms were lashed to his sides, and someone had tied his legs at the ankles. There wasn't a lot of shouting or talking. Just grunting. Heaving breath. His own, and other people's. A few words of encouragement. A few oaths. The strong smell of burlap panicked him with each breath. He heard a voice he didn't recognize say, I got him. I got him. Don't worry.

Honor among thugs.

You quieten down now, Tom, and we'll take off the sack. It was Kenny Prettyboy talking. Tom didn't move and the feed sack was pulled slowly off, taking his hat with it. He gulped air. Sonny Day, reaching to put Tom's hat back on his head, couldn't stop giggling. A big stranger—white—wearing a battered grey stetson, held a gun to his head. Howard Buckman and Kenny had their guns drawn and cocked as well. Tom turned to look around him and they all jumped, dancing in place and talking in low voices to him like he was a wild horse they were trying to break. Hey—easy now. Easy there. Come on.

There were seven or eight of them, all but one of whom he knew. Kenny held the buggy whip tight around him. It felt like it was cutting into his arms with his slightest motion. To his right he could see Wingate and Axley standing on the sidewalk facing the street. They blocked the light at that end. A little way down, near the rear of the buildings, stood Sax. He was taking a glass of water from George, who stared, pop-eyed, at the scene. Sax motioned the boy away with his head, and was approaching Tom now, talking quietly. He held the glass before him like a sacrament. Okay now, Tom, this ain't gonna hurt a bit. We done got you some medicine. Now you jes drink this on down and ev'thing be fine.

Tom started to turn his head away, but felt the gun at his temple. Then Solomon put his gun to the other side of Tom's head, so that he was held in a sort of stanchion.

Sax forced the rim of the glass between his lips and pushed it against his dentures. A little hot water dribbled down Tom's chin. Sax pulled the glass away to guard its precious contents. Look, Tom, you gotta do better'n that, or...

Or I'll jist shoot you where you stand, said the white cowboy. He spoke quietly, the stench of his breath lingering at Tom's nose and mouth.

And so Tom Johnson stood, powerless in the circle of his enemies. Someone forced him down onto his knees, yanked his head back and held it at an angle. He felt Sax push the rim of the glass between his lips again. Saw the silverish slick on top of the water. They wrenched his mouth open. He felt the liquid and spat so hard his dentures flew out. After that Sax poured it down a little at a time as Tom sputtered and coughed.

*   *   *

The train seemed almost to veer out of control as Tom made his way down the aisle. His stomach still felt tender after all that voiding from both ends, but he was just so thirsty. By God, that poison oughta be gone anyhow, he thought. Cain't be much a anything left inside a me. He stopped to get water from the fountain at the end of his passenger car. After six pointed paper cups full he decided to go buy himself an apple from the snack bar at the end of the last colored carriage. He was shaky, but he thought he could make it, as long as his stomach didn't start griping him again. Tom leaned, trembling, on the edge of the counter. The clerk looked longer at him than usual, and Tom wondered if he hadn't cleaned himself up properly.

He put a nickel on the counter. Gimme a apple, he said, looking down at his stained shirtfront, and then away from the man's stare. Feeling too weak to use his pocketknife, Tom pushed through the doors between the cars, raking his gums across the skin of the fruit. He had only managed to take one bite of it by the time he passed the toilet. Several people were gathered in the aisle, complaining to the porter about the state of the washroom. There was a definite stench emanating from it, even with the door closed. Suddenly Tom pushed the people aside and lurched into the toilet, throwing up again. In the commotion, the apple rolled down the aisle. A few minutes later, a young, pregnant mother of four woke from a brief nap to find her three-year-old daughter eating it.

Where'd you git that from, Sulene? Ain't I done tol you don't take food from no strangers?

I foun it, she answered, her mouth full. On de flo.

The mother reached for the apple. Here, gimme that! That's dirty! Sulene began wailing for her lost apple, as the mother tried to arrange for her eldest child to take it to the water fountain and wash it off. But the train was grinding to a stop and the aisles filled with people.

Above all the racket the conductor called, Fort Smith! All off for Fort Smith!

Tom, back in his seat again, tried to focus his eyes on the people who poured past him in two directions. Some were pulling suitcases from over his head. He grabbed the arm of a boy who was stretched over him reaching for baggage.

Where my suitcase?

The boy twisted away. I ain't got your suitcase, you old drunk. Let go a me!

Tom sat half forward in his seat as the train began moving again. An elderly woman across the aisle looked at him closely, and said, God bless you, son, but yo color ain't none too good.

My suitcase, he replied weakly. He settled back and closed his eyes to prevent the dizziness caused by the passing landscape, and fell asleep. He was collecting suitcases from the overhead rack and as they came down they fell open, showering everyone with hundred dollar bills and people were grabbing the money up by the double handfuls. The train had stopped in some brightly lit place short of its intended destination and everyone on the platform outside was waiting for him. He was trying to get to the door. But the money was dry. It was so dry and slippery he couldn't get anywhere. And at the end of the car stood Axley and Wingate. They were talking to each other out of the sides of their mouths, amused at his struggle. And suddenly he knew he had to get off the train.

When he woke up it was dark outside. The old woman across the aisle was gone. They were just pulling away from some station and a series of bright lights came and went like hammers to his aching head. His stomach was cramping, his mouth burned, and he was short of breath, but the strongest sensation he felt was thirst. No one had taken the seat beside him. Unbending his legs with care, he stood up to go to the water fountain, but it took him some time. The train rocked back and forth in a way that alarmed him. He had never known a train to do that.

Scuse me. S-sorry, he said over and over as people pushed him back into the aisle from their seats, some with a curse to help him along. He was scrabbling with a paper cup, drinking as much as he could, when the train started to slow down again.

Lonoke! the conductor cried out. All off for Lonoke!

When the train stopped at the platform, Tom felt the cool evening air through the open doorway, and he moved toward it. I... I gotta get off the train, he mumbled to the other departing passengers. They frowned or smiled pityingly, but no one replied. When the way was clear, he made it to the door. He stumbled on the steps and fell, smearing cinders all over himself and tearing his pants at the knee. But he was well away from the train by the time it started moving again. He watched it haul its kite's tail of lights down the track and out of sight. Heard its plaintive farewell whistle.

The other passengers were disappearing inside the depot, but Tom, sweating profusely, only wanted the cool, wide night. The stars were easier on his eyes than electric lights, though everything hurt him. He wandered down the track, stumbling occasionally and looking away from the bright depot. On the other side of the track was a row of one-story buildings, mostly dark. Only one was lit up, and, unnoticed by Tom, a silhouette materialized in that square of brightness as he staggered past. Then the door opened.

Hey, you! Look over here! Look at me!

Tom, in turning to look, swayed and was firmly caught in the sheriff's grip. You been drinkin, boy?

Naw suh.

Sure sure, course not. Well, we'll see about that, old man. You're comin with me.

The bright lights inside the sheriff's office drove Tom to hide behind his hands.

Good god, Charlie, what the hell you brought us this time? He smells like a latrine!

How many drunk niggers you smelt lately, Joe? This is what they smell like.

I... I ain't been drinkin, said Tom, his voice reedy. The officers smiled and rolled their eyes at each other. I been... been poison. I'm a... m-millionaire. His stomach was cramping again.

Now the officers laughed out loud. I tell you what, Charlie, this may be the best one yet. We better hope he's drunk, cause otherwise he's plum crazy.

They threw Tom into a cell, but he fastened his hands onto the bars and kept calling out to them that his suitcase had been stolen. That he had been poisoned for his money. That he needed help.

When he threw up again they rounded up some clean clothes. Joe went through his pockets. He pulled out a pocket knife and with it came the telegram from the *Greenberry Daily Leaf* to Judge Arch Wingate.

Well, I'll be damned, he said, reading it over. Looka-here at this, Charlie.

CHAPTER FORTY-SEVEN

Judge Wingate stepped from the train with a hearty smile for the little group that had gathered to welcome him back to town. Lexie was there with Archie and David, as was the *Daily Leaf* reporter. But, to his surprise, Paul Sanderson from the Western Union office across the street was also there, and called out to him over everybody else.

Judge Arch! Telegram just came for you, Judge. I think you'll want to read it right away, sir.

What on earth can it be that it can't wait'll I've said hello to my wife?

Sorry Judge, Sanderson said, pushing in front of the crowd and pressing the piece of paper upon him all the same.

The newsman stood with his pencil poised over his notebook, and was immediately rewarded. Wingate's face grew red. What the.... Why, this is ridiculous, he sputtered, looking at Sanderson. He boarded the same train as I did yesterday. We always travel on the same train. I just assumed he was in his section up front there. Now he sometimes gets off back at Slayden's Crossing, but this time he was coming into Greenberry—he knew y'all wanted to interview us. He looked at the reporter, who was writing furiously. Craning his head to where the colored passengers were getting off up the platform at the front of the train, he looked as if he still expected to see Tom among them.

The telegram was from Charles Drake, sheriff of Lonoke County, Arkansas. It said they were holding a Negro named Tom Johnson who claimed he was a millionaire, and who had a telegram in his pocket which had been sent to Judge Arch Wingate of Greenberry, Kentucky. They were awaiting his instructions as to what to do with Johnson.

As soon as Wingate looked up from the telegram again, the reporter began asking questions. The conductor called the all aboard and the judge's little group moved toward the depot. Where's Tom Johnson, Judge Arch? What's happened?

Wingate opened his mouth to answer, but glancing at the departing train, said first, I hope my luggage is on that cart over yonder. The crowd around him, which was growing, laughed, but the judge shook his head, truly dazed it seemed by the message in his telegram.

Well. It appears he got off the train in Arkansas—unbeknownst to me, of course—and failed to catch it when it left.... He looked again at the telegram. ...Lonoke. He is in custody—for safe keeping only, of course—at the sheriff's office in Lonoke, Arkansas right now.

Is he alright? When did you last see him?

He's fine, as far as I know. We boarded the train together yesterday, as I said. That's the last time I saw him. We sometimes bump into each other at Memphis when we change trains, but not always, and I thought nothing of not seeing him there.

How was he in Oklahoma... when you last saw him?

Uh... I'd say he was a bit nervous. Except for that he was fine. He's been feeling nervous about the trial and all that, you know. Tommie's been under a lot of pressure. There's more than twenty Indians and Indian-Negroes trying to claim his Oklahoma land. He shook his head, frowning slightly. It's scandalous, but this often happens with valuable oil properties out there, and naturally, now that the case is drawing to a close, the pressure is mounting. Tommie hadn't been sleeping very well lately. I was getting quite worried about him in fact. He's been getting more and more... I would say restless. Worked up over all this—naturally enough. Wingate glanced over and saw Lexie toss her head impatiently, her face a perfect mask of boredom.

What do you plan to do about this, Judge Arch?

Wingate sighed heavily. Well, we'll have to get him home somehow or other, won't we? After all, he's a valued client. He could even be in danger—he's had several threats on his life out there, you know.

Threats on his life? the reporter repeated with relish.

Wingate nodded, then shook his head slowly. Filthy lucre. Makes people behave in terrible ways sometimes. I've been shocked by the greed I've witnessed among those people. But we'll take care of him, don't worry. I'll call Sheriff... He consulted the telegram again before putting it in his pocket. I'll call Sheriff Drake right away.

Lexie lit another cigarette and paced the hearthrug. Arch had been on the telephone ever since they got home. She stopped to look at herself in the mirror over the mantel. She liked this new color of lipstick. Tropical Dream. The name had sold her on it right away. It reminded her of the promises Arch had made, for after the Johnson case came through. They would be richer than she'd ever thought possible, he had said. He might even get a promotion and they could live somewhere exotic for a while. The color went well with the floral print dress she'd worn to welcome her prodigal husband home, but he'd been too busy to even notice.

That's right, Miz Johnson, he was saying now. They've agreed to take him as far as Memphis, and I'll pick him up from there tomorrow.... The police station, but that's only for safekeeping. He's not being held; they're just keepin him safe there. Free board, you might call it. But listen, I'm gonna want you—or actually your son would probably be better—to go with me down there and pick him up. Yes, now I think about it, a man would be better, since we may have to stop for the night. So you get me a male relative...Who?... Well whichever. All I need is for somebody from Tommie's family to go along with me down there and pick him up.... Y... Yes, I'll let you know all the details as soon as I can make plans. Look, I've only just set foot back home myself. Haven't even gotten a chance to say hello to the wife, what with all this folderol over Tommie getting himself stranded in Arkansas! He looked over at Lexie and smiled. Good. I'll call you tomorrow then. Gimme your number again?...Okay then. Good-bye.

He settled the receiver back into its cradle. Well, that's enough of that! Where are the boys?

Outside riding their bicycles.

Good. He started toward her, smiling, but he hadn't even gotten past the corner of the couch when the phone rang. Freezing in place, he spat out an oath as he turned to answer it.

Hello? Yes, put him through.... He gusted a heavy sigh. Hello Ted. He looked over at Lexie, his eyebrows dropping with resignation. Well, I can't really go into the whole thing through the telephone.... I guess so. When?.... Right now? But.... Alright. Yes I know, I know. I'll be right over.

Leaving her unfinished cigarette balanced on the lip of a crystal ashtray, Lexie turned tightly enough to flare out her skirt as she left the room.

CHAPTER FORTY-EIGHT

Richard was extremely relieved when they pulled up in front of the Memphis Central Police Station. Hours and hours alone with Judge Wingate had taxed him into emotional and conversational bankruptcy. They had maintained a strained formality, having exhausted their few topics of conversation—cars, the court case, and the weather—after the first hour or so. The passing scene afforded the odd comment, but mostly they were quiet, Richard having to battle the urge to rattle on and on just to break the silence. The judge was definitely not a person to run off at the mouth with. Richard looked forward longingly to Tom's being in the car for the return journey. He knew Tom didn't much care for the judge, but at least he was used to dealing with him. And boy, did he owe him for this trip! A million dollars might not cover it, he thought, as the judge lit another cigar and told him not to bang the door against that lamp-post when he opened it.

Richard stood to one side while the judge spoke to the policeman behind the high desk in the lobby. The place was full of people—criminals, Richard supposed, or victims. They were almost immediately greeted by an officer, a Commissioner Fenton, who shook hands with both of them, and then directed his comments almost exclusively to the judge as he led them through a series of hallways.

He had him a bad night last night. Seemed to be havin fits, like. Even hallucinations. We got a doctor in, and he give him something to calm him down, so I think he'll be okay to travel with you.

When, exactly, will this sedative they've given him wear off?

Well, tell you what. How bout we give him another dose for the road? That way, as long as y'all don't stop overnight nor nothin, I'd say he'll be fine. Fenton paused at a desk as they passed and said, Git that doctor back here quick as you can. We gonna need another shot a whatever he brung last night.

Richard was straining to catch every word over the echo of their footsteps. You say he was havin hallucinations?

Sure seemed like it. Either that or some mighty bad nightmares. Kept shoutin at somebody to keep away, when they wasn't nobody near him.

We got him in a cell away from the other... away from the prisoners, off by hisself. Here he is.

They had arrived in front of a barred cell with a bare lightbulb hanging from the ceiling. Tom sat on the edge of a metal bunk with his head lolling down, his mouth hanging open. He had soiled himself.

Tommie?

At the sound of Wingate's voice Tom's head jerked upward. Richard gasped involuntarily. Tom's complexion was grey, his lips blackened with dried blood, the inside of his mouth dark and blistered. His eyes seemed unnaturally large, the whites of them yellow.

Oh my God. Tom, what's wrong? What's happened to you, man? Tom stared at his brother as if he didn't know him, and dropped his head back down. Richard turned to the commissioner. What happened to him?

He shrugged. He was like this when we got him.

But... where's his teeth?

Didn't have none.

Well...can't he have some water to drink? Can't I go in there with him?

Be my guest, he said, raising his eyebrows. You go on in there, but I'll have to lock the door behind ya, you understand. And Judge Wingate, you and me'll go git the water. It'll gimme a chance to go over the paperwork with you.

He unlocked the cell and Richard walked in slowly, frightened of the look and the smell of his own brother. He went back to the bars as the two white men walked away. Uh, scuse me! Could I have...please some soap and water... and a, and a towel?

Sure. Jist gimme a minute.

Richard walked slowly across the cell and squatted down in front of him. Tom? Tom, it's me, Richard. Don't you know me? Your brother, Richard. I don't know what's happened to you, Tom, but I come to take you home. Without even knowing he was going to, Richard began to cry.

CHAPTER FORTY-NINE

Mary was in bed when Judge Wingate knocked at the door. She was expecting them to stay overnight on the road somewhere and get back the next morning. By the time she lit a lamp, got her robe on and opened the door Richard was crossing the porch, supporting Tom with some difficulty. She cried out at the sight of him.

This is how we found him, said Wingate, shaking his head. No tellin what happened back there in Arkansas.

Mary took Tom's other arm and helped him to the nearest chair.

Richard was as serious as he had ever been in his life. Mary, I'm gonna go get my car, drive to Greenberry and bring Ben back jes quick as I can. He ought to be here, and Mama too, and as many of em as possible. I'll get Dr. Taylor, too, an...

No, please. I insist, Wingate interrupted. I'll send Dr. Bradley Scott out first thing in the morning. He's the top medical man in town. Come on, Richard, let's go. There's no time to lose.

Mary was crying. Can you... can you send for Clara and Gladys fo y'all go into Greenberry?

Gladys over at Mama's?

She come today.

I'll get em, he said, following Wingate out. Quick as I can. And I'll send Parmalee back here too fo I go to town.

Tom had dozed off again under the sedative and Mary bent over him in wondering sorrow. She could not stop crying. Oh Tom, she said, moving her head back and forth. What've they done to you? Leaning down she kissed his forehead and he stirred and opened his eyes. The whites were as yellow as beaten eggs. She put her hand on his unshaven cheek and tenderly edged his ruined lower lip with her thumb.

Lemme get you some water, baby.

His eyes followed her as if she were a wasp about to sting him. As if he had never seen her before. She was in the kitchen pouring a glass of water, her hands shaking badly, when she sensed him in the doorway behind her. Just as she turned around he grabbed the skillet from a nail on the wall and held it up like a weapon.

Don't come no closer or I kill ya.

She suppressed an urge to scream and stood still, praying to God for help. They stood like this, outside of time, until she heard a car cut its motor in front of the house. Tom, she said as softly as her quavering voice would allow. Tom, Richard's bringin yo mama. Help is here, Tom. Ain't no need to be scared. It's gonna be okay now. Yo mama's here.

She could hear them on the porch, and was afraid he would throw the heavy iron skillet at them as they came in. Put the skillet on the table, baby. Jes set it...

He jerked around at the sound of the door opening. To her immense relief Richard came in first. Tom? he said, seeing the skillet in his brother's hand and assessing the situation at once. He put up a hand for the women to stay behind him. Tom, it's me again—Richard. Ain't nobody gonna hurt you, Tom. Mama's here and Gladys too. You wanna see em?

Mama? Tom said. Mama? He dropped the skillet with a loud clank that caused him to startle.

Clara put her head around Richard, who had warned her of Tom's condition. Hello son. I come to help ya. She moved slowly around Richard and into the room. Let's get you all cleaned up and in yo own bed, okay son? Won't that feel good? Safe and clean in yo own bed?

Clara moved closer and closer, talking gently but firmly, until she could take his hand. Tom let her lead him into the bedroom. Gladys, stood just inside the door for a moment, her face stricken. Then she went to Mary, who broke like a storm in her arms.

CHAPTER FIFTY

Rachel pushed Reggie away from her and stepped out of the shadows. As usual now, the gates were locked after dark. Reggie thought she had a key and she didn't want him to think otherwise.

Go on home now, Reggie.

I jes wanna be sho my lil...

Shhhh! Reggie's brother Jerry was one of the biggest bootleggers in town and they'd both had some of his whiskey. The effect on Rachel was to make her think she and Reggie were shouting at the top of their lungs.

I jes wanna be sho you's safe inside them big ol gates fo I leaves you.

Naw now. I done tol you. They see you roamin round here again they gonna have you arrested. Now git on home fo we both of us gets in a heap a trouble.

I'll only go if you promise you gonna marry me and come with me to Nashville, like we talked about.

Reggie, she whispered, you don't nevah listen to what I say. I ain't marryin nobody, and they ain't no place in Nashville where I could live like this. She waved her arm loosely to take in the splendor of Wincoyne behind its tall wrought iron fence. So no. You go find yo'self another girl. He stayed where he was, his face all tender solicitation. Go on now, start lookin. She got tickled, despite her declared resolve.

Laughing because she was, and willing to risk the streetlight, Reggie walked over and kissed her again. Then he danced her back into the shadows. Oh Rachel. Oh honey... he murmured a moment later, punctuating his words with more kisses. I ain't gonna let you go... til you tell me...yes... You... jes gotta... tell me yes.

With an effort she broke free of him again, but her voice wasn't quite as firm this time when she told him to go on home. And when he did finally turn and walk off down the sidewalk, she felt a pang. He had a confident spring in his walk, turning every few yards to see if she was still watching, and cutting a little swaggering caper when he saw that she was. He could always make her laugh. Oh yeah, Reggie Cruickshank was trouble. Precisely the brand her mother had always warned her about. Rachel Slayden, you find yo'self a *good* man. Don't you be no fool!

As soon as he turned the corner, she walked around the perimeter of the estate to where the fence was a more manageable height, and climbed over it. On her way through the grounds she passed the wishing well. Stopping beside it, she put her hands on the bricks and looked down, knowing it wasn't a real well; there was no water and so there could be no reflection of the moon and stars in it, no reflection of her face. Just darkness.

The house stood beyond in all its fine masonry and European tile, the finest house for miles and miles around. Her bedroom windows were dark. In fact the only light came from the sunroom. Probably Mrs. Wingate sitting out there, she thought, waiting for Mr. Wingate to come home. As she got nearer, she heard male voices, and glanced over at the driveway. The judge's car was parked under the porte cochère. Her heart tripped sharply. The sunroom windows were open and threw lamplight across the grass like a hand of giant cards. The two men were in there. After a moment's hesitation, she moved closer and closer, daring to take her place behind an elm, from where she could hear what they were saying.

...good as done.

'Good as' isn't good enough, Arch. If you make a hash of this you'll have to go down alone.

Oh is that right? Well thanks for the support. What happened to the we're-all-in-this-together spirit? The judge was never as good as the banker at keeping his voice down.

One of us has to maintain his reputation, surely you can see that, Arch.

Okay fine. Why cain't it be me?

Because, my dear jug-headed brother, you're the one they all connect with him. You're all over the papers. This is your big case. Now think, Arch. Think it through. What do we do if he recovers?

Recovers! He cain't possibly recover. You haven't seen him. I can hardly believe he's made it this long.

Exactly. Which is why I don't trust your judgement of the matter. You said he wouldn't last twenty-four hours. Now listen. We can get Bradley to administer something with a needle, can't we?

Bradley's already seen...

When the telephone jangled its alarm from the table at the end of the wicker settee, Rachel barely caught the scream that rose in her throat. Mr. Wingate got up to answer and stood facing the outside. She held herself as still as she could behind the tree, grateful she was wearing dark blue and trusting that their lighted room blinded them to the outside world.

Hello?... Put her through. Yes Lexie, he's right here. Hold on.

The banker sat back down, and the judge reached over to take the phone from where he was sitting. Lexie?...Uh huh.... I see. Well, you better gimme

the number.... Okay. I'll call him right away. Thanks.... What's that?....
Well a minute ago I would've said soon; but now I don't know when I'll
get home. Sor.... Lexie? Hm. She hung up on me.

Oh well. She'll probably just go on to bed like Maddie did. What was
that all about?

Johnson's brother just called to say they can't manage him. The sedative
Scott gave him today has worn off and he's having fits again. They want
us to take him away.

Away where?

Hoptown.

Perfect. Hoptown's perfect! He'll be well out of harm's way there.

True enough.

Plus, we can easily have him dosed there to the full effect.

But, hold on, Ted. What if they do tests on him to figure out what's
wrong, or an autopsy?

We don't know what happened in Oklahoma, or Arkansas.

The judge nodded, then picked up the handset again. I better make that
call. Operator? Yes, hello. Listen, um, get me Tom Johnson's place out in
Slayden's Crossin....

Rachel stood as still as the tree. Her heart pounded as she tried to consider her options. Who could she tell? Who would believe her? Or even if
they did, who would act against the Wingates?

Hello, Richard? Is that you?...Yes, I heard. My wife told me. That's too
bad.... No, no, I understand. Listen, if the Memphis police couldn't control
him, you folks could hardly expect to.... W... Well, but don't be too hard
on yourself, Richard. You've done the best you could. Listen, I'll get the
papers ready tonight. Mary will have to sign them—be sure and tell her
that.... Okay. Dr. Scott and me'll meet y'all at the courthouse first thing in
the morning to take him off your hands.... Just you and Mary. And Tommy,
of course....8 o'clock sharp. He won't need to bring a thing and it won't
take very long, I'll see to that.... No, I'm afraid we can't bother Dr. Scott
with this tonight if we're askin him to meet us in the morning. Ya'll'll be
alright for a few more hours. Jist get him to bed. But I'll see you in the
mornin and we'll get him over to Hopkinsville. Not at all, it's the least I
can do. He settled the receiver back into its cradle.

Good. I'll call Bradley as soon as you leave and tell him to meet you at the
courthouse at 8, and be prepared to drive over to Hopkinsville to oversee
the admissions process.

Tell him to bring along another dose or two to keep him sedated. Last
thing I need is to have him grab the steerin wheel or some damn thing.

I will. Oh and listen Arch, get Johnson's wife to make the bank the official administrator of her estate while you're at it. One more paper to sign won't make any difference to her right now. This could be working out even better'n we'd planned. Come into my office a minute, I've got a copy of the form in there.

Rachel stood where she was until the two men left the room. She leaned her cheek against the tree, just above where it forked. When the sunroom went dark, she waited to see the study window light up, then flew to the door beside her room. As quietly as possible, she let herself into the house. Once she was inside her room, she closed the door and stared at it in the half-light. Its elegance filled her with regret. But nothing was worth staying in this house for now. Falling to her knees beside the bed, she reached under it and drew out the battered old suitcase Mrs. Wingate had given her.

GLADYS: V

When Uncle Tom come home from Memphis that time he was brought to Mary. Had to put him to sleep jes to bring him there. His clothes was all tore up and he was filthy dirty, his mouth all blistered and cooked, like. My grandmother give him black bottle, cause he'd get so vicious when he had them spells. He was a stout man, strong anyway, but the poison they done give him caused him to be so strong and violent we had to keep two men guardin him all the time. His rages'd come and go. When he was in one of em he'd grab the lamp off the dresser, or whatever come to hand, and threaten to throw it if anybody said anything to him or come near him. And you know them coal oil lamps, they'd burn the house down if you's to throw one of them. So we couldn't keep him there at home. He had to be sent off to Hopkinsville, though it like to killed us to do it.

But during that one day that he was back home, ever once in a while he'd come to hisself. His mind'd clear, like. Once when I was by the doorway and I could tell by his face—by his eyes—that his mind was clearin, I says to him, What happened to you, Uncle Tom? and he answered me. He said that a bunch of em had tried to get him to go to a big supper and eat and drink, but he wouldn't do it—didn't trust em. He knew, you see, that they's out to poison him fo that money. So jes fo he was to board the train from Oklahoma to come back home that last time, a bunch of em—his lawyers was there and even his own 'dear' uncle and a gang of em—they helt him down and forced him to drink this water. Look like it had silver floatin on top of it, he tol me. I know now it was mercury.

Well after he'd explain a little bit, he'd take one of them fits again and we'd lose him. Wasn't no way we could handle it. He had to go off to the Insane Asylum at Hopkinsville. The judge signed the papers, and Mary did too, but doin it it broke her. He lasted two weeks—can you imagine that? Two weeks in his condition. He tore his bunk near out of a concrete wall, and the sink basin too. After that they put him in one of them straight jackets. His death certificate said he died of 'Acute dilation of the heart', which a nurse tol me one time means that he...he sort of blew up from the inside.

The day he was sent home fo his burial, Dr. Scott come to Mary's house and asked permission to do a autopsy. Course wasn't nobody wanted that more'n we did, to get us some answers. So Mary and Clara, they give permission, and he unfolded a little portable table he carried around with him fo home operations and autopsies. He done it right there in the livin room.

I was standing right beside Uncle Tom's head when Dr. Scott cut him open. He had cleared the house out, cept for me and my grandmother. We was used to such work and refused to leave. Wasn't nothin gonna make us leave. My grandmother, she stood it like a rock. Nevah said one word and nevah looked away neither. He sliced Uncle Tom open from throat to groin and pulled his ribs back—broke em to do it. And then that doctor gasped. Them kidneys, they looked like little black sacks of stones and his liver was all blackened on one end. I seen it my own self.

My God, he said—to hisself like. I can quote you what he said like it was yestiddy. He said, My God, he's done had the deadliest poison you could buy in the drug sto.

Then he scooped out his liver and intestines and put em into a sorghum bucket—a ten gallon bucket—and said he was gonna send it off to Louisville fo testin. That was the last we evah heard about it until we read in the newspaper that they wasn't no evidence of poisonin found in him. That's what it said: no evidence of any poisonin. We knew bettah, but who was gonna believe us ovah them?

That July, Wingate the judge went back out to Oklahoma fo the last court date and presented as evidence the death certificate... of Sam Ford. Borned of Creek parents Doc and Molly Ford, it said, and died in Kentucky of acute dilation of the heart. I have been out to Oklahoma myself and seen that death certificate of Sam Ford, and it is as neat a forgery as you evah did see, based on the real death certificate of Tom Johnson, the one my grandmother always kep. They jes changed a few of the details to suit they story.

Oh yeah, I hired me a lawyer and went out there to see about the claim. This was in the late forties and early fifties, after Mary done died. Me and my husband made three trips out there in all. Ol Axley was still alive then, but he was bedridden. I couldn't get in to see him, but my lawyer did and he come back and tol me wasn't nothin to be done. I felt like Axley'd paid my lawyer off to drop it, cause as soon as he come out of Axley's house he changed his tune, and all he'd say after that was he couldn't help me. I had used up my savin's to get that far, and had to let it go.

Aftah the case closed in 1929, them Wingates jes got richer and richer. Ted Wingate's bank was one of the few banks in the whole United States that didn't have to close at the end of that year when the Great Depression struck. When all them other bankers was floatin upside down in they swimmin pools or jumpin offa bank buildins, ol Ted Wingate wasn't a bit worried. He was sittin pretty. They quoted him in the Daily Leaf after the big stock market crash, sayin how well his bank was fixed. 'We got $20 million capital.' That's the figure he quoted—it was right there in the paper.

As for the other Wingate, he moved to Washington DC and become a Federal Judge. He even moved down to Panama fo a few years and was a Federal Judge down there. He had him a fine big house, too, when he come back to town, though it wasn't as big as the banker's. The judge's house was right near banker Wingate's mansion, with fat white columns on the front of it and all. I used to walk by them big houses sometimes and jes look at em.

But Maddie Wingate, she went crazy and had to go to a asylum fo awhile herself. She didn't go to Hopkinsville like Uncle Tom did. They took her to a Catholic Insane Asylum in Louisville. They give her shock treatments to quieten her down. They say she wasn't nevah the same after that. And both of Judge Wingate's boys died. The little, sickly one, he died when he was still a young man. And the other one died aftah he's a grown man, but not til he saw both of his chilren commit suicide. So they ain't a one of they line left to benefit from all a that money.

But that still wasn't the end of the story.

A white couple come to Slayden's Crossin a year or so after Tom died, looking fo Mary. They's wantin to talk to her about how her husband'd been done out of his money, and they got her to sign papers. Got her to sign her name as Mary Ford, wife of Sam Ford. Clara said she and ev'body else tol her not to do it—not to take no part in it—but that this white couple had doped her. And I seen her in them days; she wasn't like herself. Jes all weak and dreamy and didn't show no gumption.

This white couple, he was a lawyer from Mi'ssippi, a tall, thin man name a Cooper. And the woman, turn out, she wasn't his wife; she was jes a frien or somethin. But they was in cahoots and both of em had been in it all along, tryin to get some a the money from the oil claim. The man, he knew Mary wouldn't go off with him if they wasn't a woman aroun. This frien of his was a short little woman like you wouldn't take no notice of—plain as a sparrow, and after Tom died they carried Mary off to Mi'ssippi to live. Out in the middle of nowhere, outside some little town that ain't even there no mo, name of Egypt. Used to be a big cotton depot. They set her up in a trailer house with a garden spot and kep her full of drugs and made her sign documents and such like.

Ben, he couldn't talk no sense to his Mama, though he tried. She'd jes smile at him and twist her hands. Then they come after him. But he didn't want no part in it. He signed over any interest he had in any Oklahoma oil lands and he got the hell outta Dodge. Moved his family to Detroit Michigan in the middle of the night one night, and never did move back here. In the 1940s, when Mary was a ol woman, she come back to Slayden's

Crossin, to her old house that Uncle Tom'd built fo her, but she nevah was the same. Soon's Ben got wind a this, he come and got her and brung her to live with him up in Michigan, which is where she died. Ben and one of his daughters, Rosa Mae, they brought Mary back to Slayden's Crossin to be buried in Heaven's Gate Cemetery, beside Uncle Tom.

Not long after that, somewhere around the middle a the 1950s, banker Wingate's wife died and he tied all his millions up in a trust fund fo the 'worthy poor' a Wills County. And he had it all written out jes who he meant by the worthy poor. I cain't say it ain't done some good. I'm sure it has, but that was Wingate, wantin to control that money from beyond the grave.

Then when Ted Wingate hisself died, a whole new court battle started over that money and it went on fo years and years. Emmett Lewis moved into that empty mansion they called Wincoyne and lived there by hisself, to keep prowlers out. His wife, she refused to move in there, so he was knockin around in that place all by hisself, like a ghost, while the white folks fought each other over the banker's fortune.

Judge Wingate and his son, Archie, they was on one side a the lawsuit, and the bank and the charity foundation was on the other side. And then Miz Wingates's family, the Coynes, why they got involved in it too. Eventually the judge and his son got caught for forging a fake codicil to the banker's will. See, Ted Wingate hadn't left Judge Wingate and his family a thing, and this codicil—that was a new word they taught us—was supposed to be sayin that, oops, the banker had changed his mind and wanted to leave half of the money to them. Y'see, they had put this piece of paper between two loose bricks in the wishing well out behind Wincoyne. I tell you true, that was all anybody in the whole county could talk about for months seem like, the codicil in the wishin well. Like a millionaire banker would leave a big change to his will between two loose bricks in a wishin well! It beat all. Course that didn't fly. The judge died soon after they got caught, and his son, Archie Junior, was run out of town in disgrace.

Oh yeah, the battle over the Wingate millions split the white people in town right down the middle fo years; it was still goin on up into the 1970s. Us black people though, we done let go of it a long time ago.

EPILOGUE, PART ONE

Although he was white, my father, Bernard 'Yardstick' Rule, was born and raised in a predominantly black part of Greenberry, near the tobacco barns. Because of this he knew stories most of the white people in town had never heard, or didn't remember. One of them was the story of Tom Johnson. You won't believe me if I tell it to you, Daddy would say, but it's the gospel truth. There was this colored fella back before the Depression, half Indian, who'd inherited land out in Oklahoma, where they'd run all the Indians off to because they thought the land out there was worthless. Wasn't many trees on it, it looked all barren. So they said, 'Here, y'all can have all of this.' But the laugh was on them, cause it turned out there was oil on that land. Oil worth millions and millions of dollars. So them Indians ended up being some of the richest people in this country—millionaires. Now if that ain't God talking I don't know what is.

Daddy would pause to let the wonder of it sink in, then he'd go on. Now this Tom Johnson—who was from here—like I say, he had him some land out there cause of being part Indian. Come to find out his land had a oil strike as rich as any of em. One day he ain't got two cents to rub together, and the next day he's a oil baron. It was all over the newspapers, and ever'body started bowing and scraping to him, even the richest people in town. 'Congratulations, Mr. Johnson. Why, what wonderful news.'

But when he goes out to collect his money, what do you think happens? He collects it and gets on the train to come home, but he never makes it back. What they said was, he ate a poisoned apple on the train. A poisoned apple. Now where'd you ever hear of a poisoned apple outside of a fairy tale? He was dead before he ever spent a penny of his millions. Now then, how do you like *them* apples? That's some of your local history for ya.

Daddy was right, I didn't much believe the story. It sounded too fantastic. But I did remember it. It wasn't until several years after he died that I decided to dig around and see whether it had any basis in fact, or was just some sort of exaggerated folk tale. I began by asking Daddy's brother, my Uncle Pat.

Hell *yes* it's true! Pat snapped. I don't know what year it happened, but it had a big, bold headline in the newspaper, I remember that much. LOCAL

NEGRO INHERITS MILLIONS—sump'n like at. You ask Klute Walker, she'll know. She could tell you the year it happened.

Grace "Klute" Walker, a black woman, was an old neighbor of Daddy's family from Boxtown, as the tobacco barn neighborhood was called. Though I had often heard Daddy and Granny mention her, I had only seen her twice. At Granny's funeral she walked to the corner across the street from St. Joseph's church. All dressed in her Sunday best, she stood as tall as a short woman can while they carried Granny's coffin from the hearse.

Daddy crossed the street and invited her to come in to the funeral, but she refused, saying she'd never been inside a white church and wouldn't be comfortable. 'I had to come this far for Miss Nell though.' She was still standing there an hour later when we came back out.

When Daddy died she was there again, but this time she came on inside the church, because this time she wasn't the only African American in attendance. Big Jody Concentine was there in his wheelchair, as was Daddy's boyhood friend George Sherrill with two of his brothers, and several others. All of them were friends and neighbors from the old days in Boxtown. I always liked your daddy, Klute Walker said, shaking our hands. He was a good man.

Drawing courage from that memory, I took Pat's advice and called her up, explaining to her who I was and what I was interested in.

Well, I might remember hearing something about it, she said artfully, but I cain't give you no details. Why don't you try calling Lorna Anderson? Now she knows evah'thang that's evah happened.

Hello, Miz Anderson? I was given your name by Klute Walker, who said you might be able to tell me....

Well now, I don't know nothin about that. That all happened a long time ago. But if you'll call up Althea Galbraith, why she be able to hep you. She's got a head for hist'ry.

And so it went. I was passed hand over hand among the women elders of the black community, each of whom said she knew nothing herself about the business, but knew exactly who would be able to tell me what I wanted to know. By the fifth call, I was beginning to imagine that they were one call ahead of me, saying, Is that you, Georgia Ruth? Listen, if a white woman calls you up asking questions about Tom Johnson, you're not to tell her a thing, you hear?

But my paranoia was unfounded. The fifth call was the jackpot. It was to Mrs. Georgia Ruth Jackson, whose existence—whose very street—was completely unknown to me though she lived on South 15th Street, in the fold of a slope beside the railroad track, only three blocks from my childhood home.

Lawd yes, I sure can tell you about that, because Tom Johnson was my cousin. And if you do find it in the papers I'd love to have a copy to take to our family reunion this June. It happened in 1928, and he died in 19 and 29.

*   *   *

Out at the library I began to swirl through 1928 on the microfilm reader, looking for a bold headline. When it slid into view on the front page of the January 26th issue I almost shouted out loud. There it was in two-inch caps: LOCAL NEGRO TO GET IMMENSE FORTUNE. It carried two sub-headings: Oil Property Is Valued at from Ten to Twenty Millions of Dollars, and Attorneys Employed to Handle Affairs.

The article reported breathlessly that Johnson, a plasterer from Slayden's Crossing three miles southwest of Greenberry, had had his breakfast interrupted most pleasantly that morning. A lawyer from Tulsa, a Mr. Ben Axley, arrived on the midnight train the night before, carrying a satchel full of papers, a title search of property in northern Oklahoma on which more than forty fine oil producing wells had been sunk. Axley had been searching for Johnson for the past four years, and told *Greenberry Daily Leaf* reporters that he could prove conclusively that Johnson was the rightful owner of the fabulously valuable property.

The article went on to assure its readers that, 'More details of this story, which sounds more like fiction than fact, will be gathered and published in the *Daily Leaf* as fast as they can be obtained. It is one of the most remarkable incidents that has occurred here in many a day, and the huge sum of money which the Negro is entitled to almost staggers the imagination.'

*   *   *

Everybody told me South 15th continued just south of Water Street, near Walnut; but though I drove up and down Water Street deliberately enough to alarm its residents, there was no Walnut Street nor any 15th Street running south off of it. 15th Street only ran north from Water. There was High Street running south. High Street ended in Idlewild, where my childhood friend Brenda had lived. Behind Idlewild was a creek, the south fork of Red Duck Creek, where I had found my best fossil, a sculpted hunk of yellowish brown that looked like the middle section of some scaled creature, maybe a lizard. Try as I might, I could never find the other parts of the fossil, but the fragment alone had fired the creek as a holy place in my imagination. I knew that area well. If Mrs. Jackson, a woman in her eighties, had occupied her home for generations, as everyone assured me she had, I wouldn't find her off of High Street. I grew up in the 1950s and 60s, a period of strict segregation in Mayfield (which I call Greenberry in the book). The racial mixing my father had enjoyed earlier in the century was not open to my generation. I was sure no African American was a long term resident in this small graph of streets. Doors to other rooms of history were here, but not the one I sought today.

After High Street, Water roller-coastered along for a while with no streets at all leading off to the south. The next corner was 14th Street. What had happened to 15th? It seemed to end on the north side of Water Street. After some irritated confusion, I drove back up Water, passing the home of another childhood friend, Debbie. Suddenly I remembered sitting in her backyard tree one idle afternoon talking about what we might get up to. She had nodded her head beyond their garage and said, I'm not allowed to go back in there. That's Darkytown.

I hadn't questioned that edict. Of the several black neighborhoods in Greenberry—Boxtown, The Bottom and Tin Cup Alley among them—the name Darkytown struck me as the least inviting. Now it gave me hope. I hadn't been able to see anything but tree branches beyond Debbie's garage, so Darkytown had remained an unexplored idea. Now I reasoned, there must be a neighborhood beyond Water with no through streets into or out of it.

I used Debbie's driveway to reverse direction and went back to South 14th, turning right at the corner. This part of 14th, visible from Water Street, was and had always been a black neighborhood; I just hadn't thought of it in connection with Debbie's term 'Darkytown'. I drove past a row of tiny houses on the left, which Daddy had once used to illustrate that there *was* a hell, when I began to question the notion as a university student.

The man that owns these places is going to hell and that's for sure, he stated emphatically. He's got plenty of money, lives in a fine big house himself; but he won't fix these shacks up for nothin. All these families have to share one outdoor toilet, and they cain't get him to make any repairs at all. He's owned em for years. He's waitin em out, and when they cain't stand it any more and move out, he'll raze em to the ground and sell off for a profit. Problem is, they cain't afford to move. Don't have anywhere to go. There *is* evil in the world; it's foolish to question it. I damn well know there's a hell for people like that. Now that's all I got to say on the subject.

Of course that wasn't all Daddy had to say on the subject; it was just all he had to say that time. I welcomed the memory. It seemed I had had the information I needed to find Mrs. Jackson all along, but my brain had been segregated along with the town, certain pockets of knowledge put away and never examined.

The railroad tracks fragmented the town's geography. Fourteenth ran into Walnut at the tracks. A little piece of Walnut ran back westward for half a block, where it connected with a tiny, isolated segment called South 15th Street. I made a close series of right-angle turns and there it was, Mrs. Jackson's neat, mint-green house, a clapboard version of the brick house I had grown up in a world away on South 16th Street.

As I mounted the first step, she came out and stood, a solidly built woman, very dark-skinned, with a striking face. Though I could sense that I wasn't invited to come up onto the porch, I reached up to shake her hand. As I did so I introduced myself and thanked her for telling me the date of Tom Johnson's big oil strike.

I have copies of the articles for you. It's all there in the newspapers just like you said.

She extended her hand to me briefly, but didn't meet my eye. In fact, as we stood talking, the closest she came to eye contact was a flicking glance that played occasionally on my cheekbones or eyebrows. I found this discomfiting, and tried to gaze less directly into her eyes, in case I was breaching some code of etiquette I didn't know about.

We talked about her cousin, Tom Johnson. I told her what I knew of his story from these articles in my hand, which I then gave to her. She told me that no one in the family had ever benefitted from his oil wells, though her cousin, Gladys, had gone out to Oklahoma years ago and hired a big-name lawyer to check out Johnson's claim. Nothing had come of it except more lost money, 'but Gladys is the one you need to talk to. Gladys Morse. Lives in Hickman. She's Tom Johnson's niece, and she knows more about all this than anybody.' She invited me to come inside the house then, while she looked up her cousin Gladys's address and phone number.

Mrs. Jackson's living room was much like my mother's: couch and chairs around a television, arrangements of artificial flowers, pictures of her children on the walls. Eventually she invited me to sit down. She had the O.J. Simpson trial turned up loud on the television, and I gradually realized I was interrupting what was, to her, vital viewing. So I knew I mustn't stay long, though she did answer my questions willingly. And she repeated the poison apple story Daddy had told me years before. The Simpson trial blared in the background, two murder stories competing for attention in the small living room, as my ink pen flew across my notebook.

When I asked her what she remembered firsthand of Tom Johnson, she said, Well, he was bright.

Thinking she was referring to his intelligence, I said in an embarrassed mumble, I'm sure he was. It was only later, after talking to Gladys as well, that I realized she had been referring to his skin color. With both Mrs. Jackson and Gladys, the first item of physical description always involved color. White was white, but black involved a range of significant variations of tone. Yellow, high yellow, bright, copper, brown, dark-skinned, etc.

After saying he was powerfully built—'broad as a door'—good-looking, of medium height and quick temper, she grew silent. Her attention had obviously strayed back to the TV, to the unfolding drama with another good-looking, quick-tempered man of color at its center. I thanked her for connecting me with Gladys, and stood to leave. But she followed me back onto the porch and said, with cold, Old Testament philosophy, 'I ain't got no bitterness over that lost oil money. Them that fashioned that poison apple and killed Tom Johnson received the Lord's own vengeance. Ain't none of they line left. They got the money alright, but it didn't do em no good. They, and all their offspring died violent deaths. Mm-mm... the sins of the fathers....' She shook her head. 'It's all done been paid fo.'

Who do you think did it?

I don't like to say, but I know alright.

Are you talking about the Wingates?

She nodded her head slowly, perhaps a little surprised, and for the first time, swung her gaze up and looked me square in the eye.

EPILOGUE, PART TWO

Armed with a map from the Creek County Assessor's office I drove toward the little town of Drumright, Oklahoma to see Tom Johnson's land claim. It was a clear, sunny day in March of 1996.

A billboard outside Drumright hails it as the 'Town of Oil Repute'. From Drumright I followed the coordinates north, and then west over the Cimarron River, and eventually turned at an unmarked road which would lead me onto Tom Johnson's claim along the banks of Tiger Creek. As soon as I turned onto the land a solid mass of dark clouds began forming in the east. They approached with alarming speed. The land here was all scrub bush as far as I could see. Then I passed a squat cinderblock bar, its one small window blocked up with purple and green neon beer signs, its little parking lot filled with pick-up trucks. The only other sign of human habitation was a leaning, derelict house whose unpainted wood had been burnished to a silver sheen by the wind.

The purple canopy had spread to take up half the sky, pushing the sunshine off to the far edge of the landscape. I turned on my headlights and hoped we weren't in for a tornado.

At the brink of Tiger Creek the road ended abruptly. Somehow it had completely buckled, a concrete bridge tipped on end in its gravel bed. Across it, in large red poorly formed letters someone had painted the eff word. Clumps of discarded clothing lay about, some having obviously been there for a long time.

I got out of the car just as fat drops of rain began to splat down. They rang off a pile of beer bottles to my left. The acrid and unmistakable odor of crude oil filled my lungs. On the other side of the uncrossable bridge was a field filled with motion. A dozen or more pump jacks rose and fell like mechanical monsters grazing insatiably to the shrill complaint of metal on metal. It was only then that I noticed pipelines running, one on top of another, along both banks of the creek. No Trespassing signs were posted everywhere. On this side of the creek, beyond the hill of beer bottles was a little drumlin crowned with more oil paraphernalia—rusted tanks, derricks, and more pump jacks.

Pelted by the rain, I stood and tried to imagine this land as it might've looked before its oil strikes. I tried to mentally erase the metal and concrete, all traces of human beings. Only then could I see that it was actually beautiful. All its lines meandered, creek and hill, branch and root. The tall, auburn grass was beautiful, the red earth and green-leafed trees, the drumlin under the living, moving sky—it was all beautiful. But somehow it had been subjected to the worst that our species can do. Cursed by greed.

I felt uncomfortable on it. Unhappy. Vaguely threatened. I got back into the car and drove away under the dark, purple sky. And precisely as I turned off of the section-township-range of that ill-fated property, the sun split through the cloud cover like some glorious, cosmic statement. The storm cleared as quickly as it had come—so quickly I was tempted to drive back onto to Tom's claim to see if I could bring the storm back.

Of course I didn't turn around; I kept driving away from it. But in front of me a brilliant rainbow built itself out of the sudden change of weather. Great columns of color rose out of the pastures on either side of the road. They looked solid enough for the cattle to use as scratching posts. For a mile or two the rainbow straddled the road ahead of me, as if any time now I would drive under its arch and into the promised land. Then it dissolved right before my eyes, as magically as it had come. Like that, it was gone, and its pots of gold with it.

NOTES & ACKNOWLEDGEMENTS

Notes & Acknowledgements is meant to be a section in which the writer thanks all the people and institutions that helped them gather the material, and to proofread the book in which it appears. As a native of Mayfield, Kentucky, releasing the second book in as many years set in my hometown (which I call Greenberry in the books), I find myself needing to begin with a strange thank you, to the town itself. On Dec. 10th, 2021, a nest of tornados—the most extensive and intense recorded in North America up to that date—leveled Mayfield. The town as it was is simply gone. Like all of us who know Mayfield, I cried for a week, looking with horror at the images on the screen. The people who still live there are struggling yet, to try to deal with the damage and rebuild. 23 people were killed. It was a vicious storm, which has left massive pain and loss in its wake.

Because I researched this book in the 1990s, and wrote it around the turn of the new millennium, many of the people mentioned below have since died. But now many of the buildings of the town are also gone. I wrote a paragraph in *The Arithmetic of Color* more than twenty years ago. It occurs as Tom is in Oklahoma, and sees the wind lift the curtains of his hotel room window. The paragraph describes the terrible damage a tornado 'out here' can do. When I came across that paragraph again while proofreading the book two months after the 2021 tornado, I was sickened by how graphically I had described the apocalypse that waited in the future for Mayfield.

So I want to begin by thanking the people and the town of Mayfield for all it has meant to me. I am thinking of the courthouse, the court square itself, the post office, the beautiful churches that are gone: Presbyterian, Methodist, First Christian, St. James A.M.E., Fairview Baptist... all of them. St. Joseph's School. The Hall Hotel, The Legion, Carr's Steakhouse. The houses and trees. The *trees*. The Ice House Museum, which has been so good to local artists, including me. The Merit Clothing Company, with it's handsome mural. The one side of shops that was still left from the original stores around the square. These and more are gone now, or seriously damaged.

The morning after the tornado, as I sat listening to Mayfield Kentucky lead the news in Canada, I suddenly realized the mug I was gripping said *The Mayfield Messenger*. The Christmas crib on the table in front of me was my mother's, bought in Mayfield. The sideboard beneath it was from my great grandparents' farm on the Paris Road outside Mayfield. The dining room table and the chair on which I sat were my grandparents', bought in 1905, in Mayfield. The painting on the wall was by Helen LaFrance. The afghan on my couch depicted scenes from Graves County. I had never realized how much of Mayfield I had surrounded myself with. I built a shrine to it, inside and out, and now the original is gone. I can hardly take in the loss. Yet I have taken it in. It stays with me, as these stories about my hometown have stayed with me my entire life. I will be eternally grateful to Mayfield, for its rich trove of stories, and its kind, talented people.

The Arithmetic of Color is a nonfiction novel, meaning that I have used the tools of fiction to tell a true story. Greenberry is Mayfield; Wills County is Graves County; Slayden's Crossing is Pryorsburg; and Harvest is Fancy Farm. I didn't change the names of towns more peripheral to the story, such as Paducah or Wingo. Though I haven't put in every member of Tom Johnson's family, I have kept the original names of everyone mentioned except Sax, whose name was also Tom. Reverend Parsons was a real man, whose work and attitudes are evident from the records. Rachel Slayden is a fictional character, but she is based on my interviews with real people. I kept Ben Axley's real name, but not those of the Wingate brothers, their wives and children. I also did not keep the real names of the people who worked for them, such as the chauffeur and the doctor. People from Graves County will know who they are, of course. I have based my depiction of the Wingates and their actions on the testimony of the people who lived in Mayfield in the 1920s. Many of these were eyewitness accounts, or things that happened directly to the people I was interviewing. I know a number of fine people who worked at 'Banker Wingate's' bank, one of them being my beloved aunt, Lucile Lenihan, another my cousin, Sandra Simmons. In no way do I want, nor is it my intention to spread the stain of Wingate's actions across anyone else who worked there.

For the sake of the story, I have taken a few liberties with time. For example, I have described Wingate's bank the way it looked in my childhood, though that Art Deco building was built in the early 1930s, just past the time span of *The Arithmetic of Color*. Another example is that the Lincoln movie theater was probably built around 1929 or '30. It replaced one over by the Merit called the Unique. It's more likely that Tom and Mary would've attended the Unique, but the Lincoln was right across the street from the home of Ellis Wilson's parents (410 East Water Street), and I wanted to mention Ellis Wilson, as his was certainly a career the community of Mayfield followed as it unfolded.

And so to the usual acknowledgements.

As did my first creative nonfiction novel, *Dark Fire* (Ironing Board Press, 2021), *The Arithmetic of Color* owes its first debt of gratitude to my father,

Bernard 'Yardstick' Rule, who introduced me to the story of Tom Johnson when I was a child. In the late 1980s, I began researching these two seminal stories he passed on to us, and I continued working on them throughout the '90s. Since they both featured the people of Graves County, Kentucky, it only made sense to ask the people I interviewed about both stories, while I was at it. Their memories of the 1920s, whether they were black, white, or of mixed race, were invaluable to me. Together they presented a much broader picture, and pointed me in directions I might never have taken. Thanking all of them will be a challenge, but I want to try, and if I leave anyone out, please forgive me.

I must begin with Tom Johnson's own family, without whom I could never have written this book. Mrs. Georgia Ruth Jackson, Tom's cousin, was the first person I met who had known him, and she knew by heart the date I needed in order to begin my research. Georgia Ruth Jackson's daughter, Ava Jackson Victorian, has been a wonderful source of family stories and photos. In support of her conviction that Tom and Mary's story should be told, she quoted Mark Twain: "History may not repeat itself, but it definitely rhymes." She also put me in contact with Tom's granddaughter, Rosa Mae Robinson, whom I visited in Detroit. Mrs. Robinson and her daughter Delores Blackman Bradley were similarly enthusiastic about my book, and offered wonderful stories of Tom's son Ben. Mrs. Bradley knew her grandfather as her sweet "Daddy Ben". She had memories of her great grandmother Mary Pryor Johnson as well, and, along with Mrs. Robinson, was able to tell me what happened to Mary after Tom died. As mentioned in the Prologue, the other of Tom's relatives who made it possible for me to write *The Arithmetic of Color*, was Gladys Morse. Gladys shared story after story with me, and answered my questions with tireless enthusiasm. Her voice was striking, as was her way with a story, and her words insisted on remaining in Gladys's own first person point of view in *The Arithmetic of Color*. The women of Tom's family sent me the family pictures that are in the book. Their generosity to a stranger like me takes my breath away, even after all these years. How I wish I could have gotten the book published before they died, so I could have laid it at their feet.

Ashley Parrish, of the Voices of the Civil Rights Movement in Detroit, reconnected me with Rosa Mae Robinson's family: her daughter Delores Blackmon Bradley, and her grandson, Derek Blackmon. They sent me a photograph of Mrs. Robinson with them so I could include it with those of my other seminal sources. Tom and Mary's line lives on!

Another woman who was very knowledgeable and generous with her memories was Jennie Hopkins Wilson, a near neighbor of Mrs. Jackson's in Mayfield. Mrs. Wilson was my source for Rachel's experience of Third Monday raids.

For most of her long life, Lucille Powell kept house for Lon Carter Barton and his family in the second oldest house in town. 'Lucy', as Miss Powell was called, was a shy person, and was very surprised when I began to ask her about *her* memories. But as she warmed up she told me about her childhood in rural Graves County. I have based Rachel's sister Hallie, on Lucy's stories of the kind of little girl she was, and how she responded to the glimpses she got of the white world.

Linda McCampbell Stewart Emerson of Pryorsburg, was another rich source of material to whom I am greatly indebted. And so was Lura Mae Emerson, wife of 'Wingate's' chauffeur. I also spoke with Dr. Leroy Brent, pastor at the time, of Fairview Baptist Church, Reverend Anthony D. Reeves, pastor of St. James A.M.E. on South 8th Street in Mayfield (the oldest church in town), and to Roth Mason of Mason Memorial Chapel. All three were very helpful.

There were many kinds of history I needed to plumb for this story: the history of Oklahoma, of the Creek Nation, Leavenworth Penitentiary and penal history in general, the history of law, medicine, the railroad, and so forth. I will list my sources below, and the people who helped me, giving their link to the story where possible.

George Almerigi (Asst. Attorney General for the Muscogee (Creek) Nation)
Beverly Alston (Union City, Tennessee, & adopted daughter of Gladys Morse)
Amtrak Headquarters (Washington, DC)
Martha Babb (Mayfield, Kentucky)
The Blackwell Morning Tribune (Blackwell, Oklahoma)
Anita Boyland (Mayfield)
Patrick Brode (legal historian, Windsor Ontario)
Clint Burnette (Mayfield)
Campbell's Archives of Creek Indian Census Cards (Okmulgee, Oklahoma)
Claude Chester, (Executive Assistant, Leavenworth Penitentiary)
Circuit Court Clerk's Office (Chickasaw County, Oklahoma)
Creek Council House Museum (Okmulgee)
Creek Nation Dept of Natural Resources (Okmulgee)
Creek Nation Headquarters (Okmulgee)
Creek Nation Realty, Land Operation Department (Okmulgee)
Dean Criswell (Mayfield)
Ada Deer, (Bureau of Indian Affairs, Washington DC)

Anne Diestel (Archive Specialist, US Dept of Justice,
    Federal Bureau of Prisons, Washington DC)
Mary Downing (Creek County Land Titles)
Eufala Indian Journal (Eufala, Oklahoma)
Federal Court Clerk's Office of Muskogee
Frisco Depot Railroad Museum (Van Buren, Arkansas)
Jack & Nancy Gamon (Broken Bow, Oklahoma)
Graves County Clerk's Office (Mayfield)
Connie Green, Bristow Public Library (Bristow, Oklahoma)
Hamilton Public Library, Quick Information (Hamilton, Ontario)
Doug Hart (Creek County Mapping, Sapulpa County Clerk's Office)
Judy & Vic Hart (Oklahoma Historical Society, McAlester,
    Oklahoma)
Historical Society for Railroad Information (Colorado)
Hugh "Chance" Jackson (Mayfield)
Mrs. Verna Jackson (Mayfield)
Kentucky Historical Society (Frankfort, Ky.)
Donna Lindsey (Medical Records, Western State Hospital,
    Hopkinsville, Kentucky)
Mayfield Chamber of Commerce (Mayfield, Ky)
McAlester News Capital
Dr. Stuart McLeod (McMaster University Medical Centre,
    Hamilton, Ontario)
Joyce McMahon (Bureau of Indian Affairs, Muskogee, Oklahoma)
Mills Library (McMaster University, Hamilton, Ontario)
Mormon Genealogical Library (Cushing, Oklahoma)
Gene Rayne Miller (First National Bank, Mayfield)
Mississippi State Records Center, Archives & Library Division
    (Jackson, Miss.)
Muskogee Daily Phoenix
Roger Myers (American Telegram, Nevada)
NAACP Headquarters (Baltimore, Maryland)
National Archives & Records Service (Washington DC)
National Archives, Southwest Region (Federal Archives Court
    Records, Fort Worth, Texas)
National Railroad Museum (Green Bay, Wisconsin)
Obion County Clerk's Office (Union City, Tennessee)
Obion County Library (Union City)
Oil and Gas Board (Jackson, Mississippi)
Oklahoma City Historical Society
Judge Parker (Fort Smith, Arkansas)

Pittsburg County Clerk (McAlester, Oklahoma)
Pogue Library (Murray State University, Murray, Kentucky)
J. Logan Pryor (Mayfield)
Rail America (Jacksonville, Florida)
Betty Rentz, Creek County Clerk's Office (Sapulpa, Oklahoma)
Dr. C.G. Roland (medical historian, McMaster University)
Barbara Rust (Oklahoma Historical Society, Fort Worth, Texas)
Mike Seki (plasterer, Hamilton, Ontario)
Shawnee Library (Shawnee, Oklahoma)
State Museum of History (Oklahoma City, Oklahoma)
Lois Strickland (Oklahoma Historical Society, McAlester, Oklahoma)
Marie Sanderson Sullivan (Mayfield)
Union City Daily Messenger (Union City, Tennessee)
U.S. Marshals Headquarters, Historical Records (Crystal City,
    Arlington, Virginia)
Vinita Indian Chieftain (Oklahoma)
Vital Statistics Bureau (Nashville, Tennessee)
Vital Statistics Bureau (Oklahoma City, Oklahoma)
Dora Waitie (Muskogee)
Barbara Whitlow (Mayfield)
Letha Woodruff (Bureau of Indian Affairs, Muskogee)
Darla Yocham (Creek Nation Headquarters, Muskogee)

And now to family and friends. Many people read versions of the manuscript over the years. Known as the historian of Graves County, Lon Carter Barton's contribution to my work cannot be overstated. He was simply brilliant, and he sent me many articles, and connected me to people who trusted me with their files and stories and such, because they trusted him. He read the manuscript closely and provided encouragement as well as fine suggestions. The same can be said for my 'beta readers': Errol Anderson, Joann Field, John Charles Goodman, Graeme MacQueen, Janet Turpin Myers, Jean Ryan, John Terpstra, Mary Terpstra, Alvaro Tortora, and Richard Van Holst. I am extremely grateful for their time, diligence and influential responses to the manuscript. Two fine writers, Jeffery Donaldson and Sheila Murray, generously read the book and I am honoured to have their comments on the back cover. Thank you, Brenda Stephenson, for connecting me with Sheila! Ernie Nelson and Ann Nelson Carr have provided invaluable stories, connections and support for my work, including selling the book in their Mayfield shop, King's Flowers. And once again I am indebted to Greg Smith of Blind Pig Press in Grimsby Ontario, for his unerring sense of book design, and his valuable guidance.

As I said previously, without Daddy, I would never have known about Tom Johnson. He was a gripping storyteller who understood the importance of remembering these things. But the whole family has been so patient and helpful throughout these long years. My mother, Elizabeth Lenihan Rule, had an excellent memory for details, and was enthusiastic about my research and my writing. I have a number of telephone messages she jotted down for me in her beautiful handwriting, and she happily kept a place for my books and papers, for when I could get down from Canada and take up the search again. My uncle, Pat Rule, was full of great stories about the 1920s in Boxtown, & helped connect me to the black community.

My astute brothers and sisters supported me in many ways, sharing their photographs and contacts, and proofreading some of the many drafts. After giving me valuable feedback, my sisters Rosemary and Angela both passed the manuscript on to knowledgeable friends. Rosemary sent it to her friend Gary Schneider of Memphis, and Angela gave it to her Minnesota neighbor, Lillie Lewis, both of whom made incisive observations. My sister Bridget, like all my siblings, has been a steady voice of encouragement. She stored copies of the book and research materials for me over the years. As well, she and my daughter Carys helped me get the clearest versions of photographs for the book, even if they were from old newspapers. They both have a superlative visual sense, and shared it with me without counting the time. Carys, along with Greg Smith, is also the cover artist. My brother Tim has increased my reach through social media, and has proven to be a font of great ideas for publicity, and a steadfast supporter. My brother Michael, who died in 1995, shared his extensive records of local history, joined me on expeditions around the county, and high-fived me with great joy whenever I uncovered another piece of the story. My son Justin gives freely of his time and talent, most notably in creating my website (www.bernadetterule.ca) and keeping it updated. My son Ross has helped me bring the manuscript to its fullest potential online. He created the e-book version of the story, helps me with audio-files, and much else. Carys came with me to Oklahoma on her Grade 5 March Break, and proved to be a stalwart companion and research assistant. Whether it was when they were children and I was deeply involved in researching and writing *Dark Fire* and *The Arithmetic of Color*, or when I returned to these projects when they were young parents themselves with far too much on their plates, my three children have been brilliant and selfless in their filial devotion, redrawing the boundaries of my expectations, time and time again.

For my beautiful, patient, talented family and friends, and for all who have helped me realize the long-held dream of bringing Tom Johnson's story to the page, my heart overflows with gratitude.

TIMELINE OF
THE ARITHMETIC OF COLOR

1928:A Tulsa lawyer gets off the train in Greenberry, Kentucky looking for a Sam Ford. Ford is a Creek Indian who has had a twenty million dollar oil strike on his land out in Oklahoma. The lawyer says he can prove Ford lives in Wills County. Judge Wingate, spurred by his brother the banker, hurries to the side of a black man in the village of Slayden's Crossing:Tom Johnson.

1897: Tom Johnson marries Mary Pryor, Dec. 11th

1898: Their son Ben is born

1899: Their daughter Alma is born

1899:Tom and Mary Johnson, with their two young children, join the migration of black people from Kentucky to Oklahoma. It is the time of the breaking up of the reservations under the Dawes Commission.

1901: Baby Alma dies of scarlet fever

1902: In order to get a land grant Johnson impersonates a dead Creek man, Sam Ford. On Jan. 22Nd, Sam Ford is granted 160 acres near the Cimarron River by the Dawes Commission.

1903:Shortly after receiving his land, Johnson murders his neighbour, Joe Elliott and is given a life term in Leavenworth Penitentiary while the inmates are still literally building that prison around themselves. Johnson begins as an uncooperative prisoner, eventually trying to escape, by jumping from a moving train.

1906: Tom is subpoenaed for a trial in Oklahoma regarding the oil strike on Sam Ford's land. He attempts to escape on the way home.

1910: The Parole Bill goes through, & everything changes for Tom. He becomes a model prisoner, setting his hopes on getting out through good behavior.

1920: Johnson is released on parole and returns to his wife, who is living back in Kentucky. While imprisoned he has learned the trade of plastering. With his new trade he builds a good life for himself and Mary.

1928: Against his will, Johnson is drawn into a dramatic and hotly contested court battle over the oil money (see first entry in the timeline above).

1929: The case all but won, Johnson dies. The Greenberry Bank is one of the few banks in the United States to ride out the stock market plunge of 1929.

FURTHER READING

Cuthbertson, G. *1300 Metropolitan Avenue: A History of The United States Penitentiary at Leavenworth, Kansas*, Department of Justice, produced to commemorate the prison's 100th anniversary, 1995.

Debo, Angie. *The WPA Guide to 1930s Oklahoma*, University Press of Kansas, 1986 (originally published by the University of Oklahoma, 1941).

Earley, Pete, *The Hot House: Life Inside Leavenworth Prison*, (Bantam Books, 1992).

Francis, L. & Fulgate, Roberta B., *Roadside History of Oklahoma*, Roadside History Series, Missoula Montana, (Mount Press Publishing Co., 1991).

Jackson, Joe, *Leavenworth Train: A Fugitive's Search for Justice in the Vanishing West*, (Carroll & Graf, 2001).

Logsdon, Donna, *A Historical Research Survey of Mayfield Kentucky*, CRA Project No. K20Q009, (Cultural Resource Analysts, Inc. 1993 and 1994).

McReynolds, Edwin C., *Oklahoma: A History of the Sooner State*, (University of Oklahoma Press, 1954).

Morgan, H. Wayne & Morgan, Ann Hodges, *Oklahoma: A History*, The State & the Nation Series (W.W. Norton & Co., Inc., 1977).

Morris, Norval & Rothman, David J., *The Oxford History of the Prison* (Oxford University Press, 1997).

Musson, Jeremy, *Plasterwork, 100 Period Details from the Archives of Country Life*, (Quality Books, 2000)

Richardson Fleming, Paula, and Luskey, Judith, *North American Indians in Early Photographs*, (Phaidon, 1988).

Taylor, J.B., *Plastering*, (Trans-Atlantic Publications, 1990).

www.ingramcontent.com/pod-product-compliance
Lightning Source LLC
Chambersburg PA
CBHW031055020726
47495CB00007B/1892